Harlequin ◇ Romances

OTHER
Harlequin Romances
by MARGARET MALCOLM

Many of these titles are available at your local bookseller
or through the Harlequin Reader Service.

For a free catalogue listing all available Harlequin Romances,
send your name and address to:

HARLEQUIN READER SERVICE,
M.P.O. Box 707, Niagara Falls, N.Y. 14302
Canadian address: Stratford, Ontario, Canada N5A 6W4

or use order coupon at back of books.

FLIGHT TO FANTASY

by

MARGARET MALCOLM

Harlequin Books

TORONTO • LONDON • NEW YORK • AMSTERDAM • SYDNEY • WINNIPEG

Original hardcover edition published in 1976
by Mills & Boon Limited

ISBN 0-373-02037-6

Harlequin edition published January 1977

Printed in U.S.A.

CHAPTER ONE

As Emma left the grey, cobbled streets and towering factory chimneys of Greystoke behind her, she felt as light-hearted as a bird on the wing. For the first time in her life she was free—really free—to make her own decisions and to shape her life as she thought best. Nor had she any sense of guilt at having made her escape. It wasn't as if she were an irresponsible child. She had had her twenty-fourth birthday some months back and it was more than time for her to discover if life couldn't be a little bit more—well, a little bit more *colourful* than it had been.

Ever since her father's death three months previously, she had vaguely considered the possibility of launching out in some way or other, but she hadn't felt that there was any need to make up her mind in a hurry. It was Frank Hall who had brought matters to a head.

He had turned up unexpectedly one hot June day when Emma, wearing a faded and crumpled old dress and with her hair tied up in a scarf whose colours had run, was sorting out the contents of the boxes and bundles in the attic of the old-fashioned house. To add to her scruffy appearance, she had pushed an errant strand of hair back under the scarf and in doing so had left a dusty smudge on her forehead. Actually she was unaware of that, but none the less it was annoying to find that it was Frank who was standing there in the blazing sunshine—Frank, immaculate and cool in a pearl grey suit, self-possessed and clearly in none too good a temper.

'Good heavens, Frank, what on earth are you doing paying social calls at this time in the morning?' she asked in genuine surprise. 'Oughtn't you to be at your office dealing with torts and malfeasances and whatnot?'

Frank was a solicitor who took himself and his profession very seriously and he ignored her somewhat flippant questions completely.

'It's necessary for me to have a very serious talk with

you without delay, Emma,' he explained ponderously. 'I've just heard something which has disturbed me very much and I want your assurance——'

'Oh, all right,' Emma said resignedly, 'but not on the doorstep. It's too hot. You'd better come in.' She turned and led the way to the back of the house. 'We'll go into the kitchen. It's cooler than either of the sitting rooms at this time of day.'

And, she might have added, a place where she would feel quite at ease, and Frank wouldn't. He wasn't a kitcheny sort of man; one couldn't possibly imagine him lending a hand with the washing up.

They sat down on either side of the big kitchen table and Emma regarded him warily. Experience had long since taught her that it was unwise to show any sign of being impressed by Frank's ponderous self-assurance, but something warned her that this time it wasn't going to be easy to maintain that degree of nonchalance which was her best defence. None the less, she made a gallant attempt.

'Well, Frank, and what's on your mind this time?' she asked lightly.

And Frank told her in one concise sentence.

'Is it true that you've decided to sell this house?'

Emma was too startled—and too honest—to give him a flat denial, but she did her best.

'And just who told you I had?' she asked with dangerous quiet.

'That's of no importance,' Frank declared. 'What I want to know is—is it true?'

'I'm sorry to contradict you, Frank,' Emma told him, 'but it's very important. You see, I only mentioned such a possibility to one person—and he had no right whatever to divulge the confidence of a possible client to anyone. My goodness, I shall expect *you* to be chattering next about *your* clients' affairs to all and sundry!'

'There is no comparison whatever between the inviolable confidence which of a necessity exists between a solicitor and his client and that between a house agent and his!' Frank declared stiffly.

'Ah, so it was Mr Vaughan!' Emma pounced on the information. 'I knew it must be because I haven't mentioned

6

such a possibility to anyone else! And at present, it's no more than a possibility. I simply asked him if, should I decide to, he thought there would be a ready market. He had no right whatever to mention the matter to you or anyone else!'

'Oh, come, Emma!' Frank protested, fingering his tie with a suggestion of uneasiness. 'Perhaps you're right where other people are concerned, but naturally, where I was concerned he would feel that it was an entirely different matter.'

'Oh? Why?' Emma demanded.

'As your solicitor, for one thing,' he explained and then, fingering his tie again, he went on blandly: 'But even more, of course, as your fiancé——'

'My *what*!' Emma shouted, jumping to her feet and sending her chair flying.

Frank frowned disapprovingly.

'Really, Emma, you must learn to exercise more self-control,' he reproved her.

'Self-control!' Emma blazed furiously. 'How can you expect me to keep calm when you've made such an outrageous statement?'

'Outrageous? Nonsense!' Frank denied crisply. 'Oh, I know we haven't announced it yet, but of course, our engagement is an understood thing.'

'Oh?' Emma spoke very softly. 'Understood by whom?'

'Oh—everybody,' Frank assured her easily. 'My mother, your sisters, other relations and friends——'

'And you?'

'Of course,' Frank declared in surprise.

'But you've left out one person, you know,' Emma remarked. 'Me!'

'But, my dear little girl, surely you've realised that for a long time it has been my dearest wish——' Frank said indulgently.

'No, I haven't,' denied Emma. 'Why should I? You've never so much as hinted that you regarded me as anyone special.'

'Oh, come, Emma,' Frank protested, 'we've known each other since we were children, and even then people used to call you my little sweetheart!'

'Did they? I wish I'd known that,' Emma retorted broodingly, 'I'd soon have put the score right! You were a nasty, bossy little boy, Frank, and whenever I could, I dodged you!'

'Well, I must admit you were rather elusive,' Frank admitted reminiscently. 'But I found that rather charming, as indeed I still do. The modern girl so often takes it for granted that a man is only too willing to be her slave——'

'Instead of the other way about?' Emma suggested, and glanced longingly across at the shelf where a row of saucepans was ranged. Short of hitting Frank over the head with one of them—the heaviest, for choice—would she ever get it through his thick skull that never, never, *never*—— She dismissed the idea regretfully. It would be a most satisfying thing to do, but there were drawbacks to putting it into practice. She would keep it as a last resource.

'Well, we'll leave the past to look after itself, shall we?' she suggested. 'The present and the future are more important, aren't they?'

'Exactly,' Frank agreed with relief. For a moment he had thought that Emma was going to be troublesome——

'Right!' Emma said briskly. 'Then I am to understand that you have formally asked me to be your blushing bride?'

Frank frowned. Her choice of phrase struck him as being in questionable taste, but he was anxious to get the matter settled without delay.

'Yes,' he said curtly.

'I see,' Emma nodded. 'Well, thank you, Frank, for paying me such a compliment, but it's quite out of the question. I can't possibly marry you.'

'*What!*' It was Frank's turn to leap from his chair. 'You can't mean that, Emma!'

'But I do,' Emma assured him. 'I can't marry you. Please, please accept that as absolutely final, Frank, for it will only be painful for both of us if you don't.'

'But why, Emma, why?' he demanded, completely nonplussed. 'Don't you realise——' He stopped short and began again. 'Have I, perhaps, been too abrupt in my declaration? I mean, as you have evidently not appreciated my feelings for you, perhaps you need a little time to grow accustomed to the idea.'

'No, Frank,' Emma told him decisively. 'If I had all the time in the world, it would make no difference, because I don't love you.'

'And you think that's important?' Frank sounded really quite surprised.

'Important?' Emma repeated. 'It's vital! I can't think of anything more awful than a loveless marriage. And that's another thing, Frank, *you* don't love *me* either!'

'I assure you, Emma, I'm very fond of you——'

'That's not enough,' Emma told him. 'It would be very, very wrong—so, I'm sorry, but I can't and won't marry you!'

For a moment or so Frank was silent. Then, very testily, he remarked:

'This is most inconvenient!'

Emma stared at him blankly.

'What an odd thing to say,' she began, and stopped short. 'Or is it?' as comprehension began to dawn on her 'Frank, you'd decided that if—*when*, in your mind—we got married, we'd live here?'

'Of course,' he acknowledged matter-of-factly. 'My present flat is big enough for my mother and me, but that's all. As a family man, I would naturally require something larger.'

'Your mother?' Emma repeated thoughtfully. 'She would continue to live at the flat?'

'Certainly not. Obviously it would be undesirable for her to live alone. She would live here—the house is quite big enough for her to have a small flat of her own.'

And, suddenly, Emma laughed. She really couldn't help it.

'You'd got things nicely planned, hadn't you? Why, I believe you've already had a good offer from Mr Vaughan for your flat, haven't you?'

'That has nothing to do with it,' Frank insisted irritably.

'Oh, but it has,' Emma insisted. 'In fact, I believe that it was because Mr Vaughan told you of the offer for your flat that you decided it would be a nice cheap way of getting a house if you married me! That's why you were so put out that I might sell it. Oh, own up, Frank, that was it, wasn't it?'

Frank glared at her.

'I have no intention of staying here to be insulted,' he began with what dignity he could muster, and that, to Emma, was the last straw.

'*You* being insulted!' she stormed furiously. 'What about the way you insulted me? To ask a girl to marry you just for what you can make out of her financially——' she choked over the words. 'It's revolting!'

'You're talking a lot of nonsense,' Frank declared coldly. 'When you have had time to think things over, you'll realise that. Until then, there seems nothing more to say.'

'Oh yes, there is!' Emma retorted. 'I told you that I don't love you and goodness knows, that's true. But I don't *like* you either, and I never have. You were a nasty, bossy, self-opinionated child and you're just the same now, only more so! And now, get out of this house before I really lose my temper. And don't come back again, *ever*! Do I make myself clear?'

Evidently she did, for without deigning to reply, Frank stalked out of the kitchen and a moment later the door slammed.

Until the sound of Frank's car died away. Emma didn't move. Then, suddenly, her legs didn't seem to belong to her any more. She slumped into the chair and buried her face in her arms. When she had first realised the depths of Frank's avaricious trickery she had been furiously angry, but now that had given place to a heart-sickening sense of bewilderment.

It wasn't that she loved Frank—nor, as she had told him, did she even like him—but she had never doubted either his professional or personal integrity. Now she knew that he had neither. He was a cold-blooded, money-grubbing opportunist who was willing to commit what, to Emma, amounted to sacrilege for the sake of mercenary gain.

After a while she sat up and considered the situation objectively. Frank, she knew only too well, wasn't a man who would accept defeat without a struggle. Sooner or later he would return to the attack, and when he did, he would marshal all the reinforcements he could.

His mother, for one. She would regard Emma's refusal to

marry her adored son as a personal affront and she would be quite ruthless about the means she would use to make her change her mind. But she wouldn't succeed because, unpleasant though it would be, Emma wouldn't hesitate to be as outspoken to the mother as she had been to the son.

What really worried her was what Frank had said about her sisters believing that they would get married. Suppose they, too, tried to persuade her, as they might well do? That would make for difficulties, for fighting people you disliked was one thing; fighting those you loved was very different.

In actual fact, Helen and Rose were Emma's half-sisters: Helen was twelve years older than she was and Rose ten. Their mother, the first Mrs Lathom, had died when they were little children. Professor Lathom had remained a widower for some years, then he had married again and the two little girls had accepted their stepmother quite happily. It was not until some years later that Emma was born, and so she had been very much the baby of the family and consequently had been more than usually petted and cherished. But as the years had gone on, Helen and Rose still regarded her as 'little sister', and not for quite a long time had she found that irksome. She adored her family and had accepted as natural the love and protection with which she was surrounded.

But for some years now neither of her sisters had lived at the old home. Helen was running a very successful tourist agency in London and Rose was married to Dr David Farrer. In other words, both of them had been very much occupied with living their own lives, and so it had fallen to Emma to run the house and care for her parents when first her mother and then her father had gradually relinquished their hold on life. And no one had questioned her ability to be in control. Emma herself knew that during those busy and sorrowful years she had grown up, and she had assumed that those nearest to her had realised that.

But now, since Frank had so crudely opened her eyes, she began to wonder if that was really so. Looking back over the last three months since their father's death, she realised that there had been a subtle change in her sisters' attitude towards her. Instead of being the marvellously competent young woman who relieved them of any need to lend a hand, she had become 'little sister' again. Helen, the brisk business woman, had doubted Emma's ability to manage her financial affairs: Rose, happily married, was quite sure that it just wasn't right for Emma to live alone in that big old house. And lately, there had been other little hints and nudges, nothing much in themselves but, Emma now realised, having one purpose in mind—to open her eyes to Frank's desirability as a husband. And all because she had inherited the house, which had belonged to her mother, and a few thousand pounds with it. Not enough for her to be regarded as a real heiress, but all the same, enough to make her something of a catch, as Frank had been quick to appreciate. Of course, if she told her sisters just what an opportunist Frank was, they'd see things differently, but that she was reluctant to do. In Emma's creed, if you refused a man's offer of marriage, you didn't tell anyone about it. It wasn't fair play, and little though Frank deserved such consideration, she made up her mind that only if it was unavoidable would she tell what had passed between them.

But in the meantime at least, she dismissed Frank from her mind. What she had to do was make some definite plans for her future without upsetting Helen and Rose more than was unavoidable. They would probably argue as to the advisability of selling the house, but after all, it was hers. So was the furniture. She would sell at least some of that. But then what? Invest most of the money, of course, keeping just enough available to pay for training of some sort. But what sort? That was the problem. Emma had no particular aptitudes other than purely domestic ones, nor any ambitions to take up any other occupation. It was really rather a depressing outlook. Her position would have been so much stronger if, with assurance, she could have said, 'I intend to be an actress or a secretary or—or a fortune-teller—and nobody's going to stop me!' But she couldn't.

'Oh well, something will turn up,' she decided optimistically, 'because it's simply got to. And if it doesn't, then I'll have to turn something up myself!'

With that settled, she made herself a cup of tea and, sipping it, decided that she was too tired to finish off the attic today. Then she realised that the sky had clouded over. Rain was imminent—and she had left the attic window open.

She trudged upstairs, but once in the room, she hesitated. She had so nearly finished the job. In fact, there was only a trunk left to deal with. It seemed a pity not to finish the attic once and for all.

It was an old leather trunk, worn and shabby and with its lock broken. But it was fastened with two leather straps whose buckles were so rusty that Emma couldn't undo them. It took a pair of pliers and a screwdriver to force them open, and even then Emma broke a fingernail. The lid wasn't easy to open either, but when she had, the effort proved to have been well worth while. For here there were no old curtains or discarded clothes; instead—Emma delved delightedly into the trunk's contents.

Right on top was a silk-swathed doll dressed in the height of Victorian fashion with a charming little bustle and the most captivating bonnet perched on her long, ringleted hair. Her beautifully modelled and tinted face was set in rather severe, almost disapproving lines, but the quality of the workmanship was unmistakable.

'You're a treasure,' Emma commented, and looked at the doll's face a little more intently. 'The odd thing is, you remind me of someone———'

But there was so much more to look at that for the moment Emma put the doll aside and continued her treasure hunt. There were three other dolls. One was dressed as a little girl, one as a baby in long robes and the last one, no more than a few inches high, was clad in the formal black and white of a maidservant. In each case, dresses and underclothes were beautifully hand-made and, rather surprisingly, all were in such perfect condition that it seemed unlikely a child could ever have played with them.

Emma drew her own conclusions. They weren't and never had been toys in the accepted sense—they had belonged to someone who had used them for models for whom to design and make clothes. There was no doubt about that, for below the dolls Emma found small rolls of beautiful materials, little pillboxes containing tiny buttons and hooks and eyes, and bigger boxes in which were scraps of ribbons and laces, small feathers and miniature wax flowers. Below them was a bigger box in which were other dresses for the three larger dolls, and right at the very bottom, she found hand-drawn, delicately tinted fashion plates and actual patterns cut out of stiff muslin.

But perhaps the greatest treasure of all was a small leather-covered book on which the initials 'L.M.W.' were embossed, and on the front page, in an elegant copperplate hand, was written: 'Lucy May Wainwright. Her Journal. Commenced on May 11th, 1865.'

Lucy May Wainwright. Emma frowned as she tried to place the name. She thought she could remember her mother having mentioned it as belonging to a family into which a many-times great-aunt of hers had married in the previous century, but she didn't remember ever having heard of Lucy May. A daughter of the marriage, per- haps——

Eagerly Emma began to read and time passed. It soon became clear that Lucy May had designed and made all those beautiful clothes herself and had revelled in doing so, but what became pitifully clear was that she was a semi-invalid. Not that she ever complained or, indeed, dwelt on her poor health, but reading between the lines was only too easy. Evidently the family had been quite well-to-do, for there were accounts of balls and parties to which Lucy May's brothers and sister went. But she never did. Nor, when her sisters got married, was she ever a bridesmaid—she just wasn't strong enough. Poor little Lucy May! And yet should one pity her? She certainly didn't pity herself. She thought that she was lucky to have such an entrancing occupation.

But now Emma found that she wasn't concentrating on the Journal. At the back of her mind an idea was stirring—something about dolls, something that she read quite lately. She worried at the half-memory like a dog with a bone—and suddenly she remembered. Someone who had a dolls' museum had been interviewed and in the resulting article, Emma remembered, there had been a reference to the increasing interest in old dolls and their resulting appreciation in value. The owner's name and the address of the museum had been given, but apart from remembering that it had sounded delightfully unusual, Emma couldn't recall any details. She simply must find that newspaper!

She spent the rest of the day and an hour of the following morning before she ran it to earth in a bundle of papers awaiting a call from the local Scouts. Thankful that they had been longer in coming than usual, she took the paper into the kitchen and spread it out on the table.

Yes, there it was, just as she had remembered.

Miss Hester Prescott,
'Fantasy',
Windyvale,
Cumbria.

Emma gave a sigh of satisfaction. She was no longer in any doubt what job she wanted. She wanted to carry on Lucy May's work, and as far as hand-needlework was concerned, she knew that she was capable of doing it. And as to how to make a contact with someone who would be willing to employ her—well, that was where the dolls came into it. Knowing nothing of their value, what was more natural than that she should show them to someone who did, like Miss Hester Prescott? That would serve as an introduction and might lead to—well, anything.

The only difficulty was that she didn't want to tell anyone of her venture until she knew if it was going to be successful or not. She knew quite well that if she told her sisters that she felt she needed a holiday, they would accept it, but they would take it for granted that she would go to a reputable hotel at some holiday resort where she would meet a lot of people and have a good time. They'd never accept the idea of her going to such an out-of-the-way place as Windyvale almost certainly was, without jumping to the conclusion that she had some special reason for her decision and wanting to know what it was.

And Emma knew that she couldn't bear to explain. They'd never understand just how, job apart, she was drawn to that house. *Fantasy!* It conjured up a picture of dreams and imagination, of romance and idealism—everything, in fact, which she had never found in Greystoke. But if that was how she saw it, Helen and Rose would regard it very differently. To them the whole idea would be unpractical and unrealistic. And worse than that, they'd say, dear little Emma might be exposed to real danger! After all, these days, one never really *knew*! People who seemed quite respectable could turn out to be downright dishonest. And Emma was so inexperienced—so, if she felt she must get a job, why not let Helen find one for her in London? Then she'd have someone to look after her. Or, for that matter, why not work for Dave as a combined secretary-cum-surgery assistant? Either would be preferable to her being on her own so far away from home.

Emma's chin set obstinately. She was determined to go and see Miss Prescott no matter what the opposition, but at the same time she didn't want to hurt her sisters' feelings. If only she could find a reason for going to Cumbria which they would find perfectly natural——

It was at that moment that she heard the morning post come flipping through the letterbox and automatically she went out to investigate.

There were three letters. Two were receipted bills, but on the third she recognised the scrawling writing of an old school friend, Kitty Mortimer.

She took it to the kitchen and slit it open. A moment later she gave a little yelp of incredulous delight, for what Kitty had written was *the* perfect solution to her problem.

'Darling Emma,

'I'm going to be married a fortnight from today to the most wonderful man in the world! His name is Rob Dickson. He's a mining engineer, and he's just landed a *marvellous* job in South America. As soon as he heard about it he proposed to me—he's been on the brink of it for weeks, poor pet!—and he cajoled the parents into agreeing to us getting married at once so that I can go with him.

'Emma, you've simply *got* to be my bridesmaid——'

There was a lot more, but for the moment Emma was too dizzy to take it in. For Kitty's home was in Durham, which if Emma's geography was accurate, was right next door to Cumbria. It would be the easitest thing in the world, after the wedding, to slip across and see Miss Prescott!

She drew a deep, quivering breath. Here was the perfect

reason for going North! A reason which Helen and Rose would never dream of questioning.

It was an absolute miracle, Emma decided in wonder. A miracle worked especially for her and proof, if she'd needed it, that the Fates were on her side and would probably be extremely annoyed if she didn't make full use of their well-timed intervention!

And so now, here she was on her way, happy, confident and without a care in the world. The sun was shining and Emma's little car, carefully checked for every contingency, was purring like a contented cat. She had had her hair styled and set with most satisfying results and she was wearing a new dark blue trouser suit which definitely did things for her. On the back seat were two cases of clothes, almost all new, for she had replenished her rather meagre wardrobe with a certain recklessness. In the boot were two more cases in which she had repacked her precious dolls as well as all the lovely bits and pieces she had found. But nobody knew about them. For the time being, they were her own delightful secret.

It was incredible how smoothly everything had gone. It was true that Rose had bewailed the fact that Emma would be driving such a distance all alone, but Dave had effectively squashed that.

'Nonsense, darling! Emma's a first-class driver, and in any case she's not going from here to Timbuctoo—just something less than a hundred and fifty miles. She'll do it on her head!'

'Well—if you're quite sure——' Rose had capitulated meekly. It was rare for Dave to contradict her, but when he did, she could never bring herself to argue. For one thing it never got her anywhere, and for another, she had implicit faith in his judgment.

'Quite,' Dave replied firmly. 'But just to reassure you, I've worked out a detailed route and if you stick to that, Emma, you simply can't lose yourself. Here it is.'

He handed it to Emma, who thanked him politely though without enthusiasm. Dave grinned and patted her on the shoulder.

'I know,' he told her in an undertone that Rose wouldn't

hear, 'you want to try your wings unaided, and who can blame you for that? Not I! But we're very fond of our Emma, you know, so forgive us if we fuss a bit!'

Dear Dave! Emma thought affectionately. But how strange that he should understand how she felt so much better than her own sisters!

The route which Dave had planned for her—and which, in fact, she had already worked out herself, though she hadn't the heart to tell him so—avoided main roads and busy towns as far as possible and she made good, steady progress for the first hour or so. Then, as she changed gear to negotiate a not very steep hill, she could feel that the car wasn't answering up as it should. It wasn't pulling properly, nor did the engine sound happy. Obviously something was wrong.

'Oh, heavens!' Emma exclaimed in dismay. 'You *would* chose a lonely spot like this, wouldn't you? There's probably not a garage for miles!'

She pulled up at the side of the road, opened up the bonnet and then went back to her seat to wait with as much patience as she could muster for the engine to cool before making an inspection.

Time passed—she wasn't quite sure how long, for she rather fancied that she dozed off, to be disturbed by the sound of another car approaching. She sat up with a jerk as it drew in behind her and a man got out. Emma had a fleeting impression that he was tall and sunburned and quite good-looking in a somewhat unsmiling, austere way. Then he spoke, and it was immediately evident that he was in a thoroughly bad temper.

'In trouble?' he asked in a tone which suggested that if she was, it was entirely her own fault.

'Yes,' Emma admitted, very much on her dignity, 'but please don't bother. I expect I can manage——'

His eyebrows lifted ironically.

'By sitting in the car and hoping it will recover on its own?' he asked. 'Or were you anticipating that some fool would come to your rescue?'

'Neither,' Emma retorted crisply. 'I was simply waiting for the engine to cool down.'

He looked mildly surprised at this evidence of common

sense and laid his hand cautiously on the engine.

'She's quite cool now,' he remarked. 'What seemed to be wrong?'

'She wasn't pulling properly,' Emma explained worriedly, 'and she didn't sound right. I think the trouble may be——'

He didn't bother to wait for her opinion.

'Start up,' he ordered, and meekly—to all appearances—Emma obeyed.

Actually she had discovered, rather to her surprise, that her resentment at his manner had given place to mischievous satisfaction. Whatever the trouble was, left to herself she would certainly have got her hands dirty and might even have messed up her elegant suit. As it was, this bear of a man would be the one to suffer. Well, let him! It was his own fault!

'All right,' shouted her reluctant rescuer, 'switch off.' He came to the side of the car. 'She's missing on one cylinder,' he announced disapprovingly.

'Oh!' Emma lifted wide grey eyes to his. 'Is—is that serious?'

'It may or may not be,' he said curtly. 'When did you last renew the sparking plugs?'

Emma didn't reply immediately. He had been driving without a coat and now, wisely, he was rolling up his shirt sleeves before getting to work. And Emma could only just check a horrified gasp, for on each forearm were terrible scars, healed but still red and angry-looking. The sort of scars a furious cat might have made, only it must have been an outsize in cats.

'Well? When did you last have new plugs?' he repeated impatiently, and Emma pulled herself together hastily. Something told her that the last thing this man would tolerate was pity for the suffering those dreadful scars must have caused.

'Some time ago,' she admitted, 'but I had her overhauled before I started and the garage people said they were all right.'

He accepted that without comment.

'It's worth while seeing if that's the trouble before looking any further,' he remarked. 'At least it would be if—I

19

suppose it's too much to expect that you carry spare plugs?'

'Oh, but I *do*,' Emma told him. And, she could have told him, a host of other small reckonings which might come in useful in an emergency. 'They said at the garage that it was advisable.'

She opened the cubbyhole in the dashboard and rummaged for a new plug. He took it in silence and went back to the job. Emma watched with interest. She rather wished she hadn't seen those terrible scars, for otherwise she would have felt nothing but gleeful satisfaction at the sight of his dirty hands—he had even got a smear of oil on his immaculate shirt. As it was, she felt absurdly guilty.

He stood erect.

'Start her up!'

Emma obeyed and the car responded contentedly.

'Yes, that was it,' he announced, closing the bonnet. He went to his own car, took out a handful of cotton waste and, wiping his hands on it, came back to Emma.

'I do wish to heaven that you women drivers would learn that there's more to making a car go than steering it and knowing which pedals do what!' he told her severely. 'But no, you take it for granted that just because you've had her overhauled, nothing can go wrong! Hasn't it ever occurred to that tiny brain of yours that a car is a very complex and in some ways delicate piece of mechanism? Or that the least you can do is to learn enough about it to render first aid!'

Emma's feeling of guilt vanished in a puff of smoke. Really, he was intolerable! Rude and full of his own masculine superiority—well, he'd asked for it!

'I think you're quite right,' she told him, 'that was why I took a course on car maintenance and repair work as soon as I passed my driving test.'

One couldn't exactly say that his jaw dropped, but it was a near thing.

'Well, I'll be——' he began explosively. 'You mean to say you could have done the job yourself?'

'Oh yes,' Emma assured him gently. 'It would have been the first thing I looked at.'

'Then why the devil didn't you say so instead of letting

me——' He looked distastefully at his dirty hands and soiled shirt.

'I did try to,' Emma reminded him, 'but you wouldn't listen. Besides, a fool—I'm using your own phrase—*did* come to my rescue, and saved me from getting dirty.' She smiled sweetly up at him. 'Thank you so much for your chivalry, kind sir. Believe me, I do appreciate it!'

And with a mocking little nod, she started up and shot off along the road.

Her rescuer watched her out of sight. Had Emma been able to see him she might have felt apprehensive, for his face was dark with annoyance and set in lines of sheer determination.

'If ever I meet you again, you little hussy, by heavens, I'll make you pay for that!' he vowed.

The rest of Emma's journey was uneventful and even the beauty of the countryside through which she was passing didn't distract her from her determination to make up the time she had lost. Nor did she spare a thought for her reluctant rescuer. He belonged to the past, for there was little or no probability of them ever meeting again.

When she reached Kitty's home she was immediately engulfed in her friend's affairs and had no time to bother about her own. Kitty, always high-spirited, was in a seventh heaven of excited bliss, and Emma had hardly had time to greet her hostess before she was hustled upstairs to see Kitty's dress and her own.

They were really lovely. Kitty's bridal white was as diaphanous as a cloud, and Emma's didn't fall far short of it in either delicacy or charm. The fragile material was patterned in the softest shades of pink and blue which swirled together like an enchanted sunset—a dress any girl would love to wear, as Emma said with very real enthusiasm.

'Yes, well, I hope it fits,' Kitty replied anxiously. 'You and I have always been so much of a size that as I was short of time it seemed safe to make it to fit me. But you're thinner than you were, Emma.'

'Well, that's better than if I was fatter,' Emma pointed out. 'I expect we can take a tuck in somewhere.'

'I expect so,' Kitty agreed, and then, with affectionate concern: 'Em, there's nothing really wrong, is there?'

'No—just that life has been a bit strenuous for some years,' Emma assured her lightly. 'Nothing I shan't get over.'

'Oh, good!' Kitty's hug was the measure of her relief. 'I was afraid it might be a love affair that went wrong.'

'No, nothing like that,' Emma told her decisively. 'I've never yet met a man with whom I wanted to spend the rest of my life!'

'No? Oh well, time enough yet,' Kitty said cheerfully. 'Who knows, you may fall for Rob's best man—his name is Adrian Wroughton, by the way, and he's quite a dish!'

'Is he?' Emma replied indifferently, and to change the subject, suggested that as soon as she had phoned through to Rose to report her safe arrival, it might be a good idea to try on her dress.

The wedding day dawned bright with the promise of even greater warmth to come but with a baby breeze that would make it tolerable.

Preparations started early since it was to be an eleven o'clock wedding, and Mrs Mortimer, experienced in such matters, knew just how quickly time could fly—and how many last-minute hitches there could be. And she proved to be right. Kitty mislaid the blue garter she had borrowed and it was only after a frantic search that it was found in, of all places, Mr Mortimer's tall hat. Then the bouquets were late in arriving and an urgent call had to be made to the florists . . .

But at last they were ready to start. Mrs Mortimer, Emma and a tiny bridesmaid were in the first car with Mr Mortimer and Kitty following them shortly after. The old church, dignified and beautiful in its own right, was made even more attractive by the masses of flowers which decorated it. A lovely, tranquil setting for a wedding.

Mrs Mortimer went to her seat and Emma waited in the porch with the squirming, excited little bridesmaid. Then Kitty and her father arrived and a moment or so later they were all walking slowly up the aisle as the organ played a welcoming march.

As they neared the chancel steps, Rob half turned to greet his bride. At the same time the best man turned as well, and for a split second Emma stopped dead in her tracks. And with some cause, for the best man was no other than her rescuer of the previous day—the man she had thought—and hoped—she would never see again!

Almost immediately Emma recovered herself, but though she carried out her duties faultlessly, she was far more aware of the tall man in immaculate morning dress than she was of the service. And when, as she walked beside him as they followed the bride and groom into the vestry, their arms touched, she was thankful for the big, gauzy hat which kept him from seeing her face.

Then, with the register signed, there was the usual babble of congratulations and the promiscuous exchange of kisses.

Emma felt a strong arm encircle her shoulders and a deep voice said softly:

'I understand it's the best man's privilege!'

The arm tightened so that Emma had to tilt her head back and she met a pair of dark, inscrutable eyes.

Then he kissed her—but it wasn't the conventionally light kiss that the situation warranted. She felt his lips seek hers, ruthless, urgent, demanding—and involuntarily, her own lips responded.

Instantly she was released.

'I think that just about evens the score!' the mocking voice said softly in her ear.

CHAPTER TWO

THE blood drummed in Emma's ears and for a moment she thought she was going to faint. She had thought that Frank Hall had plumbed the depths of masculine effrontery, but this man—*this* man——!

To use such an opportunity to pay off a trivial score in such a way! It was abominable, absolutely beyond the bounds of decency!

She raged at the memory of that burning kiss; but outrageous though it had been, that wasn't the worst of it. His simulated passion had stirred a responsiveness in her—and he knew it! That was what humiliated her beyond endurance. She felt cheap, defiled—as he had meant her to.

And there wasn't a thing she could do about it. Or was there? In the brief time she had at her disposal Emma's brain worked with a speed and a subtlety she had not known she was capable of. There was only one thing to do—one way in which she could rob him of his triumph and regain her own self-respect.

She must behave as if nothing out of the way had happened, as if she had been blandly unaware that he had exceeded the bounds of good manners. After all, on such an occasion, what did an odd kiss here or there matter? Yes, that was it, and she must waste no time before putting her stratagem into practice. She plucked up courage and though her lips still burned she forced herself to smile casually at him and then with genuine warmth as Kitty turned to her to have her veil arranged.

'Ready?' Mr Mortimer asked. 'Then off you go!'

Someone must have given the signal to the organist, for as Kitty and Rob left the vestry, the strains of the Wedding March greeted them. With a slight, conventional bow Adrian offered his arm, and Emma, perfectly composed now, laid her hand lightly on it.

At this moment there was a slight contretemps. Babette, the little bridesmaid, announced firmly that she intended

24

holding the best man's other arm. Her mother remonstrated and tears seemed imminent, but then Adrian intervened.

'But why not?' he asked, smiling down at the little girl and offering his arm, to which Babette promptly attached herself.

And so he went down the aisle, entirely at his ease, with a bridesmaid on either arm—to the amusement of the waiting guests and to Emma's bewilderment. In any other man she would have accepted such indulgence as a gesture which was rather heart-warming, but in this man——! How could one possibly credit him with such sensitive consideration for the little girl's feelings? It was absolutely out of character, she thought.

However, she had no time to consider that now as, drifting with the tide of events, she posed smilingly for photographs outside the church. Back at the house, still smiling, she stood in the receiving line and finally, feeling that the smile had become permanently glued on, she sat down to lunch—next to Adrian. But even that didn't shake her determination to rob this detestable man of the triumph he had felt at settling the score between them. She accorded him the pleasant but impersonal politeness which good manners dictated, and though Adrian gave no sign of surprise at her composure, she had the satisfaction of knowing that he had no choice but to follow her lead. Or perhaps, having regained his masculine self-esteem, he might, in any case, have behaved decently. But of one thing Emma was quite sure: he wasn't in the least repentant. He'd probably acted on impulse, but having had time for reflection he would feel no regrets.

And yet, when the time came for him to reply to the toast of the bridesmaids, no one would for a moment have suspected that he felt anything but genuine admiration for Emma as well as Babette. There wasn't the least hint that his tongue was in his cheek as he paid them quite charming compliments in a brief but witty speech. In fact it was difficult to sustain her contempt for him—but Emma managed it.

Once the meal was over it was quite easy to avoid him. As the bride and groom moved among their friends, Emma did the same, renewing her acquaintance with relations and friends of the Mortimers' whom she had met on previous visits. Now and again she caught sight of Adrian doing much the same thing, somewhat hampered by Babette, shamelessly adoring, who had attached herself to him like a devoted shadow.

At last it was time for Kitty to change into her going-away garb, and with Emma in attendance she went up to her room. For a long moment she stood in front of her mirror, taking in every detail. When at last she turned away, there were tears in her eyes.

'I'll never look like this again,' she said tremulously. 'Oh well, I suppose it wouldn't do to live permanently with one's head in the clouds!'

'Do you really want to?' Emma asked curiously, and Kitty shook her head.

'No, not really,' she admitted. 'But even with my feet firmly on the ground, I don't ever want to forget what I've felt today!'

'You won't,' Emma told her with conviction. 'And nor will Rob. You're lucky, Kitty.'

'I know I am,' Kitty responded contentedly, and hugged Emma. 'I hope, one of these days you'll be just as happy, Emma!'

'Oh, me?' Emma shrugged her shoulders. 'I'm not too sure I shall ever get married. I don't think I'm the sort of girl that men find attractive.'

'What utter rot!' Kitty declared forcefully as she began to take off her veil. 'Adrian's fallen for you all right!'

'He certainly made a very charming speech on Babette's and my behalf,' Emma agreed, carefully turning away so that Kitty should not see her face, 'but——'

'But you didn't really have much of a look in, did you?' Kitty laughed. 'Young Babette saw to that, the little minx! She simply monopolised him whenever she got the chance. Not that that was surprising. Adrian always gets on well with children and animals—they adore him. And as for men—they think there's nobody like him. You know, a real man's man, a born leader and all that. Can you cope with this zip? I can't quite reach——'

As Emma complied, she asked casually:

'And how about women? Men's men are rarely women's men, are they?'

'No, perhaps not,' Kitty agreed, her voice muffled as she pulled her dress off over her head. 'And, as a matter of fact, I've never heard Adrian's name linked with any girl's. All the same——' she emerged and spoke more clearly, 'it wouldn't surprise me if there had been someone once—and it came unstuck.'

Emma had no time to ask more questions, if indeed she had felt so inclined, for at that moment Mrs Mortimer came into the room.

'Well, how are you getting on, girls?' she asked briskly. 'There's not too much time, you know.'

'Be ready in a brace of shakes,' Kitty assured her, but paused to give her mother one of her impulsive hugs. 'It was a lovely, lovely wedding, Mummy darling! You and Daddy have been quite wonderful!'

Mrs Mortimer returned the hug, but possibly afraid to show too much emotion, she made it brief and almost immediately hurried out of the room.

Kitty mopped her eyes.

'That's the worst of getting married,' she remarked shakily. 'Much as the parents like Rob, they feel they're losing me.' She paused. Then her face cleared. 'Oh well, they'll see the bright side of it once the grandchildren start arriving, that's one comfort! Come on, let's get cracking!'

Ten minutes later when, elegant in an apricot-coloured trouser suit and with a little pillbox hat perched on her dark hair, Kitty ran downstairs, no one would have guessed how near she had been to tears. Happiness radiated from her as she and Rob said their last farewells and dashed to the waiting car amid a hail of confetti and rose petals.

Then, at the very last minute, as the car started up, Kitty's laughing face appeared at the window. She was holding her bouquet in her hand.

'Catch!' she called urgently—and threw it straight into Emma's arms.

There was an instant congratulatory chorus of: 'You'll be the next bride!' as Emma, cherishing the dainty flowers to her heart, made her escape.

As a result she failed to notice that one pair of dark,

27

puzzled eyes followed her intently until she was lost to sight.

Gradually most of the guests made their farewells and left. When only the relatives and near friends remained, they automatically divided into two groups. For the womenfolk there was a welcome cup of tea served in Mrs Mortimer's own little sitting room, while the men followed Mr Mortimer to his study, from which the pleasant sound of clinking glasses could be heard. Babette, subdued by a threat that unless she had a rest now she would certainly not be allowed to stay up for dinner, capitulated meekly. She was fast asleep in a matter of minutes.

Peace reigned throughout the house.

An hour or so later, refreshed and revived, preparations were made for the dinner dance at which Kitty's and Rob's parents would be joint hosts and hostesses. It was to be held at the one-time 'big house' of the district, now a hotel, which specialised in catering for festivities of this sort.

Emma, who had been there on a previous visit, knew just what a delightful setting the hotel would be and on that account looked forward to the evening's entertainment. But there were doubts in her mind as well—doubts which revolved round Adrian Wroughton. It was true, of course, that that charming little speech of his was quite a likely indication that, having settled his score with her, he would be quite content now to bury the hatchet and behave like a civilised being. But with a man like that, could one ever be really sure?

Certainly Emma couldn't, and the last look she gave herself in the long mirror was almost as searching as Kitty's had been earlier in the day. She was still wearing her bridesmaid's dress, but had abandoned the big hat, and after trying out various styles, she had parted her hair centrally and gathered her curly dark hair into an attractive Psyche knot in the nape of her neck. The result, she felt, was reasonably satisfactory, but it was her general appearance which held her critical attention.

In her own opinion she was neither outstandingly plain nor pretty, though admittedly in this lovely dress she looked her best. Well, to her own eyes she did. But what about other people's? What sort of a girl did she seem to them, not so much in the matter of looks but as a person? Would they realise as, to her own bewilderment Emma did, that she had at least two personalities? One was the girl who, through force of circumstances, had seen very little of the world and was consequently unsure of herself and at a disadvantage socially. The other, so recently discovered, was a very different cup of tea. Not perhaps fearless, but certainly on the lookout for adventure and with every intention, as Dave had said, of trying her wings unaided.

Yes, that was it! And her first tentative attempts had added considerably to her self-confidence, which had even seen her through her first encounter with Adrian. She had gone on her way feeling that she had done no more than defend herself against his churlishness. But he hadn't seen it that way, Emma realised. So what sort of girl did he think she was? The sort who took advantage of her sex to make use of a chance-encountered man? That almost certainly, but what else? As a shallow-minded, cheap sort of girl to whom any man's kisses were welcome? No, hardly, because if he had thought that he would have looked for some other way of paying her out. He had believed that she would resent that abominable kiss of his—her cheeks burned afresh at the memory of it—that she would feel defiled by it. As she had—and yet she had responded to it. So what did he think now? Was he disappointed that his revenge had fallen flat, or did he despise her?

'Oh, what's the good of worrying?' Emma asked herself impatiently. 'After all, either way he probably feels nice and superior, so what more can he want?'

And, indeed, it seemed that he wanted nothing more. Not that he actually avoided her, but he certainly didn't seek her company more often than he was compelled to. They didn't sit next to one another at dinner and he only asked her twice to dance with him. On each occasion Emma accepted as, indeed, she really had to, and to her relief he behaved impeccably. He held her securely but without the least suggestion of offensive familiarity; he made occasional polite conversation and he thanked her with every appearance of sincerity at the end of each dance. Emma began to breathe a little more freely.

It was well on into the evening when Babette's parents, Tom and Chris Roberts, asked her anxiously if she had seen their child lately. Regretfully Emma had to admit that she hadn't, and nor apparently had anyone else for over half an hour.

'We've hunted everywhere,' explained her distracted mother. 'We thought perhaps she might have felt tired and gone up to our room—we're staying here for the night, you know—but she wasn't there and none of the staff have seen her. Oh dear—if only the grounds weren't so big—she may have wandered off *anywhere*!'

'I'll help look,' Emma volunteered, but with the best will in the world she met with no success until she suddenly remembered a little conservatory which opened off the residents' drawing room. This was not part of the premises reserved for the dinner dance, but Babette was too young to appreciate such a distinction, and with its pretty little fountain it would certainly be an attractive place to a child.

And her guess was right. Babette was there—but she was not alone. She was fast asleep, cuddled confidingly in the arms of Adrian Wroughton. His eyes, too, were closed, but he could not have been asleep, for at the slight silky rustle of Emma's dress his eyes opened.

Evidently he saw the anxiety in Emma's eyes, for he smiled reassuringly.

'She's all right,' he said in a muted voice. 'Just dog-tired, that's all.'

'I'll tell her parents,' Emma whispered thankfully. 'They were afraid—oh, here's her father!'

'Thank the Lord,' Tom said with very real fervour as he held out his arms. 'Sorry you've been lumbered, old man!'

'Oh, that's all right,' Adrian said cheerfully as he stood up and very carefully transferred the sleeping child to her father's arms. 'We had quite a natter before she dropped off—gave me an opportunity of getting to know my future bride better than I did!'

'Oh, she's proposed to you, has she?' Tom said resignedly. 'Little baggage! When am I to welcome you as a son-in-law, Adrian?'

'Oh, not just yet,' Adrian explained. 'We've arranged that if in, say, ten or twelve years she still feels the same way, she'll let me know.'

'I bet she will,' Tom replied with considerable feeling. 'And heaven help you, my lad, if you've got hitched up elsewhere in the meantime! Well, I'd better let Chris know the search is over. She's just about frantic.' He turned to leave them, but paused as he reached the doorway. 'I'll send a maid out to you with drinks—you've earned them! Lager for you, I suppose, Adrian? And you, Emma?'

'Oh——' Emma would have liked to refuse the offer which meant, inevitably, a tête-à-tête with Adrian, but it would be so difficult to explain. 'Something long and soft. A lemon squash and soda, something like that.'

'OK,' Tom promised, and went off.

For a moment there was silence. Then Adrian said politely:

'Do sit down, Miss Lathom. Thank you,' as she complied and he followed suit. 'You know, even in these days of equality, a man feels somewhat diffident about sitting while a woman is still standing!'

Without comment Emma sat down in the chair he indicated, but her heart beat a little faster. There had been an unmistakable challenge in his final remark which made it only too clear that the hatchet was only very imperfectly buried, and could be grubbed up with very little effort. All right, if that was the way it was to be, she accepted the challenge, but on her own terms. She would only assert herself if he made it necessary, but if he did start anything, then as far as she was concerned, there would be no holds barred.

The maid arrived with the drinks at that moment and the silence between them continued until each glass was half empty. Emma wished that it could go on. It was pleasantly cool out here, and the tinkling of the little fountain added to her sense of well-being. Perhaps her companion felt the same way for when he did speak, his first remark was entirely innocuous.

'That's just what I wanted,' he remarked appreciatively. 'And yours, Miss Lathom?'

'Perfect,' Emma replied. 'I hadn't realised how thirsty I was, nor how pleasant it would be to relax. It's been quite a strenuous day. But, thank goodness, I didn't have to make a speech——that would have been the last straw! And that reminds me, Mr Wroughton, I'd like to thank you for the pretty things you said about Babette and me. As a matter of fact, I thought yours was the best speech of them all.' And if that wasn't an olive branch, she'd like to know what would be!

But his reply completely took the wind out of her sails, for he remarked complacently:

'Yes, quite good, wasn't it? It always goes down well!'

So it was no more than a stock speech, not in the least sincere! Emma fumed.

'Oh, so this isn't the first time you've been a best man?' she asked, ignoring the other aspect of his confession.

'Heavens, no! It's the'——he counted on his fingers—— 'sixth or seventh, I'm not quite sure which. And you? Have you been a bridesmaid before?'

'Oh, yes, this is my third effort. I was bridesmaid when one of my half-sisters got married and again for a cousin,' Emma explained.

'Three times?' There was a quizzical note in his voice. 'Isn't there a superstition about that?'

' "Three times a bridesmaid, never a bride," ' Emma quoted, sipping her drink placidly.

'It doesn't sound as if the prospect daunts you,' Adrian commented drily. 'Oh, but I was forgetting! You caught the bride's bouquet, and I gather that means you'll shortly be getting married.'

Emma smiled and shook her head without comment.

'Do I take it that you don't regard the prospect of marriage as attractive?' he asked deliberately. 'You have, perhaps, an antipathy for men?'

Now he really was asking for it!

'I wouldn't go as far as that,' she said reflectively. 'I was very fond of my father and my brother-in-law is a dear. But I must admit that I find the majority of men rather mentally immature.'

'How intriguing,' Adrian commented with exaggerated interest. 'Tell me more about my despicable sex, Miss Lathom!'

'Oh, not really despicable,' Emma assured him tolerantly. 'It's just the way things are, and really one should be sorry about it. I mean, it must be intolerable to go through life with such an inferiority complex that one is compelled to be self-assertive all the time to hide it!'

Blank silence. Had she hit the nail on the head so accurately that he simply couldn't find anything to say? Or—— She stole a look at him through her lashes and saw that he was—amused! Her satisfaction collapsed like a punctured balloon. How stupid she had been to be so outspoken. Of course he would simply dismiss what she had said as the outcome of silly feminine prejudice, not worth bothering about!

And that was exactly what he did, for, ignoring her criticisms, his next remark was in the form of a question.

'Am I right, then, in concluding that you're a careerist?'

'Good gracious, no!' Emma assured him. 'Nothing so impressive. In fact, I've never had a job.'

'A lady of leisure?' he asked ironically.

'Hardly,' Emma explained, and wondered why she was bothering to do anything of the sort. 'You see, I was needed at home. I'm very much the youngest of the family and so Mother and Father were getting on and neither of them was in good health for some years.' She paused and then concluded abruptly: 'It's two years since my mother died. Father died only three months ago.'

He didn't reply immediately, and when he did he offered no sympathy, but he certainly showed surprising intuition.

'So now you're free to live your own life?' he suggested. 'What are you going to do about it?'

'Get a job,' Emma said curtly, in the hope of discouraging further questions.

But her lack of responsiveness only served to make him more curious.

'What sort of job?'

'That I prefer not to discuss,' Emma told him with finality.

He peered at her though half-closed eyes.

'You know, I don't believe you trust me!' he drawled. 'Are you afraid that if you told me I might nip in and beat you to it?'

Emma laughed outright. This man—and dolls! Could anything be more absurd?

'Have I said something funny?' he asked mildly.

'Yes, you have.' Emma tried to check her amusement, but without much success. 'You see, what I have in mind is so essentially a feminine occupation that it struck me as being quite absurd!'

'You know, with everything you say you're increasing my curiosity to an almost unbearable degree,' he complained. 'Do put me out of my misery!'

But Emma was adamant.

'No,' she said decisively, and yet, once again, found herself telling him far more than was necessary. 'You see, at present, it's a job that only exists in my mind. I may well have considerable difficulty in persuading—someone—that it's a good idea. And until I've done that—if I do—I'm not telling *anybody*! I mean, no one likes to have to admit that they've met with failure, do they? I'm sure *you* wouldn't!'

'You're quite right, I wouldn't,' he agreed in an oddly grudging way, and then he lifted his head alertly. 'Listen! I think the show is just about over. Isn't the band playing "Auld Lang Syne"?'

'Yes, it is,' Emma agreed, jumping to her feet. 'We mustn't be left out of that!'

She hurried out of the conservatory and, at a more leisurely pace, Adrian followed. When he reached the al-ready-formed circle, Emma had already found a place in it and he made no attempt to join her. But afterwards, when little groups of people were still lingering in desultory con-versation, he sought her out.

'I understand that you're staying on with the Mortimers for a day or so,' he remarked, and when Emma, wondering what was coming now, agreed that she was, he went on matter-of-factly: 'I, on the other hand, am only staying overnight with Rob's people and leaving very early in the morning. So this is goodbye, Miss Lathom,' and he held out his hand.

Involuntarily Emma put hers into it and was immediately aware of the disconcerting strength of the man, which almost amounted to magnetism.

'Goodbye, Lady of Mystery,' he said softly. 'I wish you luck over your job!'

Then, without giving her a chance to have the last word,

34

he released her hand, bowed very slightly and strolled away, completely master of himself—and the situation.

Lady of Mystery, indeed! Emma thought crossly. Why, somehow or other, he'd inveigled her into telling him far more about herself than she had ever intended, whereas what more did she know about him than she had done before their tête-à-tête? Literally nothing—unless one excepted his complaisant admission of insincerity and his acknowledgement that he wouldn't like to admit to failure. And neither piece of information had done anything more than confirm her earlier impression of him.

He was the mysterious one! Why, she'd no idea where he lived, what his work was or whether he had a family. In fact, for all she knew, he might be married! Not that it mattered in the least if he was, but what did puzzle her was that though she was quite sure now that he actively disliked her, yet he had shown such interest in her affairs. Well, why?

She didn't take long to solve that problem. He hadn't really been interested—hadn't even been curious—but he was shrewd enough to know that so long as he asked the questions, he wouldn't have to answer any!

She was quite sure of it—he had something to hide!

Emma spent the whole of the next day helping Mrs Mortimer fill little boxes with cake which were destined for people who hadn't been able to be at the wedding, and in packing the wedding presents. And that wasn't an easy job, for none of the available boxes seemed to be the right size or shape.

'They never are,' Mrs Mortimer sighed. 'It's just the same at Christmas!'

However, they finished at last, and Emma was free to carry out her promise to Rose to let her know when to expect her back the following day. Now she had to be told that Emma had totally different plans—plans of which Rose would inevitably disapprove. But as she dialled Rose's number, Emma squared her shoulders. This was her chance —and she wasn't going to waste it through cowardice.

Rose answered so quickly that Emma was sure she had been purposely sitting close to the telephone waiting for the call, and her first words confirmed that.

'Oh, darling,' she began agitatedly, 'I've been so worried! I thought you'd have rung up much earlier. There's nothing wrong, is there?'

'Not a thing,' Emma assured her soothingly. 'It's just that Mrs Mortimer and I have been busy all day clearing up. We've only just finished.'

'Oh, Emma! I'm so relieved!' Rose sounded really tearful. 'I'd decided to wait just another ten minutes and then I was going to ring you!'

'Oh, Rose!' Emma protested with a not very successful laugh. 'You do let your imagination run away with you, don't you?'

'Well—perhaps,' admitted Rose. 'But awful things can happen, even at a wedding!'

'Well, they didn't at this wedding,' Emma told her cheerfully, 'everything went like clockwork. Kitty's dress was simply lovely,' she added, hoping to divert Rose, 'and so is mine. You'll love it.'

But it was no good, Rose would not be diverted.

'I'm looking forward to seeing it,' she said more cheerfully, and then, inevitably, asked the question Emma had been dreading. 'What time will you be home tomorrow?'

'Well, as a matter of fact, I won't be returning tomorrow, Rose,' Emma told her. 'You see, I've decided——'

'You're not coming home!' The telephone crackled as Rose's voice rose shrilly. 'But you *promised*, Emma! There *is* something wrong—I know there is. For heaven's sake, tell me!'

So, holding on to her patience with some difficulty, Emma explained that the scenery in this part of the world was so beautiful that she had decided to spend a while touring to see more of it. Which was all quite true, even if it wasn't the whole truth.

Rose was outraged. Emma was not only being most inconsiderate, she was almost certainly being dishonest as well, for in her opinion, Emma had planned to do this from the very first—which, as it was true, Emma couldn't deny.

'And,' Rose concluded forcefully, 'you must come home tomorrow!'

'No, Rose, I'm not going to,' Emma told her with a resoluteness which surprised her as much as it did Rose. 'It's absurd for you to make such a fuss! And as for being dishonest, I would have told you if I hadn't known you'd try to stop me! No, don't interrupt, because I've got to say this and you've got to listen! I'm of age and in full posses- sion of my faculties and I'm very, very tired of being treated like a mentally handicapped child. At the moment, all I'm planning to do is have a holiday of my own choice. There's no reason on earth——'

There was a confused noise at the other end of the line and then Dave spoke.

'Hallo, Emma, Dave here. Now what are you up to, you baggage?'

Briefly Emma explained, and to her relief Dave chuckled.

'Yes, I thought you might have something like that in mind,' he told her.

'You did?' Emma said blankly.

'Naturally! It's the first time you've got off the leash and of course you intend to make the most of it. And you've every right to decide to have a holiday. Heaven knows, you've earned it! But be fair, it's come as a bit of a shock to Rose.'

'I know,' Emma admitted, 'and I'm sorry, but——'

'But not sorry enough to give up the idea,' Dave finished for her. 'Well, why should you? But you'll keep in touch?'

'Of course,' promised Emma.

'Fine! That seems to be the lot, then—no, wait a minute, Rose wants to know something. Oh yes—you are on your own, aren't you? There's no man involved either now, or one that you're meeting later?'

'No, there is *not*!' Emma shouted furiously. Men? She'd had more than enough of them!

'All right, all right, don't deafen me!' Dave protested. 'What? Oh, Rose says if you won't come back, you must promise not to speak to any strange men, but'—there was the unmistakable sound of an unregenerate chuckle—'I've pointed out that that's hardly complimentary to me!'

Emma giggled appreciatively. There had been nothing

conventional in the way Dave and Rose had met. They had happened to travel in the same railway compartment and Dave, leaning out of the window, had got a piece of grit in his eye which Rose had skilfully extracted for him. Dave had decided then and there that this was his girl, and had seen to it that they didn't lose touch; six months later, they were married. And Rose, at that time, had been several years younger than Emma was now!

'Well, that seems to be everything,' Dave said cheerfully. 'Have a good time, Emma, and don't worry your pretty little head about anything. You're all right!' And he rang off.

Emma was relieved at having got that over, but she was somewhat exasperated. What a fuss about nothing! And the extraordinary thing was that where her own children, years younger than Emma, were concerned, Rose was tolerant to the point of being downright indulgent—if either Jeremy or Anne exceeded the bounds of acceptable behaviour, it was Dave, mildest of men, who had to crack down on the culprit while Rose found excuses for them.

'It's partly my fault. I've been much too meek and mild. But there's not going to be any more of that!' Emma told herself resolutely.

As the car ate up the miles, Emma began to sing for sheer lightheartedness. The world was such a beautiful place! The sun shone in a clear blue sky, a baby breeze that barely ruffled her curls kept her pleasantly cool, the car was— touch wood!—behaving beautifully, and as for the scenery——!

Emma had never seen anything like it before, and she revelled in the contrasting grandeur of the sheer heights which dominated and seemed to protect the fertile valleys that nestled beneath them. And as if that weren't enough, there was the added beauty which only water can give. Rivers, large and small, great lakes and tiny tarns—breathtakingly satisfying. And the waterfalls—at first Emma had been puzzled by what looked like broad white ribbons stretched from the top to the bottom of the craggy mountains: then she realised that actually they were masses of tumbling water so impressive as to be almost sobering.

But not quite. Nothing could quench Emma's high spirits for long.

> 'Sigh no more, ladies; ladies, sigh no more;' she carolled joyously.
> 'Men were deceivers ever, men were deceivers ever;
> One foot on sea and one on shore,
> To one thing constant never:
> Then sigh not so, but let them go,
> And be you blithe and bonny—and be you blithe and bonny,
> Converting all your sounds of woe
> To Hey nonny nonny—hey nonny non——'

She stopped her song abruptly. She had worked out her route very carefully, and despite all the twists and turns had had no bother in finding her way which was quite well signposted. But now she had passed a signpost on which there was no mention of Windyvale. She drew up at the side of the road and studied her sketch map. It looked simple enough, but somehow she had missed Windyvale. Or had she? That tiny village shop, the very few cottages, a smithy and—yes, the briefest glimpse of a church tower almost lost to view among the trees—was that Windyvale? She turned the car and went back to inquire. The shop seemed to be the best place to ask for information——

An old-fashioned spring bell rang as she opened the door into the smallest shop imaginable, which none the less seemed to stock simply everything except, probably, the one thing one wanted. An immensely fat woman surged and billowed from the sitting room at the back and regarded Emma with eyes which, though they weren't exactly hostile, were certainly both wary and curious. The woman waited silently for Emma to speak.

'I'm looking for a house called Fantasy,' Emma explained. 'I'll be glad if you'll direct me——'

'Up the road a piece,' the woman jerked her head in the direction to which the car was pointing. 'You turn in at the big gates and then turn off on the left. There's a signpost. You can't miss it——'

Unless you're an absolute fool, her tone indicated, and

Emma, after thanking her, beat a hasty retreat. She felt as if she had been turned inside out, put under a microscope and discarded as being beneath contempt. Not an encouraging start!

However, she found the gates without difficulty. They were open and led to a drive overgrown with weeds and made dark by trees that almost interlaced overhead. Feeling like a trespasser, Emma crawled along looking for the signpost. It simply wasn't there, but having little choice, Emma kept doggedly on. Quite suddenly the tunnel of trees ended and she was in the sunshine again, and right ahead of her was a magnificent stone mansion.

Fantasy? Surely not! It looked far too solid and dignified for such a name! Somehow she'd lost her way again . . .

It was at that moment that a young man came round the corner of the house. He was fair and extraordinarily handsome and he smiled in a friendly way at Emma.

'Hallo!' he greeted her, 'gorgeous day, isn't it?'

Emma flushed, because it was quite unmistakable from his expression that he attributed much of the day's gorgeousness to her unexpected appearance.

'Yes, isn't it?' she agreed, and as their eyes met she found herself smiling in response. 'I'm looking for a house called Fantasy. Is this——?' She looked doubtfully at the impressive mansion.

'Bless the girl, no!' A shadow seemed to fall over his face. '*This* is Heartbreak House.'

'Oh!' Emma regarded him uncertainly. 'Not really! I mean, nobody would call their home that, surely?'

'No, it's my name for it,' he explained glumly. 'It suits it better than its real name—Windyvale Hall.'

'Then why?' Emma wanted to know. 'It's lovely!'

'At first glance, yes,' he agreed. 'The walls are pretty sound, but there's hardly a sound piece of wood in it, and as for the roof'—he shook his head despairingly—'I've got myself very truly into debt to pay for putting it into anything like a state of repair.'

'You mean, it's yours?' Emma asked.

'It is,' he confirmed grimly, 'and if ever anyone had an old man of the sea on their shoulders, I have! It would take thousands of pounds to put it right, which I haven't got, so unless I marry an heiress—I suppose you're not one, are you?' he concluded hopefully.

'No, I'm not,' Emma denied emphatically, 'and I don't believe you'd really marry anyone just for their money, would you?'

He smiled.

'No, you nice child, I wouldn't,' he admitted. 'Now, about Fantasy—you should have turned off the so-called drive at the signpost——'

'But there wasn't a signpost—truly there wasn't,' Emma insisted.

'Oh, great Scot!' He clapped his hand to his forehead. 'That's right. It blew down in a gale a week or so ago and I promised Aunt Hester I'd repair it—but I haven't. Tell you what, I'll come with you as far as the turning.'

He trotted briskly beside Emma as she slowly made her way back down the drive.

'There you are!' He pointed along what Emma had taken for a garden path. 'Just a few hundred yards, you can't mistake it. It's an architect's nightmare, more politely described as a *cottage orné*. It was built some time in the seventeen-hundreds by an ancestor of mine for his *chère amie*. But don't worry, it's perfectly respectable these days! Aunt Hester is more like a character out of *Cranford* than one can believe possible. And besides, there's dear Winsome Baker to preserve the decencies.'

'Who's she?' Emma asked apprehensively.

'Aunt Hester's watchdog-cum-slave,' she was told, 'something of a Tartar. But for heaven's sake, don't let her imagine you're scared of her, because if you do, she'll despise you. Anyway, her bark is a lot worse than her bite. Well, best of luck!'

He sketched a gay salute and Emma pressed slowly along the narrow track. And sure enough, there was a little house which could clearly be called nothing but Fantasy, for it *was* a nightmare. Vaguely Gothic as to windows, some of which had stained glass, its walls were topped with crenellated battlements, and its many grotesque chimneys suggested that they were intended more for decoration than use.

But for the moment Emma had little time to spare for

41

these fascinating eccentricities, for quite suddenly her courage deserted her. The whole venture seemed preposterous and she would have given anything to turn tail. It took every scrap of resolution she possessed to walk up to the forbidding-looking front door, guarded on either side by a snarling stone lion.

She lifted her hand to the knocker, but before she had touched it, the door was opened wide as if, disconcertingly, her arrival had been anticipated.

CHAPTER THREE

THE door had opened as if Emma were an expected visitor, but there was no welcome on the face of the forbidding female who stood just inside.

She was tall and gaunt, her hair was skinned back so tightly from her forehead that her eyebrows were lifted in permanent query, and she was slightly cross-eyed. She was, in fact, quite the plainest woman that Emma had ever seen.

She waited in grim silence for Emma to speak and, cross-eyed or not, her sloe-black eyes raked Emma's face with the same wary curiosity which the woman at the village shop had shown. A positive dragon of a woman! But Emma, grateful for the warning that the fair-haired young man had given her, stood her ground.

'My name is Lathom,' she explained. 'I shall be glad, if Miss Prescott is at home, if she'll spare me a few minutes——'

'Why do you want to see her?' the dragon demanded suspiciously.

Emma was tempted to ask her straight out what authority she had to be so obstructive, but decided that an oblique attack was preferable.

'Are you Miss Prescott?' she asked, with a slight but meaningful emphasis on the pronoun.

'No, indeed,' the dragon denied hastily. 'My name is Baker. I'm her housekeeper.'

For a moment Emma was too taken aback to reply. Baker? *Winsome* Baker? Oh, surely not! As a name for such a desperately plain woman it would have been amusing if it hadn't been so cruel.

'Will you let Miss Prescott know that I would like to see her?' she asked, more gently than she had spoken before.

Even then the dragon hesitated.

'Oh, very well,' she capitulated at last. 'But just you be careful and don't worry her. That I will not have!' She paused again. 'You'd better come in, I suppose, while I find

43

out,' she concluded ungraciously, standing aside for Emma to enter the small hall which, in its way, was as absurdly pretentious as the outside of the cottage was. To begin with, the staircase, quite out of proportion to the hall which it dominated, had banisters ornately carved within an inch of their lives. The marble floor was patterned in outsize black and white squares and the few pieces of furniture were so large as to suggest that they had originally been made for a much larger house, as was quite likely the case.

The housekeeper, who had disappeared through a much-varnished pinewood door, suddenly appeared again.

'She'll see you,' she announced reluctantly, and made way for Emma to go into the room. 'The young—lady, Miss Hester.' But having made the announcement, she showed no signs of leaving.

'Thank you, Martha,' the occupant of the room spoke gently but with unmistakable dismissiveness, and the housekeeper faded away without protest. 'And now,' the gentle voice went on, 'what can I do for you, Miss Lathom?'

Emma's first impression of Miss Prescott—and one which was never to change—was that a more perfect description of her could not be found than that she was exactly like a character out of *Cranford*.

She was probably, Emma thought, somewhere in her late forties or early fifties. Her wavy grey hair, cut in front to a little fringe, made a demure frame for a still pretty pink and white face. Her eyes were deeply blue and her nose was attractively tip-tilted. But what really impressed Emma was the gentle sweetness of her expression; it suggested more leisurely, less acquisitive days than those Emma had known all her life. A simplicity of outlook—and yet there was strength there as well. And now Miss Prescott was smiling encouragingly.

'I read that interview you gave to the press, Miss Prescott,' Emma explained, put completely at her ease, 'and I've got some dolls which I think—I hope—you'll find interesting.'

'I should certainly like to see them,' Miss Prescott declared eagerly. 'Have you brought them with you?'

'Yes, they're in the car,' Emma told her. 'I'll fetch them.'

'Ask Martha to help you,' Miss Prescott suggested, and looked amused. 'You'll find her just outside this door on guard—in case you turned out to have criminal intentions, you know. She always anticipates the worst. In fact, sometimes I'm not sure she doesn't hope for it!'

'Martha,' Emma repeated uncertainly. 'Is—is that her real name?'

Miss Prescott looked surprised.

'No, it isn't,' she said. 'Her real name is—one that she considers unsuitable, so she prefers to be called Martha. But how did you guess that, my dear?'

'It wasn't a guess,' Emma confessed, rather wishing that she hadn't asked the question. 'On my way here I missed your turning'—she was discreet enough not to say why—'and went straight on to Windyvale Hall. There was a man there who referred to you as his aunt——'

'My nephew, Timothy Prescott.' Miss Prescott made a comically rueful grimace. 'And he told you what her name really is, of course, the bad boy! Actually, he's the only person who dares to call her by it, and oddly enough, she seems to enjoy letting him do it! But then Tim has a way with him——' she sighed faintly as if she wasn't too sure that Tim's 'way' was altogether a good thing. 'Well, fetch your dolls, my dear, I'm all impatience to see them!'

So, with Martha's competent if reluctant help, Emma brought the two cases in and laid them on the big worktable which formed most of the furnishing in what was obviously Miss Prescott's workroom. Carefully she unwound the silk wrappings from the lady doll and heard Miss Prescott catch her breath as it was laid in front of her.

'My dear——!' she exclaimed in an awestruck way, but as Emma produced the other dolls, she seemed to be lost for words. Emma waited anxiously for the verdict, and at last, reluctantly, Miss Prescott dragged her eyes from the dolls; though even then, her fingers lingered caressingly on them.

'My dear'—she began, her pleasant face alight with excited interest—'as I expect you know, you have nothing short of treasure trove here! In fact, I've never seen——'

she shook her head wonderingly.

'I wasn't sure,' Emma explained rather unsteadily. 'I thought they were quite good, but I don't really know anything about antique dolls, so I didn't know that they are as good as you say.'

The blue eyes twinkled.

'But you shouldn't have told me that,' Miss Prescott remonstrated. 'Don't you see, I might take advantage of your ignorance and try to cheat you?'

Emma laughed at the idea.

'Oh no, you wouldn't do that, Miss Prescott,' she said confidently. 'It would make you feel far too uncomfortable inside yourself if you did.'

'You're quite right, it would,' Miss Prescott agreed seriously. 'But it's pleasant to know that you appreciate it. And now, tell me all about these lovely dolls. How did they come into your possession? And how does it come about that they and their clothes are in such perfect condition?'

Nothing loth, Emma plunged headlong into an account of her discovery in the attic and the history of Lucy May Wainwright's hobby.

'You see, it couldn't be more than that,' she explained, 'because though her designs were used by Miss Bobbin, who must, I think, have been the local dressmaker, they didn't tell anybody about it. Lucy May talks about that in her diary. I may not have got the words quite right, but it was something like: "Dear Papa and Mama would be so mortified if they knew that my work has a commercial value, even though, of course, I accept no payment from Miss Bobbin." '

'Poor little girl,' Miss Prescott said sympathetically. 'Compelled to hide her genius under a bushel simply because her parents were snobs! Because she *was* a genius, you know. To us this dress is far too fussy with all its buttons and bows, but of its period, it is in singularly good taste. And as far as the actual stitching is concerned, it's exquisite.'

'I like some of the other dresses better,' Emma said, opening the box which held them. 'This evening gown, for instance'—she held up an entrancing confection in white moiré silk, swathed with pale pink tulle caught here and there with tiny wax flowers—'I think even Mrs Ponsonby must have looked charming in this!'

'Mrs Ponsonby?' Miss Prescott asked with interest.

'I think she was Miss Bobbin's wealthiest client,' Emma explained. 'Lucy May often refers to her—not always very flatteringly. I think she used the biggest doll as her model for Mrs Ponsonby, for if you look, you'll see that her corset has been carefully padded to give her a more buxom figure and she—Lucy May—speaks of Mrs Ponsonby as being both stout and florid—as well as being very autocratic and self-opinionated.' And suddenly Emma laughed.

'Yes?' Miss Prescott encouraged, smiling.

'I was laughing because of what Lucy May says about some material which her Mrs Ponsonby bought. It was bright purple velvet, and Lucy May and Miss Bobbin were absolutely horrified. They did their best, but apparently Mrs Ponsonby looked like an over-stuffed, upholstered sofa!' She laughed again. 'And that reminded me of a woman I know called Mrs Hall. I used to be afraid of her, but not after reading that description?' Miss Prescott smiled, then her attention reverted to the dolls as she touched their delicately tinted cheeks with gentle, caressing fingers. 'Quite beautiful,' she murmured and then, abruptly, she became practical. 'And now, my dear, will you tell me what you plan to do with your little family? I mean, do you regard them as a nucleus for a larger collection? Or do you want to sell them?'

'I haven't really made my mind up yet,' Emma confessed. 'I felt the first thing to do was to find out just how valuable they are. That's why I decided to show them to you.'

'Yes, I understand,' Miss Prescott admitted slowly. 'But that's just what—yes, Martha?' as the housekeeper, after a rather aggressive knock, sailed into the room.

'About lunch, madam,' she explained tonelessly, carefully avoiding so much as a glance in Emma's direction. 'I'll be ready in a quarter of an hour.'

'I'm glad you reminded me, Martha,' Miss Prescott replied, and turned to Emma. 'I hope you can stay and share the meal with me, Miss Lathom?'

'I'd like to very much,' Emma replied rather doubtfully, for all that her rather early breakfast seemed to belong to a very distant past. 'If you're quite sure it won't inconvenience you——'

'Quite sure,' Miss Prescott insisted, and then, dismissing the subject as needing no further discussion, she pointed to the dolls. 'Look, Martha, at these lovely dolls Miss Lathom has brought for me to see!'

'Very nice, I'm sure,' Martha—née Winsome—sniffed without looking at them, and made a stiff-necked exit.

'Oh dear!' Emma said uncomfortably. 'I'm afraid that really it isn't convenient—I do hope it doesn't mean I'll be eating what Martha would have had——?'

'Nothing of the sort, my dear,' Miss Prescott assured her briskly. 'There's almost the whole of a cold chicken to cut from, plenty of salad from the garden, and this year we've had so many raspberries that we simply haven't known how to make use of them all! No, you needn't worry, Martha won't go short, though she would without hesitation if she thought that it would help me in any way.' She paused and touched Emma's hand as gently as she had touched the dolls' cheeks. 'Don't take offence at her manner, my dear, because people who live in a little pocket in time and place like Windyvale are inclined to be suspicious of newcomers. It's a survival, I suppose, from the days when a stranger could so easily be an enemy. And in Martha's particular case—she is so loyal, so devoted to me, that in her the instinct of suspicion and caution has become something of an obsession.'

'Yes, I think I understand,' Emma said gently. 'As a matter of fact, Mr Prescott warned me that she might be a little—difficult. He said that she was your watchdog and your slave,' and instantly wished she had not repeated Tim's remark, for Miss Prescott's face clouded.

'Tim is very clever at finding the *mot juste*,' she conceded, 'but he should have told you as well that underneath that prickly exterior is the warmest heart in the world, as many people in trouble have discovered, sometimes to their surprise. And now,' she went on, 'I expect you'd like to wash before lunch?' She stood up and felt for an old-fashioned crutch walking stick, which until then Emma had not noticed leaning against her chair. 'If you will forgive me I won't come upstairs with you—I'm rather lame and I avoid stairs as much as possible. But you'll find the bathroom door is immediately opposite when you reach the landing and my bedroom is next door to it. Please make use of both of them. I shall be waiting for you in the hall when you come down.'

Emma found her way without difficulty and found that a guest towel had been put ready for her use. Evidently, however much she might resent casual visitors, Martha was punctilious where such details were concerned.

Because Emma didn't want to keep Miss Prescott waiting too long, she hurried through her tidying-up and so had little time to pay much attention to the appearance of the bedroom beyond realising that though everything was spotlessly clean and neat, there was an unmistakable air of genteel shabbiness about the room. Evidently Tim was not the only one who was hard up, and Emma wondered with some concern just how much that would affect that still rather nebulous plan of hers. She hurried downstairs, but Miss Prescott, sitting in a huge chair like a theatrical throne, was so deep in thought that she didn't notice Emma had joined her until she was quite close at hand.

'Oh—my dear——' she gave a little start: 'How quick you've been! I thought girls always took an infinity of time over their make-up.'

'Well, so do I,' Emma confessed, 'on special occasions'—and then realising that her choice of words was hardly complimentary to her hostess, she added hastily: 'Like weddings or dances, I mean. Otherwise, in the daytime and in the country, I don't really like heavy make-up.'

'Nor do I,' Miss Prescott agreed so emphatically that Emma wondered if she had someone particular in mind who did use heavy make-up.

Miss Prescott got rather awkwardly to her feet and, limping badly, led the way to a room on the opposite side of the hall from her workroom. It was a combined sitting room and dining room, and was the biggest room that Emma had so far seen.

'Originally this was Madame's *salon*,' Miss Prescott explained as they sat down at the table. 'I expect Tim told you that this little house was originally built for the *fille de joie* of the Prescott of some two hundred years ago?'

'Actually, he said *chère amie*,' Emma replied. 'But I suppose it comes to the same thing.'

'Oh yes,' Miss Prescott agreed tolerantly, 'exactly the same. The French have so much prettier names than we have for that state of affairs,' and she sounded regretful that such should be the case.

'You—you don't sound as if you're at all shocked,' Emma ventured.

'I'm not, really,' confessed Miss Prescott. 'For one thing, it was such a commonplace state of affairs in those days— and such a long time ago—that somehow it seems less reprehensible. Besides, in this particular case one is inclined to be especially tolerant. You must ask Tim to show you the portrait of the Mrs Prescott of those days. A woman with a flat, stupid sort of face and apparently with a gift for always doing and saying the wrong thing. She must have been an absolute millstone round the poor man's neck, whereas Madame was pretty and amusing and very intelligent. She must have been, for her lover was faithful to her till the day of her death.'

As she was speaking, Martha came in with a dish of hot new potatoes, buttered and sprinkled with fresh parsley. She set them down in front of Miss Prescott where a large platter of delicately sliced breast of chicken had already been placed. Both looked most appetising, and so did the salad in its quaint old china bowl.

'Ring if there isn't enough,' Martha requested witheringly, as if she suspected Emma of such excessive gluttony that despite the generous supply of food she wouldn't be satisfied.

'Thank you, Martha,' Miss Prescott said serenely. 'Just bring in the salad cream, please, and then everything will be perfect.'

The request was so gently made that it could not possibly have been regarded as a complaint, but none the less, afraid that Martha would take umbrage, Emma held her breath. But she need not have worried. Martha did not apologise, but her manner when she made good the omission was so chastened as to give the impression that she had. And evidently Miss Prescott accepted it as such, for before Martha had left the room she offered the sauce to

Emma, remarking that it was home-made.

'One of Martha's specialities,' she explained. 'It has spoilt me for any other variety!'

It was, indeed, delicious, and Emma was able to say quite truthfully that it put the finishing touch to what would in any case have been a most appetising first course. The raspberries followed, plump and juicy and served with thick yellow cream and were so good that Emma gladly accepted the offer of a second helping after Miss Prescott had confessed that she intended doing just that herself.

'We are so lucky,' she remarked. 'Tim still runs—well, one can hardly call it the Home Farm because it's on such a modest scale these days, but he's able to let me have all the milk and cream I want as well as eggs and the occasional chicken.' She laughed resignedly. 'What with his supplies and Martha's good cooking, I ought to put on weight at an alarming rate! But I don't, which is fortunate for me, though it worries them! They're quite convinced that I shall fade away before their eyes simply because I happen to be one of Pharaoh's lean kine! But I know just how they feel because—forgive me—but you're far too thin for your height, and from the moment I met you, I was consumed with a desire to feed you up! Have you been ill, my dear?'

'No,' Emma assured her, 'not ill, but——' And then, somehow, it was the easiest thing in the world to tell Miss Prescott just how demanding life had been for the last few years. 'Please don't think that I'm complaining,' she begged in conclusion. 'I truly wanted to make Mother and Father as happy and comfortable as I could and I don't in the least regret that I took it on. Really I had no choice, because I felt that it was my job, and when you feel like that what else can you do?'

Miss Prescott nodded her acceptance of this point of view, but drew her own conclusions.

'None the less, those busy, demanding years have left their mark on you,' she said gently. 'Though I think it possible that you're finding it most difficult of all to deal with the reaction which inevitably comes when a strain—I will not say a burden—is removed?'

'Yes,' Emma agreed eagerly, 'that's just it. I—I feel

almost as if I'm a stranger to myself. As if I've suddenly stepped into a new world. And it could be something of an adventure to stand on my own feet and find out what I'm really like.'

'Of course it could be, and that's how you ought to feel in the circumstances,' Miss Prescott approved warmly. 'It's possible, though, that you may have difficulty in persuading others to accept your attitude.'

'I already have,' Emma sighed regretfully. 'My two half-sisters—I know perfectly well that it's because they're so fond of me and because they're really anxious about my future, but they simply can't understand that even if I make mistakes, it's really safer in the long run than letting other people make all the decisions for me.'

'Far safer,' Miss Prescott concurred vigorously. 'And so you've run away?'

'Not exactly—yet,' Emma told her, and explained about Kitty's wedding, concluding: 'So that meant I could leave home without question for a day or so, but I made up my mind to see whether—whether it was possible for me to stay away longer. Yes, I suppose I am hoping to run away more or less permanently.'

'I see.' Miss Prescott stood up. 'And now, shall we go into the garden? Martha will have arranged my chaise-longue for me. I always rest after lunch, though I don't of necessity sleep.'

The comfortably cushioned chaise-longue had been set in the shade of a vast tree and beside it was an inviting chair also supplied with cushions. A small table had been conveniently placed and even as they settled themselves, Martha came out with coffee and still more cream.

'And now,' Miss Prescott began briskly as they sipped their coffee, 'since I think it probable that your dolls play quite an important part in your plans, I'm going to give you a brief account of the history of dolls made in the last century and early part of this. Of course, dolls of earlier centuries still survive, but they are rare and have a rarity value which puts them beyond my slender purse! Now, to begin with——'

For the next twenty minutes or so Emma listened entranced as, without too much confusing detail, Miss Prescott warmed to her subject, which she had evidently studied very thoroughly and which was very dear to her heart.

Emma learned that doll's heads of the period had been made of *papier mâché* or wax, fine porcelain or bisque, while their bodies had been made of kid, leather or stuffed cotton. Some had real hair, others mohair: there were dolls with fixed eyes and others whose eyes closed when they were laid down. And, Miss Prescott explained, most of the dolls of the nineteenth and early twentieth century were produced either in France or Germany.

'There was, in fact, considerable rivalry between the manufacturers of the two countries to dominate the market, and as a result every effort was made to make realistic and attractive dolls. First Germany, then France and finally Germany again reigned supreme for varying periods. Now, as you know, I have only briefly looked as your dolls, and I must examine them more closely before I give you a definite opinion as to their origin and date. However, I'm reasonably sure that they are all French and, judging by the quality of the heads, that they're very likely of the best French period—probably the eighteen-sixties and seventies. Now, can you help to fix the date more definitely?'

'I think so,' Emma said eagerly. 'Lucy May kept a journal which she started in 1865 and it goes on until about 1878. There aren't many entries in the latter part of the book, though—I think her health was failing by then.'

'Poor little girl,' Miss Prescott said gently. 'Well, that's likely to be very helpful, and, if you don't mind, I'd like to read the journal?'

'Of course,' agreed Emma, 'and you'd like to examine the dolls more thoroughly?'

'Yes, I would. And that reminds me, if you are interested, I would like to show you my little museum—it's housed in what were the old coach-house and stables behind the cottage.'

'I'd love to see them,' Emma told her, 'If—if it won't tire you too much,' she added diffidently.

'I'm going to be quite frank with you,' Miss Prescott replied. 'It would tire me today——'

'Oh dear!' Emma interrupted anxiously. 'I'm afraid I'm

the cause——'

'Not in the least,' Miss Prescott declared firmly. 'It's simply that I had rather a disturbed night last night for some reason or other. Actually, your visit has cheered me up considerably.'

'I'm glad,' Emma said simply, and Miss Prescott smiled.

'Yes, I really believe you are,' she acknowledged. 'Well, now—I can be lazy for the rest of the day without feeling conscience-stricken! But that does bring us to the question of where you are going to spend the night. Have you made any plans?'

'No, I haven't,' Emma confessed. 'Is there anyone in the village who would put me up? I didn't see any sign of a pub——'

'You wouldn't. There is one—the Prescott Arms,' Miss Prescott explained, 'it's just by the church, but so tucked away in the trees that it's very easy to miss. Mrs Bailey has one spare bedroom that she occasionally lets, but her son is at home on leave from the Merchant Navy at the moment and he's using it. In any case, although Mrs Bailey keeps everything spotlessly clean and is a good cook, it would be quite delightful if you would stay here. Will you?'

'I'd love to,' Emma said warmly. 'But I feel I'd be taking too much for granted. I mean, first of all I turn up uninvited; then I eat you out of house and home, and finally I practically compel you to ask me to stay! Are you really sure—and won't Martha be put out?'

'Quite sure,' Miss Prescott assured her, looking amused. 'And as to Martha——'

At that moment Martha came out to collect the coffee tray and Miss Prescott turned to her confidently.

'Oh, Martha, I've persuaded Miss Lathom to stay with us overnight, so will you please see that the Rosebud Room is ready for her?'

'I saw to that half an hour ago,' Martha announced with a mixture of triumph and resignation. She turned to Emma. 'If you'll give me your keys, miss, I'll take your cases out of the car and unpack for you.'

Meekly Emma handed over the keys, but when Martha had gone, she drew a deep breath.

'I feel as if I've been unexpectedly awarded a prize for

good behaviour,' she remarked in awestruck tones. 'What have I done to gain Martha's approbation—for I gather I have?'

'Oh yes, very definitely,' Miss Prescott assured her. 'You see, though Martha is prone to initial prejudices where strangers are concerned, fortunately she is also a very shrewd and quick judge of character—in fact, I've rarely known her make a mistake. But how she arrives at her conclusions, I've never discovered. All I can tell you is that now you're in her good books, you'll stay there! And now, my dear, if you'll excuse me, I'm going to have a little sleep.' She settled herself more comfortably on her cushions. 'Don't bother about not making any noise—I'm so deliciously sleepy that I don't think anything will disturb me!' And smiling drowsily, she closed her eyes.

But despite Miss Prescott's assurance, Emma had no wish but to relax in her comfortable chair and drink in the soothing peace of her surroundings. Near at hand a herbaceous border blazed in the sunshine, bees buzzed industriously from flower to flower. A soft breeze wafted the perfume of lavender bushes to an almost intoxicating degree, and a tabby cat sprawled at its ease on the grass, occasionally washing itself in a leisurely way. It was absolute peace such as Emma had never experienced before, and she surrendered to its spell. Her eyes closed and she hovered in a blissful state halfway between waking and sleeping.

'Who in the world are you?' a woman's voice, disagreeably strident, demanded rudely.

The newcomer had approached silently across the lawn and the first indication of her presence was when she spoke. Startled and a little confused, Emma sat erect and tried to collect her wits.

A tall, slim young woman of about her own age was standing beside her chair. She wore extremely well cut khaki jodhpurs with a brown, open-necked shirt, and she carried a riding crop in one hand. Except that she was more sunburned her colouring was very similar to Emma's, but there, Emma sincerely hoped, the likeness ended, for though the girl was undeniably striking in appearance, her expression robbed her face of any possible claim to good looks—hard, supercilious, arrogant.

'I——' Emma began, but Miss Prescott had also been awakened and intervened.

'Good afternoon, Lorraine,' she said punctiliously but with a marked lack of enthusiasm. And then, to Emma: 'Emma, my dear, may I introduce Mrs Heywood, a near neighbour. Lorraine, this is a young friend of mine, Miss Lathom.'

Emma, appreciating that Miss Prescott's formality was quite deliberate, responded as convention demanded.

'How do you do, Mrs Heywood?' she said politely.

Lorraine Heywood, however, barely acknowledged the introduction.

'Is Tim here?' she demanded imperiously of Miss Prescott. 'I must see him at once, it's important.'

'Tim here—at this time of day?' Miss Prescott looked surprised. 'But surely you know, Lorraine, that Tim hasn't time for social visits until evening, and not always then. Have you tried going to his workshop?'

'I've just come from there,' Lorraine replied impatiently, 'but there's no sign of him.'

'No?' Miss Prescott said equably. 'Then I'm afraid I can't help you, Lorraine.'

Lorraine's eyes narrowed.

'Can't—or won't?' she demanded offensively. 'I think you know perfectly well where he is, but you won't tell me!'

Emma was almost bursting with anger at this rudeness to such a gentle soul as Miss Prescott and longed to fly to her defence. But Miss Prescott was quite able to deal with the situation herself.

'It's a pity that you should think that, Lorraine,' she said with quiet dignity, 'but since you do, I can think of nothing to say which would make you change your mind, so I suggest that we don't discuss the matter further.'

Lorraine's face was a study in conflicting emotions. Clearly she was not satisfied, but the very gentleness of this unmistakable dismissal completely spiked her guns. She turned abruptly and strode off. For a moment there was silence, then Miss Prescott said regretfully:

'My dear, I'm very sorry about this, but there are limits

to what one should tolerate without protest, and Lorraine had exceeded those limits—not for the first time. But though I might have overlooked her bad manners to me, I will *not* have my guests embarrassed!'

'Oh, dear Miss Prescott, please don't worry about me,' Emma begged. 'I'm only concerned in case you've been really upset. Are you quite sure you're all right?'

'Oh yes, there's nothing the matter with me that a cup of tea won't put right,' Miss Prescott assured her, rallying gamely, 'and that Martha will be bringing out very soon now.' And then, without raising her voice or turning her head: 'You can come out now, Tim!'

And to Emma's astonishment, a rather sheepish Tim emerged from a big mass of rhododendrons, brushing twigs and leaves from his fair hair.

'How in the world did you know I was there, Aunt Hester?' he asked in amazement.

'Because I have eyes in the back of my head, of course,' Miss Prescott explained briskly. 'Well?'

Tim dropped a light kiss on the top of her head.

'You were a brick not to give me away, Aunt Hester, but I'm sorry I let you in for Lorraine's Haughty Lady act. It's all the more annoying because it was so unreasonable. All she wanted was for me to go over to the farm to tinker up her car!'

'Indeed!' Miss Prescott said, trying not very successfully to hide a wish for more information. Tim grinned understandingly.

'I wouldn't have had any warning that she was on the warpath, only Jessup rang me up—about something else—and he happened to mention that he was closing the garage for the rest of the day because he had to go to a funeral over at Felbrig and that meant he wouldn't be able to do anything about Mrs Heywood's car until tomorrow. So I took the hint and went to ground. And now,' with an abrupt change of tone, 'may I ask you to present me to your guest since, though we have met informally, we haven't yet been introduced?'

For a moment Emma thought that he was speaking with his tongue in his cheek, but as he bent slightly over her hand and said how glad he was to make her acquaintance, she felt a little thrill of excitement. There was something very pleasant about having a good-looking young man treat her with such courtesy, and yet at the same time, subtly express a very flattering admiration for her. It made her feel important and rather special.

But just then Martha came out of the house and Tim instantly transferred his attentions to her. Despite the heavily-laden tray she was carrying, he managed to slip an arm round her waist and kiss her heartily.

'Winsome, my love, you're as welcome as the flowers in spring—and as charming,' he declared fulsomely, and Emma, who had been waiting for the heavens to fall, heard an extraordinary sound issue from Martha's lips. She was giggling like a teenager.

'Give over, Mister Tim, do!' she requested, contriving to give him a vigorous nudge in the ribs. 'You don't want me to drop the tray, do you?'

'Bring another cup and saucer,' Miss Prescott said resignedly.

'And a plate,' Tim coaxed shamelessly, giving Martha another hug. 'I'm starving!'

'I suppose that means you haven't had any lunch,' Martha retorted severely. 'If you're not careful, Mister Tim, you'll outgrow your strength!'

'You know, I've cherished a hopeless adoration for that woman for years,' Tim declared fervently as Martha went back to the house. 'And what do I get in return? Nothing! She treats me as if I'm still a grubby schoolboy—and a mentally handicapped one at that! Oh well, while there's life there's hope,' he concluded, and set himself to entertain his aunt and Emma who, at Miss Prescott's request, prepared to pour out tea. When Martha returned she brought not only the cup, saucer and plate but also a dish of substantial sausage rolls.

'There, put yourself outside those, Mister Tim, and you won't do too badly,' she announced with satisfaction. 'You'll be staying to dinner, I hope?'

'Am I, Aunt Hester?' Tim had the grace to look slightly embarrassed at this informal invitation.

'Why not?' Miss Prescott shrugged placidly. 'Martha will enjoy stuffing you till you practically burst, and you can pay for your food by amusing Emma and me.'

'With pleasure,' Tim said, so lugubriously that Emma laughed.

Aunt and nephew exchanged a quick, appreciative glance; it was such a soft, infectious sound which struck pleasantly on the ear. And, as the hours passed, they were to show that it was matched by a sense of humour that bubbled up with the spontaneity of a mountain spring.

At six o'clock Tim announced his intention of returning to the Hall to change out of his working clothes into something more suitable for the evening's revels, which made Emma give serious thought to what she should wear. She finally decided on a yellow organza dress with a green sash, which she had bought in Greystoke, and tied her curls with a matching ribbon. When she came downstairs she was glad that she had taken trouble with her appearance, for Tim looked really stunning. He wore no jacket, but with black evening trousers, an elegantly frilled white shirt, a deep crimson tie and a matching cummerbund he looked such a figure of romance that Emma temporarily lost her breath.

It was a perfect evening. Martha gave them a delicious meal, they had coffee in the still sun-drenched garden, and when the sun finally set in a blaze of glory, Emma felt that she had seen the absolute peak of beauty. But she was wrong. The sky slowly turned to blue velvet spangled with stars so big and luminous that Emma could hardly bear it.

'We don't have stars like that in Greystoke,' she said shakily. 'At least, I suppose we do, but there are so many street lamps that they don't show up.'

'Ah, but these are put on at great expense by the management especially for your benefit, Miss Lathom,' Tim told her with a grave complacence which made Emma laugh, as he had meant it to. 'Later we've arranged for a full moon, which I hope will meet with your approval!'

And sure enough, in due time, the moon appeared and threw long, mysterious shadows across the smooth lawn. Unfortunately, however, an evening breeze sprang up and though she was wearing a shetland shawl round her shoulders, Miss Prescott shivered and decided that it was time for her to go indoors. Tim promptly stood up and so did Emma. She would have liked to stay longer, but felt that good manners compelled her to follow her hostess's lead. Miss Prescott, however, had other ideas.

'Just give me your arm to the door, please, Tim,' she requested. 'But don't go yet. Beauty like this shouldn't be wasted just because my old bones have to be pampered. Goodnight, Emma, my dear. Send this boy packing if he bores you.'

But there was no question of that. It was true that neither of them found much to say, but the silence held no embarrassment. Rather it provided a bond between them as each, appreciating the tranquil beauty of the night, felt that words would be both superfluous and clumsy.

Now and again a bird twittered drowsily, and little night animals scurried across the lawn, too intent on their own business to be aware of human presence—Emma, her eyes full of happy tears, was spellbound.

And then, almost under his breath, Tim said one word: '*Fantasy!*'

The spell was broken and Emma felt a sudden chill.

Fantasy! Yes, that was it. Something beyond reality, something to dream about——

Miss Prescott had spoken of Windyvale as being a little pocket in time and place, unchanging, not the sort of place to welcome strangers. And yet Emma had an absolute conviction that, stranger or not, she belonged here. It was Greystoke that seemed remote and unreal—almost a nightmare from which she had miraculously escaped and to which it would be intolerable to return.

Somehow—*somehow* it had got to be possible for her to stay here. It was the deepest wish of her heart and surely, when one felt as passionately about anything as all that, it had just *got* to come true!

At least, she resolved fiercely, it wouldn't be her fault if it didn't!

CHAPTER FOUR

EMMA woke the next morning to find the sun pouring into her room. She linked her hands behind her head and gazed contentedly at the dappled shadows which danced so entrancingly across the ceiling. A wonderful world to find waiting for her, particularly after having had such a splendid night's sleep. She marvelled at that, for she had come to bed with a mind so active that she had expected to lie awake for hours. Instead, sleep had come almost as soon as her head touched the pillow—sleep of a quality to which she had been a stranger for far too long. The fact was that though she wouldn't admit it even to herself, she had been very near to a breakdown and, as Miss Prescott had surmised, the most difficult condition to deal with had been the reaction that followed when she no longer had to drive herself to get through all that the day held. She had found it almost impossible to sit with idle hands without experiencing a feeling of guilt, and instinct had told her that unless she could make a fresh start somewhere where life was geared to a slower tempo than in a manufacturing town like Greystoke, she might never overcome that frightening nervous tension.

And surely in Windyvale she had found just such a place, a little Eden if ever there was one. And yet—Emma's face puckered—not without its serpent! Mrs Heywood—an unpleasantly domineering type, in her way, another Mrs Ponsonby or Mrs Hall. It didn't need much intelligence, even if Miss Prescott and Tim hadn't made their opinions clear, to see that she was quite incapable of seeing any other point of view than her own. Not a woman with whom one could hope—or wish—to be on friendly terms. Almost certainly more likely to be an enemy. On the other hand, and Emma cheered up at the recollection, Miss Prescott had sent her packing in no uncertain manner. And, which was even more satisfactory, Tim made no bones about not liking her. A serpent, undoubtedly, but perhaps not such a dangerous one as all that.

A light tap on the door interrupted Emma's thoughts, and calling, 'Come in!' she sat up in bed as Martha entered with a tray of morning tea.

'Good morning, miss,' she said briskly. 'I hope you slept well?'

'Very well indeed, thank you, Martha,' Emma smiled as she took the tray and balanced it carefully on her knees. And then, as Martha still lingered, she asked what time breakfast would be.

'Well, that depends on whether you want it in bed or downstairs,' Martha replied unhelpfully.

'I'd prefer to come down for it,' Emma told her, hoping to goodness that she had said the right thing.

It appeared that she had, for Martha simply said:

'Well, suppose we say in about an hour? That'll give you time for a bath. There's plenty of hot water.'

'If that won't interfere with Miss Prescott's arrangements?' Emma asked tentatively.

'Oh no. She has her breakfast in bed and gets up late these days,' Martha explained with a sigh which emboldened Emma to ask a question.

'Martha, I don't want to appear inquisitive,' she said diffidently, 'but why is Miss Prescott so lame? Is it arthritis?'

'Partly.' Martha's voice was harsh and grating. 'But the trouble began when, years ago, she had an accident in the hunting field. Something startled her mare and she bolted. Miss Hester was thrown, but one foot was wedged in the stirrup, so'—she swallowed convulsively—'she was dragged quite a distance and it did something to her hip they said couldn't be cured. Then, over the years, she's got more and more arthritic. She's got a scar, too, across her forehead. That's why she wears a fringe.'

'Oh, Martha!' Emma exclaimed pitifully.

'Yes, it gets you down when a thing happens to someone like her, doesn't it? *She* never hurt a fly, whereas some people I could name——' She left the sentence unfinished, but Emma couldn't help wondering if she had Mrs Heywood in mind who, in her opinion, deserved to meet with disaster. Quite likely, Emma thought, though one shouldn't jump to conclusions. 'And now, miss, what about your breakfast? A cooked one, of course. I don't hold with no more than toast on an empty stomach. So what would you like?'

Emma to her own surprise, was literally ravenous, but didn't like to admit it, and decided that she would rely on Martha's notions of what constituted a good breakfast.

'A surprise, please,' she was inspired to reply. 'It's always more exciting coming to table not knowing before-hand what you're going to eat——'

'Particularly if you're used to planning and cooking it yourself,' Martha agreed, and Emma realised that she wasn't the only one who could read between lines. Quite unintentionally, she had given more information about her-self than she had intended doing. Not that it mattered, but she realised that if there was anything she really did want to keep private, she would have to be very, very careful where this shrewd woman was concerned.

'Well, I must get on with my work, I suppose,' Martha remarked, but as she reached the door she paused. 'About —what I told you about Miss Hester,' she said gruffly. 'She can't bear to feel that people pity her or that they have to make allowances for her which may be a nuisance to them. So, if you please, miss, don't bring the matter up unless she does first. Just take the way she is for granted.'

'I'll remember, Martha,' Emma promised. 'And thank you for explaining.'

Left to her own devices, Emma finished her tea and then got up. She had a marvellous bath, for not only, as Martha had said, was there plenty of hot water, but the old-fash-ioned bath with its mahogany surround and brightly pol-ished brass taps was the biggest she had ever come across. Nostalgically she recalled her childhood, when a perfectly ordinary bath had seemed so spacious that there had been plenty of room for celluloid ducks and fish and even a boat or two. There had been one particularly large fish which had a small hole in it so that it slowly filled with water and sank to the bottom of the bath in a most fish-like way. She had given it a special name—yes, of course, Moby Dick. She hadn't thought of Moby Dick for years——

When she went downstairs she was greeted by a mouthwatering odour, and as she reached the hall Martha popped her head out of the kitchen.

'You'll find your cereal ready in the sitting room,' she informed Emma. 'Or you can have fruit juice if you'd rather?'

'No, I'd rather have cereal,' Emma said greedily, and went in search of it.

She found that Martha had taken as much care in arranging the table just for her as she had done when Miss Prescott was present. On a freshly laundered cloth, as well as the dish of cereal, there was a jug of creamy milk and two bowls, one containing caster sugar and one brown. The silver of the place-setting gleamed in the sunshine and, as a finishing touch, there was a little vase of flowers.

Emma sat down, spread the table napkin which matched the cloth and tucked into the cereal. She was just finishing it when Martha came in with a covered plate and basket of small rolls which gave off a deliciously yeasty smell. Martha set the basket down and then, placing the plate in front of Emma, whipped off the cover with a triumphant: 'There!'

Emma gazed enraptured. Two delicately grilled rashers, two small sausages, a grilled tomato, a perfectly fried egg and a piece of crisply browned bread constituted Martha's idea of a cooked breakfast.

'Oh, Martha, how gorgeous!' she exclaimed appreciatively. 'I—I haven't been eating very well lately, but I shan't be able to resist this!'

'That's right, miss, you eat it all up,' Martha said in such a nanny-like way that Emma was surprised she didn't add *like a good girl!* 'I'll bring your coffee and the hot milk right away.'

When, feeling that she almost needed to let out her belt, Emma got up from the table, she wondered if she should offer to help with the washing up, but decided not to. So far she was no more than an overnight visitor and Martha might well feel that she was making herself too much at home. Better wait until—if ever—Martha invited her into what she undoubtedly regarded as '*her* kitchen' on some pretext or other.

Martha, returning at that moment, confirmed her decision.

'Miss Hester says she hopes you'll excuse her, but she'd like to spend another half-hour examining your dolls,' she announced. 'She said perhaps you'd like to sit in the garden. I've put the chairs out.'

So with an easy conscience Emma went out into the sunshine, first of all to explore the little garden which was bounded from the rest of the Hall grounds by a low white picket fence, and then to sit contentedly in one of the chairs. The other—the more comfortable one—was already occupied by the cat who was performing its morning ablutions. Emma passed the time of day by tickling the little creature under the chin, an attention of which it seemed to think well, though in a somewhat preoccupied way.

Emma, too, was preoccupied, but in an apprehensive way. She had been at Fantasy for less than a day, but during that time one thing had become unmistakably clear. Tim wasn't the only one who was hard up; Miss Prescott suffered from the same handicap. Her silver, her linen, her furniture—all were beautiful, but all were old and worn. The silver was thin with wear, the fine linen sheets on Emma's bed were frighteningly fragile and had already been darned in many places. The tapestry seats of chairs had long since seen their best days and the design was blurred to little more than a monochrome. It was the same story with carpets and curtains. The carpets were threadbare and the curtains so faded as to be almost white. The meaning was obvious. Even allowing for a cherishing of old and familiar treasures, there was no money to spare even for necessary replacements. Emma sighed. It didn't augur well for her hopes and plans.

Nor was she reassured when Miss Prescott had Martha summon her to the workroom, for though she was greeted with a smile and an inquiry as to whether she had slept well, Emma could see that her hostess was not entirely at her ease. However, she didn't hesitate to come straight to the point.

'I've examined your little family very thoroughly and also, I have read Lucy May's journal through twice,' she began. 'And everything I have learned confirmed my first impression. You own a treasure trove. One, in fact, of which any serious collector would be envious.'

'Oh, I am glad!' Emma exclaimed with relief. 'I was so afraid you might feel that I'd wasted your time bringing them to you.'

'Far from it,' Miss Prescott declared emphatically. 'I only wish that——' She stopped abruptly and then continued: 'I was mistaken in thinking that the three large dolls are all of French origin. The little maidservant, by the way, is a doll's-house doll, German. The least valuable of your collection, but none the less of considerable interest because of her clothes. They're typical of Lucy May's period and show the difference between the lavish clothes of the rich and the simple ones of their servants. Now—Mrs Ponsonby.' She smiled as she said the name and lifted the doll from the table. 'She's French, and was known as a Parisienne doll or sometimes a fashion doll. She isn't marked with the maker's name, but the fact that she has a swivel neck means that she was made after 1861 and I think that someone with more knowledge than I have could without doubt determine who made her. Your little-girl doll is also French and she's marked with the name Jumeau, a firm which was making dolls for a period which covered Lucy May's working lifetime. She, too, is a luxury doll. Then the baby. She was made in England by an Italian family firm. She has a poured wax head, and is rare because she is marked with the maker's name. Quite beautiful workmanship. So there you are, my dear. You own three dolls, each desirable and consequently valuable. But of course, there's more to it than that.'

'Is there?' Emma asked breathlessly. 'What you've already told me is tremendously exciting. But please, do go on!'

'Well, to begin with, not only did they belong to one person but their history is authenticated by Lucy May's journal, and that's important because with the interest in period dolls increasing to such an extent, reproductions are on the market and, of course, that sometimes raises doubts as to their genuineness. Then there are the clothes, exquisitely made and, again, vouched for as to period by Lucy

May. And finally her journal, which gives a very human note to the little collection. Yes, a treasure trove indeed! But'—very earnestly—'I cannot impress on you too emphatically the desirability of keeping them together as a unit. That will enhance their value considerably beyond what they would fetch if you sold them individually. Do you understand?'

'Yes, I do,' Emma assured her, considerably impressed. 'But——'

'No, wait a minute, my dear,' Miss Prescott requested, lifting her hand in gentle restraint. 'Let me finish the story.' She pondered a moment and then spoke very deliberately. 'As to their exact value, that I cannot tell you, and I don't think anyone could, for I doubt if three such unique dolls have ever been on the market at one and the same time. The value of any article depends on what someone is willing to pay for it, and at an auction sale, the rivalry between collectors would certainly put the price up. Nearer than that I'm not prepared to give an opinion, other than to tell you, in general terms, that their value could well be over a thousand pounds.'

'Miss Prescott!' Emma gasped incredulously.

'Yes, I mean it, Emma,' Miss Prescott assured her. 'So, you see, that means you have to be very careful how you dispose of them. You must not let anyone take advantage of your ignorance as'—she shook her head ruefully—'as, I admit, I was tempted to! And when you see my collection, you'll understand why. I have some very good specimens, but the Victorian ones are of a later date than yours and mainly German. The Edwardian ones are all German, so yours would fill a long-felt want. But, to my great regret, it's out of the question for me to make you an offer. For one thing, in fairness to you, it would obviously be unwise for you to make a private deal with me or anyone else. Even so, I might be tempted to make you an offer were it not that'—momentarily she pressed her lips tightly together—'I have recently had calls on my purse which means that for me to make an offer, however humble, is quite out of the question. I'm truly sorry, my dear,' she concluded regretfully.

'Dear Miss Prescott, if I were to sell them at all, I would

sooner it was to you than to anyone else,' Emma told her warmly. 'But if you remember, I told you when I first showed them to you that I wasn't sure that I wanted to sell them. Now, after what you've told me, I'm quite sure I don't.'

'You mean, you're going to start collecting yourself?' Miss Prescott asked with interest. 'I'm not surprised. You have a wonderful foundation to build upon.'

'Yes, that's what I feel, and the idea attracts me very much,' Emma confessed. 'But, you see, I *am* ignorant, and from what you've told me, I realise how much I have to learn before even thinking about making a bigger collection.'

'That's very true,' Miss Prescott nodded approvingly. 'So what do you intend to do?'

Emma drew a deep breath and surreptitiously crossed her fingers.

'What I should like to do would be to learn at first hand from someone who really knows the subject,' she explained diffidently.

'A sensible decision,' Miss Prescott said judicially.

'Only I can't see why anyone should want to bother to teach me,' Emma went on, 'so I thought—if I offered to loan the dolls to an existing collector without, of course, expecting any payment, then perhaps they might be willing——'

The words choked in her throat and Miss Prescott seemed bereft of speech as well. Emma summoned all her courage in an attempt to make herself clear.

'You, please, Miss Prescott,' she croaked desperately.

Even then Miss Prescott found nothing to say, and Emma's heart sank. She had somehow found the courage to make her proposition, but she had failed. The silence lengthened until it seemed to Emma that it would never end unless she did something about it, and she stood up.

'I'm sorry, Miss Prescott,' she said miserably, 'it's a silly idea—I shouldn't have asked you—please forget all about it.'

But Miss Prescott caught her by the hand.

'My dear, please sit down,' she begged in a voice that shook a little. 'You don't understand. It wasn't because I rejected your suggestion that I didn't answer. It was because your generosity literally took my breath away.'

'Then you will teach me?' Emma exclaimed delightedly. 'If you don't find me too big a duffer. You see, I've never been good at exams. Nor have I any gift in the way of drawing or painting. So, once I left school, I just stayed at home, and I was very happy doing that because ...' she considered, 'I don't think I've really got it in me to enjoy working with masses of other people and being in competition with them.'

'Of course not,' declared Miss Prescott. 'You are essentially an individualist, Emma, and so you must find an individual way of expressing yourself. And this'—with a comprehensive gesture at the dolls on the table—'may well be the way. Now let's be practical. Are you a good needlewoman?'

For answer Emma opened her handbag and took out two pieces of material. One was velvet which had one edge invisibly hemmed while the right side was elegantly braided. The other piece of fine muslin was in effect a sampler on which Emma had worked a variety of stitches, had made a row of pin-tucks, had hemmed two sides and had whipped lace or hand-made frills on to the other sides.

'Beautiful!' Miss Prescott approved warmly. 'Quite beautiful, and a perfect answer to my question. You're a first-class needlewoman, and that's important. You see, not only are there our own dolls to be considered but there have been two developments arising from that interview I gave, one of which I hadn't anticipated. I've had a number of letters from owners of dolls who want me to undertake the repair of old clothes or the making of new ones. Now, while I would enjoy doing that, I had reluctantly decided that it would be out of the question unless I had assistance. The other development is that far more people have visited or want to visit the museum than was previously the case, and that means conducted tours which are frankly more than I can manage. So I had decided that I must have an assistant—if I could find the right one. And,' she patted Emma's hand gently, 'I believe I have! My dear, what is it? You look quite troubled,' she concluded anxiously.

'It's just that though I'd love to do it—take people round, I mean—I don't see how I could,' Emma said regretfully. 'I don't know enough to be able to tell people what they'd want to know about the dolls.'

'But each of them is numbered,' Miss Prescott explained, 'and they're all catalogued. At first you'd have to refer to that, but you would, I'm sure, soon learn to do without it. And now, as regards your salary——'

And despite Emma's protests, she found that when Miss Prescott made up her mind that a certain course was right, there was no deflecting her from it.

'And,' Miss Prescott went on, 'since in my opinion I shall not be paying you nearly as much as I ought to, you'll continue to live here as my guest. Unless, of course, you would prefer not to?'

'Oh, Miss Prescott! I'd love to—of course I would. But——'

'Then that's settled,' Miss Prescott interrupted briskly. 'And now, would you like to see the Museum?'

By the time Emma had been at Fantasy for a week she felt so much at home that it was impossible not to feel that she really belonged there.

For Miss Prescott she had felt an instant liking, and the feeling quickly deepened to one of affection which was encouraged by the fact that Miss Prescott didn't hide her liking for the girl who had so unexpectedly come into her life. As for Martha, after her initial suspicions she had changed her mind with flattering speed, although Emma still didn't know why. However, when she was promoted to helping with the washing up, she knew that she had really been accepted, if not exactly as one of the family then certainly as a very welcome visitor.

And Tim? He had declared that her prolonged stay was the best bit of news he'd heard in a month of Sundays. But while Emma didn't exactly doubt his sincerity, she was inclined to take his enthusiasm with a grain of salt. And while that was no doubt partly due to Miss Prescott's comment that Tim had a way with him, it was also due to Emma's own conviction that though he might dance attendance on her and pay her charming compliments, she would be wise not to take either too seriously. Not that she wanted to. Tim was an amusing and interesting companion and he undoubtedly contributed in no small measure to her enjoyment of being at Fantasy, but——

And there she left it, not at all sure why it was that she felt so certain that Tim would never expect—or want—more from her than a lighthearted companionship with no complications about it. The result was that she felt quite safe with him as he, she felt with a flash of intuition, did with her.

To herself Emma admitted that she had never been happier in her life. She went to bed each night able to look back on a happy, satisfying day and woke with the conviction that today would be just as good as yesterday had been.

There wasn't a cloud in her sky. Two men, Frank Hall and Adrian Wroughton, both of whom had been unpleasantly troublesome in their different ways, she relegated firmly to the past. Lorraine Heywood, who she had thought might prove to be a serpent in this little Eden, had not shown up again at Fantasy, though for all Emma knew, Tim might have seen her either at the Hall or elsewhere. But if he did, he didn't comment on the fact in Emma's hearing. In fact, she noticed that neither he nor Miss Prescott ever mentioned Lorraine's name in any connection. It was almost as if, to them, she didn't really exist. And Emma was more than content to have it that way.

Much of her time she spent with Miss Prescott. They worked together, making by hand little garments fully as skilfully as any Victorian needlewoman could have done. Emma enjoyed the work wholeheartedly, particularly as Miss Prescott kept her promise to teach her about the history of dolls over the centuries; and because she herself was so genuinely interested in the subject, she was able to pass her enthusiasm on to Emma.

The Museum, too, was an abiding delight. It had, so Miss Prescott explained, started in a very modest way, being simply a collection of family dolls which had survived more for reasons of sentiment than for their possible value. It had been Miss Prescott's mother who had first realised their historical interest and had added to the collection with gifts from friends and occasional purchases.

'When my parents died and my brother—Tim's father—inherited the property, his wife wasn't at all interested in the collection. She was essentially an out-of-doors sort of person. So they came to me, and at the same time my brother made Fantasy over to me, and the old stable and coach-house has made a perfect place to display the dolls and some other toys.'

And with that Emma agreed wholeheartedly. Nothing could have provided a better background for the glass display cases than the solid old stone walls. The lighting had been improved by the making of additional windows between the cases, and what had been double wooden doors had been replaced by glass ones with wrought-iron grilles.

But all that Emma had taken in at a glance. What interested her was the dolls, and she was surprised by both the quantity of them and the variety. Armed with Miss Prescott's catalogue she identified each doll by the number attached to it, and though she wondered apprehensively whether she would ever be able to memorise all the details about them, she realised with a feeling of rising pleasure that the superficial interest which she had first felt for the subject was deepening with every day that passed. By the greatest of good luck she had found something more than just a pleasant job—she had found a way of life which delighted her, and she was determined to make it permanently her own if only that were possible.

But having decided that, she had to let her sisters know of her decision, and that was the most difficult letter she had ever had to write. At first she thought of all the objections she would have to counter and tried to answer them before they were made, but the result was that she appeared to be making unconvincing excuses for her actions. She tried again, and this time she gave a simple account of just what had happened, beginning with finding the dolls in the attic and concluding with the agreement she and Miss Prescott had arrived at. She mentioned casually that Miss Prescott's nephew owned the Hall, which she knew would reassure Rose—and probably turn her thoughts to matchmaking—but one thing she left out; the part that Frank Hall had played in stiffening her deter-

72

mination to leave Greystoke. Instead she explained that she was not only really interested in the work but that she felt fitter than she had done for years. Country air and country food helped, of course, but also the more leisurely tempo of life suited her. Never, she hoped, would she have to live in a town again. She made no reference to her intention of selling the house, hoping that they would realise for themselves that if she didn't intend to live in it, it was the only thing to do.

She posted her letter—she had written to Rose asking her to pass on the information to Helen—and waited apprehensively for their replies. When they came, to her surprise and relief, if neither Rose nor Helen expressed approval in so many words, they did at least accept her decision without protest and even went so far as to increasing her luck. She felt rather lightheaded as she put their letters away in her writing case. After having been 'little sister' all her life, it was exhilarating and reassuring to be accepted, at last, as a grown-up capable of running her own life. It eased her conscience, too, for though she had truly believed that she was making a wise decision she had been unhappy at the thought of worrying Rose and Helen and hurting their feelings, as might well have been the case.

And now, with that milestone passed, she could enter wholeheartedly into her new life, and the days slipped by in cloudless succession. Gradually, with little bits of information gleaned from a variety of sources, Emma formed a picture both of Windyvale and the people who lived there. It appeared that the road by which she had arrived had at one time been no more than a village street whose purpose was simply to serve as a link between the houses on either side of it. Now, widened to take an increasing burden of traffic, it had the reverse effect. It divided the village in two, and at peak periods one crossed it at one's peril. On one side was the village shop, the smithy and the few cottages which Emma had passed by unnoticing. On the other side, sheltered by quick-growing trees planted as a shield against the noise and fumes of traffic, was the church with the pretty little Prescott Arms pub nestling in its shelter and half a dozen other shops. They included a butcher's, a baker's and, if not a candlestick maker's, at least one where one could buy practically everything that the general store across the way didn't stock—from old-fashioned flat-irons and carpet-beaters to the latest thing in paraffin stoves and the paraffin to fill them, as well as being an agency for Calor gas. Emma found them all fascinating and she welcomed any excuse which would take her to the village, but it was the people who interested her most. Almost everybody seemed to be related to everybody else and it didn't surprise her in the least to discover that Mrs Medler who ran the general store was a cousin of Martha's. It explained why Emma's original appearance at Fantasy had not been unexpected. Old-fashioned in many ways Windyvale might be, but its inhabitants appreciated modern inventions like the telephone to the utmost.

Miss Prescott, despite her lameness, invariably attended morning service at the old church and Emma enjoyed going with her, not only because the atmosphere was so peaceful but because it gave one a sense of continuity. Almost all the people who attended service were descendants of families who had lived there for centuries—the stones in the churchyard attested to that, as did the rather ornate memorial to the Prescott family in the church itself.

One result of her churchgoing was that Emma made the acquaintance of the Vicar and his wife, Mr and Mrs Torrance. They were pleasant people, getting on in years, who, though neither of them had been born in the locality, had been at Windyvale so long that any prejudice on that score had long since been forgotten.

Emma was invited to tea at the Vicarage either with or without Miss Prescott, as it suited them, and it was from Mrs Torrance that Emma heard something of Miss Prescott's past.

'We do so admire the way she adapted herself to circumstances,' Mrs Torrance confided on an occasion when Emma had come to the Vicarage on her own. 'She was so very active and full of life before her accident some twenty-five years or so ago. Many people would have been crushed by such a blow, but not Miss Hester. Not only does she never complain, but she prefers that no one should express pity for her either by word or deed.' She looked inquiringly at Emma, who nodded.

'Yes, Martha warned me of that. It's not always easy to remember because one does so want to make things easier for her. Anybody would.'

'One person didn't,' Mrs Torrance replied with a grimness unusual in so kindly a person. 'Just before the accident we were all expecting to hear of her engagement to a young man who was a friend of her brother's. But nothing came of it. He went to Canada or America and we understood that when he had established himself, Miss Hester would go out to join him. But she never did—and he has never been back. Of course, one can see that a crippled wife would be a handicap to a young man with his future at stake, but all the same——'

'Oh, poor Miss Prescott!' Emma said compassionately, her eyes smarting. 'I simply don't understand how she can be so sweet and uncomplaining. You'd expect her to be bitter and resentful.'

'Yes, you would,' Mrs Torrance agreed. 'But if she isn't, I can tell you who is—Martha, on her account. If ever you hear *her* giving vent to a diatribe on the iniquities of men, you can be sure she's got one particular man in mind! Dear me, I'm afraid I'm nothing but a gossiping old woman—intolerable in any of our sex, but quite disgraceful in a Vicar's wife!' she concluded self-reproachfully.

'But I'm glad you've told me,' Emma assured her. 'I could, in all ignorance, have said something that might have pained her. Now I'll be on my guard.'

About Lorraine Heywood she learned little, except that she had been old General Heywood's second wife, having come to Windyvale as companion-housekeeper-nurse to the first Mrs Heywood in her last illness. Lorraine and the General had been married some six months later and he had left her all he had: 'in grateful recognition of her care and devotion to my wife, Agnes, and to me.'

Martha had told her that, but had stopped short of any comment. Probably, Emma thought, there had been some local scandalmongering, but if so Martha didn't repeat it, except to say that some people earned money the hard way—which could have been interpreted in more than one way.

Tim was more forthcoming, but always about his own

affairs. He was, it appeared, a mechanical engineer and was obsessed with the belief that much could be done to improve the braking system of heavy motor vehicles; and to this end he spent long hours in the workshop he had fitted up in an outhouse at the Hall.

'You see,' he explained to Emma, 'there's bigger and heavier stuff on the road than there's ever been before. And that means that it's absolutely vital to have a braking system which is reliable in even the most demanding circumstances. Of course, there are systems already which do the job well, but they're pretty expensive. So's mine, for that matter. All the same, I'm certain I'm on the right track —if only I can cut down cost without reducing reliability...' And he frowned in an abstracted way, as if he had forgotten that Emma was there and had become immersed in his problem.

'And when you've done that?' Emma asked sympathetically. 'You'll market it and be very rich?'

'If I ever market it,' Tim said gloomily. 'There's one firm that's quite interested in a general way, but they jib at the cost. Told me to go away and see what I could do to make it cheaper. But even if I do, they want me to back it myself with a good deal of cash, and that I simply haven't got. If only I could find some mug willing to give me a good price for the Hall——' He brooded heavily over such a possibility but finally shook his head. 'Not a chance!'

'But, Tim, wouldn't you hate to sell the Hall?' Emma asked. 'I mean, it is your home——'

'I'm afraid sentiment goes by the board when all I can do is live in a corner of the place while the rest of it crumbles about my ears,' he replied bitterly. 'Of course, I'd prefer to sell it to someone who would patch it up and live in it, rather than let a developer build masses of dismal little hovels on it. Aunt Hester feels the same way. Oh well'—he shrugged his shoulders—'there it is! I can only hope that when my guardian pays me a visit, as he'll be doing in a week or so, that he'll come up with a solution. He's an ingenious chap.'

'Your guardian?' Emma repeated in surprise. 'But surely you're of age, Tim?'

'Oh lord, yes, I had my twenty-fifth birthday months

ago. I should have said *ex*-guardian, although actually he only signed off when I was twenty-four because that's how Father left things. I was only a kid of eighteen when he died and pretty scatterbrained in his opinion, so he took no chances. He was probably quite right, and he certainly chose the right bloke to be my guardian. Actually, he's only eight or ten years older than I am—a cousin—but he's not only as honest as they come but he's pretty shrewd, too. He handed things over to me in better shape than they were when Father died. It's only in the last year or so that everything got so difficult——' His forehead creased in anxious lines. 'I'm not a good hand at business, but I don't think it's been altogether my fault——'

'But, Tim, if you've been so worried, why didn't you consult your cousin before?' Emma asked reasonably. 'Surely he'd have helped——'

'Sure he would,' Tim agreed promptly, 'only he's been out of the country doing his own job. He's a professional photographer——' And laughed when he saw Emma's surprise. 'Oh, not the sort who takes wedding groups and pictures of simpering graduates in caps and gowns clutching their certificates. He's nuts on nature study, and he knows his stuff! He's done television films and he's written books with masses of first-class illustrations. He's just about tops in his line—not that he ever throws his weight about. As a matter of fact, it's the most difficult thing in the world to get him to talk about his work but if you *can* persuade him to—well, I for one forget all about my own job, listening to him. And that's saying something. Oh, he's a great chap, Emma! You'll like him!'

Emma, promptly possessed by the conviction which comes to most people when they are told that they will like a certain person, was quite sure that she would find this paragon intolerable. However, she held her tongue discreetly over that, not least because Tim had gone on to say that though his cousin would be staying at the Hall, he would certainly be coming over to Fantasy to see Miss Prescott.

'Not that they're related,' he explained. 'He and I are cousins on our mothers' side, while I'm her nephew on my father's side. But he lost his parents when he was just a youngster and spent much of his time at the Hall both during school holidays and later. As a result, he's always been a sort of extra nephew to Aunt Hester, so to speak. They think a lot of one another in a quiet, not very demonstrative way. But then he's not the sort of chap who ever shows his feelings very much, unless he ever catches anybody cheating or being deliberately cruel. Then, my word, the balloon goes up!'

At that moment Martha came out to say that dinner was ready, and Tim dropped the subject. Nor did he refer again to his cousin's pending arrival and, rather to Emma's surprise, Miss Prescott made no mention of it. However, since she wasn't really interested in the man beyond rather vaguely regarding him as an intruder, Emma gave him no further thought.

Consequently it came as a surprise, even a shock, when returning from a trip to the village some ten days later, she went straight to the workroom to let Miss Prescott know the result of the expedition. The door leading from the hall to the workroom was half way open and as Emma, heavily laden, pushed it wider with her knee, a man spoke—and it wasn't Tim.

'But, Aunt Hester'—there was both protest and alarm in the very individual voice—'you surely don't mean that, knowing absolutely nothing about this girl, you've taken her into your home!'

'Yes,' Miss Prescott replied serenely, 'I have done just that! And if to you that seems rash, my dear boy, then all I ask is that you should suspend judgment until you've met her!'

It was at that moment that Emma's not very well balanced load chose to slither and slide to the floor.

Miss Prescott's visitor jumped to his feet and turned towards the door.

And Emma found herself face to face with Adrian Wroughton.

CHAPTER FIVE

EMMA's first reaction was one of resentment, though not directed against either Miss Prescott or Tim, for she was sure that it was only by chance that neither of them had happened to speak of Adrian by name. It *could* be only chance, since she hadn't spoken of those two earlier meetings, let alone mentioned whom they concerned. She didn't even blame Adrian himself for this incredible third encounter, for she was certain that it was as annoying to him as it was to herself.

No, it was the Fates, the gods of chance, whom she would like to take to task in no uncertain manner. If *they* thought it was amusing to overwork coincidence in this embarrassing way, she didn't. On the contrary, it was just sheer bad manners to interfere to such a degree in the affairs of human beings who couldn't do anything in self-defence.

Then she realised that Miss Prescott was looking from one startled face to the other with some concern, having drawn the obvious conclusion.

'But I think you already know one another, don't you?'

Emma tried to answer, but the words simply wouldn't come, and it was Adrian who answered.

'We have met—twice,' he explained precisely. 'But I hardly think it would be accurate to say that we know one another. Don't you agree, Miss Lathom?'

Was that meant to be some sort of an apology? Was he telling her that he had come to the conclusion that his first judgment of her had been unfair? Emma didn't know, but because Miss Prescott was so clearly disquieted by the tension which had invaded her room, she determined not to add fuel to the fire of her earlier clashes with Adrian.

'Yes, I think you're quite right,' she agreed matter-of-factly, and turned to Miss Prescott. 'As he has explained, Mr Wroughton and I have met twice already. On the first occasion he was kind enough to come to my aid when my

79

car was giving trouble. The very next day, we met again at the wedding I told you about where I was principal bridesmaid and, to my surprise, Mr Wroughton was the best man. As I think you'll agree, such a coincidence was surprising enough, but for there to be still another——' She shook her head as if words failed her, as indeed they did, for the expression on Adrian's face wasn't encouraging. There was a faintly sardonic twist to his mouth and mockery in his eyes such as she had seen in them more than once before. He still thought that she was a sophisticated individual who saw everything only from her own point of view. Hence, in his opinion, her desire to give Miss Prescott a commonplace explanation for their behaviour which would not imperil her position at Fantasy. Not that she had said anything which was not true, but she had certainly not told the whole truth. Would Adrian, she wondered, be content to leave it at that?

Apparently he would, for he added nothing to her explanation and Emma wondered why. Not out of consideration for her, she was sure, but of course if he told tales out of school, then he must know that she would do the same.

The distress faded from Miss Prescott's expression. Indeed, she appeared to be rather amused.

'Most disconcerting,' she acknowledged. 'No wonder you were both taken aback! Anyone would be in such circumstances. But'—she turned to Adrian—'I'm really quite glad you have already met, because it means that it won't take so long for you really to get to know one another. And that's a good thing,' she concluded significantly.

Clearly she had in her mind the request which Emma had overheard, that Adrian should suspend judgment until he had met her new assistant. Now that she knew they had already met, she had evidently decided that Adrian would have to admit that his suspicions were unfounded. Did she but know, the very reverse was practically inevitable!

There was rather an awkward little silence. Emma stooped to pick up her various packages and Adrian, with a murmured: 'Allow me!' began to help. When the task was completed and Emma had voiced her thanks, the uneasy silence still persisted until, in rather a forced way, Miss

Prescott asked Emma what success she had had in the village.

'Really very good,' Emma responded hurriedly. 'Miss Hodges had the Shetland wool you wanted waiting for me, and she's had the invoice for the baby ribbon, so that should be along any day. And then'—in her enthusiasm she temporarily forgot Adrian's presence—'I met Mrs Torrance and she told me that she had come across a yard of so of what she described as spot muslin—a white dress muslin with little embroidered spots all over it that had evidently been left over from a dress she remembered having as a child, and she said you could have it if you liked. So I went with her to the Vicarage to collect it—that's why I was such a long time—and I think it might do nicely for that little girl doll we were wondering about. With a coloured sash——'

'Dolls!' Adrian interrupted suddenly. 'That reminds me, Aunt Hester, I've got a present for you!' And from his jacket pocket he took out a very small package wrapped in tissue paper and handed it to Miss Prescott.

'Oh, Adrian!' she exclaimed with the delight of a child as she took it and removed the paper to reveal a tiny wooden egg.

'It opens,' Adrian remarked, watching her intently, and very carefully Miss Prescott removed the top half of the egg. The lower half was solid, but a small hole had been bored lengthwise in it, and projecting from it was a tiny Dutch doll; not three-quarters of an inch tall, but even so, both arms and legs were jointed.

'Oh, Adrian!' There was no mistaking Miss Prescott's delight. 'I've heard of these egg-dolls, but I've never seen one before. Where did you get it?'

'It was given to me by an old lady up in Scotland,' Adrian explained. 'She had had it when she was a child—it's at least seventy years old. I told her about your collection and she said she'd like you to have it so that she could be sure it would be properly looked after.'

'Indeed it will be,' Miss Prescott declared emphatically. 'And when I write to thank her for it, as of course I shall, I'll assure her of that!' She held the little egg out to Emma in the palm of her hand. 'Look, Emma, isn't it delightful?'

'It is, indeed,' Emma agreed in all sincerity, yet somehow for a reason which she could not fathom, she could not bring herself to touch the pretty trifle. She picked up her parcels from the table where Adrian had laid them and remarked rather breathlessly that there was just time to put everything away before lunch.

'So there is, dear,' agreed Miss Prescott, 'but you'll need to say goodbye to Adrian now, because he's not staying for the meal.'

Emma did as she was told, but since she was so laden she had a good excuse not to shake hands with him.

'Thank you again for helping me, Mr Wroughton,' she said, and gave him a smile which, however, did no more than curve her lips slightly.

'My pleasure, Miss Lathom,' Adrian assured her gravely, and held the door open for her to pass through.

It wasn't until she was tidying up for lunch in her own room that she realised, to her amazement, that she was disappointed because Adrian was not staying to lunch.

'But that's absurd,' she told herself impatiently, 'because it isn't as if I'd *enjoy* his company, and I certainly don't want any more opportunities of wrangling with him, least of all in front of Miss Prescott! Oh dear, why does life have to be so complicated, particularly just when I thought it would be so simple?'

But there seemed to be no answer to that.

Emma saw nothing more of Adrian—or of Tim, for that matter—for the next few days. Where Adrian was concerned that was something of a relief, though she could not rid herself of an uneasy feeling that his presence in the district constituted a threat to her future at Windyvale.

As for Tim, she missed him very much. He had formed the habit of arriving at any time of the day and though, if she was busy, Emma sent him packing in no uncertain manner, she enjoyed his cheerful company, and after consulting Miss Prescott, had agreed to several mildly exciting outings with him. This sometimes meant a visit to the Prescott Arms for a pre-lunch or dinner drink, and twice he had taken her for runs in his shabby but splendidly-maintained car.

Miss Prescott had smiled when Emma had brought the matter up.

'My dear, don't you know that these days girls and men go their own ways without reference to older folk?'

'Yes, perhaps they do,' acknowledged Emma, 'and perhaps I'm old-fashioned, but after all, Tim is your nephew and I'm your guest and I'd be happier to know that you've no objection.'

'None whatever,' Miss Prescott assured her. 'Young people need each other's company and it could be very dull for you here with only Martha and me for company. By all means accept Tim's invitations.' She paused and then went on deliberately, 'Your own good sense will tell you if the time should ever come when it would be wiser for you to refuse them.'

Just what she meant by that Emma wasn't sure, but secure in her belief that Tim's interest in her went no deeper than friendship, Emma enjoyed his companionship without anxiety and with a clear conscience. It *was* nice to go about with someone of her own age and it was a new experience for her, all the more pleasant because he made it very clear that he enjoyed being with her.

But she missed it all the more now that, with Adrian at the Hall, he seemed to prefer his cousin's company to hers. Emma did her best to accept the situation without resentment; after all, she told herself, it was only natural that the two men should have a lot to talk about. For one thing they hadn't seen one another for some time and, as Tim himself had told her, he wanted to consult Adrian about his financial affairs. Yet at the back of her mind was a lurking suspicion which refused to be ignored. Did Adrian disapprove of her friendship with Tim, and was he doing his best to undermine it? She couldn't feel it was beyond the bounds of possibility where Adrian was concerned, but surely Tim was hardly likely to allow himself to be dragooned into behaviour which went against his inclinations?

And when the two men came to dinner one evening, Emma decided that she had been silly to worry. Not only did Tim treat her with the camaraderie she was used to from him, but Adrian accorded her a degree of attentiveness and amiability that made Emma wonder if, after all, she had been mistaken about him. Perhaps, however reluctantly, one had to admit that he had had some cause for annoyance with her. On the other hand, of course, his good manners could simply be in deference to Miss Prescott. Still, whatever the cause, it was pleasant not to feel one needed to be on the alert all the time for some underlying and not very pleasant meaning to anything he said.

Later, when he and Tim were leaving, Tim suddenly said:

'All right if I pick you up pretty early on Wednesday, Emma? Round about half past nine?'

'Wednesday?' Emma repeated vaguely, and Tim clicked his tongue disapprovingly.

'I like that!' he complained. 'Here I plan a treat for you and you forget all about it! Just like a woman! A tour of our beauty spots plus a slap-up picnic, girl! Or do you want to back out of it?'

'Of course not,' Emma denied hastily. 'I've been looking forward to it ever since you suggested it. It's just that I'd thought of it by the date rather than the day. Yes, I'll be ready.' She hesitated. 'Can I do anything about the picnic supplies?'

'Oh, that's all arranged,' Tim explained airily. 'I had a word with our Winsome and she's coping.'

Emma was considerably taken aback at the possibility that in fact Miss Prescott would be paying for their picnic, although it was possible that the matter had been arranged on a cash basis. She certainly hoped so, and though she didn't want to make Tim lose face by asking him then and there, she made up her mind to find out later and if her worst suspicions were confirmed, she would make it very clear to him that unless either he or both of them paid for their fun themselves, there would be no more outings. All the more so because Adrian's expression of sardonic amusement made what he thought quite obvious. It was, however, a relief to see that Miss Prescott was showing no sign of either surprise or annoyance. But then it could be that, like Emma herself, she didn't want to make Tim look small. Equally, it could be that she was used to Tim's casual ways.

But when Wednesday came, bright and beautiful, Emma put her doubts to the back of her mind, though her eyes widened when she saw the size of the picnic hamper which Martha had prepared.

'There, that ought to keep you going,' Martha commented with satisfaction. 'Even if Mr Tim hasn't had breakfast—and he probably hasn't. Well, it's ready, anyway—though he'll probably be late anyhow.'

And he was. Half past nine came and went. So did a quarter to ten. Emma began to feel somewhat vexed since Tim had laid such stress on an early start. She was on the point of ringing him up when she heard the sound of an approaching car and hurried to the door to give Tim a piece of her mind. But as she flung the door wide, she came face to face not with Tim but with Adrian.

She stared at him in startled silence, her imagination running riot as she tried to think of an explanation for Tim's absence and his cousin's presence.

'No need to worry,' Adrian assured her coolly, 'nothing catastrophic has happened. Simply, Tim has unexpectedly had to go to Carlisle on business which couldn't be postponed. He asked me to give you this.' And he handed her a sealed envelope.

Emma ripped it open and her expression hardened as she read it. Tim had scrawled a hasty apology for his default and had gone on to suggest, outrageously, that Adrian should stand in for him.

'How disappointing,' Emma said in a brittle voice. 'Still, these things do happen, don't they? And I'm sure Tim and I will be able to arrange another outing some other time.' And that, if he knew what Tim had suggested, ought to make it clear to Adrian that as far as she was concerned, today's picnic was entirely abrogated.

Unfortunately, it did nothing of the sort.

'I'm sure you will,' he agreed cordially. 'In the meantime, there is today to be considered, isn't there? I do hope you'll accept me as a substitute for Tim, however inadequate.'

'How very kind of you, Mr Wroughton,' Emma replied coolly, 'but I really can't let you put yourself out——'

'Oh, I wouldn't be doing that,' Adrian assured her

blandly. 'I've really nothing else to do today.'

'All the same——' Emma began, but at that moment Miss Prescott limped into the hall. She took the situation in at a glance and looked inquiringly at Adrian. Without hesitation he explained, using much the same words as he had done to Emma. But he added:

'I'm trying to persuade Miss Lathom to allow me to take Tim's place, but so far without success. Will you come to my aid, Aunt Hester?'

Miss Prescott hesitated and Emma seized her chance.

'I feel it's too much to expect of Mr Wroughton that he should put himself out on my account,' she said firmly. 'I would prefer simply to cancel the arrangement——'

'And what about all the food I've prepared?' a tart voice demanded from the back of the hall. 'Up at six I was so that everything should be nice and fresh, and now to have it all thrown in my face! Nice, I must say!'

'Oh dear!' Miss Prescott looked appealingly at Emma. 'That *is* a point, you know.'

Even then Emma would have stuck to her guns if she hadn't happened to look at Adrian. There was no mistaking the meaning of his ironical expression. He was amused because he thought that her refusal to spend a few hours in his sole company was due to a lack of self-confidence. In other words that she was afraid, not so much of him but of herself. Clearly he had never forgotten her response to that outrageous kiss . . .

Her head went up defiantly.

'Yes, I see what you mean,' she conceded coolly. 'And of course, the last thing I want to do is hurt Martha's feelings. So'—she turned deliberately to Adrian—'thank you, Mr Wroughton, for finding a way of avoiding it. Shall we start?'

'By all means,' Adrian agreed nonchalantly. He kissed Miss Prescott, said 'Thank you, Martha' in the general direction of the kitchen, and lifting the hamper, stood back for Emma to precede him.

While he was stowing the hamper carefully in the back of the car, Emma got into the passenger seat. She noted with satisfaction that though the car was not in the luxury class it was comfortably roomy, which meant that though she and Adrian would be sitting side by side, there would be no contact between them as there would be in a small car like her own. Even so, as he got in beside her, fastened the safety belt and started up, Emma was acutely conscious that they were sharing a small, isolated world from which, for the time being, there was no escape. But though that might have been alarming, to her surprise it was actually exciting. Just why Adrian had been willing, even determined, to take Tim's place she didn't know, though she was quite sure that it hadn't been for the pleasure of her company. So what had been the reason? Almost certainly she would find out before they returned to Fantasy, and despite her resolution not to cross swords again with him, there was something stimulating in the knowledge that even a state of armed neutrality needed co-operation from Adrian himself—and that, she was convinced, he wouldn't give. For all his recent superficial politeness, at heart he still disliked and mistrusted her. Well, all right, if that was the way he wanted it, then she would be entirely justified in defending herself against his suspicions, whatever they might be.

In the meantime, it didn't surprise her in the least that Adrian drove in silence, though it did confirm her belief that he had something so unpleasant to say that he wanted to be able to give all his attention to it without being distracted by his driving.

That suited Emma. One couldn't indulge in pleasant chit-chat when, in all probability, there was a first-class row ahead.

However, she was fair-minded enough to admit that if she was right, Adrian didn't allow his prejudices to affect his driving, which was neither timid nor reckless. Smooth and alert would be the best way to describe it. His anticipation of possible difficulties was just that little bit quicker —which marks the good driver out from the bad. And despite the beauty of the surrounding countryside, Emma found herself watching his hands with fascinated interest. Not only were all their movements controlled and certain, but the hands themselves—odd that she had never noticed before how supple and sensitive they were. Or how strong. Hands, she thought, that an artist would enjoy painting.

Still neither of them spoke and as the day grew warmer,

Emma, soothed by the steady hum and rhythm of the car, found it difficult to keep her eyes open. After a while she didn't try to.

She woke with a start to find that the car was stationary at the side of the road, and that Adrian, his hands still on the wheel, was staring straight ahead almost as if he wasn't sure what to do next.

'Oh, my goodness!' Emma exclaimed as she gathered her wits. 'How long have I been asleep?'

'Over an hour,' Adrian told her in a voice entirely devoid of expression, and without turning to look at her.

'How inexcusably rude of me,' Emma said hurriedly, and feeling at a disadvantage and wanting to reduce a somewhat embarrassing situation to a more commonplace level, she added formally: 'I really must apologise——'

'Not at all,' Adrian replied politely. 'I feel that you've paid me a compliment.'

'Oh?' Emma said guardedly. 'I don't quite see——'

'No? But surely your going to sleep indicated that you trusted me.' He paused very briefly and then qualified the statement. 'Or rather, trusted my driving.'

It was, of course, one of those oblique challenges of his which she had encountered before, but Emma refused to rise to the bait.

'I think you're a very good driver indeed,' she told him sincerely. 'I wasn't in the least tempted to indulge in passenger-seat driving. Is this where we're going to picnic?'

'It's rather pleasant, don't you think?'

It was far more than pleasant. Tim had taken her to quite a few delightful spots, but this was the most beautiful of all. Adrian had parked by the side of a small tarn set like a jewel amid the surrounding hills. Its smooth surface, made brilliantly green by the reflection of nearby trees, sparkled in the sunshine, and the air was sweet with the fragrance of the pine trees. Birds twittered and sang as if they had no fear of the intruding humans, and beneath their feet the short grass was studded with tiny flowering plants so beautiful that it seemed a shame to walk on them.

'It's beautiful,' Emma acknowledged softly. If Tim had been her companion she would have said that it was quite perfect, but despite her appreciation of the beauty,

Adrian's presence hovered like a threatening storm cloud. Involuntarily she shivered as she got out and followed Adrian to the big flat outcrop of rock on which he was preparing to unpack the hamper.

'Don't unpack too much,' she requested in a high, unnatural voice, 'at least, not on my account. I'm not really hungry.'

Adrian glanced at her briefly.

'No? Something made you lose your appetite? An uneasy conscience, perhaps?'

'No, not that,' Emma replied, ignoring the insult. 'I'm just not ready for a meal yet. Martha always gives me such marvellous breakfasts——'

'At my aunt's expense,' Adrian retorted harshly. 'As this picnic would have been——'

'But won't be now because you'll insist on paying Miss Prescott for it,' Emma suggested quickly, 'even though you'll hurt her feelings very much by doing so.'

Adrian frowned as he poured out two cups of hot black coffee from the thermos and handed one to her.

'I hope not to do that, but there are circumstances in which such a consideration has to be ignored. When, for instance, advantage is being taken of someone who's too generous for her own good!'

'As you feel advantage is being taken of Miss Prescott?' Emma asked. And then, determined that if a battle was unavoidable, at least he should be the one who fired the first shot: 'Have you anyone in particular in mind you feel is guilty of such an offence?'

'Of course I have,' Adrian retorted sharply as he sat down beside her on the short sweet grass. 'You!'

'I thought it might be,' Emma admitted, placidly sipping the fragrant coffee. She would not let him gain the advantage of her by losing her temper, but she wondered if he realised just how near she was to throwing the hot coffee in his face. 'Do tell me why you feel that way.'

'Good lord, isn't it obvious?' Adrian demanded impatiently. 'You turn up at Fantasy from nowhere with a hard luck story, and in no time at all you con my aunt not only into giving you free board and lodging, but also into paying you a salary. Isn't that enough to give concern to anyone who has her welfare at heart?'

'It would be, if it were the whole story, but it isn't. Surely Miss Prescott has explained that to you?'

'Oh, I know you're doing odd jobs for her,' Adrian admitted with a shrug, 'but——'

'But I don't think you really listened to what she said,' Emma interrupted bluntly, and setting her cup down safely on the grass, she half turned so that she faced her opponent. 'In fact, as both Mrs Torrance and Martha can confirm, Miss Prescott had spoken of her need to have an assistant *before* I came, because, one way and another, the work was getting too much for her——'

'And the coincidence of your turning up was like an answer to prayer?' Adrian suggested sardonically.

'Hardly that, but it was certainly the solution of a problem,' Emma conceded. 'And you must remember, Mr Wroughton, that not only might she have had difficulty in finding an assistant who would be genuinely interested in *her* interests, as I am, but almost certainly such a person would have been a stranger to her again, as I am. Moreover, I doubt if many, if any, other people, would have been able to add to the Museum as I have.'

'But only on loan,' Adrian pointed out quickly.

'But a *free* loan,' Emma countered crisply. 'And my dolls are, so Miss Prescott assures me, both valuable and interesting.'

'I know all that,' Adrian admitted impatiently. 'But'—he paused—'it's this confounded coincidence of us meeting three times in so short a period that makes me feel that there's something fishy going on!'

'Yes, I thought it might be that,' said Emma, lifting her cup again. 'But when you come to think of it, the first two occasions on which we met weren't so very surprising. I mean, we were using the same road because our destination happened to be the same. I expect, had we but known, probably so were a lot of other guests. And do remember I didn't ask you to stop—you did that, if not of your own free will, at least because you felt that there was no alternative.' She looked at him inquiringly.

'Well?'

'Well—I irritated you,' Emma reminded him frankly.

90

'Perhaps that wasn't surprising in the circumstances. But don't you remember what you said—in the vestry?' To her annoyance the warm colour surged to her cheeks at the memory, but she went on steadily: 'You said that—you felt you had evened the score. But you haven't behaved as if you had. You still seem to feel that you owe me a grudge.'

'As you feel towards me!' he retorted, and Emma nodded.

'Yes,' she said, 'it's this last coincidence. It's just too much. It makes me wonder if, for some reason which I simply can't fathom, you have some not very pleasant objective in following me.'

'What!'

Adrian jumped to his feet and stood glaring down at her, his hands clenching and unclenching. Clearly she had disconcerted him, but with a considerable effort he controlled his anger.

'You need have no fears on that score,' he assured her coldly. 'Until I actually met you at Fantasy I had no idea that you were there.'

'So you tell me,' Emma said very softly, 'but can you prove it?'

To her satisfaction she saw that he was taken aback by her attack.

'No,' he admitted at length. 'I can't, Any more than you can prove that there isn't something——' he paused.

'Something fishy was what you said earlier,' Emma reminded him. 'I suppose by that you mean something sinister. Actually there isn't anything of the sort, though, as you say, I can't prove it. And of course, the fact that you're an old friend of Rob Dixon's and I one of Kitty's doesn't help in the least, because though Kitty and I have kept up our friendship since we left school and I've visited her home—oh, three or four times, I suppose, and we've occasionally written to one another at Christmas and on birthdays—that's not really enough for us to know one another intimately as adults. And you?'

'Yes, the same with Rob and me,' said Adrian, sitting down beside her again. 'When we have met we've got on well enough together, but our meetings have been few and far between. As for letters, we rarely write to one another.

Men don't, you know.'

'So where does that leave us?' Emma asked.

'Back in square one, I suppose,' Adrian admitted impatiently. 'In other words, we've reached an *impasse*. Each of us mistrusts the other——'

'And each of us has some cause for doing so?' Emma suggested.

Momentarily Adrian hesitated.

'All right, perhaps we have,' he conceded. 'But even granting that, there's a difference—look, Miss Lathom'—and he turned to her with an impulsiveness which he had never shown before in his dealings with her—'if this present situation concerned only you and me, I'd accept it as pure coincidence—rather annoying and perhaps even a little embarrassing, but nothing more. But now another person is involved—Aunt Hester. And it's on her account that I'm disturbed. You see'—he hesitated as if he would really have preferred not go give any explanation for his anxiety, but finally he continued: 'I've always kept a friendly eye on Aunt Hester's finances. At her request, I may say. A year or so ago, knowing that I wouldn't be visiting her until now, I went into everything even more thoroughly than usual, and I was satisfied that her affairs were in good shape. There appeared to be no reason why she should have any money troubles. Not that she's ever been wealthy or ever will be, but still, all right. Now I find that during my absence'—he hesitated again, evidently choosing his words with care—'an appeal was made to her for a loan of a bigger sum than she could afford. And when I say a loan, I have my doubts if it will ever be repaid. But being the generous soul she is, she fell for it,' he concluded savagely.

'Actually, Miss Prescott did tell me that she had had calls on her purse which prevented her from offering to buy my dolls,' Emma told him. 'But she didn't go into details.'

'And nor do I intend to,' Adrian said grimly. 'Indeed, I've already said more than perhaps I should have done, but it seemed unavoidable if I'm to make you understand why I'm concerned on Aunt Hester's account.' He looked at her inquiringly.

'Yes, I do understand,' Emma assured him earnestly. 'I'd

be worried if I were in your place. And I wish that there was something I could do to reassure you about me. But I don't see that there is.' She shook her head helplessly.

'No, there isn't,' Adrian agreed. 'Except—I wish you'd tell me just why you came to Windyvale and why you're so anxious to remain.'

'It's really quite simple,' Emma told him, and gave him a succinct account of what had led up to her arrival at Fantasy. When that came to an end, she went on: 'As to why I want to stay—it will probably sound rather pretentious to you, but I think—I'm quite sure—that it's time I stopped being the little sister, and learned to stand on my own feet. Grew up, in other words.'

'And you think that dressing dolls will enable you to do that?' And surprisingly, there was no irony, only genuine interest in the way he said it.

'I think more the fact that I've found a job for myself with no one pulling any strings for me,' explained Emma. 'A job that I believe I'm capable of doing reasonably well—though that I've still got to prove. But certainly one I'm enjoying as I couldn't possibly have enjoyed an office job.'

'You don't think you'll get bored, living in the back of beyond?'

'If you'd lived in a busy manufacturing town like Greystoke all your life, as I have, you'd know that Windyvale is sheer heaven!' Emma told him feelingly. 'Oh, do try to understand, Mr Wroughton! It means so much to me!'

He didn't reply, and Emma's heart sank.

'After all, now that you're back, you can always keep an eye on me to see that I behave,' she pointed out desperately.

Still he didn't answer, then without warning, he caught her wrist in a tight clasp.

'Ssh! Don't move,' he said urgently, hardly above his breath. 'Look over to the right—on that big rock——'

Cautiously Emma turned her head in the direction he had indicated, and caught her breath. Sunning herself luxuriously on the warm outcrop was a vixen, and playing round her were four part-grown cubs. Sometimes they blundered into her, or daringly, played with her bushy tail, to be rewarded with a warning snarl or a smart cuff of their ears. But in the main, they chased one another, rolling over in a tangle of legs and snapping jaws, snarling and barking in high, staccato ferociousness.

'Oh-h!' Emma breathed, and watched entranced. Yet, somewhere at the back of her mind, she was supremely conscious of the warm grip on her arm.

'It looks like a good romp, but actually, they're learning how to defend themselves against an attacking enemy,' Adrian explained in a whisper. 'Very necessary if they're to survive, as the vixen well knows. That's why, although she's not making it too obvious, she's keeping one eye on them. One of them is bound to be the leader among them because he's the stronger and the more artful, and she wants to know which.'

'And the other eye?' Emma wanted to know.

'Oh, she's keeping that one skinned in case of trouble,' Adrian explained. 'A vixen with a young family is never off duty. She'd go for any predator, however much bigger than she is, in their defence.'

For perhaps another ten minutes they watched the delightful little family with absorbed interest. Then, suddenly, the vixen was on her feet, her ears pricked. In one swift movement she hustled her cubs before her, nipping and shoving them to make it clear that there was danger at hand. And the cubs evidently understood, for they obeyed without protest and the little family vanished from sight.

'She probably winded us,' Adrian remarked. 'Pity I couldn't explain that she was in no danger from us. I've had one lesson from an irate mum and I don't want another!' And quite unselfconsciously, he rolled up one shirt-sleeve to reveal those terrible scars. 'I got that up in Scotland a few months back from a wild cat. I almost trod on one of her kits, and she went for me tooth and claw. I was lucky to get off as lightly as I did!'

'You don't sound as if you blame her in the least,' Emma commented wonderingly, and Adrian shrugged his shoulders.

'I don't,' he agreed, 'it was my own stupid fault. I was so intent on watching an eagle soaring above me that I didn't look where I was putting my feet. Besides, she was only behaving as Nature dictated.' He paused. 'As, I suppose, we all do,' and he smiled at her quizzically.

It was a real smile. His eyes smiled as well as his lips, and Emma knew that in some mysterious way the sharing of the charming little experience had brought them closer together than any amount of explanations could have done. She smiled in response and for a moment there was silence. Then Adrian asked: 'And now what?'

'Well'—Emma said apologetically—'I'm afraid it's something of an anticlimax, but actually I'm hungry! Pretty well starving!'

'Come to think of it, so am I!' Adrian declared, and stood up. 'Let's see what Martha has provided. A lot, I hope, because I warn you I intend to be frankly greedy!'

It would have been an exaggeration to say that from then on the two of them became close friends, but most certainly they were no longer enemies—though that didn't mean that they were always in agreement, or that they didn't argue when that was the case. But it was argument which wasn't prompted by malice, and though it was rare for either of them to give in they frequently found it possible to agree to differ. Both Adrian and Tim were frequent visitors to Fantasy, and although the two men were so utterly unalike in temperament, Emma enjoyed their company, though in such different ways that she felt she was two people in one as she adapted herself to their moods. And then, just as she was feeling that life at Windyvale was even more delightful than she had hoped, everything changed.

Adrian had to go to London on business and didn't know how long he'd be away.

'We shall miss him,' Miss Prescott said with a sigh. 'Still,' brightening up, 'we still have Tim.'

But that was just what they didn't have. Four days passed after Adrian had left—a week, and still no sign of Tim. Miss Prescott began to get anxious, and finally suggested that Emma should go over to the Hall to make sure that everything was all right. But at that very moment, as if on cue, Tim burst unceremoniously into the room.

And what a Tim! His shirt was crumpled and grimy, he

badly needed a shave as well as a wash, and his hair stood on end.

'Tim, my dear boy——' Miss Prescott exclaimed anxiously, but Tim brushed her protest aside.

'No, there's nothing wrong,' he declared exuberantly. 'It's just that I've been busy! I'—he hesitated—'it's no good me going into details because you wouldn't understand, but what it comes to is that I couldn't see my way round some difficulties on the thing I'm working on—and now I have! And how I could have been such a mutt not to have seen it before—well, there it is. Of course I've still to make road tests, but it's going to be all right! I know it is!'

And once again his spirits bubbled over. He dropped a kiss on Miss Prescott's cheek, leaving a dirty smudge, and then, seizing Emma in his arms, he danced her round in a mad fandango.

'Emma, my lamb, I've simply got to celebrate or I shall go off pop!' he declared as they came to a breathless halt. 'Come out with me this evening, there's a dear! There's a dinner dance at the Falconbridge Hotel. Let's go to it, shall we?'

And Emma, infused with some of Tim's exuberance, agreed.

It was a delightful evening. Tim, immaculate now but still in high spirits, made a gay and amusing companion, though as the evening wore on he had difficulty in suppressing a yawn, and when questioned admitted that he hadn't had much sleep for a week. Emma promptly suggested that they should leave early, and Tim gratefully agreed. All the same, he insisted on taking her to the door of Fantasy.

It was as they stood for a moment in the porch that Tim struck the first discordant note of the evening.

'Goodnight, Emma love,' he said softly. 'Thank you for a lovely evening,' and bent his tall head with the obvious intention of kissing her.

Instantly Emma's mood of enchantment vanished.

'Oh no, *please*!' she begged, backing against the door.

'No?' Tim regarded her troubled face with considerable interest. 'Well, that's up to you, sweetie-pie! I mean, if the thought of my kisses make you feel as if black beetles are crawling up and down your spine, then we'll defer them indefinitely. But you must admit that what with the moon and the flowers smelling like the most expensive sort of perfume, to say nothing of your great big eyes shining like stars, it's almost too much temptation for an impressionable chap like me! However'—he took her hand in his and bowed ceremoniously over it—'goodnight, Miss Lathom! Happy dreams!'

Stricken to dumbness, Emma went indoors and, with hands that shook a little, locked and bolted the door.

Tim, however, didn't immediately go home. He stood staring thoughtfully at the door for an appreciable time, giving those last few moments earnest consideration.

By his easy-going code, a kiss here or there was not of any great importance; simply a nice way of rounding off an extremely pleasant evening, as this had certainly been. But evidently this little girl didn't feel that way about it.

'I wouldn't mind betting that some chap or other *has* kissed her—and she didn't like it,' he reflected, 'probably a scruffy type, all whiskers and clammy hands. Enough to put any girl off! Or it could be that she's already hooked on some other fellow. I wonder——'

He gave the matter a moment or two's further thought, then, philosophically, he decided that perhaps it was just as well that Emma had been so unresponsive.

'She's a poppet,' he admitted, 'but I've got too much on my plate to think of settling down. Lord, but I've got to work! But it's going to be a success. I know it is!'

CHAPTER SIX

For the next week Emma was so busy that she had little time to think about either Adrian or Tim. For one thing, half a dozen dolls whose clothes needed either repairing or replacing arrived, either by post or were brought by their owners. These latter always wanted to see the museum, and it was Emma's job to take them round.

She was still rather nervous of acting as cicerone, and took good care always to have Miss Prescott's catalogue near at hand in case she was asked questions which she couldn't answer. But she soon found that visitors fell into two classes. There were those who knew something about dolls and could judge for themselves which were the most interesting; and there were those who knew little or nothing, and gave their uncritical admiration to what caught their eye.

The second variety, particularly if they were children, were almost invariably first attracted to a case containing dolls dressed in national costumes. They were the sort that tourists bring home when they have been abroad. Indeed, that was how Miss Prescott had come by them and, as she rather ruefully admitted, she wouldn't of her own free will have given them so much space.

'But when friends are so kind and thoughtful, you can't hurt their feelings by telling them that really they're rather out of place among rare and valuable dolls. And anyhow, they're very colourful.'

'The children all fall in love with them,' Emma agreed, 'And next in favour are the little Japanese dolls with coloured paper kimonos and the neat little pieces of black felt for hair! I must say, I rather like them myself.'

'So do I,' Miss Prescott admitted.

It was one of Miss Prescott's 'good days' when walking didn't trouble her as much as it sometimes did, and she and Emma were making a tour of the museum principally for her to see the rearrangement of the dolls so that the

'Lucy May Wainright collection' could have a showcase to itself. But now that she had approved of what Emma had done she was reluctant to go back to her workroom, and was making a slow tour of the museum.

'Have you a special favourite, Miss Prescott?' Emma asked with interest, and Miss Prescott nodded.

'Oh yes,' she said unhesitatingly, ' "Cherry Ripe", and opening a case, she touched the doll in question with gentle fingers.

'Cherry Ripe' was certainly attractive, though, as Emma knew, not by any means the most valuable doll in the collection. She was very pretty, golden-haired and blue-eyed and with a particularly sweet expression. She was dressed in a high-waisted, full-length muslin gown with a cherry-coloured sash. Strings of the same gay colour tied her Dolly Varden hat under her dimpled chin and as a final touch, on one arm she carried a little basket filled with miniature imitation cherries.

'She's sweet,' Emma agreed sympathetically, 'though not, perhaps——' she stopped short, not wanting to hurt Miss Prescott's feelings.

'Not the most valuable?' Miss Prescott smiled. 'Oh no, she's not. But she is especially precious to me because she was a gift——' she paused, and then went on dreamily as if she were thinking aloud, 'given to me in love by—someone who could ill afford to buy her. Yes, she's my greatest treasure.'

Naturally Emma wondered who the 'someone' was. The man to whom Miss Prentice had once been engaged? But, according to Martha, he had jilted her with absolutely heartless speed after she had had her accident. Yet presumably they must have had their happy times together and these were what Miss Prescott wisely preferred to remember. Emma wondered if she could be so wise or so forgiving in such circumstances—somehow, she doubted it, and promptly felt ashamed of herself. She was distracted from considering the matter further because Miss Prescott said briskly:

'And now we really ought to get back to work. You said you were going down to the village, didn't you?'

'Yes, I've got the Edwardian bride doll packed and ready

to post,' Emma replied. 'I ought to be able to catch the post if I start off now.'

She reached the village shop which was also the Post Office with plenty of time to spare, as Mrs Medler remarked as she laid the parcel on the counter.

'The van isn't due for another ten minutes or so,' she said reassuringly. 'And anyway, Joe Potter, he won't be on time. Courting Molly Turner at Dingle Farm, he is, and he always stops to have a cup of tea with her. Well, we were all young once,' she concluded tolerantly, 'but if the Inspector catches him dawdling on his rounds, he'll likely have something to say. And so I've warned Joe, repeated. And how are you liking it at Fantasy, Miss Lathom?'

'Very much,' Emma replied, not in the least put out by the sudden change of topic. She was a stranger and would be for a long time to come so, naturally, local people were interested in her. 'Miss Prescott is a dear person to be with, and Martha looks after me in the kindest way.'

'They both like you, too, from what I hear,' Mrs Medler commented, leaning her arms on the counter so that her vast body surged towards Emma. 'Well, that's natural enough. They'd got into a bit of a rut, just the two of them alone together, and it's stirred them up a bit to have someone young about the place. But I'd have thought a pretty young lady like you would find it dull living with two old maids!'

'Well, I assure you I don't, Mrs Medler,' Emma told her. 'I'm enjoying myself very much.'

'Yes, well, come to think of it, perhaps it isn't as dull as all that,' Mrs Medler acknowledged, adding significantly: 'Not seeing that you're not short of gentlemen visitors, or so I understand.'

Tim and Adrian, of course, Emma thought resignedly, and was just about to give a casual, noncommittal reply when she saw that Mrs Medler's round red face had become absolutely devoid of expression, though it seemed to Emma that her boot-button eyes were trying to convey a warning. And at that moment the bell jangled as the door was opened and Lorraine Heywood came into the shop.

Mrs Medler heaved herself off the counter.

'Yes, madam?' she asked with punctilious politeness.

'What can I do for you?'

But for the moment Lorraine, looking most attractive in a beautifully cut trouser-suit of air force blue, ignored Mrs Medler as she saw and recognised Emma.

'Hallo,' she said casually. 'I heard you were still in Windyvale. Not bored with our simple rural pleasures yet?'

'Not yet,' Emma assured her crisply, and turned to Mrs Medler. 'Thank you, Mrs Medler. That's all today, but we'll have some more parcels ready in a day or two for me to bring to you.'

'You'll be welcome,' Mrs Medler replied matter-of-factly, yet with just the faintest emphasis on the first word which suggested that some other people might be less welcome.

Not wanting to get involved in what might become an embarrassing situation, Emma's one thought was to get out of the shop as quickly as possible. She bade Lorraine a pleasant farewell and her hand was actually on the handle of the door when Lorraine intervened.

'Don't go,' she requested, but though the two words were drawled in a casual way, there was something faintly imperious in her manner. 'It would be rather fun if we were to go over to the Arms to have a drink together, don't you think? Unless, of course, you're too busy?' and her beautifully shaped eyebrows arched quizzically.

She thinks I'll make an excuse to get out of it, Emma thought, inwardly fuming. She thinks I'm afraid of her, I suppose. Well, I'll show her!—'That would be very nice,' she said equably. 'I'll wait for you outside.'

She spent the brief time before Lorraine joined her telling herself that she'd been a fool to fall right into the trap Lorraine had laid for her, with the realisation that, short of showing the white feather, there was nothing else she could have said. At least she had the satisfaction, when a little later they were sitting together in the attractive little bar, of seeing that Lorraine herself wasn't quite at her ease. Indeed, as they sipped their sherries she had nothing to say and hardly seemed to listen to Emma's discreetly commonplace remarks.

Then suddenly Lorraine drew a deep breath as if she had made up her mind about something. She leaned forward, and interrupting Emma in the middle of a sentence demanded abruptly:

'How long do you intend staying in Windyvale?'

'How long?' Emma repeated consideringly. The question hadn't altogether taken her by surprise, but she had no intention of being hustled into replying. 'Well, that's something that's never been discussed. But, in general terms, I suppose the answer is—for as long as the arrangement suits both Miss Prescott and me.' She smiled disarmingly. 'I'm sorry I can't be more definite.'

For a moment Lorraine stared at her with an intensity which was offensive, so clearly did it indicate that she was trying to read Emma's thoughts. Then she shook her head.

'You're wasting your time,' she pronounced very positively. 'Can't you see that?'

'Oh, I don't think so,' Emma said reflectively. 'I'm not only thoroughly enjoying my work, I'm learning a lot from Miss Prescott. And quite apart from that, I think Windyvale is beautiful and I'm feeling fitter than I've done for a long time. I was really run down when I came here, you know. So one way and another I really don't feel that I'm wasting my time.'

Lorraine stared at her in silence for a moment. Then, once again, she shook her head.

'Sorry, but you haven't convinced me! Oh, I admit you've learned to say your little piece very effectively, but I can't believe that you'd be content to bury yourself alive in an out-of-the-way dump like this if you hadn't some other much stronger motive than those you've admitted to.'

'Oh?' Emma regarded Lorraine with genuine interest. 'That sounds as if you don't like living in Windyvale!'

'I don't,' Lorraine said shortly, 'but we're not talking about me——'

'And nor,' Emma said firmly, 'are we going to talk about me. Now—another sherry? Or do you appreciate that you'd just be wasting your time to continue this conversation?'

'Yes, I'll have another drink, because I don't think I'm wasting my time. Though I can see that I shall have to be rather more outspoken than I'd hoped would be necessary.'

Emma went to the bar to collect the drinks, wishing heartily that, since Lorraine had paid for the first round, manners didn't dictate that she must make a return gesture. However, she returned to the table determined not to let Lorraine get the better of her. But it wasn't going to be easy; she knew that.

Lorraine murmured a word of thanks as Emma set a glass down in front of her, but she left it untouched, apparently lost in thought. Emma, having no intention of starting the ball rolling, filled in time taking note of the other occupants of the bar. Actually it was too early for there to be many customers. There were two couples and, out in the car park, two cars, so Emma concluded that the four people were just passing through Windyvale and were consequently not of very great interest.

The remaining customer was rather different. He was, perhaps, in his early fifties, fresh-complexioned and with a very trim Van Dyke beard which gave him a distinguished appearance. He was wearing lightweight tweeds, not in their first youth but undoubtedly the product of a good tailor. But what interested Emma most was that he had an air of permanence which the other customers lacked. Possibly that was because he was reading a newspaper in a leisurely way which suggested that he was in no hurry to leave.

'He looks as though he belongs,' Emma thought with passing interest. 'Perhaps he's boarding here—I know Tom Bailey has rejoined his ship, so his room could be free——'

She had no more time to consider the matter, for Lorraine suddenly returned to the fray and Emma gave her all her attention.

'I don't know if you've realised it,' Lorraine began, 'but this village is a hotbed of gossip—and not always very kindly gossip at that, as I know to my cost. But what *you* may not know is that everybody is agog to know which of them you're setting your cap at. I must say it interests me, too.'

'*Them?*' Emma repeated the word vaguely.

Lorraine's hands moved impatiently.

'Don't try that little innocent line with me,' she advised, 'because it doesn't take me in for a minute. But if you want it in words of one syllable, who have you set your sights on, Tim—or Adrian?'

'I think you're being incredibly vulgar,' Emma replied icily, 'but in the hope of ending this distasteful conversation, I'll tell you—neither of them. And now——' she pushed her still unfinished sherry away and stood up, 'If you'll excuse me——'

Lorraine's hand shot out and she gripped Emma firmly by the wrist.

'You'd better stay and hear what I've got to say—for your own sake,' she warned.

Emma was in a predicament. She could, of course, have compelled Lorraine to let go, but only if she used force, and she was reluctant to make something of a scene in such a public place. So, with a shrug, she sat down again.

'That's better,' Lorraine said with satisfaction, and went on briskly, 'Now then, if it's Tim, then you're backing a loser. Oh, he's charming, I grant you. And he's got what could be a delightful home—if he could afford to spend a lot of money on it. But he can't. He hasn't got two pennies to rub together, and if he had he'd spend them on his stupid inventions, not the house. And not on getting married, either, believe me!'

It was on the tip of Emma's tongue to ask her if she spoke from personal experience, but to indulge in a riposte would only serve to cheapen herself in her own eyes. So, setting her mouth firmly, she remained silent.

'Actually, he's worse than broke,' Lorraine went on scornfully, 'he's deeply in debt. To Miss Prescott, among others.'

Remembering what both Miss Prescott and Adrian had said about Miss Prescott's finances, Emma thought that this might quite likely be true. And though she did her best not to give a hint of what she was thinking, there must have been a slight change in her expression, for Lorraine gave a little exclamation.

'But that doesn't come as a surprise to you, does it?' she asked shrewdly. 'So, since I'm sure you're an essentially practical person, Tim is out! But that still leaves Adrian, doesn't it? Well, financially he's a much better bet than Tim, I grant you. But even so you're wasting your time. He's not the marrying sort, you know.' She paused and then asked pensively: 'Did you know that he and I were once engaged?'

Emma felt as if she had been dealt a violent blow somewhere in the region of her heart, but far from disconcerting her, it had the effect of keying her up to such a degree that she knew what her answer must be.

'Oh yes?' she said indifferently. 'How interesting!' and knew instantly that she had scored a point because Lorraine's eyes, which had been watching her narrowly, widened very slightly in surprise.

'Of course,' Lorraine admitted, just a little too quickly, 'that's ancient history now. But all the same, Adrian has come back—and he's paid me several visits.' Her complacent expression made the significance of the remark quite clear.

'I see,' Emma said politely. 'May I offer you both my congratulations and good wishes?'

'Oh——' That really did disconcert Lorraine. 'It's perhaps a little early for that——'

Emma wondered why, in that case, Lorraine should have taken her, of all people, into her confidence. After all, as Lorraine had said, Windyvale was a gossipy place and she couldn't be sure that Emma wouldn't pass the news on. Or, despite her protest, was that what she really wanted?

'I expect you're wondering why I've said anything about it, particularly as we hardly know one another,' Lorraine went on as if she had read Emma's thoughts. 'But that's just it. If I don't warn you, no one else will, because of course Adrian counts as a local—and they all gang up against strangers, as I know to my cost. You'll never hear the truth about Adrian from any of *them*!'

'And I shall from you?' Emma asked sceptically.

'Oh, I know,' Lorraine shrugged drily. '*Never believe a warning from a woman about a man because she's probably got some ulterior motive!* Well, perhaps I have, but all the same, you'll be wise to listen to me because no one else knows the whole story. Except Adrian, of course. You see, we never announced our engagement——'

Emma was sure that it would be wise to take anything Lorraine said with a generous pinch of salt, but she felt compelled to listen. After all, it might explain that feeling

105

she had always had that something had once happened to Adrian which had made him so intolerant of women.

'I expect you know that I came to Windyvale about two and a half years ago,' Lorraine began, 'as a companion-housekeeper. Both Mrs Heywood and the General were quite old, you know—in their eighties. And Mrs Heywood, in particular, was very frail and failing rapidly, so I was her nurse as well. She died just about six months after I'd come, poor old soul. It was what everybody had expected; in fact, it was surprising that she lived so long.' She paused as if she were marshalling the order of events. 'It was during that six months that Adrian and I met and fell in love, but we didn't tell anyone because I was afraid—and Adrian agreed—that if Mrs Heywood heard of our plans, she might be worried that I intended leaving her in the lurch. Then, as I said, she died and I stayed on to look after the General for the time being. There was a certain amount of gossip, of course, but that was sheer nonsense. Poor old darling, he'd been badly shocked by his wife's death and his own health deteriorated badly. He simply had to have someone to look after him, so I was doing my best to find someone to take my place so that I would be free to marry Adrian.' Once again she paused and smiled apologetically at Emma. 'I'm afraid it's rather a long story, but you need to know all this if you're to understand what happened then.'

'Go on,' Emma said briefly.

'Well, to my amazement, when he heard what I was planning, the General suggested that instead of marrying Adrian, I should marry him! Of course I refused, and then he told me that if I'd agree he'd leave me everything he had, and that my young man and I wouldn't have long to wait for it! Even so I told him it was out of the question, but all the same I felt—confused. I mean, I could understand the General's point of view. He knew and trusted me, and he was too old to accept change easily. But there was something about the idea——' she grimaced fastidiously. 'Isn't there a word which means taking money for doing something that ought not to be for sale?'

'Venal,' Emma supplied automatically. 'It means being mercenary beyond the point of—of decency.'

106

'Yes,' Lorraine said eagerly. 'That's just what I mean. So, like a fool, I tried to sort things out in my mind by telling Adrian. I thought—I hoped—he'd tell me that pathetic though the General was, what he suggested was impossible. But instead of that'—she closed her eyes and gave a convulsive little gulp—'he told me quite calmly that I'd be very silly not to marry the General! Oh, not so that he, Adrian, would benefit as regards the money, but because he'd come to the conclusion that he'd made a mistake in getting involved with me! Yes, that was how he described it, and he explained why. He'd realised, you see, that as a married man he wouldn't be free to go careering about all over the world as he had done, and that as he was making a name for himself, he didn't want to be tied down. He was kind enough to say that he'd felt rather concerned about backing out, but now that he knew my future could be assured, our engagement could be broken without any hardship for me. So'—her voice dropped to a dreary note —'that was that! He went away—and I married the General. You see, nothing seemed to matter any more. And the General was a dear old man, I was really fond of him. Then he died and he had kept his word. He left everything he had to me—"*in gratitude for her care and devotion to my wife, and to me*". And it was true,' she declared passionately. 'I *did* look after both of them. I tried my level best to make them feel safe and happy.' She drew a deep breath. 'Well, do you believe me?'

Emma moved uneasily. It was a convincing story, and what Lorraine had said in no way contradicted anything Emma had already heard from other people. And yet she knew that she wasn't really satisfied. Somewhere at the back of her mind was the conviction that she knew something which made Lorraine's story ring false, but for the life of her she couldn't think what it was.

'Well?' Lorraine repeated insistently.

'You—you must have felt terribly hurt and bitter at being treated like that,' Emma said hesitantly, avoiding a direct answer to Lorraine's question. 'I'd have thought you'd never feel like trusting Adrian again, and yet you say that you and he——'

'Yes, I suppose it does sound strange to an onlooker,'

Lorraine admitted eagerly. 'Adrian is a hard, self-centred materialist, and I know it. And if I'd any decent pride, I'd have nothing more to do with him. But pride and love don't go together, you know, and I love Adrian. What's more, I believe that in so far as he can love *any* woman, he loves me. And I'm willing to settle for that!'

It was said so simply, so earnestly, that to Emma it carried more conviction than anything else Lorraine had said. There was a little silence. Then Lorraine spread out her hands.

'Well, there it is,' she said wistfully. 'That's the whole story and you probably think I'm every sort of a fool. Sometimes I think so myself, but'—she shrugged her shoulders—'what else is there for me to do? Here I am, still young and comparatively well-to-do—but I must be the loneliest person on earth! I've no friends because everybody has decided that I'm a calculating gold-digger. And I'm not! I never was!'

'No, I see what you mean,' Emma said awkwardly, wishing to goodness that she could put an end to this incredibly embarrassing conversation without appearing too abrupt. Then the old wall-clock struck midday, and she seized her chance.

'Goodness, as late as that?' she exclaimed, standing up again. 'I really must fly! I've been far longer than I'd anticipated, and I don't want Miss Prescott to worry that something dreadful has happened to me!'

'No, of course not,' Lorraine agreed, and this time she made no attempt to detain Emma. 'Thank you for listening so patiently. You do understand why I felt I had to tell you, don't you?'

'Not altogether,' Emma equivocated, 'but you've given me something to think about! And now I really must go . . .'

She beat a hasty retreat, but found that she was not yet free. She was actually in her car and had switched on the ignition when the bearded man who had also been in the bar came to the side of the car, and spoke to her through the open window.

'Excuse me for addressing you, ma'am,' he said deferentially, 'but I overheard you mention Miss Prescott's name, and I concluded from what you said that you live

108

with her. Is that so?'

His pleasant voice had a Canadian accent and Emma liked his manner as much as she had liked his general appearance, but she really was in a hurry and in addition, she was not in the mood for talking politely to strangers, however nice.

'Yes, I live with her,' she admitted, 'but——'

'Then I'd be most grateful if you could spare me a few minutes——'

'Look, I'm truly sorry but I simply haven't time,' Emma told him firmly. 'Another day, perhaps——'

And shot away without giving him a chance to protest, nor did she spare him another thought. She had too many other things to consider.

That Lorraine had had some definite reason for telling her that old story was of course, very clear. And she had no difficulty in knowing what it was. In fact, Lorraine had all but told her in so many words that she wasn't in the least sure of Adrian. She was afraid that he was finding Emma herself more attractive, and she wasn't taking any chances. That was why she hadn't scrupled to present Adrian in such an unpleasant light by telling a story so greatly to his discredit. But surely, if one really loved a man, as Lorraine said she loved Adrian, then one would want to bury such a bitter memory deep in the past, particularly if there were a real chance of a reconciliation.

'At least, that's how I'd feel about it,' Emma reasoned, 'but *she* didn't. I suppose she thought that if I *was* setting my cap at him it would put me right off. Yes, she was warning me to keep off the grass! It would serve her right if I asked Adrian if it was true. No, that wouldn't help because, true or false, he'd deny it. I think it was probably a mixture of truth and falsehood that she told me—if only I knew which was which!'

But she didn't, and though still at the back of her mind was the conviction that she really did know something which discredited Lorraine's story to the point of making it extremely improbable, she was nowhere nearer remembering what that something was. It was horribly tantalising.

As it was so near lunch time there were few people a out who might have further delayed Emma, though she did get a glimpse of the Vicar and Mrs Torrance; but they were just vanishing into a shop and didn't see her, which was fortunate, for Mrs Torrance, as she herself admitted, did so enjoy a good gossip.

Mrs Torrance. Gossip. A light seemed suddenly to flash in Emma's mind—that day when she'd had tea with Mrs Torrance and the kindly old lady had reproached herself for just that very weakness. And practically word for word, Emma recalled the conversation. They had been talking about Miss Prescott and Mrs Torrance had spoken of her broken engagement. The man in question had gone to Canada—or it might have been America—and the arrangement had been that when he had established himself Miss Prescott would join him. But she never did because of her accident. The man had jilted her and he had never come back to Windyvale.

Of course, Mrs Torrance had said, *one can see that a crippled wife would be a sad handicap to a young man with his future at stake, but all the same——*

And Lorraine, speaking of Adrian had said:

He'd realised that, as a married man, he wouldn't be free to go careering about all over the world and he didn't want to be tied down——

Not identical words or identical circumstances, but in each case the man concerned had put ambition before loyalty and had behaved with utter callousness towards the woman he professed to love.

Coincidence? Emma dismissed the idea impatiently. There had already been so many coincidences affecting Adrian and herself that she simply couldn't credit the possibility that there should be still another one. What was far more likely was that Lorraine had heard the old story and had adapted it to suit herself.

'Which explains why it all sounded so glib,' Emma decided. 'It was a lesson that she'd learned by heart!'

She drove the rest of the way to Fantasy with a delightfully light heart——

But she was so late in getting back that, with a busy afternoon ahead, she had to hurry over lunch. Half a dozen schoolgirls in the charge of a mistress were coming to see the museum and later on, another collector was coming to see Miss Prescott. Emma would have to show this visitor round the museum, for even in the short time that she had been at Fantasy it was only too clear that Miss Prescott's condition had deteriorated. It caused Emma considerable anxiety, but she felt that as a comparative newcomer it wasn't for her to suggest that Miss Prescott really ought to consult a specialist. That would surely come better from Adrian or Tim, and would probably carry more weight.

The girls, all in their very early teens, arrived exactly on time, and though Emma greeted them smilingly, she gave them a quick, searching look. By now she had had sufficient experience of young visitors to come to the conclusion that although the majority of them were reasonably well-behaved, there was more than likely to be one awkward customer. And it was advisable to determine who that was as soon as possible. With this particular contingent that wasn't very difficult. Five of the girls were ordinary to the point of being dull, but the sixth——!

She was a scrawny little thing, inches shorter than her companions, but she made up for that with a cocksure air that boded trouble. Her black hair was chopped off short so unevenly that one suspected it was an amateur effort achieved with nail-scissors. Her very dark eyes were small and beady, and her expression was unmistakably both resentful and critical.

There was going to be trouble, Emma thought with a sinking heart, and the child's first remark confirmed that.

'I'm not interested,' she announced scornfully as Emma began to point out particularly interesting dolls. 'Dolls are for kids, not teenagers!'

'That will do, Susan,' the mistress expostulated sharply. 'If you can't be polite, please remain silent. You're spoiling other people's pleasure.'

Susan shrugged her thin shoulders.

'Well, I never asked to come,' she retorted. 'Who wants to look at a lot of tatty old dolls anyway? I think that old lady must be dotty! Fancy wanting to play with them at her age!'

'If you are referring to Miss Prescott, she's certainly not dotty,' Emma told her coldly, 'nor does she play with them.

111

She is, in fact, the possessor of a very interesting and valuable collection of dolls of all periods——'

'Valuable?' Susan interrupted incredulously. 'Are they really?'

'They certainly are,' Emma confirmed, and saw that for the first time she had really gained the child's interest. She also saw that the dark eyes glinted with unchildlike shrewdness.

'Which are the most valuable?' was the next question, and again the mistress in charge intervened.

'Really, Susan——'

'I'd better tell her,' Emma suggested placatingly, 'I expect it will interest the other girls as well. It fascinates most people.'

So, painstakingly, she pointed out four or five of the most desirable dolls—four of them belonged to Miss Prescott, the fifth was her own Mrs Ponsonby.

'How about that one?' a fair-haired girl asked shyly, pointing to 'Cherry Ripe'. 'I like her best.'

Emma smiled responsively.

'So do I,' she admitted. 'And so does Miss Prescott. "Cherry Ripe" is her greatest treasure!'

After that the tour went on without any more interruptions from Susan, though she showed no further interest in the exhibits. When it was time for the party to go, the mistress thanked Emma for her interesting explanations and apologised for Susan's troublesomeness.

'She's something of a problem child,' she confessed, 'extremely intelligent but a born rebel. Miss Ford, our headmistress, thinks it's probably due to the fact that both her parents are dead and the relation—or step-relation—who has charge of her isn't really interested, poor child. So we try to make allowances for her, though sometimes I wonder——' she shook her head doubtfully.

'Please don't worry,' Emma begged her. 'After all, it was only just at first that she was rather troublesome. Afterwards, I don't think she said a single word.'

'She didn't,' the mistress confirmed, 'but she was thinking hard, and I couldn't help wondering——' she stopped uncertainly. 'You see, it's just that in order to avoid trouble we try to be one jump ahead of her. But in this case, I really can't think of anything——'

'No, nor can I,' Emma agreed. 'Probably it was just that she was disconcerted at being put in the wrong, and she didn't want to make any more mistakes.'

'Yes,' the mistress agreed, 'it could be that.' But she didn't sound entirely convinced.

Miss Craven, the other visitor that afternoon, spent quite a lot of time talking to Miss Prescott and it was some time before Emma escorted her round the museum. Naturally, she did not need to ask the questions that most visitors did, since her knowledge of the subject enabled her to identify various dolls without assistance. When they came to the Lucy May collection, however, she asked a lot of questions and listened with absorbed interest to Emma's account of how she had found them. But though she remarked that Emma was extremely lucky to own them, she was as reluctant to place a value on them as Miss Prescott had been.

'But one thing you can be sure of, the greatly increased interest in antiques of all sorts can only mean that *their* value will increase. So, if ever you do decide to sell, take great care to seek really good advice—and let me know! I would certainly want to be at any sale in which they figured!'

A few days later Emma had to go over to the Hall with a message for Tim from Miss Prescott.

It was Tim's custom to bring farm supplies over to Fantasy once or twice a week and he was due on the following day. But since she had given him her order, Miss Prescott had decided that she needed a chicken in addition to other supplies. She wrote a note to this effect and handed it to Emma.

'Give it to him if you can, dear,' Miss Prescott requested, 'but if you can't find him, then just leave the note on the kitchen table. The back door is never locked.'

When Emma reached the Hall there was no sign of Tim, and thinking that he was probably in his workshop in what had been the stables she went round to the yard at the back of the house. She had almost reached the half-open door when she stopped short.

Tim was there all right; she could hear his voice, but to her surprise, she could hear Adrian's as well. Evidently he had got through his business more quickly than he had thought possible. Her heart gave an inexplicable little lift, and she wondered if it would be an intrusion if she went in to greet him.

But even as she hesitated, she heard Tim say with satisfaction:

'So, by and large, you found out all we wanted to know?'

Adrian's deeper voice replied:

'I think there are still a few odds and ends to be cleared up, but on the whole I've a fairly good idea of just how things are. But it's not altogether a reassuring story. The house is undoubtedly hers, but there isn't much hard cash. It's the story one so often hears—a pension and annuities which terminated at death. Apart from that, admittedly some thousands of pounds, but not what one could possibly call a fortune.'

Emma stood completely petrified. Neither man had mentioned any names, but they didn't need to. The information which Adrian had obtained described her own circumstances so exactly that there was no room for misunderstanding. Adrian's 'business' had been to poke and pry into her own affairs. She listened shamelessly now.

'Oh!' Tim said blankly. 'That's disappointing.'

'It is,' Adrian agreed grimly. 'And there's something else. She's definitely planning to sell the house, but she'd put it into the hands of a big London firm instead of employing a more local one, as would have seemed the natural thing to do. So, presumably, she wants to keep it quiet until she can announce a *fait accompli*.'

And that, too, was true. After finding out that Frank Hall and Mr Vaughan, the Greystoke house agent, were hand in glove, Emma had decided that it would be wiser to find an agent with whom Frank had no influence; and though Adrian had misunderstood her motive for bypassing Mr Vaughan, that was of no importance.

Yes, it all fitted. There was no need to wait to hear more. She stole quietly to the back door, left the note on the kitchen table and let herself out of the front door.

CHAPTER SEVEN

EMMA fled down the drive, but she didn't take the turning which led to Fantasy, for she realised that anyone who saw her would immediately know that something was wrong. She simply couldn't face Miss Prescott's kindly concern or Martha's inevitable curiosity until she had had time to pull herself together. So she kept on to the big gates, crossed the road and made her way across fields to the sanctuary of a little spinney. There she flung herself down on the soft, mossy turf and buried her face in her arms.

She couldn't cry, but she was racked with terrible dry sobs that shook her from head to foot and tore at her heart with a physical pain. Gradually the sobs died away and she lay very still, spent and spiritless.

Nothing seemed to matter. Lorraine had been right, Adrian *was* hard, self-centred and a materialist.

What a fool she had been to let him put her off her guard with what she now could see was a shrewdly calculated pretence at friendship! Why, he had never overcome his original dislike and mistrust of her. What other reason could there be for him going to the trouble of presumably visiting Greystoke to find out all about her at first hand?

Or was there another reason? Emma stiffened with dismay as she remembered her first encounter with Tim. He had told her then that he was badly in debt and that his only hope was to marry an heiress. Then—in so many words—he'd asked her if *she* was an heiress. Of course she had denied that she was, but had there been something in her manner which suggested to Tim that she was wealthier than she was prepared to admit?

If that was the case, then had Adrian, acting on Tim's behalf, decided that it was worth while going to some trouble to find out just what she had got? Unconsciously she moaned protestingly. That Adrian should be guilty of such mendacity bruised even more than the possibility of his not trusting her. And what made it all the worse was

that Tim, dear, friendly, happy-go-lucky Tim, should be
involved. There could be no doubt about that. With her
own ears she had heard his reaction to Adrian's revelation
that she had only a limited amount of capital—certainly
not enough, even if she sold her house for a good price, to
put the Hall to rights and have an income left to live on.
What was it that Tim had said?

'That's disappointing——'

It all fitted together like the pieces of a jigsaw puzzle.
There wasn't a pin to choose between them—or between
them and Frank Hall. And then there was the man who had
jilted Miss Prescott. Even her own father had accepted
quite placidly the fact that his home belonged to his wife,
not to him.

Were all men the same? Emma wondered bitterly. Cynical opportunists with no other thought than their own
material gain?

'They *are* all the same!' Emma declared passionately,
beating her clenched fists on the ground. 'Ambitious, heartless and money-grubbing! I'll never trust another man for
the rest of my life!'

'That's rather a sweeping condemnation, isn't it?' a mild
voice asked.

Emma turned and sat up in one swift movement. She had
not realised that she had spoken aloud, but even before she
faced him, she knew who the intruder was. It was the
bearded man who had spoken to her at the Prescott Arms.
His voice was unmistakable.

'It may seem so to you,' she retorted belligerently, 'but I
happen to be speaking from personal experience. And now,
will you please go? I prefer to be alone.'

'Yes, I expect you do,' he agreed matter-of-factly, 'but
that doesn't mean that you should be. Besides, it's only fair
that you should give me a chance to defend my sex, isn't
it? Or are you afraid that I may convince you that you're
wrong?'

'Certainly not!' declared Emma. 'Say what you like, but I
warn you, you won't make me change my mind!'

'I'll take a chance on that,' the man replied cheerfully,
and sat down on the stump of a tree which had been felled.
'Ah, that's better! I'm not as young as I was and I've

walked rather further than I intended. Now then—you say that *all* men are ambitious, heartless and money-grubbing. Well, I grant you that it's a description which some men deserve—and, for that matter, some women. But all of them? Oh no, that's not true! *I* know that, also from personal experience, and that covers a longer period of time than that from which you can speak.'

'You may have been luckier than I have,' Emma admitted grudgingly, 'but that doesn't alter——'

'Doesn't it? Oh, surely! However, we'll leave that for the moment.' He paused. 'Have you any idea what the population of the world is? No? Well, to be honest, nor have I, but I think we can agree that it's a good many million. And let's say that half of them are male. Now, that's still a good many million, isn't it?'

Emma made no response. She could see, of course, where his reasoning was leading, and resented the way in which he was cornering her.

'So,' the quiet voice went on relentlessly, 'for you to claim that you're justified condemning all men on *personal* knowledge is just not feasible. Now is it, my dear?'

Again Emma was silent and very gently, her inquisitor went on:

'So I think that what you really mean is that far too high a proportion of the men you *do* know answers to your description of them. Am I right?'

'Yes,' Emma admitted wearily, 'quite right. And now, having gained your point, will you please go?'

'Now less than ever,' he declared, and there was an inflexibility in the way he said it which convinced Emma that he meant just what he said. 'Confound it, child,' with a sudden display of irritability, 'quite obviously you're desperately unhappy. How can I leave you without trying to do something to help you?'

'I expect you mean to be kind,' acknowledged Emma, 'but nothing you can say will alter facts, will it?'

'No,' he conceded. 'It won't, but sometimes just telling somebody all about a trouble clears things in your own mind.' Then, as Emma remained silent, he leaned forward and very gently patted her shoulder. 'Trust me, my dear, I shan't betray your confidence.'

Emma's stormy eyes met his searchingly. His expression was very grave but, preoccupied though she was with her own affairs, she still had the mother-wit to appreciate the strength and kindness which the lines of his face revealed. It was the face of a man who had himself known trouble but had not allowed it to conquer or embitter him. Despite all her prejudices it *was* the face of a man one could trust and, surprisingly, she knew that it would be an unutterable relief to confide in such a man.

The next moment it all came tumbling out, from the day when she had found the dolls to today's débâcle. And never did anyone have a more attentive audience. Not once did he interrupt, though several times he nodded as she laid particular emphasis on some point or other, and once—when she told him of the incident in the vestry—his eyes twinkled, though he was careful not to let her see that.

'So that's why I've made up my mind never, *never* to fall in love with *any* man,' she concluded vehemently. 'It's the only way to be safe!'

'Ye-es,' he conceded thoughtfully, 'you may be right. But isn't it just a little late in the day for you to come to that decision?'

'Late?' Emma repeated sharply. 'I don't understand.' But her eyes dropped from his.

'I think you do, my dear,' he told her compassionately. 'Because—forgive me—I think the truth is that you've already fallen in love.'

Emma's lips parted to give an absolute denial—but the words died on her lips.

'Yes,' she admitted forlornly, 'I have.'

There was a short silence, then Emma stood up.

'Thank you very much for listening so patiently,' she said. 'But you do see now that there's nothing you can do to help?'

'I'm not so sure of that,' he told her. 'Not until I know what you're going to do.'

'Oh——' Emma said listlessly, 'leave Windyvale, of course. What else is there for me to do?'

'Not that!' he insisted. 'Don't you see, my dear, you've already run away once from Greystoke—and rightly so, it seems to me. But to run away a second time would be to brand yourself a coward in your own eyes, and that you would find intolerable.'

'It wouldn't be nice,' agreed Emma, 'but it would be better than staying here now that I know——' She bit her lip, trying to keep back the tears that were now all too ready to flow.

'It might perhaps seem easier to go,' he admitted. 'But I'm going to ask—no, beg you—to stay. Not for your own sake but for Hester Prescott's.'

'For Miss Prescott?' Emma shook her head. 'I don't understand.'

'I'll explain. Sit down again, my dear, because it will take some time—that's better! Now, I've registered at the Arms as John Symonds, but actually my name is John Halliday.' He looked at her keenly. 'That doesn't mean anything to you?'

'I'm afraid not,' Emma confessed. 'Should it?'

He smiled fleetingly.

'Well, the fact that it doesn't means that Windyvale has lost its grip!' he explained wryly. 'My beard and my accent are evidently a better disguise than I'd dared to hope. Otherwise someone would have tumbled to my identity— and talked!' He paused. 'You see, as a young man I lived here. Hester and I were engaged——'

Sheer consternation possessed Emma. She had taken it for granted that this man was a stranger who would shortly be leaving Windyvale and who, once he had gone, would lose all interest in her affairs. Because of that she had talked with absolute freedom, but now she realised just how indiscreet she had been. And there was something else as well.

'Were you, indeed!' Her voice was brittle with disgust. 'In that case, it may interest you to know that the way you treated Miss Prescott is still another reason why I feel the way I do about men!'

'Is it?' he sounded genuinely surprised. 'Why?'

Emma's hands moved impatiently.

'Oh, don't try to deny it,' she said scornfully, 'that only makes it worse! Because of the heartless way you jilted her after her accident, of course!'

'Did Hester tell you that?' Mr Halliday demanded

sternly, and when Emma shook her head: 'No, of course she didn't, because she, of all people, knows it isn't true!' He took his wallet out and extracted a much worn envelope from it. Then, as he took a folded sheet from it, he went on: 'I've never shown this to anyone before, but now I think it's essential that I should. Read it, please!'

Wonderingly Emma unfolded the paper and saw that it had been written in Miss Prescott's beautiful script.

'Dear John,

'I have thought things over very carefully and I have come to the conclusion that I cannot marry you. Perhaps I have mistaken a very real and deep friendship for love. Anyhow, to join you in Canada would mean tearing up all my roots here, and I cannot do it.

'Forgive me if you can, John, and please do not try to make me change my mind. I know that it would be wrong for me to marry you.

'Hester.'

'She jilted you!' Emma exclaimed incredulously. 'I can't believe it!'

'It seems utterly out of character, doesn't it?' Mr Halliday agreed sombrely. 'Until you appreciate the significance of the date.'

Emma looked again at the letter. It had been written twenty-five years ago.

'I've checked up very carefully,' Mr Halliday said quietly. 'She wrote it a month after the accident—about which I knew nothing until a week ago, by the way. Now do you understand?'

'Yes,' Emma's voice shook uncontrollably. 'It's obvious, isn't it—knowing Miss Prescott. She'd been told that her condition was hopeless and she loved you too much to want you to be tied to a cripple for the rest of her life. And so, because she knew that you would never let her down if you knew the truth, she pretended she didn't love you. And all these years——'

'Yes, all these years she's faced pain and loneliness alone, my poor little girl,' Mr Halliday said painfully. 'While I—do you know what I've done?'

Beyond words, Emma shook her head.

'I'll tell you,' Mr Halliday said grimly. 'Of course I wrote to Hester, begging her to reconsider her decision, but I got no reply, and so I turned to the only thing that is any help in such circumstances—work. Hard, demanding work. I put all I'd got into it and as a result, success came to me to a greater degree than I had ever thought possible.' He sighed heavily. 'For years now I've been a wealthy man. But wealth, I discovered, is of no value if you've no one to share it with. My whole life was purposeless and there didn't seem to be anything I could do about it. And then by chance, I heard that the owner of the Hall—Tim Prescott—wanted to sell it. I made inquiries, less out of interest for the fate of the house or, for that matter, for its owner, but because it seemed to me more than likely that Hester might also be in financial difficulties. So I came to find out—and I found out far more than I'd anticipated.' His voice broke and for a moment there was silence.

'So now what are you going to do?' Emma asked tentatively.

Mr Halliday squared his shoulders.

'Do? Isn't that obvious?' he demanded in surprise. 'I shall insist that we get married at once. If her condition *is* hopeless, then at least I shall have the right to make life as easy and comfortable for her as possible. But medical and surgical science has made tremendous strides since she was told that her condition was hopeless and, thank God, I can see to it that she has the very best opinion about that now.' He seemed to consider and went on a little uncertainly, 'Of course, she *may* have consulted a specialist since that original verdict—do you know if that's the case?'

'No, I'm sorry, I don't,' Emma confessed. 'But I tell you who would know—Martha.'

'Yes,' Mr Halliday said thoughtfully, 'so she would. Only I can't be the one to ask her. For one thing, I want Hester to be the first one to know me in my true colours and for another——' he hesitated. 'Martha and I never got on very well together. She was always deeply devoted to Hester and, I always felt, prejudiced against me. Perhaps I was wrong, but certainly if she believes it was I who jilted

Hester———?'

'It wasn't she who told me that,' Emma said quickly, 'but I think she does believe it.'

'In that case, she'd hardly be likely to welcome my return,' Mr Halliday said reflectively, 'and it would probably seem right to her to warn Hester that I'm back. And to be entirely frank, I'm gambling on the fact that if she isn't prepared for my reappearance, she may—well——' he hesitated, smiling wryly as if ashamed of the thought that was in his mind.

'You mean, you don't want her to have time to brace herself so that she can keep up the foolish pretence about not caring for you,' said Emma. 'A good idea, Mr Halliday. All right, I'll find out and let you know. And I'll remember that until you've seen Miss Prescott, you're still Mr Symonds.'

'Good girl!' He looked tremendously relieved. 'And you'll stay on at Fantasy? You see, for one thing it would ease Hester's mind if you were there to look after things while she's in hospital—if that's what happens. And for another, if Martha's difficult, you could keep her from making real trouble——'

Emma promised to stay. It wouldn't be easy, she knew that, but she also knew that Mr Halliday had been right. She *would* despise herself if she ran away for a second time. But there was an even more compelling reason than that for her to stay. Until now she had refused to believe that meeting Adrian again at Windyvale, had been more than sheer chance. But now she had a conviction that it was something more than that. She was *needed* here—not on Adrian's account, but for Miss Prescott's sake. She must stay on at least until the tangle of this old romance had been sorted out, as surely it must be.

Nor did it occur to her that believing as she did that love was a delusion and a snare and that men were despicable and untrustworthy, it was singularly illogical for her to have fallen in so readily with Mr Halliday's unabashed scheming.

As it turned out Emma didn't have to make any excuse for asking questions about Miss Prescott, for Martha herself brought the subject up.

'I'm real worried, Miss Emma,' she confided, her plain face bleak with anxiety. 'Miss Hester's not so well. You must have noticed it.'

'Yes, I have,' Emma admitted regretfully. 'She's not nearly so mobile as she was when I first came here. I think she must be finding it more painful to walk.'

'That's it,' Martha agreed dismally. 'And I'll tell you why. I'm just about certain that she's had a fall that she's kept quiet about. P'raps not a very bad one—she'd have had to let on if it had been—but bad enough.' Martha's eyes filled with tears. 'If only she'd *do* something about it—but I don't believe she's even told the doctor. He hasn't been to see her, not since she had 'flu in spring.'

It was then that Emma felt it was safe to ask whether, once the original verdict had been pronounced, Miss Prescott had ever consulted a specialist about her condition.

'No, she never has,' Martha declared unhesitatingly. 'And that I know for certain, for I've never left her for a single day. You see, Miss Emma, she's not the sort that's always grizzling about her troubles. She's always said that the less one thinks about one's troubles the better, because otherwise they fill one's mind as well as affecting one's body. So the only thing to do, she says, is to accept things as they are, not only because that makes them more bearable but what's more, one isn't such a bore to one's friends.'

'How very brave of her,' Emma said softly. 'And of course she's quite right—up to a point. But I think the time has come when something *must* be done. And, unless very soon she herself comes to that conclusion, I think someone will have to tackle her.'

'That's what I think,' Martha agreed. 'But who? Not me, because I've tried it and it wasn't any use. She just smiled and told me I was imagining things, and wouldn't talk about it any more. You know, Miss Emma, for anyone as kind and sweet as Miss Hester, she's uncommon obstinate. Once she's made up her mind——' And Martha rolled her eyes expressively.

Just how true that was, Emma had reason to know. Who but a very fine, sweet person who was also very obstinate could have so firmly dismissed the man she loved, for his own sake?

123

'Well, Martha, let's leave it just a little longer,' Emma suggested, feeling rather guilty because she knew that she had no intention of doing anything of the sort. 'There is, after all, the possibility that if Miss Prescott feels that she is becoming more of a burden to other people, she may decide to do something about it.'

'Yes, there's that,' Martha admitted, cheering up slightly. 'But it's awful hard just to stand by and do nothing. Oh well, there it is. I had wondered if either of the young gentlemen might be able to get round her, but they both seem too wrapped up in their own affairs to bother even to come to see her. Men!' And with a contemptuous toss of the head she made her departure.

For a moment Emma shelved Miss Prescott's affairs to consider Martha's concluding remarks. It was quite true that since Adrian's return neither he nor Tim had visited Fantasy. Because they were genuinely busy? Or because, now that they knew she wasn't a 'catch' financially, they had decided that it would be wiser not to seek her company?

But there was really no point in wondering what kept them away. It was just one of those facts which had to be accepted. Indeed it was perhaps just as well, since it saved her the necessity of having to avoid them.

But now—about Miss Prescott—she decided that she would go to the Arms at once in the hope of encountering Mr Halliday, but just in case he wasn't there, she wrote a note telling him what she had learnt from Martha.

It was as well that she had taken the precaution, for as Mrs Bailey explained, Mr Symonds had gone out for a walk and wasn't expected back until tea-time.

'A nice gentleman,' she commented as she put Emma's letter in the slot beside Mr Symonds' key. 'No trouble at all. Funny thing is, he reminds me of someone, though for the life of me I can't think who.'

'Oh?' Emma hoped to goodness that she was showing sufficient interest in this pronouncement to allay any suspicions Mrs Bailey might have. 'I expect you'll remember sooner or later.'

'Sure to,' Mrs Bailey agreed confidently. 'Funny, the way

things come back to you if you don't keep nagging at them.'

'Yes, isn't it,' Emma agreed. Then, as Mrs Bailey was summoned to the rear premises by her husband, she was able to make her escape without discussing the matter further. She only hoped that memory wouldn't return to Mrs Bailey before Mr Halliday and Miss Prescott had met.

As she turned out from the car-park she heard the sound of horses' hooves coming towards her, drew well over to the side of the road to leave comfortable space for them to pass and switched off the engine. Only at the last moment did she realise that the riders were Lorraine and Adrian, and wished to goodness that she had been just a little later in leaving the Arms. However, it was too late to wish that, and she managed a tight little smile as Adrian gravely lifted his crop in acknowledgment of her courtesy. Lorraine acknowledged her with a smile which was at once both complacent and derisory. As clearly as if she had spoken she was underlining what she had already said. Adrian was *her* property.

They passed and Emma was just about to start up when a child appeared in the road apparently from nowhere, and spoke to her. Astonishingly, it was Susan, the child who had been so contemptuous of the dolls' museum.

'I thought they'd come this way—and I was right,' she announced triumphantly, picking hedge brushings from her tousled head. 'That's one up to me!'

'You mean you were spying on them?' Emma asked.

'Oh *no*!' Susan declared with such an air of superiority that Emma felt she was the child—and a mentally deficient one at that—and Susan was the adult. 'It isn't spying when you're a detective. It's routine investigation. How else can you get evidence?'

'Oh!' Emma said weakly, 'I didn't know you were a detective.'

'Well, I'm not yet, of course,' admitted Susan regretfully, 'but I'm going to be when I'm a bit older. And it's never too soon to start learning and practising if you know what you want to do, is it?'

'I suppose not,' Emma agreed, still feeling at a disadvantage with this strange little creature.

'Of course not,' Susan insisted with conviction. 'That's why, when I knew that Aunt Lorraine and Mr Wroughton were going riding, I considered all the evidence——'

'*Aunt* Lorraine! Emma exclaimed. 'Is Mrs Heywood your aunt?'

'Not really,' Susan explained impatiently, 'but General Heywood's first wife was my great-aunt Rose. And she was my guardian. Then she died and he married Aunt Lorraine, and that meant he was my guardian. Then, when he died, it was Aunt Lorraine. There was no one else, you see. But it's not an arrangement that either of us likes.'

No, Emma thought, it wouldn't be. Lorraine, she felt, would probably regard the guardianship of any child as a nuisance, and this shrewd, self-opinionated young person must be a constant thorn in her side. As for Susan—it wasn't difficult to appreciate that she would resent the sort of authority which Lorraine would insist on asserting.

'But, as I was saying,' Susan went on determinedly, 'knowing how they like to be alone I guessed—deduced, I mean—that they'd come this way because it takes you to the open country where they wouldn't be likely to meet anyone. And I was right!' she concluded triumphantly.

'I'm sorry, Susan, but I do call that spying, and I think it's bad-mannered and underhanded,' Emma told her firmly.

'Oh?' Susan didn't sound in the least concerned. 'I don't see why. It hasn't done them any harm, because they don't know about it.'

'No, but——' and Emma stopped short, not seeing any way of convincing Susan that though she might not have harmed Adrian and Lorraine, the inquisitiveness which she was deliberately cultivating might do unpleasant things to her own personality.

'If I'd *really* wanted to spy on them, it would be quite easy,' Susan went on scornfully. 'I did once—I hid in a cupboard one day when Mr Wroughton came to see Aunt Lorraine. But it was so boring. All they talked about was the alterations they were going to make at the Farm when they got married, so I haven't bothered any more. It seems to me that people in love always are rather soppy. That's why I don't ever mean to get married. Or if I do, it will be to a policeman, then we'll have interesting things to talk about.'

Emma didn't wait to hear more. She started up and slid carefully away from this cold-blooded child who poked and pried into other people's affairs for her own entertainment.

So that was that, Emma thought grimly. If she had wanted confirmation of Lorraine's claims, Susan had certainly supplied it, for though one might have doubted the veracity of some children, that was hardly possible where Susan was concerned. With her obsession for 'evidence' she was almost certainly a very reliable witness—she would have scorned to be anything else.

Not that it really mattered. Even if Adrian hadn't cared for Lorraine, Emma had no illusions that he loved her or was ever likely to. That she had no choice but to accept, and in the meantime, far more urgent of consideration than her own affairs were those of Miss Prescott. Just what would Mr Halliday do when he read her letter? Would he come at once to Fantasy? Emma thought he probably would, though she wished that she had been aware of Mrs Bailey's half-recognition of him in time to have included a warning in her letter. That would certainly have brought him to see Miss Prescott post haste!

Emma pondered. There was just a possibility that Mrs Bailey, when she handed over the letter, might refer to the matter, in which case Mr Halliday would be sure to realise that there was no time to waste.

But Emma decided to take no chances. She would see to it that she had an opportunity of speaking to Mr Halliday before he saw Miss Prescott—or encountered Martha. Accordingly, at lunch time she told Miss Prescott that, if she didn't mind, she would like to spend the afternoon gardening.

'There's so much simply crying out to be done,' she explained and then, as Miss Prescott looked rather troubled, she added reassuringly: 'I'll wear gloves so that my hands don't get roughened.'

'Oh, my dear, I wasn't thinking of that,' Miss Prescott said quickly, 'it's just that I feel I'm taking too much advantage of your generosity. I mean, you didn't undertake to look after the garden, you know.'

'But I really enjoy gardening,' Emma assured her quite truthfully. And, she could have added, even if she hadn't, this afternoon she would have been willing to do even the most distasteful task if it meant being able to intercept Mr Halliday.

Miss Prescott smiled and patted her hand.

'Dear Emma, I don't know what I'd do without you. You're such a comfort to me!'

Emma smiled in response, but she felt uneasy. Suppose Mr Halliday's sudden appearance after all these years was too much for Miss Prescott in the present state of her health? Or supposing that, after all this time, she wouldn't welcome his return? That could be—after all, it was twenty-five years since they'd parted. It was a long time for love, unnourished, to endure.

However, it was too late to worry about that. The die was cast. Nothing, Emma was quite sure, would persuade Mr Halliday to abandon his avowed intention. He wasn't the sort of man to change his mind once it was made up.

She had been working in the garden for over an hour when she heard the sound of a car approaching. She got up off her knees and listened anxiously. The car stopped, just within the turning off the main drive, Emma guessed. A moment or so later Mr Halliday appeared, walking, and Emma went a little way to meet him.

'I got your letter——' he began, and regarded her with anxiety. 'Something wrong?'

'I don't know,' Emma told him hurriedly. 'It's just—did Mrs Bailey say anything about thinking she'd seen you before?'

'No, she didn't,' Mr Halliday replied. 'But I noticed that she rather stared at me. I suppose that was why. Well, that settles it! Take me to Hester right away!'

Silently Emma led the way into the house, but when they reached the door of the workroom she paused. Was she being loyal to Miss Prescott in conspiring with Mr Halliday like this? Was it too late, even now, to prevent him invading Miss Prescott's quiet life so unceremoniously? She lifted appealing eyes to Mr Halliday's face—and her anxiety was stilled. It was a strong face, no denying that. But there was such kindness there, such evidence of warm, human compassion——

She opened the door. Miss Prescott was sitting by the window sewing a tiny dress. She looked up and smiled.

'I've brought—an old friend to see you, Miss Prescott,' Emma said in a voice that she didn't recognise as her own. Then she stood back for Mr Halliday to come in.

For a moment there was complete silence. Then Mr Halliday held out his arms and said just one word:

'Hester!'

At first there was nothing but incredulity in Miss Prescott's face. Then, as recognition came, such utter joy dawned that she seemed to become suddenly young again.

'Oh, John—*my* John!' she breathed, and the next moment she was safely in his arms.

With tears stinging her eyes, Emma shut the door gently but very firmly. Nothing and nobody would disturb the two happy people she had just left. She turned—and came face to face with Adrian. Instinctively she backed against the door, spreading her arms defensively.

'You can't see Miss Prescott,' she told him bluntly.

'No?' He spoke quite pleasantly, but his dark brows lifted inquiringly. 'But it's really rather important that I should.'

'It can't be as important as that she shouldn't be disturbed just at present,' Emma insisted, and then, realising that he wouldn't be content to take her word for it without an explanation, she went on hurriedly: 'You see, an old friend has come to see her and they've a lot to say to one another.'

Through half-closed eyes, Adrian scrutinised her resolute face with considerable interest.

'I think something rather odd is going on, and I mean to find out what it is,' he told her determinedly. 'So suppose you come and sit down—no, I give you my word I won't barge in until you've explained—but an explanation I will have! That's better!' as, rather blunderingly, Emma went over to the hall chair. She was, in fact, trembling violently both from sheer reaction and from this unwelcome encounter with Adrian. 'Now then, who is this mysterious old friend, and why are you so determined to keep me out?'

'It's not just you. It's *anybody*,' Emma explained.

'All right, so it's anybody.' Adrian accepted that. 'But again—why? Which brings me back to my first question—who is this visitor?'

'Well——' Emma began uncertainly, and then, realising that after all secrecy was no longer necessary, she blurted out: 'Well, if you must know, his name is Halliday. John Halliday.'

'John Halliday?' Adrian repeated, and shook his head. Clearly the name meant nothing to him. Then his expression changed to one of alarm. '*John Halliday!* Do you mean the blighter who jilted Aunt Hester years ago? You do? Heavens above, Emma, what have you done? Don't you know that he must be the last person she'd want to see? Here, let me go!' as Emma, forestalling his obvious intention of breaking his word, clutched him firmly by the arm.

'Not until you've listened to me,' Emma retorted, and stood up to face him resolutely. 'Mr Halliday didn't jilt Miss Prescott. It was the other way round.'

'You mean she jilted him?' He was taken aback but clearly not convinced. 'Well, if she did she must have had a very good reason!'

'She felt she had,' Emma said softly. 'You see, she'd been told that she'd be a cripple for the rest of her life and she didn't think it was right that he should be burdened with a wife in that condition. But she didn't tell him that—in fact, she didn't tell him about the accident—because she was afraid that he'd refuse to break their engagement. So she pretended that she didn't love him enough to give up her life here and go to Canada to join him.'

Adrian considered this, then he shook his head. 'But, Emma, it's common knowledge that he jilted her——'

'Common guesswork!' Emma retorted scornfully. 'How could it be anything else? Naturally Miss Prescott wouldn't explain to anyone, because she'd be afraid that somehow Mr Halliday might hear the truth. And he's been out of touch with Windyvale because he believed that was the way she wanted it. So until he did come back, he didn't know anything about the accident. Oh, do stop being such a doubting Thomas!' She stamped her foot impatiently. 'It isn't just what Mr Halliday has told me, he showed me the letter that Miss Prescott wrote to him. So you've got to believe it!'

'All right, so I've got to believe it,' Adrian acknowledged without enthusiasm. 'But I still don't see why he's left it all this time—unless, that is, he's hard up and thinks he can sponge on Aunt Hester. Because if that's so——'

'Oh, for goodness' sake!' Emma exclaimed in sheer exasperation. 'What a beastly mind you've got! I don't believe you ever think of anything but money! Can't you understand, he stayed away because he believed that was what Miss Prescott wanted! And he's come back because he heard that the Hall is up for sale and that made him wonder if it was because Tim was hard up, which could mean that so was Miss Prescott. So he came to see for himself. He's been staying at the Arms as Mr Symonds, and since you're so anxious about money, he's got plenty—so now do you see?'

'No,' Adrian told her, 'I don't. What I mean is, the situation is just as it was—Aunt Hester is still a cripple. In fact, her condition is worse than it was, so how can it be anything but a torment to her that he's come back? She'll never marry him!'

Emma smiled tolerantly as if pitying his masculine obtuseness.

'Oh yes, she will,' she assured him with complete conviction. 'You see he knows now that she loves him—she gave herself away completely as soon as she recognised him. So he won't stand any nonsense. They'll get married and he'll see to it that she has the very best and latest advice and treatment—which is more than you've ever bothered about for her,' she concluded with a hint of venom.

'On the contrary,' Adrian told her with surprising mildness, 'I've tried very hard to persuade her to seek advice—still, that's not important now.' He pondered, his face troubled. 'Emma, of course she ought to see someone about her condition, but suppose it's true that there's nothing that can be done?'

Emma put her hands over her ears.

'I won't listen—I won't believe it,' she declared vehemently. 'They can do so many more things now that they used not to be able to do. Why, they can even replace a painful joint with an artificial one. I know that's true, because I know of someone who had it done and it made a wonderful difference. And that's what I hope and believe will happen to Miss Prescott—and so ought you,' she concluded rather incoherently.

'My dear Emma, I do hope that with all my heart,' Adrian assured her, 'but I also realise that there may be bitter disappointment ahead for them. One has to face facts, you know!'

'But it's not a fact either way yet,' insisted Emma, 'and I do think you'd be a much happier person if you weren't so pessimistic! I believe you really prefer to think the worst of people and things, without any real evidence!'

Adrian regarded her reflectively.

'No,' he said deliberately, 'incredible though it may seem to you, I'd very much prefer to be an optimist. But if experience has taught one that——' He shook his head, and then in a surprisingly gentle voice went on: 'This is a world of reality, Emma, not a fairy tale which inevitably has a happy ending. Haven't you learnt that yet?'

'Of course I have,' Emma assured him matter-of-factly, and almost told him that he himself had helped to teach her that. 'But just because one has to accept that, it's all the more important that one should never believe the worst without real proof!'

But Adrian didn't appear to be convinced.

'Fair enough—as far as it goes,' he conceded. 'All the same, I think you still incline towards a preference for fantasy. Indeed, I'm not at all sure that one reason at least why you were attracted to Windyvale was the name of this house. I think it was a flight to Fantasy from ugly reality on your part. Am I right?'

'Perhaps,' Emma conceded with a shrug.

Adrian shook his head.

'It can't be done, Emma,' he told her harshly. 'No doubt it seemed to you that in such lovely country as this life must be finer and simpler than in a grim manufacturing town like Greystoke, but, believe me, that's unfortunately not the case. Human beings are much the same no matter what their surroundings—a mixture of good, bad and indifferent. And one just has to make the best of it—not always with much success.'

If he really believed, as he appeared to, that it was a pity that some people lived to very low standards, then how could he possibly justify his own cynically egotistic behaviour?

Emma's lips parted to make a bitterly scathing retort, but at that moment the door of the workroom opened and Miss Prescott, leaning on Mr Halliday's arm, came out into the hall—a smiling, happy Miss Prescott from whom the years had fallen away.

CHAPTER EIGHT

EARLY in the morning, a few days later, Miss Prescott and Mr Halliday were married by special licence in the little church.

It had been decided that it should be a very quiet affair with only the two principals and Mr Torrance, Tim, Adrian, Emma and Martha present, although, as a gesture of courtesy, Mrs Torrance had been included. But somehow or other the news had got round—and one had only to glance at Mrs Torrance's face with its expression of mingled triumph and apprehension to know how that had happened. As a result, early though it was, everybody in Windyvale who could possibly turn up had done so and Mr Torrance had a bigger congregation than he usually had on Sundays.

In order to save Miss Prescott exertion it had been suggested that she should remain seated in a wheelchair throughout the service, but this she had sturdily refused to do. However, she did make the concession that instead of awaiting her at the chancel steps Mr Halliday should escort her up the aisle, and with him on her right and Tim on her left—he was giving her away—she managed very well.

No one had dressed up for the occasion, but Emma and Martha had united in insisting that there must be flowers even if Miss Prescott couldn't conveniently carry a bouquet. And so attached to her shoulder was a charming bridal spray of stephanotis and lilies of the valley.

To Emma's relief, there had been no suggestion that she should act as bridesmaid, and so she sat with Martha—a very subdued and rather tearful Martha—in one of the front pews. Adrian, acting as Mr Halliday's best man, sat on the other side of the aisle until the bridal pair arrived and Emma took very good care not to look in his direction, though she had an uncomfortable feeling that more than once he glanced across at her. Was he, as she was, remembering that other wedding which they had both attended?

134

she wondered.

It was a very short and simple service and very soon they were back at Fantasy. Martha had made a wedding cake and Tim had laid on champagne, but there were no speeches. Simply Adrian lifted his glass with a brief expression of good wishes to which Mr Halliday responded with equal brevity. Then, after the new Mrs Halliday had had a short rest, they left in the big car which Mr Halliday had hired.

'And jolly good luck to them,' Tim remarked heartily as the car vanished from sight.

'Indeed, yes,' Adrian echoed in a sombre tone which suggested that he felt the newly married couple would need all the luck that was going.

Emma said nothing. She wished them luck, of course, but she was conscious of a strange outgoing of some fundamental part of herself—as if she were endeavouring to give her own young strength and courage to help in the ordeal that lay ahead for both Mr and Mrs Halliday.

'Hallo!' Tim said with concern. 'You look down in the mouth, Emma. Something wrong?'

'I think, perhaps, Emma is a little oppressed by a belated sense of culpability,' Adrian commented drily. 'She played quite a big part in bringing this marriage about, you know.'

'Is that so?' Tim regarded Emma with interest. 'Well, that's surely nothing to worry about. After all, there *is* a good chance that something can be done for Aunt Hester. And if it can't—well, at the very worst, she's got Halliday to look after her now. And he'll do that, I'm confident. I mean, he's a thoroughly decent chap, and what's more, he's got plenty of cash!'

Adrian made no comment, but Tim seemed to think that he knew what was in his cousin's mind.

'Oh yes, he has,' he insisted rather as if he found amusement in making the statement. 'Don't you worry your head about that, Adrian! Emma, love——' he slipped his arm through hers, 'I know what you want—another spot of champagne. Come on!' He coaxed her back into the house. 'How about you, Adrian?' he asked over his shoulder.

But Adrian, his expression very thoughtful, had already

begun to walk away from Fantasy, and was apparently out of hearing.

Fantasy, without Mrs Halliday's serene presence, was a rather depressing place to be, though both Emma and Martha did their best to keep the feeling at bay by working hard. Martha announced that she was going to spring-clean the house from top to bottom.

'I couldn't do it properly in the spring,' she explained, 'not with Miss Hester having 'flu.' She sighed heavily. 'I s'pose I'll have to get use to calling her Mrs Halliday, but it won't come easy.'

'I'm sure it wouldn't matter in the least if you continued calling her Miss Hester,' Emma told her encouragingly. 'Both she and Mr Halliday will quite understand.'

But Martha had her own ideas about that.

'No, it wouldn't be proper,' she insisted primly. 'She's a married lady now and it's her right to be referred to as such. For me to do anything else would be downright bad manners—and I hope I know my place too well for that! Well, I suppose the sooner I learn that things aren't going to be the way they were, the better. Because they won't be.'

And, perhaps more from Martha's point of view than anyone else's, that was very true. Her devotion had taken the form of unremitting care and service. Perhaps at times she had rather imprisoned Mrs Halliday in the web of her protectiveness, but most certainly one couldn't deny the sincerity which had dictated her self-denial. It had been a labour of love and now, married to Mr Halliday, her adored Miss Hester would turn to him for much of the help that Martha had previously given her.

Nor was the situation rendered any easier for Martha by the fact that it was only with very great difficulty that she had been persuaded that Mr Halliday was not the hard-hearted villain she had always believed him to be. In fact, Emma was rather of the opinion that she hadn't really been persuaded at all, and that her suspicions of him wouldn't fade for a long while to come—not until he had had time to prove himself, in fact. And just how long that would take was anybody's guess.

Emma herself had plenty to keep her busy, both with needlework and conducting visitors round the museum, in which interest was steadily increasing. Miss Craven, who had already paid one visit, dropped in unexpectedly and though she was disappointed at not seeing Mrs Halliday, she listened with deep interest to Emma's account of what was happening. She was also able to identify the makers and the age of a doll which had been sent for redressing, information which her owner had requested but which was beyond Emma's knowledge.

Miss Craven accepted Emma's invitation to stay to tea, but she seemed to be increasingly preoccupied, and only as she was leaving did the explanation for that emerge.

'Miss Lathom,' she said hesitantly. 'From what you've told me, this change in Miss Prescott's—Mrs Halliday's—way of life has come about in a very short space of time?'

'Yes, it has,' Emma confirmed, wondering what this was leading to.

'In that case, she has probably not had time to make plans for the future—when she returns in better health, as I most sincerely hope she will.'

'I think that might well be the case,' Emma admitted cautiously. 'I mean, quite apart from the fact that naturally her marriage and the operation have taken precedence over everything else, just what she'll be capable of in the future is still uncertain. So even if she has thought about it, I don't see that she can have come to any decision yet.'

Miss Craven nodded.

'In that case——' she began, paused and started again. 'I find it very difficult to tell you what's in my mind without it sounding as if I'm trying to take advantage of Mrs Halliday's absence,' she confessed, 'so I'd better put it in very general terms. It's just this, Miss Lathom, if at any time and for any reason you feel free to leave Mrs Halliday, then I'd like you to know that I shall be glad to offer you a similar position to the one which you have here. But only in those circumstances. Do you understand?'

It was so unexpected that for a moment Emma found herself incapable of replying. None the less, the offer was reassuring, implying as it did that Miss Craven thought well of her abilities.

'Yes, I do, Miss Craven,' she replied, 'and thank you for telling me. It's very encouraging. But I'm sure you won't expect me to say more than that, because as things are, I can't let Mrs Halliday down so long as she needs me.'

'Of course you can't, my dear,' Miss Craven agreed sympathetically. 'And I may tell you that one reason why I'd like you to come to me is that I had no doubt what your answer would be. Loyalty is none too common a virtue these days, I'm afraid, but it's one that I particularly value. So, in the meantime, think no more about it.'

It was only after Miss Craven had left that Emma realised what she had done. From her personal point of view nothing could be wiser than that she should leave Windyvale as soon as possible. And yet, when the opportunity to do so had offered, she had rejected it out of hand.

'But what else could I do?' she asked herself resignedly. 'It's out of the question for me to desert Mrs Halliday, and if I did I don't think Miss Craven would want me! So I'd better do what she said—forget all about it for the present.'

The first news from the Hallidays came in a letter which Mrs Halliday wrote—very tactfully, as Emma appreciated— to Martha.

'Dear Martha,

'I am sure you will be glad to know that I stood the journey very well. I have already been initially examined by the specialist, and he is of the opinion that it is well worth while that a further, more detailed examination should be made in hospital. Further than that, of course, he cannot go at present, but it is encouraging, isn't it?

'Will you please pass on this news to Miss Lathom, and to Mr Adrian and Mr Tim? Either Mr Halliday or I will keep you posted as to further developments, though I must warn you that if an operation is decided upon, there will have to be a delay before it is undertaken so that I can be under close observation and a decision made as to just what the operation will be.

'Thank you so much for the lovely cake, dear Martha.

And thank you all for your good wishes which I know I have.

'Mr Halliday joins me in these thanks.

'Yours affectionately,

'Hester Halliday.'

'Well, that's good news, so far,' Emma said with resolute cheerfulness when a tearful Martha had given her the letter to read.

'Yes, I s'pose so,' Martha agreed, sniffing dismally. 'But suppose things don't turn out well? After all, even the best of doctors sometimes make mistakes——'

'But we're not going to think about things like that,' Emma insisted bracingly, though the same fear was troubling her. 'And now, what about letting Mr Adrian and Mr Tim know, as Mrs Halliday asks? Telephoning would be the easiest and quickest way.'

'You do it?' Martha begged shakily. She had calmed down considerably, but still had not got complete control of herself. 'I'm not that good on the telephone at the best of times, and the way I feel now——'

'All right,' agreed Emma, 'and while I'm doing it, what about you making a nice cup of tea for us both? I know I could do with one!'

And while Martha obediently trotted off, Emma went to the telephone and dialled the Hall number. She had hoped that it would be Tim who answered her call, but it was Adrian's unmistakably deeper voice which replied. Still, it didn't really matter—Adrian couldn't possibly think that she was making an excuse to speak to him.

He listened in silence while she read the letter. Then, after a little pause, he said quietly:

'Well, that's as much as can be expected at the moment.'

'Oh, surely it's something better than that!' Emma protested quickly. 'The specialist *might* have said that there simply wasn't anything to be done.'

'Yes, that's true,' Adrian agreed, 'he might.' Again he paused. 'Well, there's one thing, Emma, you and I have disagreed over quite a number of things, but over this we're in complete agreement. All our loving hopes are with Aunt Hester, and—who knows?—that may help her!'

He spoke so simply, with such convincing sincerity, that a lump came into Emma's throat and she couldn't speak.

'Emma?' There was more than a hint of anxiety in the way he said it.

'It's all right,' Emma assured im shakily. 'It's just that I was being thoroughly feminine and tearful. Stupid, because it won't help Mrs Halliday in the least!'

'No, it won't,' Adrian agreed, 'but it will probably do you good, particularly as I expect it's partly reaction from having to prop Martha up?'

'Perhaps,' Emma admitted, 'but she's pulled herself together now. As a matter of fact, she's making us a nice cup of tea——'

'The universal panacea!' He sounded amused, though not in an unkindly way. 'Well, all right, I'll pass the news on to Tim—he's out at the moment. And, Emma——'

'Yes?' she asked rather breathlessly as he paused.

'I shall be away from Windyvale for a week or so and as I shall be on the move all the time I can't give you an address. But I don't want to be out of touch, so may I ring you up from time to time?'

'Of course you may,' Emma replied warmly. 'And it's going to be good news—it's got to be, Adrian!'

'If faith has anything to do it——' Adrian began, and was silent as if he, too, found words impossible. 'Well, off you go, Emma, and have your tea. You've earned it. 'Bye!'

Emma rang off and made her way slowly to the kitchen. She was conscious of a tremendous feeling of elation not unmixed with bewilderment. For the first time since they had known one another Adrian had given expression to a depth of feeling for another human being such as she had not known he was capable of—and he had admitted that feeling to *her*. It was difficult to make up her mind which fact gave her the greatest satisfaction—and which was the more bewildering. But one thing at least she did not attempt to deny. This facet of Adrian's personality was the most endearing she had yet encountered, and the effect of it was to plunge her more deeply in love with him than ever.

Emma's optimism proved to have been justified. The news

of Mrs Halliday continued to be good—in fact, as good as it could possibly be.

First came the news that an operation had been definitely decided upon. Then an interval of anxious waiting which was terminated at last when Mr Halliday rang up to say that the operation had been carried out and that the result so far was everything that had been hoped for and that, incredibly, she was in no pain at all.

'They say she'll be on her feet and walking in a few days.' His voice broke. 'It seems like a miracle. She sends you all her love.'

Adrian rang up that evening, and when Emma had told him the good news he left her in no doubt as to his relief and satisfaction.

'And so your faith has been justified,' he remarked reflectively. 'You must be glad of that, Emma.'

'Yes, I am,' she agreed. 'The only thing is now that everything has gone so well so far, I'm more frightened than I was to begin with. After all, the real test will be when she begins to walk. Supposing—oh, Adrian, supposing——'

'Hey, that won't do,' Adrian told her chidingly as her voice trailed miserably away, 'you can't let Aunt Hester down now!' And then, astonishingly: 'Or me!'

'You?' Emma echoed in astonishment. 'But what——?'

'But surely you realised that I had very grave doubts about the whole business? Yes, of course you did! You berated me for being a pessimist, and you were so convincing that you converted me to your way of thinking. So how can you go back on that now?'

He sounded quite put out, and Emma laughed.

'What's so funny about that?' he demanded indignantly.

'Just the idea of you needing me to encourage you,' Emma explained. 'I mean, you've always seemed so—so self-sufficient.'

'Have I?' Adrian apparently considered the accusation. 'Well, admittedly I prefer to stand on my own feet if that's in any way possible, but if anyone ever tells you that they never need to depend on other people, write them down as vainglorious or else as a downright liar! We all have our moments of—of uncertainty. Understand, Emma?'

'Yes, Adrian,' Emma said meekly, though she wasn't at all sure that she did. Such an admission from Adrian—it was incredible! 'And thank you for propping me up. I feel much better now.'

'That's my good girl,' Adrian said lightly. 'I'll ring you up in a few days' time. Keep your chin up—'Bye!'

And he was gone.

And then came a letter from Mrs Halliday herself.

'It's true! After all these years I can walk erect and without pain! It seems like a miracle. It *is* a miracle.

'I've been given an entirely new hip-joint! Of course, to start with I have to have support when I'm walking. At present I depend on a sort of three-sided metal frame, but soon, when I'm more confident, I shall be promoted to using two sticks. Then one. Then no support at all. Yes, a miracle!

'I shall be in hospital for about another two weeks. Then, purely as an extra precaution, John insists that we shall stay at an hotel near to the hospital for a week or so. After that, we'll be coming home—and you'll all see for yourselves!'

When Adrian next rang up Emma answered him excitedly.

'It's all right! Marvellously all right. Listen!' And she read Mrs Halliday's letter to him.

'That's fine,' he said when she had finished. 'Could hardly be better, could it?'

Emma didn't answer immediately. She had expected a similar reaction to her own from him, but it wasn't there. He sounded pleased, of course, but in an impersonal, pre-occupied way that was unpleasantly chilling.

'No, it couldn't be, could it?' she said flatly. 'Well, that's all there is to tell you. Will you be ringing up again?'

'I'm not too sure,' Adrian explained, still in that abstracted way. 'There's a possibility that I may be flying to America in a few days' time—it isn't finally decided yet. But, in any case, I'll be back in time to welcome Aunt Hester.'

And with that Emma had to be content. She told herself that she was being silly; that no doubt Adrian had other things on his mind besides Mrs Halliday's affairs, perhaps worrying things. The uncertainty about the trip to America, for instance.

Windyvale was frankly delighted by Mrs Halliday's 'miracle'. Once the news got around, Fantasy was inundated with telephone calls and visitors, with the result that Emma's time was severely interrupted, and she despaired of ever getting through all the work she had set her heart on finishing before the Hallidays returned.

Tim, too, was something of a problem. He was always popping over, sometimes most inconveniently, and the worst of it was that one could never know in what mood he would be. Sometimes he would be on top of the world, sometimes in the depth of gloom, until at last, in sheer exasperation, Emma tackled him.

'Obviously you've got something on your mind, Tim,' she insisted, 'and my guess is that it's something that may or may not turn out the way you want it to, and that's why you don't want to talk about it. All right, that's your business. But——'

'You're quite right,' interrupted Tim, 'and if I could tell anyone I'd tell you, Emma, but honestly I can't. You see, it doesn't only concern me, and I've given my word to hold my tongue in the meantime. I'm sorry I'm being such a pest. I'd better take myself off.'

'No, don't do that,' Emma said, appeased. 'Just tell me one thing, if you feel you can. How long will it be before you know if—whatever it is—will be all right or not?'

'Oh—a few weeks, with luck,' Tim told her listlessly. 'But that seems like an eternity to wait——'

To that there seemed no adequate reply, but fortunately at that moment Martha announced that dinner was ready, and a little later Emma was relieved to see that whatever Tim had on his mind, it wasn't affecting his appetite.

Emma spent the day before the Hallidays' return in the museum. Wanting it to be just as spick and span as possible she had to replace several dolls that she had dressed in a way which she hoped would please Mrs Halliday. She gave them a final appraising look as she put them in place. She had had to do a new set of cards for them because now, in addition to the date and maker's name, she had added that the clothes were new.

The job took longer than she had anticipated because three times she was called to the telephone and twice a caller had brought a 'welcome home' present and had to be seen and thanked. After that Martha had to be placated, for the gifts were of food and she had taken umbrage at what she regarded as an aspersion on her own preparations, which had filled both the refrigerator and pantry to overflowing.

By the time Emma was able to get back to the museum she had to scurry over the final tasks, and even then there was another interruption to come just as she was about to go back to the workroom. Of all people, Lorraine Heywood walked into the museum, her arms full of a great bunch of flaming dahlias. By her expression she was obviously put out over something, and Emma's heart sank. Not another person with a grievance!

'Hallo,' Lorraine greeted her casually. 'I thought you might like these, but I gather from Martha that they're completely superfluous, as you've already been given so many flowers that you've run out of vases. She seemed to be in a bit of a huff. What's the trouble this time?'

Emma thanked her for the flowers, which were really lovely, and assured her that she'd certainly find a container for them somewhere. Then, very briefly, she explained what had upset Martha.

Lorraine shrugged her shoulders.

'That's the worst of these terribly loyal people,' she commented disparagingly, 'they end by getting so possessive. It wouldn't surprise me in the least if Mrs Halliday has real trouble with her being jealous of Mr Halliday. Almost inevitable, I'd say!'

Emma was saved from the necessity of replying to a statement which she felt might be only too accurate, for once again, the telephone bell rang.

With a murmured: 'Excuse me!' she ran back to the workroom to take the call. It was Mrs Torrance at her most loquacious. Cuthbert thought that it would be only proper for him to refer to dear Mrs Halliday's wonderful recovery in a special prayer of thanksgiving, but she, Mrs Torrance, had her doubts.

'You see, while I quite sympathise with Cuthbert's point of view, I feel it's just possible that Mrs Halliday might feel embarrassed at being singled out in such a public way. Now, what do you think, my dear?'

And having put the question, Mrs Torrance began to suggest all the possible and impossible answers that Emma might give. Emma waited as patiently as possible. One had to wait until Mrs Torrance had run out of steam—a lengthy matter. However, at last she paused from sheer lack of breath, and Emma was quick to give her what was really the only possible answer.

'I think that's something that only Mrs Halliday can answer,' she said firmly. 'And after all, tomorrow is only Wednesday. Surely the Vicar can discuss the matter with her on, say Thursday. That'll surely give him time——?'

'What a very sensible idea!' Mrs Torrance exclaimed. 'You know, that's something neither Cuthbert nor I thought of! I'll tell him what you say.' And she hung up with a thump that made Emma rub her ear.

'Mrs Torrance, for a dollar!' Lorraine's voice remarked behind her, and Emma turned sharply.

Lorraine was leaning against the frame of the door which led to the museum and Emma thought, not for the first time, what a gift this girl had not only for choosing clothes which suited her but for wearing them with a positive genius for making the very best of them. Today she was wearing beautifully cut fawn trousers with a bright yellow polo-necked sweater. The result was an elegance of which Lorraine was doubtless well aware, and yet Emma had the feeling that there was an unusual degree of tension about her. She was on the point of asking if anything was wrong when Lorraine held out her hand. The key of the museum lay on its palm.

'I hope you don't mind me having followed you,' she said with a diffidence unusual in her, 'but the fact is, those dolls give me the jitters! All those blind, staring eyes—ugh, I don't know how you can stand them! I locked the door since I imagine you don't leave it unlocked if there's no one there.'

'No, we don't,' Emma agreed gratefully, though she was not a little surprised at this evidence of thoughtfulness on

145

Lorraine's part. 'Thank you very much, Mrs Heywood.'

'Not at all, Miss Lathom,' Lorraine murmured, and with a final word of farewell, went out to her car.

The Hallidays were expected back in the early afternoon and both Adrian and Tim arrived at Fantasy in time to greet them. Conversation was a little strained because, in their different ways, everyone was feeling an emotional tension to which they were reluctant to admit.

'I suppose the trouble is that we're all afraid we're expecting so much that we're bound to be disappointed,' Tim said suddenly, and Emma drew a sharp breath. So far as she was concerned that was certainly the case, but it was a fear which Adrian apparently didn't share.

'That's hardly reasonable, Tim,' he pointed out. 'All that we're anticipating is based on what Aunt Hester has herself told us, and that specifically includes her ability to walk erect, without pain, and with a decreasing need of support. What more do you want?'

That was so true that Emma could relax, but Tim wasn't satisfied.

'All right, if you're so confident about that, what's on *your* mind?' he snapped. 'Because there *is* something—that's obvious.'

'Yes, there is,' Adrian admitted coolly, 'but it's a personal matter which I have no intention of discussing, and nothing to do with Aunt Hester. So, if you don't mind, we'll leave it at that.'

And though it was clear that Tim resented being told to mind his own business, it was left at that, for at that precise moment they heard the sound of an approaching car and with one accord they flocked to the front door and stood waiting—hoping——

The car stopped. First of all Mr Halliday got out, then, turning, he offered a hand to his wife. Mrs Halliday accepted his help—but only relied on it to a degree that any woman might have done. Then, with her hand resting lightly on his arm, she walked the short distance to the house.

And it was true! Mrs Halliday walked unfalteringly and, her face wreathed in smiles, made it perfectly clear that she was in no pain.

'I told you,' she declared exultantly, looking from one awestruck face to the next. 'I told you it was a miracle! Now you can see for yourselves!'

Adrian was the first to regain the use of his tongue.

'We can, indeed, Aunt Hester,' he agreed somewhat unsteadily as he put an arm round her and kissed her warmly. 'And if we can hardly believe our eyes—well, miracles don't happen very often, do they?'

For a brief moment Mrs Halliday looked keenly at him. Then, smilingly, she shook her head.

'More often than you might think, my dear!' she told him with conviction, and turned to greet the rest of them.

Tea was a gay, even hilarious meal, for spirits rocketed and everyone talked at once—with the exception of Mr Halliday. He, not in the least put out that his wife was the centre of interest to his own exclusion, beamed on them all with the contentment of a man who has got his heart's desire at long last.

When the meal was over—which took rather a long time since, as Tim said: 'The table was groaning with the weight of food and now I'm groaning because I've eaten far too much!' But it was over at last, and Mrs Halliday stood up.

'And now I want to show you the museum, John. And particularly how well I've looked after your Cherry Ripe.'

Thankful that she had spent so much time furbishing up the museum, Emma got the key and handed it to Mrs Halliday, who led the way to the Museum and opening the door, went straight to the case where Cherry Ripe had always displayed her charms.

'You see, John——' she began, and stopped short. 'Why, she isn't there!' she exclaimed in bewilderment. 'Have you put her somewhere else, Emma? Or—or has something happened to her?'

'Not that I know of, Mrs Halliday,' Emma felt the colour draining from her face. 'She was there yesterday morning. I'm quite sure of that, because I adjusted her skirt.'

'Then——' Mrs Halliday's happy face clouded over, 'if you haven't moved her—who can have done?'

'I don't know,' Emma confessed helplessly. 'I mean, the

147

cases aren't locked, but the windows and door have patent locks and the keys for them are in the safe in the work-room. So I don't see——'

Methodically Mr Halliday and Adrian inspected the windows and door and found them all properly locked. There was an uneasy little silence which Adrian broke with a question.

'Are any other dolls missing?' he asked briskly, and only then was it realised that two other dolls were missing. One was 'Mrs Ponsonby', the other one of the few French dolls belonging to Mrs Halliday.

'And how do they compare for value with the remaining dolls?' Adrian asked. 'I mean, does the choice suggest that whoever is responsible knew just what they were doing, or was it quite haphazard?'

'That's what puzzles me,' Mrs Halliday confessed. 'Up to a point, the selection suggests considerable knowledge, but not entirely——'

'I think, my dear, that it would be a good idea if we were to go back to the house so that we can discuss the matter in greater comfort,' Mr Halliday intervened gently, and drew his wife's arm through his. 'Will you lock up and bring the key with you, please, Emma?'

Silently they trooped back to the house in a very different mood from that in which they had left it such a sort time previously.

'And now, my dear, will you tell us what's puzzling you?' Mr Halliday suggested when they were all seated.

'It's just this—my French doll and Emma's Mrs Ponsonby are among the most valuable dolls in the collection,' Mrs Halliday explained. 'That suggests expert knowledge, particularly as the French one, though it has a rarity value, is rather tatty in appearance. I don't think it would be the choice of anyone without such knowledge. But where dear little Cherry Ripe is concerned, though she's so charming and quite my favourite——' she laid her hand gently on Mr Halliday's arm, 'commercially she isn't as valuable as at least half a dozen others. So, she would appeal to someone without real knowledge, but not to an expert. So why——?'

'And who?' Adrian turned to Emma. 'Since you've been

showing people round, has anyone asked you which are the most valuable dolls?'

Emma's hands moved in a little gesture of helplessness.

'I think almost everybody who visits the museum asks that,' she explained despondently, and looked at Mrs Halliday.

'That has always been my experience,' Mrs Halliday confirmed with a nod,' and sometimes visitors are very much disappointed at being told that a doll which to their eyes has no appeal may be far more valuable than one which they have found attractive.'

'Oh, so you do give the information if it's asked for?' Adrian said quickly. 'And you?' he turned again to Emma.

'Yes,' she admitted briefly.

'But why not?' Mrs Halliday asked sharply. 'It's something which does interest people, and until now there's never seemed to be any reason why they shouldn't be told. I've certainly never told Emma not to give the information if she's asked for it. And indeed, in her early days here, she must have heard me answer questions about value.' She looked inquiringly at Emma, who nodded.

'Yes, I did,' she agreed gratefully.

Tim, who until now had taken no part in the discussion, moved restlessly in his chair.

'Well, to me it's pretty obvious that someone—and I don't see that it matters whether they knew their stuff or not—sneaked into the museum when Emma wasn't there and pinched the dolls,' he declared loudly. 'Damn it, you can't expect her to have eyes in the back of her head! And anyway, the dolls are insured, aren't they, Aunt Hester?'

'Oh yes,' she acknowledged worriedly, 'but that's not really the point, you know, Tim——'

'Of course it isn't.' With an effort Emma kept her voice steady. 'What matters is that someone has robbed Mrs Halliday.'

'And you,' Tim interpolated sharply.

'Yes, and me,' Emma agreed, but as if her loss was not of great importance. 'And what matters most to me is that it happened at a time when I was in charge, so of course I feel responsible.'

Mrs Halliday took one of Emma's hands in hers and gave

it a little squeeze.

'My dear——'

Emma's lips quivered at the kindness in Mrs Halliday's voice, but she could find nothing to say. Indeed, for a long moment they were all silent. Then Mr Halliday gave a little cough.

'Now, what we all want to do is get to the bottom of this mystery,' he said in a brisk, matter-of-fact way that had the effect of easing the tension in some degree. 'So suppose we consider what we know for certain. First of all, Emma, you say that you're quite sure the dolls were there when you were in the museum during the morning?'

'Quite sure,' confirmed Emma.

'Good! That's one fact established. The next is that now, only a few hours later, they're missing. Now, my dear, in that interval was the key out of your possession, no matter for how short a time?'

'Yes, it was,' Emma admitted regretfully. 'I had to answer the telephone, and while I was away the museum key was in the lock of the door.'

Tim gave a sharp ejaculation.

'Well, there you are!' he declared loudly.

'Yes, but there was someone in the museum,' Emma explained quickly, 'Mrs Heywood.'

'Lorraine?' Tim exclaimed incredulously. 'What the deuce was she doing there? She's not interested in dolls!'

'She'd brought over some flowers as a welcome to Mrs Halliday,' Emma replied reluctantly, 'and she came to the museum to see me because—well, because Martha had told her that we had enough flowers already.'

Again there was silence. Then Tim said significantly:

'Lorraine!'

Emma turned on him sharply, all the more determined to be fair to Lorraine because it was so tempting not to be.

'No, Tim, it couldn't have been her,' she declared emphatically. 'She left the museum just a short time after I did and she joined me in the workroom. She said the dolls gave her the jitters because of what she described as their blind, staring eyes, and told me that she'd locked the door of the museum and gave me the key. When she'd gone, I checked to make sure that it was locked, and it was. And there's another thing. She was wearing slacks and a knitted jersey, so there simply can't be any question of her having the dolls with her. She'd no way of hiding them.'

'She might have had a confederate and handed them out through one of the windows,' Tim suggested, but Emma shook her head.

'No. The windows and the outer door were all locked. I know because I was just about ready to leave the museum, and I'd checked them.'

Tim looked considerably put out.

'You know Emma, anyone would think that you want——'

He was interrupted by an imperative knocking at the front door.

'Oh *dear*!' Mrs Halliday said plaintively. 'Not a time when we can do with a visitor——!'

They heard Martha trot along the hall, then the sound of a man's voice and Martha's unwelcoming rejoinder, followed by a shrill little squeal.

With one accord Adrian and Tim made for the hall, but before they could reach it, the door of the sitting room was flung open and, of all people, Frank Hall strode into the room.

CHAPTER NINE

FRANK at Fantasy! Emma was too dumbfounded to speak. Then, completely ignoring the other people in the room, he came towards her, smiling confidently and with hands outstretched. Automatically Emma backed away from him, her hands behind her back.

'Frank Hall, what on earth have you come here for?' she demanded with unflattering bluntness.

But Frank still smiled.

'Why have I come, darling?' he asked with glib self-assurance. 'To put an end to this wretched misunderstanding between us that's gone on far too long!'

'What misunderstanding?' Emma asked unhelpfully.

Frank's hands moved in a deprecating gesture.

'My dear, it's surely too personal a matter for us to discuss before strangers,' he suggested reproachfully. 'If we could talk alone somewhere——'

'What misunderstanding?' Emma persisted stonily.

Frank shrugged his shoulders.

'Perhaps misunderstanding isn't exactly the right word,' he conceded. 'A lovers' tiff would be a better description.'

'No, it wouldn't,' contradicted Emma, 'it would be utterly misleading. You and I have never been lovers in any sense of the word. And as for misunderstanding—I didn't misunderstand you, Frank. You asked me to marry you, not because you loved me in the least but because, when Father died, the house became mine and you thought that if we were married we—and your mother—could live in it and you would save money! And you can't deny it because you admitted it in so many words!'

'Really, Emma——' Frank began, and though he changed colour slightly he sounded really offended.

Until then the other people present had remained silent since, embarrassing though the situation was, there seemed nothing that they could do about it. Then Adrian stood up and intervened with an authority which brooked no resistance.

'I quite appreciate, Mr Hall, that to you your personal affairs are of paramount importance,' he said icily, 'but you've arrived at a singularly inopportune moment at which to ride in such a roughshod manner over any other considerations.'

Frank stared at him as if he had only just become aware of his presence.

'What other considerations?' he demanded arrogantly, and Emma held her breath. Just what was Adrian going to say to that? Tell Frank it was no business of his, or——? She was not left long in doubt.

'There's been a burglary here,' Adrian explained unhesitatingly, bringing out the word with chilling emphasis. 'And not unnaturally, we would like to know who's responsible for it.'

'Oh?' Frank sounded completely lacking in interest. 'Well, in that case, you should get in touch with the police, if you haven't done so already. In any case, what has it to do with Emma?'

Just what Adrian would have replied no one would ever know, for, surprisingly, Emma herself answered him.

'It has a lot to do with me, Frank,' she told him coolly, 'I'm deeply involved. In fact, you might say that I'm suspect number one! I had opportunity, sufficient knowledge of the value of the articles stolen, and a motive! All rather difficult to explain away, as you, I'm sure, will be the first to appreciate. I certainly can't think of a way to exonerate myself.'

'But—but——' Frank stammered, for once in his life completely at a loss. 'But that's absurd! There *must* be some explanation——'

'All right.' Emma sounded almost bored, 'I'll tell you all about it and then you can judge for yourself.' And precisely and methodically she recounted all that had happened, and Frank listened with growing consternation.

'So, you see,' Emma concluded, 'everything points to it having been me, doesn't it?'

Frank moistened his lips with the tip of his tongue. He was badly shaken, but he contrived to rally sufficiently to raise an objection—and quite a reasonable one.

'It hardly sounds convincing to me,' he announced judici-ally. 'I mean, why, if you're the culprit, should you have removed one of your own dolls? That hardly makes sense!'

'Oh yes, it does,' Emma contradicted drily. 'Don't you see, the fact that *my* doll is missing is the one thing that serves to divert suspicion from me? Rather clever, don't you think?'

'Emma, for heaven's sake!' Frank protested agitatedly. 'You're all but admitting——' he wiped his forehead with an immaculate linen handkerchief. 'As a solicitor, I most earnestly beg you not to say any more.'

'Oh, but you won't understand properly if I don't,' Emma told him resolutely. 'I told you that I had a motive and until you know what that is, you won't appreciate what a jam I'm in.' She turned away from him and faced Mrs Halli-day, sitting silent and troubled at the table. 'While you were away, Miss Craven called unexpectedly——'.

'You told me that in one of your letters,' Mrs Halliday reminded her, her lips hardly moving.

'Yes, I did,' Emma agreed, 'but what I didn't tell you was that Miss Craven said that if ever the time came when you no longer needed me and I felt free to make a change, she would like me to work for her. Well——' her voice hard-ened defiantly, 'I *would* like to leave Windyvale. It is, after all, a rather dull, insignificant sort of place——'

'My dear——' Mrs Halliday's voice shook. 'But you must surely know that if you wish to go, you're absolutely free to do so! Much as I should miss you, I wouldn't dream of trying to keep you against your will. You must surely know that!'

'Oh, but it's not as simple as that,' Emma explained. 'You see, Miss Craven has very definite ideas about loyalty, and if I were to leave you now, at a time when I can be of use to you, she would think I was being unfair to you and I'm all but certain that her offer wouldn't still be open.'

'And so——?' Adrian asked curiously.

Emma turned on him impatiently.

'Oh, don't you see, even now?' she demanded. 'Isn't it obvious? With one of my dolls missing, I have every reason for being too upset to want to stay on here. And what's more, I could reasonably take my other dolls away with me

154

instead of keeping my promise to loan them to Mrs Halliday.'

'Yes,' Adrian agreed thoughtfully, 'all quite true, don't you agree, Mr Hall?'

'Yes—no. I don't know,' Frank stammered uncomfortably. 'It all seems rather involved to me.'

'Oh no, not really,' Emma told him, 'it's actually all quite simple. Or at least, it would have been if you hadn't come, Frank. As it is, to most people there must seem to be a considerable likelihood that you're my accomplice.'

'Emma!' Frank almost shouted her name. 'Of all the outrageous ideas—I must protest——'

'Yes, but look, Frank,' Emma explained, 'the dolls have vanished—what would have been easier than that I took them out of their cases and handed them over to you? Easy and absolutely safe. Or would have been if no one had known that you were in the neighbourhood. But as it is, don't you see that it looks as if you'd decided that it would be better if I had an excuse for leaving Fantasy at once?'

'I protest most strongly!' Frank said again, even more loudly. 'Until you told me about it I knew nothing about the theft, and it's preposterous that I should be in any way incriminated. Emma, I insist that you make it absolutely clear——' but his voice trailed away inconclusively as Emma pursed her lips and shrugged her shoulders. 'Very well,' he said furiously, 'in that case, you can get out of this mess by yourself. I absolutely refuse to have anything more to do with it! What's more, if any further attempt is made to incriminate me, I shall know just what steps to take, and I warn you——' he glanced menacingly at his silent audience, 'you'll find the result both unsuccessful and unpleasant! I have nothing more to say!' And without so much as a glance at Emma, he strode purposefully out of the room.

No one spoke. Then, with an exclamation of disgust, Tim jumped to his feet and flung one of the windows wide open.

'Sorry if you feel cold, Aunt Hester,' he remarked as she shivered slightly. 'But one needs fresh air when there's been a skunk in the room. Emma, my dear——'

But Emma, ignoring him, turned to Adrian.

'Well, did I forget anything?' she demanded recklessly.

'No,' he admitted reflectively, 'no, I don't think so. Indeed, you suggested some points which hadn't occurred to me, and they do incline me to think that there are one or two questions——'

'Just a minute, Adrian,' Tim interrupted with unwonted authority. 'Before you ask Emma any more questions, there's one to which I want an answer.' He came over to Emma and took her unresisting hands in his. 'Emma, will you marry me?'

It was so totally unexpected that Emma could only stare blankly at him, and she was only vaguely conscious that the other three people present were tense with suspense. Only Adrian found anything to say as his face hardened ominously.

'This is hardly the time, Tim——' he began, but Tim waved him aside.

'Oh yes, it is,' he contradicted belligerently. 'If you think I'm going to stand by and see Emma bullied and brow-beaten without doing anything about it, you've made the mistake of your life! Well, Emma? What about it?'

With an effort she pulled herself together and gave him the only possible answer.

'Dear Tim,' she said tremulously, 'I can't begin to tell you how touched I am that you should suggest such a thing. It's wonderful of you to have such faith in me, but it's out of the question——'

'I don't see why.'

'But I do,' Emma told him, gently but very firmly. 'It's quite impossible for me to think of marrying anyone while this is hanging over me. Surely you can see that?'

'No, I can't,' Tim denied flatly. 'But if you won't, you won't. But understand, I'm not taking that as final. My offer stands.' He bent and kissed first one of her hands and then the other. Then, his fair head held high, he went quickly out of the room.

There was a brief, strained silence. Then Emma turned impulsively to Mrs. Halliday.

'Mrs Halliday, I can't tell you how sorry I am about all this,' she said with desperate earnestness. 'It was bad enough before Frank came, but now—I simply *had* to do something to convince him once and for all, and I couldn't

156

think of any other way. His mother was the Miss Ponsonby I told you about,' she concluded, which, to the two men seemed utterly inconsequential but which they saw made sense to Mrs Halliday.

'Ah!' she said with interest. 'I did think that might be possible. Evidently a strong family likeness—no wonder you resorted to desperate measures! Don't you see'—she addressed the two men with a hint of impatience—'that man previously pestered Emma to marry him, but he had too good an opinion of himself to accept his dismissal. So she scared him into backing down by telling him this rigmarole—isn't that the way it was, Emma?'

'Yes!' Emma acknowledged, thankful that one person at least understood what had been in her mind. 'I knew that Frank would never—never——'

'Risk being involved in possible criminal proceedings?' Adrian suggested ironically. 'No, you're right, of course. He put his own integrity before anything else. Well, it's a very practical point of view, of course, very different from Tim's——'

'We'll leave Tim out of this,' Emma told him resolutely. 'He's paid me the greatest compliment I've ever had, and I won't listen to him being sneered at. And nor,' she went on steadily, 'will I hold myself answerable to anyone but you, Mrs Halliday, because, since you're my employer, only you have the right to dismiss me!'

'That's quite true, Emma,' Mrs Halliday confirmed. 'And I hope everyone will appreciate the fact.' She didn't look at Adrian, but unmistakably the warning had been for him.

'Thank you, Mrs Halliday,' Emma was finding it increasingly difficult to keep her voice steady, but she persisted gallantly. 'Before you tell me what you intend to do, may I explain how I feel about it? Thank you,' as Mrs Halliday nodded. 'Actually, my mind is in confusion. How *can* I stay on when I've made my position even worse than it was— and that was bad enough. How can I help knowing that, however generously you judge me, you must be left with some doubts at least? That's humiliating almost to the point of being unbearable. And yet——' she squared her shoulders and held her head high, 'I'm not going to run away'—and now it was at Mr Halliday that she looked and received an encouraging little nod of approval. 'So I leave it to you to decide, Mrs Halliday, and I'll accept your decision without question. No, on one condition. Whatever you decide and whatever is the outcome, I want you to keep my other dolls on indefinite loan——' Her voice broke, and she waited silently for the verdict. Mrs Halliday didn't hesitate.

'I would like you to stay here, Emma,' she said firmly. 'Not only because I have complete faith in you but because I'm convinced that we'll get to the bottom of the mystery and my faith will be completely vindicated.'

'I should like to add my complete agreement to that,' Mr Halliday announced. 'And, my dear'—he turned to his wife—'may I suggest that it would be wise if no one—literally no one besides ourselves is told of this matter?'

'I quite agree,' Mrs Halliday replied promptly, and both of them looked towards Adrian. He however, shook his head.

'I don't see how you can just let the matter slide,' he replied deliberately. 'In fact, I'd better warn you that I have every intention of getting to the bottom——' He stopped short, and he and Mr Halliday exchanged a long intent look. Evidently a message passed between them for, after a moment's deep thought, Adrian nodded. 'Yes, I see your point. And of course you're quite right. Very well, I'll hold my tongue and I'll see to it that young Tim does the same. In fact, I'll push off at once to make sure——' But for a moment he paused. 'About us coming over to dinner this evening. Would you prefer that we didn't?'

'And make it clear to Martha that there's something wrong? Certainly not!' insisted Mrs Halliday. 'Why, it would be all over the place in next to no time! She's a dear, loyal soul, but she's a gossip. We shall be expecting you at seven o'clock—and please don't arrive looking like mutes at a funeral!'

She was just as outspoken when Emma suggested that she should not be present.

'My dear, that won't do at all!' It was astonishing how authoritative this sweet, gentle little woman could be when she felt the occasion warranted it. 'Oh, I know you could say that you have a headache or something like that, but you were so right in refusing to run away, so how can you not accept this challenge—yes, I admit it's that—to prove that you really meant what you said?'

And, since Emma could think of no reasoning which could refute such a logical argument, she gave in. But as she dressed for dinner she wondered how on earth she could get through the evening without breaking down.

She was in an impossible position from which, despite the trust which had been shown in her, she could see no way of escape—she herself had made such a thing out of the question. Of course, thanks to her having deliberately misled him, Frank would never bother her again. That was the only bright spot in the gloom—but what a price she had had to pay to achieve that end! For, whatever the rest of them felt, Adrian undoubtedly believed her to be guilty, and sooner or later would come the questions Tim had prevented him from asking, and somehow he would make her incriminate herself still further. As for that odd look which he and Mr Halliday had exchanged—she dismissed that as not very important. Mr Halliday, she knew, was for all his self-restraint—or perhaps because of it—a man of strong character. Even without words, he had influenced Adrian to fall in with his wishes. Something of a triumph when dealing with such a dominant personality as Adrian's, but that was all. It wouldn't really help Emma to evade him.

She looked critically at herself in her mirror. With hands that shook a little she added more make-up than she normally used, then, bracing herself and with her head held high, she went downstairs.

Time passed—and nothing happened. Sometimes Emma could forget what hung over her for hours at a time, then memory would come flooding back, and over and over again she would ponder every detail of those fateful hours during which the dolls must have been stolen and always she came to the same conclusion. She hadn't what that odd child, Susan Heywood, would probably have called a clue. All she knew for certain was that on the earlier occasions when she had been called away from the museum, she had locked the door and had put the key in her apron pocket.

Only when Lorraine had been there had she left the door unlocked—but Lorraine had joined her in the workroom almost at once and, as Emma herself knew, beyond doubt she had left Fantasy empty-handed.

And so one could get no further. It was a completely baffling state of affairs, or so Emma felt, and it didn't help in the least to wonder if, after all, there was some way in which Lorraine had tricked her. But if there was, just what it could be Emma had no idea at all.

Of course, one might say that Lorraine had a motive for creating the mystery—when no other explanation appeared possible, Emma herself was practically bound to be suspected. In which case, what more likely than that she would leave Windyvale—which was just what Lorraine wanted!

But that Emma was determined to keep to herself. How could she possibly explain that Lorraine suspected her of being a rival where Adrian was concerned? Adrian would very promptly ridicule such an idea and Lorraine would almost certainly deny that she had ever even considered such a thing. Besides, there was the dreadful possibility that it might occur to someone—perhaps Adrian himself—to accuse Emma of wishful thinking.

No, she was trapped and there was nothing she could do or say to get herself out of this horrible impasse. It was only with difficulty that she kept to her decision not to run away. Somehow she would stick it out.

But, as it happened, events over which she had no control compelled her to change her mind. Her niece, Anne, Rose and Dave's daughter, rang her up one morning with the frightening news that Dave was in hospital following a serious car accident.

'It wasn't Daddy's fault,' Anne explained shakily, 'a child ran across the road just in front of his car and in swerving to avoid her he crashed into one of those big lamp-posts in the High Street. He's been badly cut with glass and his left arm is broken, but the worst of all is that his head was injured. They've done an emergency operation, but they can't tell us yet——' she left the sentence significantly unfinished. 'Oh, Emma, what are we to do if anything happens? It's always been Daddy who's been the strong one, and now we feel so terribly alone. Aunt Helen's been very kind, but she doesn't really understand what being part of a family means. Oh, I do wish you were here, and so does Mummy!'

Emma didn't hesitate. Face to face with such an emergency as this, her own troubles paled into insignificance. Nor did she give a thought to what others might think about her sudden flight.

'I'll start at once,' she told Anne. 'Tell your mummy that, darling.'

'Yes, I will,' Anne promised gratefully. 'We're both at the hospital. Will you come straight there?'

'Of course,' Emma agreed steadily. 'I'll be just as quick as I can. Goodbye for the present, Anne dear. And be brave for your mummy's and daddy's sake.'

'I will,' Anne said in rather a wobbly voice, and rang off.

Emma went straight to the sitting room where Mr and Mrs Halliday sat. They looked up quickly concerned at the sight of Emma's tense face. She came straight to the point.

'My brother-in-law has been badly injured in a car crash and they can't say yet whether he'll recover. My sister is badly shocked and she wants me, so of course I must go to her immediately.'

'Of course,' Mrs Halliday agreed simply, and stood up. 'Go and pack while I see about some sandwiches for you to take with you, and, John, will you bring Emma's car round to the front door?'

'I will,' Mr Halliday replied, and held out his hand. 'Can I have the keys, Emma?'

She ran upstairs and fetched them from her handbag. Then, having handed them over to Mr Halliday, she hurried upstairs again. She changed from the dress she was wearing into her trouser suit, hurriedly packed a few essentials and went downstairs again. The Hallidays were waiting for her in the hall.

'You'll find sandwiches and a flask of coffee on the back seat,' Mrs Halliday told her, giving her a warm hug which said far more than any words could have done. 'Let us know——'

'I will,' Emma promised gratefully, and went to the front

door which Mr Halliday had opened, only to stand there completely dumbfounded.

The car was there all right—but so was Adrian. He was sitting in the driver's seat, and since he had buckled the safety straps, clearly had every intention of staying there.

'No!' Emma protested, conscious that her voice was shrill to the verge of hysteria.

'I'm going to drive you home,' Adrian told her, and he spoke with unmistakable determination. 'It's the only sensible arrangement, so don't waste time raising stupid objections. Get in!'

'No!' Emma repeated even more resolutely. And then, as Adrian showed no sign of yielding, she went on pleadingly: 'But you must surely see that I can't possibly be beholden to *you*, of all people!'

'I'm perfectly well aware that you would prefer Tim to go with you,' Adrian told her, grim-faced, 'but unfortunately he's not available and I am. And you're in no condition to drive such a distance on your own.'

'I'm perfectly capable——' Emma protested, but, as she might have known, without making any impression.

'Hold out your hand,' ordered Adrian, and when Emma obeyed, her trembling hand gave her away completely.

'Now listen, Emma,' Adrian went on sternly, 'this is an emergency. All that matters is that you should get to your sister as quickly and as safely as possible, and in my opinion you're in no condition to fulfil those two obligations. So it's far wiser that I should drive you. Now, isn't it?'

It was, Emma knew that perfectly well, but she still couldn't bring herself to give in.

'Oh, for heaven's sake!' Clearly Adrian's patience was wearing thin. 'Be your age, Emma! Our personal differences aren't in the least important now, because this is a matter of life and death. Yes, I know, that's pretty brutal,' as she flinched, 'but unfortunately it's the truth. Well? Which matters most to you? Your sister's need—or your pride?'

Silently Emma opened the rear door, put her case and topcoat on the seat beside the packages already there, and finally took her place beside Adrian.

'Straps,' he reminded her, showing no sign of the triumph which her capitulation must have given him. Then, when he was sure that she had fastened the buckles properly, he slid competently into gear and they were off. On the way to the village Adrian spoke only once.

'I see that you're pretty well off for petrol,' he remarked, 'and Halliday checked the radiator for water, so we won't need to stop in the village for supplies.'

He sounded relieved, a feeling which Emma shared. Once one was stationary in Windyvale there was always someone at hand who wanted to talk—and ask questions. And this was an occasion when such a hindrance would be intolerable.

But their luck was out, for as they approached Mrs Medler's shop Lorraine strolled out. Her eyes widened as she recognised the oncoming car, and with unmistakable purpose she stepped well out into the road and lifted her hand. And since the only alternative was to risk running her down, Adrian had to stop.

'Hallo, where are you two off to?' she asked with an assumption of gaiety which, to Emma at least, was quite unconvincing. Lorraine was, to put it mildly, curious. Suspicious would perhaps have been a better word and she was determined to have her question answered. Emma, however, remained silent. How could one speak of such heart-burning anxieties to such a callous person as Lorraine? But Adrian evidently had no such inhibitions.

'Emma has had bad news from home,' he explained crisply. 'It's necessary that she should get there as quickly as possible. So, if you please, Lorraine, don't hinder us.'

For a moment Lorraine stared at him speechlessly. Then she transferred her gaze to Emma, and laughed.

'That's clever of you!' she said appreciatively. 'About the only excuse you could use to get you out of trouble!'

'Excuse?' Emma repeated blankly. 'I don't understand——'

'No?' Again Lorraine laughed. 'Well, of course, having told that story, you've got to stick to it, haven't you? And possibly the Hallidays have fallen for it, but I must say I'm surprised that you have, Adrian! Except, of course, that it does mean you're getting rid of her without any fuss and publicity. Yes, something in that, I suppose!' And with an impudent gesture of farewell, she retreated to the pavement. 'Be seeing you, Adrian!' she called mischievously.

Grim-faced, Adrian started up again and they drove in silence for a couple of miles before, suddenly, he laid a hand over Emma's tightly clenched in her lap.

'Stop worrying, Emma. Lorraine was being very foolish—as I'll make clear to her when I get back.'

A queer little sound that was half sob and half laugh forced itself between Emma's lips.

'Yes, of course, you'll be in a position then to know that I've told the truth about Dave, won't you? Now I understand why you were so determined to come with me!'

Adrian didn't answer immediately, but his grasp tightened on the steering wheel. Then, without apparent emotion, he remarked reflectively:

'It would give me considerable satisfaction to put you across my knee and give you the spanking you richly deserve. Or, as a possibly more telling chastisement, I might kiss you. At present I haven't made up my mind which makes the greater appeal, but I swear, Emma, that if you don't stop behaving like an arrant little fool, it's going to be one or the other! So I advise you to hold your tongue!'

And Emma took the advice, partly because she was too startled to do anything else, and partly because she was quite sure that, given the provocation, he would carry out his threat one way or the other. And despite her load of anxiety, she was conscious of a lifting of her spirits, for what he had said could only mean that he didn't share Lorraine's opinion. And that was undeniably reassuring.

Unconsciously she gave a little sigh of relief and settled herself more comfortably in her seat. She was more tired than she had realised, though that was hardly surprising, for she hadn't slept at all well since the discovery of the theft. But now, lulled by the steady drone of the engine and the knowledge that though they were travelling at a considerable speed Adrian would take no foolish risks, she dozed off.

She was awakened some time later because they were

stationary, and she struggled into a more upright position.

'Why have we stopped?' she asked anxiously. 'Is anything wrong?'

'Nothing more than that the car needs a refill—and so do we,' Adrian explained, and then Emma realised that he had stopped in the car park of a pleasant old pub at the side of which were petrol pumps. 'Go in and order something quick while I see to the petrol, will you? Soup and hot snacks. They specialise in them.'

'But we've got sandwiches and coffee,' Emma pointed out, 'so we needn't waste time——'

Adrian gave vent to a heartfelt groan.

'Emma, can't you ever do as you're asked without argument?' he demanded in sheer exasperation. 'I want a let up from driving, however brief. So get on with it—oh, and order a couple of sherries. Medium dry for me.'

Without further ado, Emma went meekly off on her errand and realised with a shiver that there was a marked change in the weather. They had started out in sunshine, but now the sky was dull and overcast and there was a penetrating wind blowing. She was grateful for the warmth which met her as she went into the cosy bar. There was a log fire burning and when she had given her order she went to sit at a table near to it. Adrian came in just as the waitress brought a full tray over and Emma saw that he carried her coat over his arm.

'I think you may need this,' he commented, laying it over an adjacent chair. 'And if you don't—well, there's no harm done. We can just take it back again.'

'But I think I shall need it,' Emma acknowledged gratefully. 'Thank you for thinking of it.'

'Not at all,' he said punctiliously, and paused. Then he raised his glass. 'My very, very best wishes, Emma,' he added with real sincerity.

This time Emma could find no words, but the quivering little smile she gave him seemed to satisfy him. During the welcome little meal they discussed final plans. They would go straight to the hospital——

'But there's one thing I've only just thought of,' Emma confessed anxiously. 'How will you get back to Windyvale?'

'Oh, as to that'—Adrian replied casually, though he was careful to avoid meeting her eyes—'we needn't worry about that just yet. I shall clock in at some hotel or other in Greystoke and stay for a few days.'

Emma knew what that meant. Unsure what the next few days would bring, he would stand by, ready to do whatever might help her. And this time she didn't argue. Such a gesture was beyond any question of pride or the desire not to become further indebted to Adrian. It was almost beyond thanks—but not quite. Impulsively she slipped her hand into his and felt his warm, reassuring response.

Back in the car Adrian was still at the wheel, although Emma had offered to take over. They covered the remaining distance smoothly and quickly, and with Emma acting as guide, negotiated Greystoke's busy streets and reached the hospital. She directed him to the visitors' car park and then, as they got out, suddenly Emma's heart failed her.

'Adrian——' she said uncertainly, and needed to say no more.

'But of course I'm coming in with you,' he said matter-of-factly, and pulled her arm through his.

An inquiry at the reception desk, a conducted walk along interminable corridors and so, at last, they reached the room where Rose was waiting—a Rose who seemed to have shrunk, and who was grey-faced and near to collapse. She jumped up and flung herself into Emma's welcoming arms and clung to her.

'I knew you'd come!' she sobbed. 'I knew I could depend on you!'

And with a sense of shock, Emma realised that Rose meant just what she said, and that never again would she be thought of as the little sister who everybody felt needed to be advised and guarded. So, after all, her flight to Fantasy had achieved its purpose.

There followed days of anxiety and suspense, days when Dave's life hung on a thread and there seemed little or no hope. Days which made Emma wonder whether without Adrian's presence they would ever have succeeded in living through them. For somehow he was always there when he was needed, but yet was never intrusive. Even Rose, in her distress, turned to him and seemed to draw strength and comfort from him.

And then at last, miraculously as it seemed, came a change. At first optimism was guarded and cautious, but little by little it was clear that Dave had weathered the storm and even the knowledge that it would be a long time before he would be able to return to his practice, couldn't dim their relief and thankfulness.

But while Emma truly rejoiced, her happiness was marred by the knowledge that quite soon Adrian would tell her that he felt he was no longer needed, and that he was going back to Windyvale.

And that was just what happened, though he did add the rider: 'Unless you feel that I could be of use if I stayed on?'

But Emma, having anticipated something like this, was prepared, and after thanking him for all he had done, agreed that really there was no need for them to trespass further on his generosity. But the moment the words were out, she was dismayed to realise just how cool and impersonal they sounded. How they sounded to Adrian she had no idea, for his impassive face told her nothing. Probably he was relieved that she had accepted his decision without argument.

Only the next day when he said goodbye did she have any doubts, for, as they shook hands, he said quietly:

'If any any time you feel that I can be of use to you or to Rose and Dave, please let me know.'

And contriving to swallow a lump in her throat, Emma promised that she would.

But in her heart of hearts, she knew just how unlikely it was that she would ever send for him. Adrian was going out of her life for good. She would probably never see him again, for she had made up her mind never to return to Windyvale.

While Dave was still in hospital, Emma had a very good offer for her house and accepted it. Then, after selecting a few favourite items of furniture for Rose, Helen and herself, she sold the remainder; and the money, Emma felt, could not have come at a better time. Dave simply must have a long rest before even thinking of getting into harness again—and since it didn't seem desirable for him to convalesce at home where it would be all but impossible for him to turn a deaf ear to calls for his professional help, that meant going away somewhere. But Dave was not a wealthy man and holidays, however modest, would be expensive. To Emma, there was a simple way out. She insisted on dividing what she had got for the house and furniture between Rose, Helen and herself. At first she met with blunt refusal, but she refused to listen. It was true that neither of her half-sisters had any legal right to a share, but what had that to do with it? The house had been their home for much of their lives, and that was what counted. And at last they capitulated.

Then, to ease matters still further, an invitation arrived from an old friend of Dave's—himself a doctor living in Devonshire—for both Dave and Rose to stay with him and his wife as long as they liked. It was really an ideal arrangement. Dave would have the peace and quiet he needed, and in addition Dr Lever would keep an eye on him to see that he didn't overdo it. What was more, he proposed to drive up from Devonshire to collect them.

So, a few days after Dave was discharged from hospital, Dr Lever arrived and the next day carried off two very grateful people.

But when they had gone there was even less for Emma to do with only herself and Anne to care for, and so she had all too much time to brood.

She had written twice to Mrs Halliday since Adrian had left, and on each occasion had received a warm, friendly reply. But on neither occasion had there been any suggestion that Emma should return to Fantasy. Probably that meant that Mrs Halliday felt it would be better if she stayed away. After all the mystery of the vanished dolls had never been cleared up, and probably never would be now. Suspicion would always hang over her.

There were days when depression became almost unbearable, and it was something which she had to cope with unaided, for she had told no one in Greystoke of the trouble and neither, apparently, had Frank. He had in fact made it very clear that he wanted to have nothing more to do with her, for twice when they passed in the street he had cut her dead, and there was a rumour that he was paying marked attention to another girl. If that was so, then for his own sake Frank had every reason to hold his tongue.

But that was the least of the things that troubled Emma. She had run away from Greystoke in the hope of starting a new and more meaningful life, but instead she had found disappointment and disillusionment. Windyvale was beautiful—it satisfied all her aesthetic longings—but people, it appeared, were much the same, whether they lived in a town or in the country: some were nice and some most certainly were not. But the most perplexing ones were those who seemed to combine both natures in one. Adrian, as she knew only too well, was hard and mercenary, and yet capable of such incredible generosity and kindness.

It was bewildering, but even more bewildering was the knowledge that, faults and all, she loved him—and always would. Why else, waking or sleeping, should he so dominate her thoughts and dreams? Why should she long so for news of him—news which never came, and for which she could never ask?

There were times when she thought of writing to Tim, but never really seriously, for the odd thing was that after that incredible proposal of his she had neither seen nor heard from him. So presumably he was regretting his impulsiveness, and pride forbade that she should be the one to make the first approach. She had got to accept that Windyvale and everyone she had met there belonged to a dream world—to a world of Fantasy. A world in which she had no place.

And having come to that conclusion, she was almost at once proved to be wrong—almost as if once again the Fates were laughing at her up their sleeves.

One day, without any sense of either foreboding or anticipation, she answered an imperative knock at the front door; and when she opened it, there stood Tim.

CHAPTER TEN

Too surprised to do anything but stare at Tim, Emma saw the confidence fade from his face to give place to uneasiness.

'If I might come in and explain——' he suggested diffidently.

In silence Emma turned and led the way to the sitting room. Tim, after a moment's hesitation, followed her, having closed the door behind him with exaggerated care.

Emma sat down in a stiff, not very comfortable chair and indicated that Tim should sit down as well, but he preferred to stand at a little distance from her, his face troubled.

'I ought to have come or at least written to you before,' he began, guessing the reason for her lack of responsiveness, 'but there have been reasons why I couldn't—truly there have, Emma.'

He spoke so earnestly that Emma knew he was telling the truth, at least as he saw it. None the less, he did surely owe her a more explicit explanation than that, and evidently Tim realised that, for after a moment he plunged headfirst into an explanation.

'So many things have happened since you left Windyvale, important things, and the most important is that I've sold the Hall for a good figure. Actually John Halliday has bought it, and when it's been repaired and redecorated, he and Aunt Hester are going to live there and move the museum over as well.'

'Oh, I am glad for you, Tim!' Emma exclaimed, too genuinely pleased for his sake to maintain her aloof manner. 'That will make a lot of difference to you, won't it?'

'I'll say!' he agreed fervently. 'It means I've paid off all my debts, which in turn means I'm clear of any obligation to Lorraine——'

'Lorraine?' Emma repeated sharply. 'What has she got to do with it?'

'Quite a bit,' Tim explained grimly. 'Not that she actually lent me the money—it was the General who did that, and on very easy terms. But when he died, Lorraine insisted that I must repay the capital at once. And that I simply couldn't do—I hadn't got it. In fact, I'd even had to borrow off Aunt Hester to pay the interest. In the end Lorraine had to accept that you can't get blood out of a stone, but she got back at me in other ways. She told me that if she couldn't get money out of me, she intended that I should be at her beck and call whenever there were odd jobs she wanted done.'

Remembering her first encounter with Lorraine, Emma could well believe that. On that occasion Lorraine had been really angry because Tim wasn't available to deal with her car.

'And I suppose she'd got something there,' Tim conceded ruefully, 'I mean, she honestly needed the money because when the General died it turned out that much of his income died with him—annuities and that sort of thing. So, other than the house and the land, for which she couldn't find a buyer, he had precious little to leave Lorraine. Yes?' as Emma gave a startled little exclamation.

'No, nothing,' she assured him hurriedly. 'Go on!'

But of course, to her that was the most important thing that Tim had so far said. It explained that conversation between him and Adrian which she had overheard, and put a totally different interpretation on it. They hadn't been talking about her affairs, as she had assumed, but about Lorraine's! She listened with bated breath as Tim went on:

'Well—Lorraine and I have never really got on well, but I must say when Adrian managed to find out for me that she really was hard up, I felt a complete heel. After all, I know only too well what it means to be short of cash, but there wasn't a thing I could do about it. But now'—he squared his shoulders as if a load had been lifted from them—'thanks to Halliday, I've paid her—and Aunt Hester. So, as I said, I'm in the clear, but of course it means far more than that . . .' He seemed to lapse into a happy dream which Emma had no difficulty in interpreting.

'And you've still got enough money left for your invention?' she suggested.

'Yes. I told you, didn't I, that there was a firm who said they'd be interested if I could put up some of the cash to float the thing? Well, now that I can do that, they're really keen. In fact'—he rubbed his hands together gleefully—'everything's cut and dried, and though I'm not going to become a millionaire overnight, I'm certainly going to be pleasantly well off! And that's really why I came to see you, Emma.' And his face became so serious that it wasn't difficult to know what was coming. 'About us getting married——'

'Yes, Tim, what about it?' Emma asked.

'Well'—he hesitated before going on—'actually, you know, when I asked you to marry me before I hadn't got two pennies to rub together, and what we'd have lived on if you'd said you would, heaven alone knows! But now it's quite different. So what about it?'

Emma traced a little pattern with her forefinger on the arm of her chair. Tim, bless him, was evidently brilliant where his work was concerned, but in other ways he was oddly immature. And one way in which that showed was his inability to hide his feelings; he couldn't now. He was waiting for her answer with considerable anxiety, but not, Emma decided thankfully, because he was afraid she would refuse him. On the contrary.

'But, Tim,' she said gently, 'I think you've forgotten, I told you I couldn't possibly think of marrying anyone until this wretched business about the dolls was cleared up—and it hasn't been. Nor can I see any prospect that it will be.'

'Oh, but didn't you know?' Tim sounded genuinely surprised. 'It's been solved.'

'What!' Emma exclaimed incredulously, half rising from her chair.

'Oh lord, yes! Adrian found the dolls,' Tim explained as if it wasn't really a matter of much importance. 'Lorraine had hidden them up in the old hay loft!'

'I see,' Emma said slowly. 'Yes, of course, she would have had time to do that. But how did anyone know that she was responsible? I mean, it might just as well have been me——'

'Yes, well, I'm not at all sure how they—or rather Adrian—got that out of her,' admitted Tim. 'I'd got so many other things on my mind that I wasn't particularly interested in the details, but apparently she gave herself away by knowing too much, and in the end she owned up. And she admitted that she did it because she hoped to get you into trouble. She seems to have had it in for you, Emma!' he concluded curiously.

'Yes, she had,' Emma acknowledged, 'but that isn't of any real importance now, is it?'

'No, I suppose not,' Tim agreed, though he looked disappointed. 'What's important is us getting married, isn't it?'

Emma drew a deep breath and took the bull by the horns.

'Tim, are you very much in love with me?' she asked bluntly.

Considerably taken aback, Tim hesitated for a fatal second which completely betrayed him.

'I—I'm awfully fond of you, Emma,' he told her with genuine feeling, 'and I think we might make a good thing of it together——' His voice trailed away inconclusively and his eyes fell.

'But you're not head over heels in love with me,' Emma stated cheerfully. 'Well, never mind, Tim, because fond though I am of you, I'm very definitely not in love with you. And I'll never marry anyone unless I am—in love with them, I mean,' she explained confusedly.

In a most uncomplimentary way, Tim looked unmistakably relieved.

'I say, are you really sure?' he asked eagerly.

'Cross my heart,' Emma told him briskly. 'And equally sure that for a long time to come, you won't want to be bothered with a demanding wife! It's your work that really matters to you, isn't it?'

'Well'—he admitted with belated diffidence—'yes, it is. I mean, when one has felt as hopelessly frustrated as I've been, it's so incredibly marvellous when everything comes right!'

Yes, Emma thought wistfully, it must be! Well, there it was, luck wasn't for everybody, but it would be mean to grudge Tim his portion because nothing similar could or would come her way.

'Gosh, I've been lucky.' Tim had reverted to that earlier abstracted mood again. 'And I've got plenty of other ideas——'

Emma allowed him to dream for a few moments, then she brought him firmly down to earth.

'Then, as far as we're concerned, that's that!' she summed up. 'No wedding bells—but I hope we'll always be good friends.'

'Rather!' Tim agreed heartily. 'I really am fond of you, Emma, but——' His expression was one of such comical ruefulness that Emma laughed outright.

'But not in love,' she concluded for him. 'Well, as I've already told you, that suits me. All the same,' she added, 'I'll never forget that you trusted me enough to ask me to marry you. It was wonderful of you, dear Tim!'

Just what she had thought he would say to that she hadn't considered, but certainly she hadn't expected that he would stare at her in blank bewilderment.

'But, my precious idiot child, don't you realise even now why I did that? It was because I thought you *were* the culprit, and you looked so helpless and scared! No, I'm ashamed to say that I wasn't the one who realised that you'd been framed. It was Adrian who tumbled to that. And it was Adrian who told me in no uncertain words just what an abysmal fool I was to doubt you for a single moment.'

Emma stared at him, white-faced and wide-eyed. The whole room—the whole world—was spinning round her with dizzying speed. It couldn't be true!

'But—but——' she stammered, shaking her head.

'It's true,' Tim insisted vigorously, 'I ought to know after the dressing down he gave me! Now look here, Emma,' as she shook her head again, 'you're just being downright pig-headed. For heaven's sake, use your wits! I know that Adrian didn't accuse you of taking the dolls *before* I left, but did he after that?'

'Not in so many words, but——'

'Now look here, my girl,' Tim enjoined her impatiently, 'it was *you* who piled up the evidence against yourself! Oh yes, it was! With these two ears I heard it! And you were most convincing—you took me in completely. And, of course, that blighter Hall! You gave him the shock of his life—which was just what you intended doing. By the way, have you had any more trouble with him? Because, if you have, I'll punch his head with the greatest of pleasure.'

'I've only seen him twice in the street since I came back here,' Emma smiled faintly at Tim's enthusiasm, 'and both times he cut me dead. So thank you very much, Tim, but there's no need for you to bother.'

'Pity,' Tim commented regretfully. 'But to get back to Adrian. Just what happened after I'd left?'

'Not very much,' Emma said reflectively. 'Adrian said that Frank was very practical in not wanting to be involved in possible criminal proceedings——'

'Which, of course, you interpreted as meaning proceedings against *you*,' Tim sighed. 'Go on.'

'Then, after Mrs Halliday had said that she'd like me to stay she—no, Mr Halliday—said that he thought it would be wiser if no one but ourselves was told of the theft. But Adrian said he had every intention of getting to the bottom of the mystery. Then——' She paused, looking puzzled. 'He and Mr Halliday looked at one another and—and Adrian seemed to change his mind, but I don't know why.' She looked inquiringly at Tim.

'Because, my innocent, he had added two and two together, just as Halliday also had. Remember Adrian said that you'd suggested some things he hadn't previously thought of? Didn't you wonder what he meant? No? Well, I'll tell you. Until then, we'd all assumed that it was the value of the dolls which had prompted the theft. But you suggested that there could have been another motive, and if that applied to you, wasn't it possible that it might apply to someone else as well? And if so, what was that motive? Well, pretty clearly, to get you into trouble. But Halliday went further than that. He realised that if nothing was said about the matter, the suspense of not knowing whether she'd achieved her purpose or not might make Lorraine give herself away. See?'

'You mean she'd try to find out—ask questions that showed she knew?' Emma said slowly. 'Yes, I do see. And that was just what Lorraine did! Or rather, she assumed things—she thought I'd made up the story about Dave's illness so that I had an excuse for getting away from Windyvale—and that I was being allowed to go so that I was got rid of without fuss and publicity.'

'Now you're using your brains!' Tim told her approvingly. 'Trouble was, that alone wasn't real proof—she could easily have said that someone told her. So when Adrian got back——'

'Oh, Tim!' Emma interrupted, aghast. 'I've only just realised! How absolutely awful!'

'Now what?' Tim asked resignedly.

'Why, that it should be Lorraine—and that Adrian was the one who found out.'

'And why should that matter?' Tim asked callously. 'He'd said that he'd get to the bottom of it—and he did. That's all there is to it.'

'But it isn't,' Emma protested, almost in tears. 'He's in love with her—they're going to get married!'

'Are they, indeed?' Tim interjected sardonically. 'And just how did you come by that interesting piece of information?'

'Why—why, Lorraine told me——' Emma stammered.

'Wishful thinking,' Tim told her cynically. 'Plus, possibly, a desire to warn you to keep off the grass! Yes, that was it, wasn't it?' As the betraying colour crept up into Emma's pale cheeks. 'Well, all I can say to that is you were a chump to take any notice!'

'Yes, but it wasn't only that,' Emma protested. 'That little girl—Susan—heard them talking about the alterations they were going to make to Lorraine's house when they got married!'

Tim ran his fingers through his fair hair until it stood on end.

'Well, I don't know the answer to that one,' he admitted, 'but I do know that that child should either be strangled or else given a gold medal, because somehow or other she was concerned in the final showdown. I don't know how, because Adrian didn't like the idea of getting such a kid involved.'

'No, of course not,' Emma agreed, but though she had no intention of explaining to Tim, she was reasonably sure of the part Susan had played. After all, she had asked which were the most valuable dolls in the museum and Emma remembered that in telling her, she had said that Cherry Ripe was Mrs Halliday's greatest treasure. And evidently Susan, in that strangely unchildlike mind of hers, had memorised the numbers. Surely it wasn't too much to conclude that in some way, Lorraine had got that information from her? Yes, that must be it!

Tim, watching her intently, realised that if he didn't understand the significance of Susan's involvement Emma did, but he was equally sure she had no intention of explaining to him. 'By the way,' he said casually, 'Lorraine's sold her house—and she's left Windyvale.'

'Tim!' Emma clutched tightly at his sleeve. 'Are you sure? *Quite* sure?'

'Absolutely, my child,' Tim assured her. 'As sure as I am that Adrian isn't. Leaving Windyvale, I mean.'

The significance of what he had said sank slowly into Emma's brain, but words failed her.

'Well?' Tim demanded. 'What are you going to do about it?'

'What—what can I do?' Emma asked shakily.

Tim shrugged his shoulders.

'Well, that's up to you,' he said, 'but if I were you, at least I'd want to know why Adrian was so sure that you weren't a sneak-thief! And I don't mean that you were quite intelligent enough to appreciate that if you married me, or even if we were engaged, there could be no question of prosecuting you. Family pride and so on. But when you turned me down, it could only mean that you weren't looking for an easy way out. In other words, you weren't guilty. 'Oh no'—he grinned as if he had an amusing secret up his sleeve—'that was true enough, but he had other reasons— better reasons—than that!'

'But what, Tim, what?' begged Emma. 'Please, you must tell me!'

'Not on your life!' he declared resolutely. 'Adrian's the one to tell you that, not me! All I'm going to say is'—he hesitated as if he was choosing his words very carefully—'I know that Halliday coming back after all that time and he and Aunt Hester still being in love is very romantic and all that, but to my way of thinking it was an awful waste of time—if you see that I mean?'

Emma's lips quivered, then they curved into a smile.

'Yes, I think I do, Tim,' she said softly. 'And thank you!'

Tim grinned as he pulled her to her feet.

'Then that's my good deed for the day,' he remarked with satisfaction, 'so I can push off with an easy conscience! Goodbye, little Emma.' And bending his fair head, he dropped a kiss lightly on the tip of her nose. 'Good luck!' he said, and left her.

Bemused, Emma let him go. Then the slam of the front door broke into her dreams.

'I've got to find out exactly what happened,' she told herself firmly, 'and there's only one way to do that. I must ask Adrian face to face. And'—she spoke aloud as if someone was trying to make her change her mind—'it's no good thinking about pride, because I'm not prepared to lose a chance of happiness just because of that!'

So first of all she went in search of Anne and explained that she'd got to leave at once for Windyvale, and Anne, puzzled but obliging, said she'd get one of her girl friends to stay with her. With that off her mind, Emma packed her case and not much more than half an hour after Tim had left, she was on her way.

It was a cold day, but the sun shone brightly, and Emma's spirits rocketed. Of course Tim hadn't said so in so many words, but what else could he have meant than that Adrian loved her? Nothing else made sense of what he'd said—and even more, of what he had left unsaid. It was going to be all right, and the car, as if it were in sympathy with her mood of optimism, had never seemed so responsive or run so smoothly. The miles reeled away.

Then, almost without warning, great clouds piled up, hiding the sun and chilling the air. A cold, persistent drizzle made it necessary to have the windscreen wipers going—and Emma's courage began to ebb.

Suppose, after all, Tim was wrong, or she had read more into what he had said than he had ever intended? After all, though it was evidently true that Adrian wasn't in love with Lorraine, it didn't necessarily follow that he loved *her*. Unconsciously she slowed down, her mind in complete confusion. When had Adrian ever done or said anything which remotely suggested that he loved her? And there was only one answer to that—never!

'Oh, what's the use?' she asked herself despondently. 'Surely, surely I'd have known——'

She was about half way to Windyvale now, and the nearer she got, the more foolish the enterprise seemed. Yet she couldn't make up her mind to abandon it. It was only when, a little way ahead, she saw the pub at which she and Adrian had stopped that she came to a decision. Once again she would stop, and by the time she left she would have compelled herself to make up her mind one way or the other. And whichever way it was, that would be final, she told herself resolutely.

The car park was fuller than before, but she managed to find a space and a moment later she entered the pub. From the bar she heard a cheerful babble of voices which was only to be expected seeing how many cars there were outside. But Emma didn't want to be part of a gay, carefree crowd of people. She wanted a quiet place to think things out.

And as she hesitated, a man came out of the bar and walked towards her with the obvious intention of leaving. And, incredibly, it was Adrian!

He came nearer and Emma held her breath; there was a strange, blind look about his eyes. Would he pass her without even seeing her? Then, as if he had been transfixed, he stood still and stared at her. Neither of them spoke, but, as if moved by a single impulse, their hands stretched out and locked together. And from that moment there was really no need for explanations. That instinctive reaching out to one another had told the whole story far more vividly than any number of words could have done.

Adrian put his arm round Emma's shoulders and guided her to the residents' lounge on the opposite side of the hall from the bar, and fortunately, it was empty. He drew her close to him and she surrendered with a little sigh of contentment. For a moment he gazed down into her happy face, then, very tenderly yet with more than a hint of deliberately restrained passion, his lips claimed hers.

Emma understood. He was telling her just how different this kiss was from that earlier one he had snatched: that had only been a means of settling a score. *This* was given in love and could only be responded to in love. And joyously, she gave him the answer he wanted.

At long last he looked down wonderingly at her and Emma saw something in his face that she had never seen before. That he was deeply moved he made no attempt to hide, but there was something else as well. All the hardness had gone and in its place was both satisfaction and—anticipation.

'Now I know I'm forgiven,' he murmured unsteadily.

'Oh, Adrian *darling*!' Emma put up her hand and gently touched the line of his strong jaw. 'Please don't talk of any need for forgiveness between us! And anyway,' she concluded honestly, 'it was no wonder you wanted to pay me out! I was beastly to you!'

Adrian laughed.

'You were rather,' he agreed. 'But I imagine that it wasn't long before we met that Hall had given you every reason to have an extremely poor opinion of men in general, and you saw no reason why you should spare me!'

'Yes, that was exactly it,' Emma agreed. 'But it's marvellous that you should understand, Adrian. I mean, it was stupid of me to condemn all men because one was so odious.'

'Perhaps it was, but it was a stupidity which I shared—only the other way round. Because I'd found one woman to be ruthlessly ambitious and hard, I concluded that no woman was to be trusted.' He hesitated. 'It's rather a long story and not a pleasant one, but I think you should know about it. Then, I hope, we'll be able to forget it. Let's sit down, shall we?'

But even when they were sitting side by side on a sofa before the fire he didn't begin his explanation immediately. Evidently he didn't find it easy.

'It's about Lorraine, isn't it?' Emma said gently, giving his hand an encouraging little squeeze.

'Yes.' He spoke abruptly. 'Some years ago, she and I were engaged, and we decided to keep quiet about it because old Mrs Heywood was very ill and it seemed possible she might be upset that Lorraine might leave her to marry me——'

From there on, he told the story in almost the same words that Lorraine had used—until he came to the point where, after Mrs Heywood's death, Lorraine had told him of the General's proposal. And what he said made it unpleasantly clear just how clever Lorraine had been, for there was a marked similarity in the two stories, and yet with a vital difference.

Adrian had felt genuinely sorry for the poor, lonely old man, but had naturally assumed that, like himself, Lorraine realised how impossible it was to agree to the suggestion. And it was then that Lorraine had told him of the generous terms that the General had offered, and had gone on to suggest that it would be foolish to reject such an opportunity. After all, the General was old and ill; his hold on life was very tenuous. So if she were to marry him, she and Adrian would only have, at the most, a few years to wait.

'At first I couldn't believe that she meant it,' Adrian said harshly. 'But she did, and when I told her that I would have nothing to do with such a plan, she was genuinely surprised. She simply couldn't believe that I could be so oblivious to the financial advantage. Well, she did eventually—when I told her that if she married the General there was no future for us. I went abroad almost immediately, and until I came back to Windyvale this summer we hadn't set eyes on each other since we'd parted. When I did come back, the General was dead and she was free, but as far as I was concerned that was of no importance. Any feeling I'd ever had for her was completely dead, but she assumed that now that there was no possibility of gossip, I'd come back to marry her. She even congratulated me on my shrewdness in staying away from Windyvale. When I made it clear that I had no intention of marrying her——' he broke off, scowling darkly. 'Anyway, it was very shortly after that episode that I had to keep my promise to be Rob's best man, though I'd never felt less like going to a wedding in my life!'

'I don't wonder,' Emma told him sympathetically, 'or that you felt all women were tarred with the same brush. No wonder you were annoyed when you came to my rescue. And then for me to twit you as I did—it was disgusting of me, Adrian, I'm sorry.'

'Oh, there was worse to come,' he assured her wryly. 'When you turned up the second time, I was furious and I decided to pay you out. But even as I told you that the score was even, I knew it wasn't true. In fact, I was hoist with my own petard!' He put his hand under Emma's chin and turned her face up to his. 'I'm not going to tell you that I fell in love with you then and there, because to my way of thinking love, the genuine article, is something that has to grow between two people, deepening as they get really to know one another. But all the same, I knew that a spark had been lit between us—hadn't it?'

'Oh yes,' Emma agreed. 'It had—and I was furious! And so were you.'

'I was,' Adrian agreed fervently, 'but I told myself that it didn't matter—that we'd never see each other again. And then—there you were at Fantasy! If I'd been furious before, I was beside myself then! I tried my utmost to believe that you were an unpleasant, designing little minx, but it just didn't work—the longer I knew you, the more I had no choice but to admit that you were sweet and honest—and utterly desirable.'

So that was why he had believed in her! To Emma it was as if the sun had come out, warming her to the very heart.

'But why didn't you ever let me guess?' she asked reproachfully.

'Because, my little love, each time I took a step towards you, you retreated. And naturally I concluded that in your eyes, I'd blotted my copybook irretrievably, and that my only hope was to wait as patiently as I was able for you to change your mind. But then I came to the conclusion that it was Tim——'

'Well, it wasn't,' Emma told him firmly. 'It never was and it never could have been, as Tim knows. I told him so this morning.'

'I know you did,' confessed Adrian. 'Tim phoned me when he left you and told me you'd turned him down flat. He also told me that you thought I was going to marry Lorraine—that she'd told you so. So I came haring down to see you and at least put things straight——'

Emma chuckled.

'I have a suspicion that Tim must be fancying himself in

182

the rôle of Cupid,' she commented, 'because he told me that if I wanted to know why you believed in me, *you* were the one to tell me! So I came to ask you—oh, my goodness——' Her eyes widened in horror. 'Supposing we'd missed each other? Suppose we'd never found out!'

'Not a chance,' Adrian declared cheerfully. 'Tim, no doubt, will take all the credit, but when two people are involved in no less than four coincidences'—he counted them out on her fingers—'well, then it's a matter of Fate or destiny—something beyond human control, anyway.'

'Yes, it must be,' Emma agreed soberly. 'It's rather—awe-inspiring, isn't it?'

'Well, I certainly think it means that it would be a very good idea if we were to get married soon,' Adrian suggested. 'In fact, very soon, Emma?'

'Very soon,' she agreed softly, her heart shining in her eyes as Adrian claimed her lips again.

At last, somewhat breathless, Emma drew slightly—very slightly—away from him.

'Adrian, Tim told me most of what's happened, I think,' she said diffidently. 'But there are still some things I'd like to get clear, and then, as you said, we can forget all about them.'

'Tell me,' he encouraged.

'Tim told me that you'd found the dolls in the old hay loft, but I don't see how that cleared me *or* incriminated Lorraine. Tim did say something about Susan, but he didn't know just where she came into it. But I did wonder—was it because Lorraine had found out from her which were some of the valuable dolls?'

'Yes, that was it,' said Adrian. 'In all innocence, Susan supplied the vital bit of evidence. You know she's quite determined to be a detective when she grows up? Well, she had decided that as part of her training she ought to cultivate a good memory, and so she'd memorised the numbers of the dolls which you'd told her were valuable. She rather boasted about it in front of Lorraine and the rest of us. We were so startled by the significance of this possible link that for a moment none of us said anything. As a result, Susan thought we didn't believe her. She was indignant and said that she could prove it—she'd written the numbers down and asked Lorraine to check that she knew them by heart—and she turned to Lorraine for confirmation. And that was that. It wasn't pleasant.'

'It couldn't have been,' Emma agreed feelingly. 'Does Susan realise what she did?'

'I hope not,' Adrian said doubtfully, 'but she's pretty shrewd, you know.'

'I know she is. All the same, she does sometimes make mistakes!'

'Oh?'

'It seems unpleasantly like telling tales,' Emma went on reluctantly, 'but actually she believed that you and Lorraine were going to get married because she heard you discussing the alterations you were going to make to the house—afterwards.'

'She told you that?' Adrian said explosively. 'The young monkey! Not but what,' he added reflectively, 'I suppose that was a natural conclusion for her to have drawn. You see, Emma, Lorraine and I did discuss alterations to the house, but not because we planned to share it. Actually, I was negotiating on behalf of an organisation which wanted to buy the house and land to develop it as a wild life reserve, with the house as headquarters. She stuck out for an impossibly high price, and when I explained just how much money would have to be spent on converting the house to offices and so on, we argued about it. That must have been what Susan overheard. You know, that infant needs to be taught the difference between genuine evidence and guesswork,' he concluded feelingly.

'Yes, perhaps she does,' Emma agreed, 'but even more, I think she needs to be loved and wanted. That's why I'd like to have her as one of my bridesmaids.'

'Oh!' Adrian sounded dubious. 'Don't you think she'd prefer to be the detective in charge of the wedding presents?'

'There's no reason why she shouldn't be both,' Emma pointed out. 'After all, what could be a better disguise for a detective than to be dressed as a bridesmaid?'

'True,' Adrian conceded, 'but you said that was just to begin with. What other plans have got for her in that fertile brain of yours?'

'Well, I was wondering—do you think it would be possible for her to spend her holidays with us?'

For the time being Adrian forgot all about Susan and her needs.

'What a darling you are!' he said caressingly. 'Who else but you——'

'Yes, but couldn't she?' Emma persisted as soon as she was free to speak.

'I think it might be arranged,' Adrian said consideringly. 'Certainly Lorraine won't be available—she's already left for America. Yes, I'll write to the headmistress and ask her to put the idea to Susan's trustees; they'll probably be only too thankful to find someone who'll accept responsibility for her during the holidays. And I don't see why, as respectable married people, we shouldn't qualify as being suitable. Particularly as we'll have a good home to offer her.'

'Oh, will we?' Emma asked with considerable interest.

'Yes, there's more to the story than I've told you so far—and the best part, actually. The sale of Lorraine's property finally went through—and I've been asked to take charge of the reserve. I haven't finally said I would, but if you like the idea?'

'Oh, but Adrian, that's *marvellous!*' Emma exclaimed enthusiastically. 'You'll love it—and so will I! Oh——' Sudden doubt shadowed her delight. 'Does that—does that mean we'll have to live there?'

'I'm afraid it does, for a while,' Adrian admitted regretfully. 'And I must say I'm not too keen, either. We don't want any reminders of Lorraine in our home! But it won't be a permanent arrangement. Ultimately my second in command will have a flat in the house and we'll move to Fantasy—but that can't be until the Hallidays are able to move to the Hall, and I can't possibly say when that will be,' he concluded warningly.

'It doesn't matter how long it is,' Emma assured him blissfully. 'With that to look forward to——'

'Thanks be!' Adrian ejaculated fervently. 'I was half afraid——'

'Well, you needn't be,' Emma assured him. 'Actually, I don't really mind where we live so long as we're together.'

It took Adrian a long time to thank her adequately for that, but at last practical matters had to be considered. Should they go to Greystoke or to Fantasy? Adrian asked the question, but Emma supplied the answer without hesitation.

'Fantasy, of course!'

Adrian laughed.

'I was almost certain you'd say that,' he commented with satisfaction, and standing up, drew her to her feet. 'All the same, sweetheart, there is just one thing——'

'Yes, darling?' as he hesitated.

'Fantasy,' he said thoughtfully. 'An enchanting name for an enchanting little house, but you do realise, don't you, that life isn't a matter of fantasy? It's something much more demanding than that!'

'Reality,' Emma said softly, 'yes, much more demanding. But far more wonderful——'

An elderly resident, intent on finding a quiet place where he could read his newspaper in peace, opened the door and peered in. Then, very quietly, he closed it again and retreated. He, too, had been young once.

Harlequin Collection Editions

Please note: The number in brackets indicates the original Harlequin Romance number.

Harlequin Collection Editions

Please note: The number in brackets indicates the original Harlequin Romance number.

Harlequin Collection Editions

Please note: The number in brackets indicates the original Harlequin Romance number.

Harlequin Collection Editions

Please note: The number in brackets indicates the original Harlequin Romance number.

Complete and mail this coupon today!

WIN A SET OF DIAMOND JEWELRY!

Love Spell and Colleen Shannon invite you to participate in a special drawing to help Callista Raleigh's descendants solve the mystery of their heritage. The lucky winner will receive a fourteen-carat gold carved rose pendant set with a ten-point diamond (no chain provided) and matching diamond-studded earrings (pictured opposite). Second prize will be a sterling silver rose pendant set with a topaz, including chain. Ten third-place prizes will be awarded: a signed copy of Colleen Shannon's Faerie Tale Romance, *The Gentle Beast*.

The poem in the front of this book contains a clue to the legacy Callista will pass on to her children and to her children's children. This legacy is a prominent symbol in the stormy romance of Callista and Drake in *The Gentle Beast*.

To qualify for the drawing, send a postcard with the solution hidden in the poem, along with your name and address to:

Dorchester Publishing Co., Inc.
276 Fifth Avenue, Suite 1008
New York, NY 10001

All entries must be received by December 31, 1996. The drawing will be held on January 2, 1997. Winners will be notified by mail. One entry per person please.

Good luck to you all!

A Faerie Tale Romance

The Mirror & The Magic

CORAL SMITH SAXE

Bestselling Author Of *A Stolen Rose*

Sensible Julia Addison doesn't believe in fairy tales. Nor does she think she'll ever stumble from the modern world into an enchanted wood. Yet now she is in a Highland forest, held captive by seven lairds and their quick-tempered chief. Hardened by years of war with rival clans, Darach MacStruan acts more like Grumpy than Prince Charming. Still, Julia is convinced that behind the dark-eyed Scotsman's gruff demeanor beats the heart of a kind and gentle lover. But in a land full of cunning clansmen, furious feuds, and poisonous potions, she can only wonder if her kiss has magic enough to waken Darach to sweet ecstasy.

__52086-9 $5.99 US/$7.99 CAN

An artist with no palate for business, Margaret Masterson can create a world of excitement on canvas, but her love life is as dull as flat paint. Then a carriage ride on a foggy night sweeps her back to Regency London and the picture-perfect nobleman she's always yearned for.

Preoccupied with marrying off his rebellious sister, Adam Coleridge has no leisure to find a wife of his own. Yet when fate drops Maggie at his feet, the handsome earl is powerless to resist the desire she rouses in him. But with time fighting against them, Adam fears that not even a masterpiece of love can keep Maggie from becoming nothing more than a passionate memory.

—52060-5 $4.99 US/$6.99 CAN

Pure Temptation

Connie Mason

"Each new Connie Mason book is a prize!"
—Heather Graham

Spirits can be so bloody unpredictable, and the specter of Lady Amelia is the worst of all. Just when one of her ne'er-do-well descendents thought he could go astray in peace, the phantom lady always appears to change his wicked ways.

A rogue without peer, Jackson Graystoke wants to make gaming and carousing in London society his life's work. And the penniless baronet would gladly curse himself with wine and women—if Lady Amelia would give him a ghost of a chance.

Fresh off the boat from Ireland, Moira O'Toole isn't fool enough to believe in legends or naive enough to trust a rake. Yet after an accident lands her in Graystoke Manor, she finds herself haunted, harried, and hopelessly charmed by Black Jack Graystoke and his exquisite promise of pure temptation.

_4041-7　　　　　　　　　　　　$5.99 US/$6.99 CAN

Dorchester Publishing Co., Inc.
65 Commerce Road
Stamford, CT 06902

Please add $1.75 for shipping and handling for the first book and $.50 for each book thereafter. NY, NYC, PA and CT residents, please add appropriate sales tax. No cash, stamps, or C.O.D.s. All orders shipped within 6 weeks via postal service book rate. Canadian orders require $2.00 extra postage and must be paid in U.S. dollars through a U.S. banking facility.

Name_____

Address _____

City _____ State_____Zip_____

I have enclosed $_____in payment for the checked book(s).

Payment <u>must</u> accompany all orders.□ Please send a free catalog.

Get Four Books Totally FREE — A $21.96 Value!

The Gentle Beast

lightened. He stepped closer to stare at Drake, his nose wrinkling at the scent of rum. "I'm occupied at the moment, but if you care to wait, I shall be with you shortly." He spun on his heel, then added to his underling, "And take him upstairs to bathe, Jerry. He offends me."

The leader, Jerry, caught Drake's arm, grumbling to himself, "I ain't no ruddy nursemaid fer a cove wi' more money than sense." But he showed Drake upstairs, waving aside the various seedy-looking characters who'd come into the hall to glare at Drake suspiciously.

At Jerry's jerk of the head, they retreated to various rooms down serpentine halls. Drake tried not to appear too interested as he passed doorways, many of them open. Jerry had just shoved him into a small chamber set up as a bathing room when Drake heard the scream.

The hair rose on the back of his neck, for he knew that voice, even as anguished as it was. "What's that?"

"Another cove wot don't mind his own business," Jerry growled, slamming the door and locking it from the outside.

Drake immediately went to the window. A sheer drop to the street below greeted him, but he saw a dim glow ten feet over. He leaned out. A curtain flapped in the breeze. He looked closer at the side of the building. A drainage pipe was attached to the wall, but when he tapped it, it swayed. Too weak to hold him. Drake looked up.

An ornate cornice held the remnants of an old sign. The sign was virtually rotted away, but the pole that had held it still looked sturdy. Drake shrugged out of his jacket and pulled the rope from the lining. He made a noose, tossed the loop around the pole, and tugged. It gave slightly, but he didn't have many options.

Colleen Shannon

Drake shoved a heavy bureau before the door. He paused to scrub the soot off his face, hands, and jacket before approaching the window. He looked out again, but the only movement he saw was the rabid dog.

Slipping up on the sill, Drake rested his weight for a moment. He took a deep breath, then dropped, using his feet against the side of the building to support some of his weight. He inched sideways. The pole screeched, then began to bend.

"Hell and damnation," he growled. He moved his feet faster, and had just grasped the opposite windowsill when the pole bent in half. The rope went slack and fell to the street below.

For an instant, Drake literally hung by his fingertips. Then his powerful legs spider-walked up the wall until he could boost himself over. Drunken snoring came from the iron bedstead. The only other amenity in the room—a full chamber pot—had drawn flies.

Norther's generosity apparently didn't extend to his men, Drake reflected. Not surprising. Good. His greed would be his undoing. Drake tiptoed to the door and opened it a crack to peek outside. The foyer was dimmer than before. Jerry had slumped to the ground, looking bored at his duty.

Two sleepy guards, their heads nodding, manned each side of the front door. Drake slipped out of the room, around a corner. A floorboard creaked, but by the time Jerry looked up, the hall was empty.

Drake felt in the dark hallways, looking for a sliver of light, praying for that scream that had grown ominously silent. He tried to retrace the sound by memory, but there were too many halls and too little time.

Drake went back to the central hall, pulled the knife from his boot, and slipped up on Jerry. "Move and you're dead," he whispered. He scraped Jerry's throat

The Gentle Beast

just enough to leave a red rash. "Help me and I'll give you more gold."

Jerry's bald head barely moved in a nod. Drake let him rise, but he held the knife to the man's throat the entire time. "Show me where the prisoner is."

Jerry hesitated. His gaze darted below, then back to Drake's pitiless blue eye. Greed and fear obviously warred in Jerry's larcenous soul, but he apparently decided the current peril outweighed the future one. He eased in the opposite direction, turned, then turned again. When Jerry finally stopped, Drake sensed they were at the back of the building. Jerry gave that same distinctive knock.

A chain scraped. The door eased open. A surprised, ugly face met Drake's fist. The man, Clyde's blood still on his knuckles, crumpled to the floor. Drake shoved Jerry inside.

Clyde's bruised face sagged on his chest. His fingernails bled where they'd been ripped away. For a moment Drake's heart stopped, but then he saw the thin chest moving slightly up and down. Drake picked up the ewer beside the bed and smashed it down on Jerry's bald pate. Jerry fell on top of the other man.

Drake pried open his fingers and put three guineas inside, closing the man's hand. Too bad it wasn't twenty pieces of silver, but doubtless Norther would catch the symbolism.

Drake wet his own clean kerchief and tenderly bathed Clyde's face. Clyde blinked, gave a moan of protest, then froze at the familiar voice.

"Quiet. We've no time to waste. Can you walk?"

Clyde tried to smile, winced, then struggled to his feet.

"Good. Now let's try this. . . ."

* * *

Ten minutes later, Jerry ushered his charge down-stairs. His steps were a bit slow, his face uncommonly dirty, as if he'd rolled in ashes, and he wore a disreputable looking hat. He seemed to have lost two stone in the past half hour, but his height was the same. The two guards struggled awake and peered at him in the dim hall.

"Felix said ta do away wi' him," Jerry growled in a voice a bit higher than usual. He shoved Drake so hard that Drake stumbled, glaring at his captor.

The two men, distracted by Drake's clumsiness, didn't react until Jerry opened the door.

"Wot's the code?"

Jerry froze. Drake caught the door as he struggled to his feet. Swiftly, he rapped out the odd sequence of knocks, hoping the two men couldn't see.

They relaxed, waving them out. The door swung shut behind them. Clyde slumped, almost falling.

Drake caught him. "Not yet, old friend. There are more guards in the street."

Breathing heavily, Clyde forced his spine straight and again struck the pose of arrogant assassin. Drake eased down the steps, paused, and pulled something from his breeches pocket. He stamped on it, shoving it partially under a step, then walked out into the yard, his steps dragging as if he weren't looking forward to his end.

Again they went through the charade of killer and victim, but the sleepy guards outside lost interest when the two men turned toward the Thames. Another unidentified corpse would wash ashore in the next few days. Nothing new to Whitefriars, for London had plenty of the cheapest commodity of all—human life.

Safely two buildings away, Drake and Clyde looked

The Gentle Beast

down at the filthy water. "Are you strong enough to swim, Clyde?"

Clyde hesitated, but when they heard raised voices and a pistol shot, he was galvanized. He jumped. Drake followed, grabbing a floating log and shoving it at Clyde. They both crouched on the opposite side of the log and let it sweep them downstream.

Drake wondered where Jerry had gotten it. The head? The heart? Oddly Drake felt regret at his part in the man's death, self-defense or no. He must be getting old. He ducked lower behind the log as the bushes rustled. They were coming.

By the time the search party came, they found only a log, far downstream, and no sign of the men who'd outwitted them.

Two streets over, away from the warehouse district, Callista felt safe enough to collect herself. She'd been so hasty to escape that she'd forgotten to check her reticule for funds. She paused under a street lantern. She stared and pulled out the bank draft. Drake Herrick's bold handwriting taunted her, but she squelched the urge to tear the paper in half.

Why hadn't she offered it back to him, begged for the return of Paris if she had to? Because what he had, he held. The motto rang a warning bell in her mind, but she was distracted before she could pinpoint the thought. Two rollicking men, supporting one another as they sang a bawdy song, rounded the corner up ahead. She shoved the draft back under her kerchief.

Paris was lost to her, too. Tears stung her eyes, but she forced them back. Time enough for regrets aplenty, when she was safe. She felt in the bottom of the bag. She grasped two coins, pulling them out eagerly. Her heart sank. Twopence. Not enough for a chair. Callista

dropped the coins back in, calling herself names for not taking at least a little of the Dragon's precious gold.

The two men paused, blinking at her. Galvanized, Callista wrapped her mantelet more closely about her shoulders and hurried up the street, ducking into a doorway shadowed by an awning. The men lurched past, leaving the street empty of all but Callista and her fears.

Peeking out, Callista tried to get her bearings. She finally spied a shop she knew and realized it would take her a good hour to walk to Marian's. If she could rouse the household so late, doubtless Marian would pay the chairman. However, she'd have to go where the activity was—two streets over, to the coffeehouse and tavern district on Ivy Lane. And a woman alone at this hour was fair game to the habitues there.

Exhausted, Callista leaned against the building and closed her eyes, wishing briefly that she'd stayed put. Such thoughts put her in a peril that was more frightening than her current predicament. "Devil take the hindmost," she snarled, and stepped out of hiding.

Boldly she strode up the street toward the faint sounds of masculine laughter.

Drake pulled a white-faced Clyde out of the water. He anxiously patted Clyde's cheeks. He'd had to brace Clyde on the log as they floated downstream to the street where he'd planned his escape route.

Clyde blinked, groaned. "I ache all over."

Drake hauled him up and turned him facedown over his shoulder. "I shall fetch you to the doctor posthaste."

"This is not the first time I have been tortured, you know. Put me down. I can walk." But Clyde's protest was feeble, and Drake ignored it.

" 'Tis the first time you have been tortured because

of me. And as God is my witness, 'twill be the last."

Drake walked without visible effort toward his hired carriage, glancing warily at every avenue. No one in sight. Gently he placed Clyde inside on the plush seats, followed, and ordered the driver to take them straight to the doctor.

Hassan would not be happy at being awakened, but Drake would pay him well. Having spent his formative years in the East, Drake had great respect for Arab medicine, and none, from what he'd seen since returning home, for English methods.

Drake brooded on the consequences of this night. Of all the thoughts clamoring for his attention, one stood out crystal clear: the true cause of Clyde's suffering stood tall, with enough curves to make even the Dragon long for what he could not have.

Aye, he'd kidnapped her, but the wench had caused him naught but trouble. She made him weak; she made him question the choices by which he'd lived his life.

Worst of all, she made him dream of the future, when his feet should be firmly set in the present.

'Twas time to let her go. The little diversion had been pleasant, but nothing would ever sway him from the vow he'd made over his father's body. . . .

Callista hurried her steps when she spied a chair. Before she could reach it, an elderly gentleman stepped inside. Callista bit her lip in frustration and looked the other way. No other chair in sight, but three men exited a tavern, stopped cold, and stared at her. They approached.

Callista affected blindness, staring through them, willing another chair to arrive.

The tallest of the three whistled when he drew close enough to see the face under the hood of the mantelet.

"Damn, but the ladies of the night get prettier all the time, what, old boys?"

The other two looked her up and down in apparent agreement.

Callista gave them her haughtiest stare. "Please be so good as to take your commerce elsewhere. I am a lady who just had a carriage accident. All I want is a chair so I can get home."

The tallest chuckled as he reached out to chuck her under her chin. "Now that is an original way to ferret out business. Can't say I've ever done it in a chair, but I am willing to try. Come along." He reached to grab her arm.

Callista stepped backward and landed a kick on his shin. The other two glared and fanned out to surround her. Callista opened her mouth to scream.

A blessedly familiar voice said, "My dear lady, what brings you out so late?" Dr. Samuel Johnson stepped away from the stoop of the King's Head tavern and approached to take her arm.

The three men goggled at him. Two removed their hats, but the third merely stared in awe at the world-renowned writer.

Callista relaxed. "I . . . merely wish to hire a chair. Thank you, Dr. Johnson. You are too kind."

"Nonsense. My coachman will take you wherever you wish to go." Those penetrating blue eyes peered at the three men. "I am quite sure these gentlemen were about to offer to do the same. Why, 'twould be un-English to leave such a lady in distress, correct, sirs?"

The tallest cleared his throat. "Indeed, indeed. Sorry, ma'am." He shoved his friends up the street.

Callista took a deep breath. "Why must you always see me at my worst?" She followed as Johnson led her up the street to his carriage and sleepy coachman. "I

The Gentle Beast

swear it is not normally my wont to flit about the streets alone after dark."

Johnson chuckled. "Did you not know that it is one of the maxims of life, my child? On those occasions when we least wish to be discovered, we always shall be." She gave the coachman her directions. He then helped them up and closed the door. As they jolted forward, Johnson leaned back against the squabs and gave her one of those acute stares she was beginning to recognize. "Had a falling out with the Dragon, eh?"

Callista twisted at her reticule. "Not exactly. We have never had a . . . falling in, you see."

Johnson lifted an eyebrow in obvious disbelief, but he allowed her the fiction. "Indeed. May I be so bold as to ask you if these rumors flying about are true?"

"What rumors are those?"

"That you and your stepfather are opening a gaming hell."

Callista blushed and looked unseeingly out the dark window. "Yes, sir, it is true." She awaited his condemnation, for his views about virtue and women were well known. However, his reply was soft. His voice expressed the understanding of one who had known poverty. It was no secret that he lived hand-to-mouth on a pension and what he could make with his writing.

"Ah, money. I cannot condemn you for your pursuit of wealth. Too many think I wrote my dictionary for sheer elucidation. No man but a blockhead ever wrote, except for money. Just as no man ever loses his fortune at the gaming tables, save by choice. Though I confess I should like to see you gain your fortune in another way, I admire your gumption."

When she still looked shamefaced, he patted her hand. "I shall badger you no more, my child. 'Tis only that I enjoy little so much as a good argument."

At this, Callista looked up. "If that is the case, sir, then may I ask your opinion of John Wilkes? Do you believe him a patriot, trying to bring about peaceable reform?"

If she had hoped for reassurance that Wilkes was not so bad, she received none from this quarter.

Johnson's gentle expression hardened. "Patriotism is the last refuge of a scoundrel. The rule of government is best done by those with education and discernment. When a butcher tells you that his heart bleeds for his country, he has, in fact, no uneasy feeling. The notion of liberty only amuses the people of England, and helps to keep off the taedium vitae."

Callista nodded. She wasn't surprised at his attitude, for he was known to be a staunch Tory. Still, she wondered if her life would ever calm again to the point that she found it tedious.

Disheartened, she leaned back wearily and said no more until they reached Marian's house. As the coachman opened the door, Johnson made to rise, but she shook her head. His leg was obviously paining him and his trembling was worse than usual. He, too, was tired.

"I am once again in your great debt, sir. If I can ever repay you in any way . . ."

He smiled, his eyes twinkling even in the muted glow of the carriage lamp. "I may visit your establishment and try your wit at cards. What say you to that?"

Callista jumped down and gave him a deep curtsy. "I should be honored. Good even, and Godspeed."

"And the best of luck in your new endeavor, my dear." Johnson waved as the coachman clucked to the horses.

Callista hurried up the steps and banged the large knocker. Thrice more she tapped before she finally heard dragging footsteps. Colter, his clothes hastily

The Gentle Beast

thrown on, opened the door a crack and peered out with one bloodshot, irascible eye. It widened when he saw who had disturbed his rest.

Flinging open the vast door, he forgot himself so far as to pull her inside and hug her. "Miss, we feared you lost for good." As if realizing what he'd done, he stepped back and blushed.

Callista smiled bleakly. Home she might be, but she was still lost. However, she only replied, "Don't wake Marian. I am quite fatigued and wish nothing so much as a good . . . hard bed." She'd had enough soft, comfortable beds for the nonce. They evoked too many memories best left undisturbed.

"The mistress will scold me proper if I don't wake her—"

"Indeed I would, Colter."

Callista looked up the stairs. Marian, her round form representing hearth and home in her old dressing gown, rushed down the stairs. Callista's calm facade crumpled. She ran to hug her oldest friend. Despite her resolve, tears came to her eyes.

Marian's voice quavered as she patted Callista's back. "I've scarce slept a wink since you left. You silly goose, running off like that. If you knew what grief you'd put us all through . . ." Marian glanced at Colter. "Hot tea in the parlor, Colter." She locked arms with Callista, as if determined to hold her friend safe, and marched them into the parlor.

"Where is Henry?" Callista asked as they sat down.

"He spends half his time at the hell, the other looking for you." Marian stirred the embers with the poker and added wood.

Colter knocked, set down a tray for them, and then exited just as discreetly.

"They only await your return to open," Marian said.

Colleen Shannon

Callista sighed. She had no illusions about what awaited her. She was not looking forward to the leers, the whispers, and the propositions. The thought of Drake, setting his arrogant brand of possession about her throat, spurred her on. "Good. The sooner, the better." She would work from dawn till dusk, and make this venture such a success that she would never be dependent upon any man again.

Marian thrust a steaming cup of England's greatest calming influence, tea, under Callista's nose. "Collect yourself. Now, tell me all."

Callista sipped, gathering her thoughts. The hot brew singed a trail down her throat, leaving her bare before emotions only truth could assuage. She opened her mouth, telling herself she owed the Dragon nothing, but she could not speak. She took another sip.

Marian squirmed on her seat, but Callista could not tell her where she'd been, even for the sake of their friendship. Anything she said would endanger Drake. Misplaced this loyalty might be, but it was as much a part of her as blood and bone. Finally, wearily, she shook her head. "Do not ask me where I was. Only know that I was safe enough, and unharmed."

Marian snapped her own cup down. "Physically, perhaps. I have never seen you so much at sixes and sevens. Do you take me for a fool? I know Herrick kidnapped you. The question is—did he take more than your freedom?"

Callista's eyes watered as she remembered all she'd offered, all he'd demanded. "Nay," she finally whispered. "He . . . wants to marry me. Or so he says."

Marian's eyes bugged out. "The Dragon? Married?" She frowned thoughtfully. "Financially, he would be quite a catch. Yet he is not accepted in polite circles."

Choking on her last sip of tea, Callista finally gasped,

The Gentle Beast

"Nor will I be after I take my place in the hell. No, Marian. I cannot marry a man who hates my father. A man who will not even show me his face. Above all else, that I cannot forgive."

Marian shivered. "I wonder if he's horribly disfigured."

"No."

"How do you know?"

Callista rose to warm her hands before the fire. From this safe distance, she answered softly, "He is a fine-looking man with only a small scar on his temple."

"But I thought you said you've never seen him."

"I . . . felt his features in the darkness." Callista squirmed at the pregnant silence, and knew Marian was wondering what else she'd felt. "Please, Marian, tell no one this, least of all Henry."

"But, my dear, if he persecutes you, we must fetch the constable."

Callista whirled on her friend. "No! Promise me what I tell you will not leave this room."

Marian was still staring at her in confused dismay when the door burst open. Henry Stanton, his wig askew, his gaunt face white with exhaustion, stared at Callista.

He gave a deep sigh. "Thank God," he said simply. Then he opened his arms.

He clasped her so strongly that Callista could scarce breathe, but she only held him tighter.

Simon followed, patting her shoulder. "You ninny, running about like that . . ." He trailed off. "Did you get Paris back?"

Callista shook her head.

Simon's handsome face fell. "Idiotic of me, to sell him like that without asking you. I'm sorry, 'Lista. Guess it's my fault you went through this, but we'll see

the bastard pays, by God we will." Simon savagely rammed the poker into the embers.

Sparks flew, winging up the chimney like a portent of the future. Henry said evenly, "The first thing in the morning, we fetch the law."

Callista pulled her hands from his. "No. I will speak of this only once. I will not testify against Drake Herrick under any circumstances."

Henry plopped into a chair, almost missing the seat. His eyes narrowed. "The devil's bewitched you. Now listen here, missy—"

Callista hovered over him. "I shall be glad to listen when you offer me the truth. I know you know who he is. Tell me." When Henry looked away, she bent and caught his shoulders, "Tell me, damn you, or I shall marry him as he wishes and wash my hands of you!"

Henry gasped. Simon half rose, then sank back in comical dismay. They both spoke at once.

"I'd sooner you wed an adder!" Henry roared.

"Alex won't allow it," came Simon's usual objection.

Callista waved an imperious hand for silence. "I remind you both that I am of consenting age. I do not intend to wed him, but I have had enough of being a pawn in a game for which I do not know the rules. I swear to you, Henry, we are at quits if you do not acquaint me with all your suspicions."

Henry rose as if he could not keep still. Callista watched him with concern. She'd scarce been gone a week, but he seemed to have aged five years.

His agitated strides finally stopped. In a measure of his disgust, he threw off his wig and ran his hand over his bald head. "I do not know for certain, but I suspect he may be the son of a man I . . . wronged."

"Who?" Simon demanded.

Marian leaned forward with bated breath, but Cal-

The Gentle Beast

lista closed her eyes as her worst fears came true. Like a death knell, the motto of that portrait crashed down on her: "What I have, I hold."

Drake Herrick was Bryant Kimball's son.

She'd known it for days, but she'd been afraid to admit it, even to herself. She had to force herself to listen through the frantic pounding of her heart.

"Bryant Kimball. I was young and ambitious. As a second son, with no hope of inheriting, or so it seemed at the time, I did not play fair. In fact, I stole the Yellow Rose from Bryant before he could give it to Mary. He wanted to marry her."

Simon looked shocked. "But you have always been so deuced straitlaced."

"Not in my youth. When I ran off to Gretna Green with Mary, and Bryant discovered I'd stolen the gem, he vowed to see me ruined as soon as he returned from the East Indies. I . . . I . . ." Henry clasped his trembling hands together and took a deep breath. "I used the last of my funds to hire pirates to attack his ship. I did not know he took his son with him. I thought the boy stayed in England. When I heard the boy had been killed as well, I. . . ." Henry swallowed.

Simon whitened.

Callista swayed where she stood, and only avoided falling because Henry led her back to the settee.

He rubbed her hands. "I've lived with my sin for over twenty years. I swear I've tried to atone by being a good father. I would die before I would cause you one moment's pain, especially in recompense for my wrongs. Callista? Speak to me."

But Callista was remembering those ugly ridges on Drake's back. She tried to force herself to visualize how he must have received them, but a black wall descended on her thoughts. The thought of his pain, even

so long ago, was more than she could bear. And to know beyond doubt, from Henry's own lips, that her stepfather had ruined Drake's life . . .

How could Drake bear the sight of her, much less ask her to marry him?

Callista began to rock back and forth in her chair. Indeed, Henry Stanton had been the making of the Dragon's fire and brimstone. Tears flowed freely down her face, dropping hot on Henry's hands.

He drew back as if they were acid. His flat tone grew passionate. "But as evil as my deed was, nothing justifies what Kimball's son has tried to do to you. Help me stop this insanity, Callista. He's so rich and powerful that even once he's behind bars, he will not stay there long. But his persecution will be out in the open then, and he will not dare continue his vendetta against you. Against me, well, I confess I am not certain I care anymore what he does to me."

Simon surged to his feet. "All you've tried to teach me was a lie! How dare you sermonize to me, then—"

Callista rose and went to her brother, dashing her tears away. "Hush, Simon. It was long ago, and cannot be undone." Her arm about her brother's shaking shoulders, Callista looked mournfully at Henry. Unlike Simon, she understood what lengths love could drive a person to. "It was because of Mama that you did this, wasn't it?"

Her arm dropped as she stood firm.

Henry stared at her. They all stared at her. Callista did not know how changed she looked, how much more mature she seemed than a bare week ago. But there was a quiet resolve to her now that made Henry frown.

Henry said, "Bryant wanted Mary beyond reason, and he would not accept her preference for me. He

The Gentle Beast

frightened her. I loved her more than my life, and in my youth I justified the act by telling myself I was keeping her, and you, safe."

"Poor little boy." Callista's eyes watered again. "No one to love him, no one to help him."

Henry waved an impatient hand. "Bah, he is a bounder to hold you against your will. I wronged him, I admit it freely, but two wrongs do not make a right."

"Exactly." Callista dried her tears, resolving to shed no more. "We can never repay him for the years of pain we must have caused him. But neither will I add to it by testifying against him."

"You may not need to. Finding the printing press will do that well enough. The publisher of the *Letters of Junius* will not be above the law, no matter how rich and powerful he is." Henry's hooded eyes stared at her.

Callista turned away, but not fast enough. He saw her panicked comprehension. Rapidly he turned to the door. "Come, Simon. 'Tis almost dawn. But I opine that Quartermain will be glad of this news, and that he can rouse a score of magistrates, if need be. The king will be delighted to have these nasty rags destroyed at last."

"Henry, no!" Callista ran after him and grabbed his arm. "You owe him mercy. If you do this, I shall never forgive you."

But Henry pulled away and flung open the front door. "And I shall never forgive myself if I do not act to keep you safe from him. He is a monster, whether of my making or no, and only when he's rotting in prison will he leave off this obsession with you. He is as bad as his father."

"But . . ." Callista trailed off as he and Simon hurried down the steps, banging the door behind them. She bit her lip so hard that she tasted blood. She whirled on Marian. "I want your fastest horse. Have him saddled

immediately, or I swear I shall ride him bareback."

"Are you mad? You just escaped. You cannot go back now."

But she might have spoken to the wind.

Callista had already headed for the stables.

By the time Drake finally arrived back at the warehouse, it was two in the morning. Drake was drained, but the Arab doctor had assured him Clyde would be all right. It was time to settle an even thornier problem. Drake slammed the panel shut behind him and glared up at the dark alcove. Doubtless she was asleep, but after his hellacious night, he would not defer to her feminine sensibilities. He snorted.

Masculine determination, more like. She'd bewitched him precisely because she had a man's stubbornness and wit encased in a deucedly female form. Well, she would bewitch him no longer. Good riddance. Let her return to Quartermain. They deserved each other.

If Clyde had been there, he would have given Drake one of his knowing looks, shaming Drake into admitting that his fury was a bit too righteous to ring true.

But Clyde wasn't there. Drake deliberately stomped as he climbed the winding stairs to the catwalk, hoping he'd awaken her. He wrenched back the alcove curtain and plunged into the darkness. When his eyes adjusted a bit, he scratched the flint on the bureau and lit the lantern. His chest heaving with warring emotions he would not name, much less admit, he ripped back the bed curtain.

It was time she heard some of those uncomfortable truths she was so good at offering to others. He couldn't wait to help her pack. Aye, she was welcome

to every stitch he'd bought her, just so he never had to see her again.

His combative expression changed as he stared at the empty bed. He felt among the covers in disbelief. He flipped open the chest and plunged his hands in the soft fabrics that reminded him of her living silk and velvet textures. She'd not taken a single one of his gifts. He opened the dragon bedpost and tipped out his cache of jewels and gold. No, nor taken his money either, though surely she was entitled after he'd held her against her will. Maybe she was still here, watching him from some dark corner with those amused green eyes that made him want to kiss her senseless.

Whirling, he ran downstairs. "Callista? Where are you?" He lit every lantern in the place, to no avail.

She was gone.

He was alone with all the treasures he'd won save the one he wanted most. He sat down heavily, fury turning to gall in his throat.

Where was his relief? His triumph? After all, now he could return to the goal that had driven him as long as he could remember. Somehow the former ennobling rage would not come. The memories of Stanton's daughter were like a balm upon his tormented soul. How would he survive without her?

In all his thirty years, no one and nothing had made him feel so alive. She made him laugh, she made him yell, she made him happy, she made him sad. He stared at the Yellow Rose pendant, sparkling in mockery from the chest where he'd flung it. Even that she had not taken.

One memory, more moving than the rest, made him reach out and grasp it. He turned it about, watching this jewel that had started it all sparkle with all the warmth and vitality now gone from his life.

"Remember, when I am gone, that I will not betray you," she had said. Remember? He clasped the stone tightly in his fist, feeling it grow warm from the heat of his despair.

No power on earth could ever make him forget. He'd struggled against it, denied it, even tried to run from it by resolving to let her go. He could hide from himself no longer. He loved her, this beautiful girl—nay, woman, as he'd longed to make her in the fullest sense. He wanted to share his bed, his belongings, his very being with the offspring of his greatest enemy.

Not even his sacred vow to make Henry Stanton pay for his sins could change the forbidden feelings he had for the man's daughter. Aye, he was his father's son, right enough. It must be their lot in life to be obsessed with the Raleigh women.

Unable to keep still, Drake ripped off the mask and stared at himself in the mirror. He saw not an imposing man too strong for handsomeness, but a fool who railed against the very fates he'd tempted. He'd learned nothing in his years in the East.

The past week had indeed forced choices, but not upon Callista, as he'd intended. His own choices were the most difficult of his life.

Happiness or revenge.

Love or hate.

Life or death . . .

Chapter Nine

Ever after, that wild ride would remain vivid in Callista's mind. The clop of the mare's hooves on the cobblestones. The wind pulling at her hair with urgent fingers, as if to hurry her on. The astonished stares she received from the few men about the streets.

Finally she reached the prison that had almost become a home. A home so dear she'd had to force herself to flee. The front door was locked, so she led the mare around to the back. She had to step aside as a large wagon almost ran her over, clipping along at a rapid pace out of the same alley that led to Drake's building.

She stared after it, but the load in the back was covered with a dark cloth. When it was out of sight, she felt warily along the apparently blank wall, then banged with all her might. "Drake! It's Callista! Let me in! 'Tis urgent!"

Silence answered. Despair seized her, but she pounded again, harder. The wind died as if it, too, had

lost hope; then she heard the faint approach of footsteps. The chain rattled, and the blank wall began to rise. She stepped back, tied the mare to a drainpipe, and ducked under the gap. The gap closed slowly, inexorably; then all was quiet, save for the sound of her own breathing.

She felt his presence, for no other man had been able to make her skin tingle with his mere proximity. She blinked in the darkness, suddenly frightened. Would he kidnap her a second time?

What I have, I hold. Again she remembered Bryant Kimball's incredibly strong face staring out of the portrait. Did Drake look like his father?

She hurried into speech, too nervous and too rushed to put a pretty face upon the ugly truth. "Henry is on his way to fetch Quartermain and the magistrates. They suspect you have the press and they will search more thoroughly this time."

Still he didn't speak. Her eyes had adjusted enough to see his dark outline, but he was so motionless that she shivered.

She backed away. "I . . . came as soon as I could to warn you—"

A silken, dangerous laugh cut her off. A lantern flickered to life, illuminating a mask this time that was grim and horrible. "Delilah, warning Samson after she betrayed him?"

She stiffened, her fear abruptly gone. "I told Henry nothing. When he asked me about the press, I turned away, but not fast enough. I was tired, and he knows me well. I cannot lie as well as you."

She saw him take three huge strides toward her. She knew better than to back away again. He was at his most dangerous. The dragon had been challenged in his lair, one of his possessions—herself—stolen.

She felt his hot breath upon her face when he said, " 'Tis not a failing I have noticed. Did you not proclaim your loyalty, say you would never betray me?"

She gasped her outrage. "I did not say a word against you. I pleaded with Henry to leave you alone! And a dressing-down I received for it, from Henry and Marian both—"

"You left me." His tone was quiet, flat, and finally she saw how much she'd hurt him.

So that was it. Callista's building anger quieted. She turned away, afraid he would see the moisture gathering in her eyes. "I did it for both of us. We only tormented one another to no purpose."

A gentle hand fell on her shoulder. She did not resist as he pulled her close to lie against his thudding heart. She subsided, knowing that her own heart answered the siren call loud and true.

"Better sweet torment than this cursed darkness without you." His voice was shaky now, and she could not doubt his honesty.

Callista felt his long torso bending so he could kiss her, and with her last remaining strength she pulled away. "We've no time for this now. Let me help you move the press before it is too late."

She hurried over to the hidden storeroom, pushing at the door, expecting to find it locked. To her surprise it swung inward. She lit a candle and plunged inside. She stared.

Riches untold shimmered from every corner. Over there bolts of silk, over here a silver service large enough to feed an army. In that corner stood a gold-leafed secretary; opposite hovered a wide bureau topped with marble and silver inlay.

She jumped when his voice spoke over her shoulder. "As soon as I found you gone, I summoned Wilkes and

his men to take everything. I knew Henry would come."

In the light of the single candle she held, she turned to look at him. He was dressed more roughly than she'd ever seen him, and his clothes bore a musty smell. They were wrinkled and dirty.

Vaguely she wondered where he'd been. But the curiosity was buried under an onslaught of foreboding. For every move they'd made, Drake had been one step ahead of them. Like a chess master, he'd used them as pawns, but this game was far from over.

What other plans did he have for them?

He would never give up his vengeance. He'd learned under incredibly difficult circumstances to care for no one but himself. If she had wed him, she would be one more rung on his climb to total victory against the man who had ruined his life. And oddly, now that she knew the truth, she could not blame him.

Something hot stung her hand. Callista looked down. The wax had dripped. Numbly she handed the candle to Drake and ran back to the warehouse door, fumbling at the chain. He did not need her. He never had, never would. She was pulling at the chain when his hand covered hers.

"Wait."

She steeled herself not to cry as she looked down at that hand that, despite the two missing fingers, was still strong and capable. She had to bite back a moan as she luridly pictured his fingers being chopped off in punishment for stealing a crust of bread.

"Callista, I . . . I . . . do not want you to go. There is something between us that will not die, no matter how we both might wish it. Maybe if we try to begin anew we can put aside our differences in hope of the future we both want. I will badger you no more to wed me, if

you will only stay. I promise not to touch you unless you wish it."

As peace offerings went, it was a magnanimous one, especially to the daughter of Henry Stanton. With every ounce of her being she wanted to take that wounded hand and kiss the hurt away. But she could not. Henry needed her far more than Drake. As long as these two strong men tried to force her to choose between them, she could only walk the narrow line in the middle, taking one side or the other as circumstances warranted.

"If I stay, what they say of me will be true in deed as well as name." She turned to look at him in the dim glow. He flinched as if she'd slapped him, but he did not deny her statement. "We both know that we cannot be in such close contact without . . . without . . . No, I promised Henry to help save our fortune by working in his gaming hell. And I always keep my promises."

A sad smile stretched her lips. "Something else we have in common, I apprehend."

A faint knocking sounded above. "Herrick! This is Quartermain. Open up in the name of the king!"

They stared at one another, memories of their short time together vivid in their eyes. Finally, reluctantly, Drake released her. "Go. You've made your choice. And in truth, it was probably the right one."

He hauled at the chain, opening the door enough for her to slip away. She stared at the space that led to freedom, then back at him. She teetered, feeling torn in twain. "Do you wish me to wait with you? If I say you have been with me this week past, it should help."

He gave her a gentle push. "Nay. You have done enough. I will be fine. I am used to being alone. Good-bye, Callista."

She slipped outside and watched the gap close. The

door bounced as it hit the ground. Then all was quiet. The moon peeked out of clouds, as if curious about the human vale of toil and torment.

The mare whickered. Only when the horse sniffed at her cheek did Callista realize she was crying. She groped for the saddle, found a stump, and mounted, his last words echoing in her ears. *I am used to being alone. . . . I am used to being alone. . . .*

Perhaps he was—but he did not say he preferred it.

By the time she arrived home, her spirits had lifted a bit. He was too intelligent, too strong, to let Quartermain or anyone else get the best of him. As for the good-bye, well, she might be confused about many things, but one thing she knew.

She would see Drake Herrick again.

Or rather, Drake Kimball.

Her heart beat faster. Now he had no reason not to show her his face. Oddly she felt that once he removed his mask, her gentle beast would change into the man of her dreams. . . .

Drake rested one palm flat on the wall, listening to her hesitant footsteps. *Call her back*, his instincts begged, but his mind, the cool, calculating mind that had kept him alive more times than he could count, told him he'd done the right thing. She was a distraction of the worst kind when he could afford none. Besides, what could he offer her? A man scarred, body and soul, so deep he would never heal. A man who had known little tenderness and less happiness.

He had possessions aplenty, but if she had been the type of woman to be satisfied with that, he'd not be standing here now aching for her. The faint knocking sounded again, louder.

Forcing himself to turn away, he put on a clean

The Gentle Beast

jacket, leisurely brushing the worst of the river debris off his pants. Despite the sick despair in his gut, part of him was looking forward to this.

Drake checked his pocket watch. Many hours had passed since he brought Clyde back. Long enough, especially with Quartermain so conveniently busy, for Norther to have done what he was best at.

Drake's smile was gracious when he flung open the door. "Good even, gentlemen. I wish I could say this is a surprise."

Quartermain shoved past him. Two magistrates followed. Several soldiers crowded in next, their muskets alert but not cocked—yet. They stared around in awe at the riches they'd never dreamed of, much less hoped to buy.

The magistrate in the lead, a round little man with prominent blue eyes, glanced impatiently at Quartermain, covering a yawn with his hand. The cit would not be hurried. The tall magistrate was as lean as his fellow was plump, and he looked irritated at being pulled from his bed.

Quartermain glanced up the stairs, as if looking for someone. "And where's your faithful shadow, Mr. Haynes?"

If Drake had still doubted who kidnapped Clyde, the comment would have alerted him. Quartermain wanted to rub it in. Drake had to turn away to disguise his grinding teeth and clenched fists. "Safe in his bed, I should imagine." He glanced over his shoulder.

Quartermain smirked before he could stop himself.

Drake looked quickly back around. *Smile, you bastard. While you can.* "We can exchange banalities all night, but I will gladly take you gentlemen about my property, as that is clearly why you have come." Drake calmly climbed the stairs.

Nonplussed, the magistrates stared at the sinister man in the mask, but Quartermain bounded up the shop's stairs eagerly enough. The soldiers took the lower floor. They flung open every door they came to, glancing about in a cursory manner, before hurrying to the next room.

Quartermain, however, was thorough. He tapped on walls, listening, his head cocked, before slowly going to the next room.

His little ritual bore fruit in Drake's office. He stiffened when he heard a hollow echo. He glanced at Drake. "Open this panel."

Hiding the mechanism with his body, Drake opened the stairway and shoved it wide, grumbling, "Deuced invasion, that's what this is." Quartermain plunged into the passage.

The thin magistrate glared at him. "Only if you've something to hide."

"Oh, I've something to hide, all right."

Two steps down the narrow tunnel that Drake had deliberately left dark, Quartermain froze. He peered up at his enemy in obvious surprise at the bold admission.

Drake finished languidly, "My art collection, of course. Here, let me show you." He brushed past Quartermain and led the way down to his lair. Quartermain had to catch himself with a hand on the wall, but he recovered quickly and stumbled after Drake.

The other men followed more warily. Drake waited until all were in the warehouse before, one by one, he lit the lamps. Even Quartermain gasped in amazement at the muted glint of silver, gold, jewels, and furs. He stared at the exquisite paintings and valuable statuary, but he recovered more quickly than the men of more humble origins.

"Yes, well, you may be rich but you are still not above

the law." He stomped about the walls, tapping, looking for a hidden closet.

Drake sat down on the settee, comfortably stretching out his arms. "Make it quick, if you please, as you pulled me out of bed."

The plump magistrate stared at him suspiciously. Drake could read him like a book. Most of the quality would have been screaming in outrage by now, the man was thinking. This bloke was a bit too accommodating.

"Guard the door," he ordered his men and forged off in the opposite direction, searching carefully. The thin magistrate searched upstairs on the catwalk, but he came back down soon, obviously disgruntled.

Drake had to quash a grin. What fun it would be when Quartermain played his ace, only to discover that he wasn't even in the right game.

Quartermain called, "Here! Here it is!" Both magistrates ran to where he tugged at the storage closet door.

"Unlock this door," Quartermain ordered.

Languidly Drake rose. He fumbled in his pocket. His usually dexterous hands were unwontedly clumsy, but finally he got the lock open.

Quartermain flung open the door, barreled inside, and froze. The two magistrates gave Drake triumphant looks and followed.

Staying put, Drake folded his arms and waited. Rich curses preceded an equally precipitous exit. Drake wondered if they knew how comical they looked, all pomp and circumstance, representatives of the Crown—turning on one another.

The plump magistrate glared at the cit. "Certain evidence, eh? You dragged me out of my home at this ungodly hour for *this*?"

Quartermain growled, "Button your lip!" He turned

to Drake, pausing for drama. "You think you're a clever blighter, do you not? Well, explain this away!" Like a wizard casting a spell, Quartermain pulled a sheaf of papers from his coat pocket and brandished them high.

Drake held his breath, staring at the papers, then eased it out slowly. Thank God. The chemistry had worked.

This time Drake couldn't contain his smile as Quartermain raged on, "This was taken from him a few nights ago. If you read it, you shall find it is the same seditious nonsense found in the *Letters of Junius!*"

The tall magistrate took the papers to a lantern. He turned them this way and that, then peered askance at Quartermain. "What nonsense is this, sir? These papers are blank."

His eyes bugging out in obvious disbelief, Quartermain jerked the papers away, shuffled through them. He frantically turned them this way and that. Slowly he looked at his tormentor. "You shall pay, and richly, for this."

"Promises, promises." Drake's smile deepened. "Would you gentlemen care for a glass of port before you leave?"

"Don't mind if I do," the plump magistrate said. The tall, thin one stomped on his foot. He winced and hurriedly retracted, "Ah, not now. Not the thing, no, no, we really must be getting on." He waved his men back up the stairs.

The tall magistrate bowed toward Drake. "Please excuse the intrusion, sir. We will not trouble you again."

"I trust not," Drake said.

The plump magistrate hesitated, peering at Quartermain's thunderous frown; then he hurried after his comrade.

The Gentle Beast

Quartermain made no move to follow. He tossed the papers into the fireplace. Drake poured himself a glass of port, then offered Quartermain one.

Quartermain accepted it, clenching it so tightly Drake expected it to break.

"Alone at last," Drake said, sipping, hoping the dig would do the trick.

Instead of cutting himself, Quartermain relaxed and drained the glass. "How did you manage it?"

"Manage what?" Drake held his wine up to the light, admiring its clarity.

"This disappearing ink business. You are ill-named, Dragon. You should be called Sorcerer."

Drake bowed, freezing when Quartermain added softly, "Or perhaps Defiler of Innocents would be a better name."

Slowly Drake straightened, all pretense of congeniality gone. "Do not speak of my affianced wife that way."

Now it was Quartermain's turn to freeze, but he recovered quickly. "Nonsense. She hates the sight of you. Even now, Henry is preparing her for her debut two nights hence. Beauty such as hers needs to be put on display for all the blades in London to enjoy."

Before he could stop himself, Drake took a step toward Quartermain. "And you call *me* a defiler? At least I would hold her safe, like the rarity she is, rather than offer her on a platter to every Jack Sharp and drunken lout in London."

Unperturbed, Quartermain turned toward the stairs, but at the opening he paused. "The lady will stay true to her blood, in the end. You are a coarse, nameless scoundrel afraid to show your face, a fact I will prove to every soul in London before we are at quits." Quartermain threw the fine crystal goblet at Drake's head.

Drake dodged it. It shattered on the armoire behind him, splattering him with glass. He pulled a deep splinter from his neck, flicking it away as if blood were cheap, particularly his own. "Oh, we are far past the gaming stage. If Callista is harmed, you die." His tone was dead calm, like the eye of a hurricane.

Quartermain's smile slipped a tad. "Watch your back." He turned to climb the stairs.

"Oh, I shall. And Quartermain?" Drake waited until Quartermain looked back. "Enjoy your happy home this eve."

Quartermain frowned and hurried off.

Drake's facade of calm shattered like the glass. He was shaking as he swept up the priceless Venetian goblet that had been rumored to belong to Catherine de Médicis. *Threaten me all you wish*, Drake thought darkly, *but if you use Callista against me, you shall find that the Dragon is well named, after all.*

You shall learn firsthand the meaning of fire and brimstone.

Two mornings later, Drake waited until the paper arrived before going to see Clyde. He thumbed through it, smiling when he saw the small article. He dressed quickly, tucking the paper under his arm. What a marvelous restorative to Clyde's health this bit of news would be.

Clyde was actually dressed, arguing with the Arab in that singsong language Drake had always admired. "I am fine. I wish to go back to the warehouse."

The Arab, Hassan Assabi, glared at him with liquid dark eyes. "Neither of us are as young as we used to be, my friend. You may still become infected."

Clyde's swollen, black-and-blue eyes still managed to

The Gentle Beast

take on that stubborn gleam Drake recognized. *"In-shallah."*

"No, you pious old mule, it's your own will you don't want thwarted." Drake also spoke in Arabic, with equal ease.

Both men turned to him in relief. It was obvious they'd been arguing for some time.

"He will listen to you," Hassan said.

At the same time, Clyde said, "Ah, I knew you would come for me."

Drake sat on the edge of the bed and pointed out the article that described a robbery at the home of one of England's wealthiest merchants. The account did not name the merchant, but from the hints dropped, it was obvious the victim was Quartermain. Art and jewels worth over fifty thousand pounds had been stolen.

Clyde read slowly, blinking to clear his blurred gaze. At the end, he looked up in confusion. "What has this to do with us? Surely you did not rob Quartermain's mansion?"

He stared at Drake's sly grin. Suddenly a comprehending smile stretched Clyde's puffy face. He winced slightly, but still could not contain his delight. "You dropped his card that night, did you not?"

Drake winked. "Clumsy of me, indeed. When I filched it from him, I had no idea it would come in so handy. Of course, Norther's mistake was quite natural—thinking it was mine, I mean."

Clyde's smile faded. "If Quartermain finds out, he will hate you more than ever."

Drake's twinkle faded. He flung off the mask, rubbing his face tiredly. "Good. I am sick of all these games. Within a week, I hope, I will be able to have done with these cursed masks and claim my rightful place."

Colleen Shannon

Clyde tugged on the bedclothes, obviously struggling with what to say. His swollen fingers were wrapped, but the soreness had apparently eased under the doctor's smelly salves.

Hassan looked at his friends with sympathetic eyes. His robes rustling slightly, he went into the next room to give the two men time alone. The door closed, leaving a pregnant silence.

Drake knew what was coming, but he stayed still, waiting, instead of fleeing as instinct bade. He owed Clyde that much. Besides, it was time to face some hard truths and quit agonizing over things he could not change.

"And what of the lady Callista?" Clyde finally asked baldly, in English this time.

Drake rose, the newspaper falling from his lap. He strode up and down, replying in the same language. "What of her? I gave her every chance, and she's made her choice patently clear."

"And was it fair of you to force the choice upon her? Tell me, what would you do if Callista asked you to choose between your father or her?"

Drake whirled on him. "My father is dead because of hers!"

"And you are the man she loves because of him."

Drake gasped, falling back a step at the low blow.

Clyde struggled to his feet, swaying. Then he stood firm as if he knew that Drake needed him more now than ever since that dark, humid night on which they'd met nigh on twenty years ago. "Yes, Henry Stanton did you and your father grievous wrongs. But from what I have seen of the man, he has spent most of the intervening years trying to make up for them. Think, Drake. Would you really be as intelligent, or as strong, or as inherently decent as you are if you had not grown up

242

the way you did? Those who live with fire are inevitably forged by it."

Drake shook his head, unable to face Clyde's inexorable logic.

But Clyde continued softly, "With rare exceptions, the landed gentry in England are a selfish, grasping lot. How many of them would risk their lives to bring change, as you have, for all Englishmen?"

Drake shrugged. "Some of them already have."

"A precious few. Perhaps your father would have been able to protect you from all the temptations young lords face in this land, but arrogance tends to beget arrogance. From what you have told me of him, he was as obsessed with Callista's mother as you are with her daughter."

Drake opened his mouth to deny it, but Clyde held up his hand. "A fact you will admit before too many more days, I predict. Do you not see, Drake, that your father never would have accepted her marriage to Henry? In that way, Henry's fears were justified."

Drake returned to his restless pacing. "I' faith, you make it sound as if I should thank Stanton on bended knee."

"No, of course not. But use the strengths God, in his wisdom, has granted you, for the good they were meant for." Clyde put his hand upon the shoulder of the young man he obviously loved like a son. "Or perhaps you will understand better if I use the words of one of England's greatest minds: 'Sweet mercy is nobility's true badge.'"

"Shakespeare, *Titus Andronicus*," Drake said softly.

For a moment they stared at each other with the wordless empathy that only joint suffering allows. During those long years in prison, Clyde's wonderful mind had been Drake's only comfort. He owed his current

Colleen Shannon

knowledge of Latin, literature, and science to this frustrated monk. The stone walls had been slate to Clyde's chunk of charred wood, Drake's mind Clyde's notebook.

Drake's chest heaved with a sigh. "I will think on it. 'Tis all I can promise."

A look of peace descended on Clyde's battered face. Then, energetically, Clyde set about packing.

Drake hovered over him. "Are you certain you feel well enough to leave?"

"Of a surety I shall not let you go to that den of iniquity alone." Clyde closed his satchel with a haughty snap.

Drake laughed, the rich, basso laugh that so few were privy to. "I am old enough to enter a hell without escort."

"What has age to do with it? Methinks I am not old enough, either, to gladly suffer such exposure to human greed and misery."

With a flourish, Drake held the door for his old teacher. "Lead on, master."

In the next room, Hassan glared at Clyde. He rose from the tiny table where he nursed a minuscule cup of strong coffee. "Leave then, you stiff-necked English fool. Do not ask me to bandage you up when your wounds reopen."

"I shan't." Clyde glared at Hassan and fumbled in his pocket. He tossed several sovereigns on the table, but Hassan swept them to the floor.

"You insult me."

Reluctantly Clyde accepted the coins Hassan gathered and thrust out. "Very well. But we shall send you what commerce we can."

Hassan threw open the door. "See that they know how to follow good advice, unlike yourself."

The Gentle Beast

Clyde swept outside, his nose in the air.

Smiling, Drake watched the byplay. Hassan and Clyde had always bickered like children. They were of the same age and intellect, but their opinions rarely matched. Hassan had been threatened with death for his outspoken criticism of the sultan of Turkey. When he had saved both Drake and Clyde after they'd suffered injury during a pirate raid, Drake had given him passage to England.

"Peace be with you, old friend," Drake said at the door. He paused to attach his mask.

Hassan bowed. "And to you." As Drake closed the door, Hassan added softly, "You need it."

At that very moment, Quartermain waited impatiently in the private room of a nondescript inn. He sipped the execrable burgundy. He shoved it aside in disgust, drumming his fingers on the scarred tabletop. When a knock sounded at the door, he growled, "Come."

Two brawny ruffians marched in and proceeded to prowl the room. They made Quartermain stand, searched him. Then one jerked his head at the other.

The ruffian returned quickly with a tall, handsome man dressed in the rich silk and lace of a lord. Then one brawny lad crossed his arms over his chest and stood, his back to the door while his fellow guarded the only window.

Not even offering so much as a how-do-you-do, Quartermain deliberately slouched back in his chair. The lord narrowed his eyes at the impeccably dressed merchant and did the same.

An astute observer would have realized how like the pair were in dress, demeanor—and depravity.

Colleen Shannon

"Who the devil are you and why do you call me here?" asked Felix Norther.

Quartermain brandished the insignia ring on his hand and pressed it into the chunk of cheese at his side. Norther stared at the imprint, then shrugged.

"So? I am to be impressed that the mysterious individual who has used my services so anonymously over the years finally reveals himself?"

Quartermain took a card from his pocket and flipped it faceup before Norther. This time he got a reaction. Norther's eyes widened. He stared at the insignia, at the card, then at Quartermain's fuming expression.

Blowing a bitter laugh, Whitefriars's master criminal sat back in his chair. "Outsmarted, by gad. By a man I can't even name."

"He's known as Drake Herrick, the Dragon, though I am certain that is not his real name. He is far richer than I, and would make a wonderful target for you. In fact, after our business is done, I shall gladly lead you to his lair. As for now, you will return my things immediately."

Norther stiffened. "I don't take no orders from no one." Then, with an effort, he recovered his cultured accent. "I shall see what my men have left and return it to you forthwith. I owe you that, given how badly I bungled your latest task."

"Haynes didn't say a word about who the Dragon really is, or why he's come?"

"Not a peep. Most odd, the man looks like a strong wind would blow him away, but he's got a constitution like a bull's. Of course, we'd barely started on him when that . . . that fiend spirited him away."

"Would you like to get even?"

Norther's handsome face set into a mean grin that

displayed the inner workings of his heart and mind. "For this, I work for free."

Callista rotated slowly before Marian's mirror, stunned at her own appearance. The gown made for her in her absence was a daring design she'd never seen before. The red silk, shimmering with her every movement as only the finest fabric could, fell in lush folds from a high waistline. It was lined with layer upon layer of the finest muslin, giving it a formal fullness that still clung a bit too lovingly for her taste. The slim design of the dress made it impossible for her to wear any of her petticoats. As for the bodice, well, really!

"Marian, did you have a hand in this design?"

Marian worried at her lip as she stared at her best friend. "Ah, not exactly. I recommended a new French designer to Henry, but I imagine you have Quartermain to thank for that, ah, scrap that shields your modesty."

Callista tugged at the meagre covering of silk and lace. Her generous cleavage only deepened. The dress had no stays, and save for a lavish fall of glittering gold metallic lace at neckline, hem, and tiny cap sleeves, it had no other ornamentation. The dress was designed as a beautiful frame, accenting the full-length portrait of the wearer, rather than as a work of art itself.

Callista leaned forward tentatively. Her breasts, full and tempting, pressed against the low neckline, but they did not pop loose as she feared. Finally, a blush high on her cheeks, she turned away from her reflection. That wanton creature was less a creation of the designer than of the man who put that fullness in her lips, that lissome fluidity in her movements. Callista could only hope that no one else would see the change in her.

Colleen Shannon

Marian cocked her head. "I cannot quite define it, but you look different, Callista."

Callista slipped her feet in the red silk slippers, her head bent. "So would you, if you were displayed for all and sundry like a prize sow in a butcher shop window."

"No, that's not it. It's not too late for you to back out, you know."

Callista barked a laugh. "True. Only if I decide eating is unimportant to me."

"But I have told you, over and over—"

"Please, Marian. My mind is decided. I cannot let Henry down at this late date, not when he's so tired and frail."

Fairly vibrating with rage, Quartermain had returned two nights ago to pull Henry into the study. Callista had made it a point to busy herself in the hall, but she still couldn't hear anything other than the sound of raised voices. Finally Quartermain had slammed out. She glimpsed Henry sitting before the fire, his head in his hands, before the door closed.

Quartermain had paused. "I am glad to have you safe again, my dear." He picked up her limp hand to kiss it. "You would please me greatly if you would accept my ring to wear on your debut at the hell." He pulled something gaudy and glittering from his pocket, lifting her hand, but Callista jerked away.

"I will not wed." Especially not you, she said to herself as she turned toward the study. "Now, please excuse me. I wish to talk to Henry."

Had she looked over her shoulder, she would have been frightened at the expression on that handsome face, but she had slipped quickly into the study. She knelt before Henry and cupped his weary face in her hands.

"Please, dearest Henry. What is amiss?"

The Gentle Beast

He caught her palm to kiss it, saying into her hand, "I have made such a mess of things, child. I am fair worn, in spirit and body. Perhaps you would be better off if I died."

At that Callista surged to her feet. "What drivel! We shall come about. We always do." When he still wouldn't look up, she sat next to him. "Henry, we have Summerlea safe again, and soon enough we shall be swimming in funds, if the ton's interest in the hell is truly as high as it promises to be. What have you to be upset about?"

Marian's secretary had been deluged with inquiries as to when and where the hell would open. The notice they'd placed would surely heighten interest further.

Apparently the hell had been the least of Henry's worries at that moment, for he had wearily rubbed his face, leaned back, and looked at her. He studied her for a long time, then said simply, "Do you love him, child?"

Callista froze. "To whom are you referring?"

"Herrick, of course."

What to say? A dozen evasions had come to mind, but the worry in Henry's haggard face tugged at Callista's conscience. She should have tried harder to escape. She should forget Drake Herrick, as he'd doubtless already forgotten her. She should think of nothing but the debut.

Callista Raleigh seldom did what she should; she was more in the habit of doing what she could. "I . . . I . . . think so."

His weary expression became bleak. "I feared so. Callista, Quartermain has just returned from Herrick's warehouse. He went there with the magistrates after I warned him to search for the press that prints the *Letters of Junius*."

Colleen Shannon

Callista bit her lip. "And? Did they find anything?"

"Nothing."

Callista had sagged back in relief.

Henry watched her grimly. "But, child, do you not see what this means? Drake Herrick is the most astute, grimly determined individual I have ever come across. And he is my deadly enemy. He will stop at nothing until I am ruined, at the least, and he may even want me dead. He will never wed the daughter of his nemesis, no matter what he tells you. Given the chance, he will use you and cast you aside."

He only put words to her greatest fear, but something in Callista still rose up to defend Drake. "He had ample opportunity to do so and did not."

Henry gasped. His face twisted in pain as he grabbed his heart. Callista started for him, but he waved her away. He took deep, panting breaths. His face gradually relaxed.

"Have you seen a doctor lately?"

"Too busy. These are just spells of tiredness, I make no doubt. They always go away quickly. Now, did he try to, er, be overly familiar with you?"

Callista blushed, but she held her head high. "He tried nothing that I did not allow. Perhaps you do not give me enough credit. Is it so hard to believe that he wants me for myself, not because I am your daughter?"

"Wants are unimportant to Drake Herrick, as, I suspect, are needs. He is just like his father. It is deeds he lives by."

Callista turned to the fire. She played with the poker, but she was blind to the sparks that flew up the chimney. *You think; I act,* he had told her. Henry was right. She should put aside this foolish infatuation. It was folly.

Some of the world's greatest advances began as folly.

The Gentle Beast

"Have you ever wondered whether, if you left off persecuting him, he might leave you be as well?" Callista put the poker back next to the rake with a forceful clang.

"I did not start this."

At that Callista turned to stare at him.

He had the grace to blush. "At least, not since he returned to England." He rose to take her hands. "Dearest Callista, you may not believe me, but it is you I fear for, not myself. If I believed for an instant that Drake Herrick truly loved you, and would treat you well, I would set aside my objections. But please remember he has lived a hard life, and his experiences have made him a hard man."

Callista pulled her hands away. "And the two of you make a fine pair!" She strode to the door, where she paused. "I am sick to my soul of this lurid battle between two bulldogs, with me as the bone. I hope you both choke before this is done!" The door had slammed behind her.

Now Marian drew Callista back to the present by handing her a velvet box. "A frippery I bought for you. I insist you wear it. Perhaps it will bring you luck."

Callista opened the box. Inside, on a white satin bed, lolled a single exquisite ruby set in a lacy filigree heart on a slim gold chain. The ruby winked like an indolent lady surrounded by white satin sheets.

"Frippery, eh?" Callista tried to snap the case shut and hand it back, but Marian looked so hurt that she sighed and pulled the necklace out. "Thank you, dear friend. Have I ever told you how grateful I am that you pushed that hateful Lizzie Hepburn in the pond after she tripped me and made me fall in?"

Marian's eyes grew misty at the memory. "Ah, what times we had at school. I fear we were a sore trial for

the headmistress. On that occasion, as I recall, we both went to bed with our stomachs gnawing at our backbones. But it was worth it, just to see Lizzie's face with moss and mud dripping down it."

They both laughed at the memory. Callista let Marian attach the necklace for her. Callista was relieved to see that the heart nestled in the deep cleavage of her bosom, obscuring the vee slightly. Callista added plain gold earbobs, and set a gold comb in her simply upswept hair.

Marian nodded her approval. "Now. You are ready. I wish I could come." She looked so wistful that Callista laughed.

"Not even the rich Marchioness of Netham could weather such a scandal. No, Marian, I need you to pull my tattered reputation back to some semblance of order."

Sniffing, Marian led the way downstairs. "Won't be the first time I have pulled you from the bumble broth. No doubt it will not be the last, either."

Henry, Simon, and Quartermain all waited impatiently in the hallway. Simon and Quartermain gasped as Callista stepped down demurely, the gossamer fabric clinging with each movement. Henry frowned and looked as if he might order her to change.

But Quartermain stepped in front of him to offer his arm. "You look just as I knew you would. The gamers certainly will not be able to keep their minds on their cards." When Quartermain caressed her bare arm, Callista lifted his hand and pulled it away.

"What they do with their minds is their business, but their hands, they keep to themselves." Callista met his narrow-eyed gaze defiantly.

Sighing, Henry intervened. His face still haggard despite his royal purple coat and white satin knee

The Gentle Beast

breeches, he tucked Callista's hand in his arm. "I have imported something from the country that might aid us in that end."

Callista frowned in a confusion that was not cleared up until they reached the hell. As Henry helped her down from the carriage, Callista was pleased at how handsome the town house looked. Gone were the overgrown weeds and the dead leaves. Lights blazed behind the freshly painted shutters. Even the chipped walkway had been repaired.

Inside, the furniture, from the antique secretary and chairs in the entryway to the rooms filled with new green baize–topped tables and handsome chairs, glowed with paste wax. Every candle and sconce in the place blazed. "You've done wonders, Henry."

Simon looked affronted. "Give me some credit, 'Lista. I managed a veritable army of workmen."

Callista hugged him. "And a fine manager you made, too. I always knew you would, if you'd but apply yourself."

Henry was looking about expectantly. Callista watched him, wondering what he waited for, but when he whistled, heavy footsteps galloped on the floor above.

A delighted grin stretched Callista's face. She ran to the bottom of the stairs, whistling. Cerberus bounded down to her, his canine face set in what looked extraordinarily like an answering grin. He jumped the last two steps and tensed to leap on her.

She said firmly, "No! Down!" He collected himself. His powerful haunches plopped down on the parquet floor, but his stump of a tail wagged. Callista patted his head fondly. "I've missed you, boy." And Paris. Again Callista grieved for her most cherished possession, but she knew Drake would treat him well.

Henry nodded in satisfaction. "None of your table partners will get too bold with him by your side." Henry glanced slyly at Quartermain. "Right, Alex?"

The cit made what might have been a disgusted sound: then he went into the side parlor they'd set up as the room where chips were purchased and redeemed.

Callista smiled at Henry. "Thank you." It was so hard for her to reconcile her kind, considerate stepfather with the ruthless opportunist of Drake's youth.

"Now, upstairs with you. When we're full, I'll ring the bell. That will be your signal to make your entrance."

And so Callista went upstairs. She threw a ball for Cerberus while she waited. She heard the door open and close numerous times and the muted sound of male voices. With every sound her nerves grew more tense.

Would he come? Did she want him to come? She needed no distractions this evening. She'd seen him two days ago, but it already seemed like an age. When the bell finally rang, she jumped.

Taking a deep breath, Callista rose. She went to the stairs. "Heel, boy." Cerberus walked beside her obediently. She put one hand on his head as she made her descent. The lights were bright after the dimness upstairs, so she concentrated on her footing, but she did notice that the excited voices died away. The silence unnerved her, but somehow she managed the long, curving staircase without stumbling.

"Beauty and the beast," someone mumbled, but it was not the voice she'd hoped to hear.

She tilted her head proudly, expecting at best disapproval, at worst lust, from these wealthy, mostly titled gentlemen.

But in the sea of masculine faces, she saw stunned

admiration, delight, and, yes, in many cases, desire. Callista searched the crowded hallway, hoping, fearing. . . . He was not there.

Torn between disappointment and relief, she nodded regally. "Welcome, gentlemen. We hope tonight will be the first among many of good company, good wine, and good games. Please feel free to go from room to room until you find a table where you are comfortable. We offer whist, piquet, and dice."

Callista entered the piquet room and sat down at the head table. Her heart drummed in her ears, but the warmth of Cerberus at her side gave her confidence. He watched protectively as men crowded about until every available chair was filled. Most of them were unfamiliar to her, but a few she recognized.

She smiled at a young friend of Heath's. He had been the second at that ill-fated duel. "'Tis good to see you again, Hampton. How is your father?" The young man's father had been ill for several years.

"Finally passed on, God rest his soul. Heath would be delighted to see you looking so well." Hampton kept a straight face, but Callista heard his unspoken thought: *But he'd not be delighted to see so much of you here.* With obvious effort, he kept his gaze away from her bodice.

Callista hoped her colored cheeks would be construed as rouge. "Thank you. Now, gentlemen, if you agree, the stakes are open at a guinea, double with every hand. Acceptable?" She glanced around the table. Some of the men blanched, but most only looked more eager.

Inwardly Callista sighed. Most of these young bucks thought she would be ripe for the picking. Women were not accounted as having good heads for cards. All to the better. The faster they made their fortune, the

sooner they could quit this distasteful enterprise.

She had barely started dealing from the card box when she heard a stir at the door. She was concentrating, so she didn't pay the disturbance much heed until Heath's friend growled, "What is he doing here? I thought he only played in private games."

And from another, "We might as well make ourselves scarce. That arrogant bastard shall make the stakes too rich."

Callista looked up.

He had come after all.

The Dragon was dressed again in the fine sapphire coat and black knee breeches he'd worn during their game at Marian's. From somewhere came the thought that he loved art more than the frivolous pursuits of vanity that so many rich men pursued. But at that moment she was too nervous to be charitable, especially considering the way he was looking at her.

Across numerous heads and a large expanse of carpet, those eyes still had the power to pin her to her chair. He stared at her until her skin prickled and her palms grew damp. He stared at her as if he owned her and everything around her, and only awaited the time and place of his choosing to shout it to the world.

And he stared at her as if they were the only two people left in the world capable of mating. Callista could not move, despite the fact that she felt the acute curiosity of the gamesters.

They glanced from her tense expression to the Dragon's masked face. The smiling sapphire mask was sewn with brilliants that caught the candle glow as he approached. Then he stood over her, staring down, his gaze appraising every brazen inch. Only by effort of

The Gentle Beast

will did she keep from splaying a hand over her almost bare bosom.

Cerberus growled, but Drake didn't even glance at him. "What are the stakes?"

Callista was beyond answering, so Hampton told him.

"A hundred pounds to the man who lets me take his seat." Drake glanced about the table.

A callow young man rose. "Done."

Drake nodded at Clyde, who sat glumly in a corner. "My manager will write you a draft. Thank you kindly."

Callista was still staring at Clyde when Drake took his seat. Why were Clyde's hands bandaged? And he, too, was masked.

Drake's voice dragged her back. "My credit is good, I presume?"

"You presume too much. As usual. Get chips like everyone else," Callista replied.

Drake chuckled. "I shall be back forthwith. You will wait for me, yes?"

Every other gamester watched avidly, their heads flinging from side to side at each verbal parry and thrust.

Damn him and his double entendres. "If it suits me. But if you think to make us nervous while we wait, it shall not work. Only the most skilled, not the most devious, win at this table."

Towering over her, Drake leaned down to whisper in her ear, "You should know by now, my dear, that I always win. Especially when I desire something strongly." That sparkling gaze touched her shoulders and breasts possessively.

Then he was gone, leaving the other men to stare

hungrily at the gooseflesh that had risen where Drake's gaze had touched.

Only pride kept Callista sitting at the table. Pride and determination to torment her tormentor until he, too, was almost climbing out of his skin with the same desire he inspired in her.

Chapter Ten

Despite Drake's absence, Callista continued dealing. Let him cry foul and seek another table, she fumed inwardly. Each of the other gamesters had time to peruse and arrange their cards. Callista did the same, but she still jumped when Drake's shadow loomed over her.

He glanced at the careless pile of cards facedown on the green baize–topped table, while the other players pressed their arranged hands to their chests. Drake's attention centered on Callista. "Vixen," he mouthed.

She stared through him haughtily. "Join us if you dare."

Gasps sounded at her boldness.

Drake's tall figure checked slightly as he sat down, but that was his only reaction. "Bullbaiting is not a sport I would encourage in you, my dear. It can be quite dangerous. I have visited Madrid and witnessed the proceedings. I might point out that your dress is

red, as is the cape the matadors use." Again that hooded, sparkling gaze ran over her possessively.

Cerberus did not like his warning any more than his mistress did, apparently, for he edged closer to Callista, showing his teeth at Drake. Callista patted the mastiff's head. "And I might point out that the matador, though much smaller and weaker than the bull, is almost always the victor. The bull, fearsome monster that he might be, usually ends up dead and bleeding in the dust."

Drake chuckled. "Olé."

"Pardon me?"

"It's a Spanish term given when the matador makes a skillful pass of the cape."

Callista opened her mouth to respond, but one of the older gamesters at the table complained, "And you may skewer one another at your pleasure, but later, kindly. I thought this was a gaming house, not the blasted Globe Theater."

Blushing, Callista mastered her ire and smiled at the man sweetly. "Certainly, sir. Let us begin the bidding."

Still, she had to force herself to concentrate. With every card that hit the table, she expected Henry to burst into the room and order Drake out, but Henry was apparently busy at the dice table. She was not surprised to find Drake the winner of the hand. She had to get a grip on herself. She was here to make money, not lose it, least of all to the same man who'd stolen so much from them.

However, he was apparently not ruffled by the speed with which he had to arrange his cards. He won the second hand just as easily.

As Callista tallied the points, the other gamesters looked at Drake sourly. "Damn, but you have the devil's own luck, Herrick," groused one.

The Gentle Beast

"Fame and fortune not enough, old fellow?" flattered another, his tone forced. "You must carry Lady Luck away with you, kicking and screaming if need be?"

"No, I prefer she come willingly," he replied. His fingers brushed Callista's as he picked up his third hand.

Callista felt her face reddening. She studied her cards and did not reply, hoping the men at the table would not catch his meaning. Only Hampton looked at her thoughtfully.

At that moment Callista could not even remember what her childhood love had looked like, and somehow that only made her angrier. Aye, Drake had reason to hate Henry, but she'd done naught to him. Why, with a word from her, he would be clapped in irons. How dare he bait her in front of all and sundry?

All through the interminable set, she fumed. He won each hand, and she finally decided she'd best escape before she said something completely beyond the pale. When she saw Simon enter the room, she beckoned. She gave Drake the agreed-upon stake from the house funds; then she shoved back her chair, forcing a pleasant smile. "Please excuse me, gentlemen. My brother Simon will take over as dealer."

Simon opened his mouth, but Callista gave a curt nod and hurried away. She didn't see Drake's telltale intake of breath as he got his first full-length look at her form, nor did she notice the way her long, agitated strides made the soft fabrics cling.

Every other man in the room noticed.

Drake's beautiful mouth tightened under the mask. He raked his winnings into his pocket and followed her. The gamesters broke out in excited whispers as soon as he left, and only Simon's glare shushed them.

In the foyer, Callista handed Cerberus to a servant. "Please feed and water him."

Colleen Shannon

Then she hurried for the stairs. A familiar voice made her turn.

"Ah, dear child, you are looking . . . well this evening." Dr. Samuel Johnson handed his hat and cane to a servant, who discreetly disappeared. The redoubtable doctor was dressed conservatively in his usual long black coat and white linen shirt, but he wore an intricate cravat for a change, and his dress shoes boasted silver buckles. His blue gaze appraised her daring gown with a blend of disapproval and appreciation that brought the roses back to her cheeks.

However, she would make no excuses. Callista went toward him, her hands outstretched. "I am taking your advice, sir. And I am honored that you came. Do you plan to game with us?"

He took her hands, squeezing them with his own trembling but self-assured ones, and released them. "I confess I wish I had learned years ago. It is not the games of chance that draw me, child, but the opportunity of good company and good argument."

"Of that we have plenty," said Drake from the doorway.

Callista turned to glare at him.

Johnson smiled. "Ah, the Dragon. Now why am I not surprised to see you here?"

Drake came forward, patting his pocket. Chips clinked together. "The house rules are fair, sir, if you wish to challenge Lady Luck in such potentially ruinous sport."

Johnson snorted. "Balderdash. Who is ruined by gaming? You will not find six instances in an age. There is a strange rout made about deep play; whereas you have many more people ruined by adventurous trade, and yet we do not hear such an outcry against it."

The Gentle Beast

Drake had the grace to shift his feet uneasily at the thrust.

Callista gave her nemisis a meaningful look. "Too true, Dr. Johnson. Mr. Drake Herrick excels at both."

Johnson glanced between the two tense figures. He smiled slightly, but before he could reply, a new arrival banged on the door. Callista waved away the servant and opened it herself. She blanched when she saw the man standing there.

How dare he come here, bold as you please?

"Well?" John Wilkes snapped. "Are you going to let me in?"

Obviously he had not forgotten their last meeting any more than she had. Callista stood back reluctantly.

Wilkes entered. He, too, sported a black coat, but his laces were of the finest and fanciest. He hesitated slightly at the sight of Johnson, who looked at him with curiosity.

"Good evening, Drake," Wilkes said. "Are you going to introduce me to England's most revered writer?" When Callista didn't offer to take his cape, he tossed it over a hallway chair.

"You have the advantage of me, sir," said Johnson, glancing at Drake. "Who is this fellow?" But Johnson's eyes were puzzled, as if he knew he should recognize the man.

Wilkes had been in the papers often enough. Callista searched desperately for a way to deny him entrance, but could think of none.

Drake, apparently, was not happy to see Wilkes either. He sent him an angry look, but he replied politely, "Dr. Samuel Johnson, meet Mr. John Wilkes."

Johnson gasped. His cheeks reddened.

Uh-oh, Callista thought. The two men had attacked one another in their published works, and surely two

263

more different individuals could not occupy the same space.

Johnson, the Tory; Wilkes, the liberal. Johnson, the loyal Englishman; Wilkes, the rebellious patriot.

Despite the firmness of his opinions, Johnson was always a gentleman, Callista knew, and he loved little so much as a good argument, as he often admitted himself. Wilkes, on the other hand, would want to curry favor with one of England's greatest intellectuals.

Abruptly Callista's panic eased. Wilkes would be too busy trying to impress Johnson to implicate Drake. Callista said sweetly, "I believe Mr. Wilkes is an admirer of the Americans, Dr. Johnson." She gave Wilkes a challenging look.

He glowered at her, and then glanced at Dr. Johnson, holding his breath.

Johnson's expression hardened. "He is welcome to his opinion, of course. But for me, well, I am willing to love all mankind—except an American. They are a race of convicts and ought to be thankful for anything we allow them short of hanging."

Wilkes cleared his throat. "Yes, well, virtue and vice are sometimes indistinguishable unless one is in possession of all the facts. And those are still being written in the colonies. Be that as it may, would you care to continue this discussion over dinner?"

Callista had not even heard the supper bell, so intent had she been on the pair.

Johnson brightened. His love of food and drink was well known. He waved Wilkes ahead of him. When the man's back was turned, Johnson wrinkled his nose at Callista and whispered in her ear, "If he does really think that there is no distinction between virtue and vice, why, ma'am, when he leaves your house, you

The Gentle Beast

should count your spoons." But he followed willingly enough as Wilkes waited for him.

When they were out of earshot, Callista couldn't contain her laughter anymore. "He has the sharpest wit of anyone I have ever known. He is simply delightful."

"And so are you. Too much so, in that dress." Drake's disapproval was stark in his voice. "I should cover you up—"

"Until you unwrap me for your own delectation?" Callista said sweetly. "But I have not given you leave." She turned to exit.

An iron-hard but gentle hand manacled her wrist. "You shall." Drake bent his head until his breath stirred the hair at her temples. "Now let us dine, ere I give in to my urge to sample that delicious expanse of skin you offer up for my enjoyment."

Callista pulled away. "You know your way about, I believe." She was pleased to see his mouth drop open in slack surprise.

She strode for the stairs, only to find herself pulled willy-nilly into an empty coat closet. The door snapped shut, trapping her in darkness scented with woolens, wax—and aroused male.

Callista tried to squeeze past him to the door, but he only pulled her against him.

"Now tell me what you mean by that remark. Do you finally know who I am?"

Callista wished she'd held her tongue, but he was enough to taunt a stone. At first she did not answer, but when he squeezed her tighter she gasped, "Yes."

She felt his immediate tension.

"And . . . do you hate me for it?"

Should she lie? Somehow the words that tumbled to her lips were inspired by a force more powerful than fear. "I could never hate you. I lie awake nights won-

dering what horrible pain you suffered, to leave you scarred like that. I waver between longing to come to you and the knowledge that the enmity between our families is too deep for us to overcome. Oh Drake, I . . ." Callista buried her face in his coat.

The big hand that stroked her shoulders trembled. "Shh. Someday I will tell you. For now just let me hold you."

And there, in the coat closet, Callista took comfort from the one man who had all but ruined her life. They did not kiss; they did not speak.

They just shared the warmth of their humanity like two souls hungering for a truth yet denied them.

The door opened. A shocked servant stood back in surprise, a greatcoat in his hands. Callista drew away, too embarrassed to look at Drake, and fled up the stairs.

She felt his gaze boring into her back, but she knew he would make some facile excuse to the servant. She slammed the bedchamber door behind her, and looked about at what had obviously been the master bedroom.

The bed, of the old, hulking Elizabethan style, would surely hold an army. The hangings were threadbare, but had once been burgundy silk embroidered with gold. The gold silk drapes at the windows were still handsome, as was the oriental carpet underfoot. Callista tried to picture Drake being conceived in that bed, but the image was beyond her.

She was bathing her flushed cheeks in fresh water before the full import of his identity struck her. "You nodcock!"

If he was indeed Bryant Kimball's son, they had bought this house under false pretenses, from an heir who had no right to sell it. Weakly, Callista sat down on the edge of the bed. Dear God, was this part of his

grand plan, too? To let them sink their last farthing in this place, come forward and prove his identity, then take it all away? Feeling queasy, Callista cupped her stomach.

No, surely his hatred was not that strong, not if he had an iota of feeling for her. His vengeance had already all but ruined them.

Ever honest, Callista logically voiced the opposite argument: their pound of flesh would become a ton ere they could make restitution for what Henry had done to an innocent young boy. What terrible trials had turned that sheltered young lad into the grim and horrible Dragon? Mayhap one day he would tell her. If she could bear to listen.

Callista's muddled emotions fogged her wits. She could not return to the tables in such a state. Blowing out all but one candle, she lifted her feet on the bed and lay back. She'd slept so poorly of late. Perhaps if she closed her eyes just for a moment . . .

She was asleep on the thought.

Drake whirled away from the bottom of the stairs and stomped into supper. Why did she always flee just when they were making progress? He was hopeful at the fact that she knew who he was, yet still seemed to care for him. That tender exchange in the closet had shaken him to his evening slippers.

He groped his way to the dining salon, glad when Clyde joined him outside the door. Clyde took one look at his face, then pulled Drake to a side chair against the wall. "What's amiss?"

Drake looked about. For the moment they were alone. "Callista knows who I am."

Clyde sighed in relief. "We are almost at an end with this comedy of errors, then. When do you take the

house back?" He waited with ill-concealed impatience as Drake did not answer immediately. Clyde's expression was expectant, as if he waited to hear longed-for words.

Drake stared at the atrocious wallpaper of puce-and-maroon stripe that now overlay the Wedgwood blue-and-cream stripe of his youth. He doubted Callista had chosen it, for her taste seemed impeccable. He visualized her shivering in Summerlea, with no money to fix the crumbling roof. "I . . . I had intended to, this very night."

Now where had that answer come from? Victory was in his grasp. This very moment, if he chose, he could make Stanton the untouchable that Drake had been in his youth.

As he struggled with himself, serenity settled over Clyde's battered face. He had removed the mask when he came into the dim hallway, and he flung it aside now as if he could not bear the weight upon his face. "Never mind, lad. You shall do what is right, in the end. Shall we dine? It seems an age since I last ate. I am hungry for the first time in a long time. If I eat, I will not have to make explanations about this ugly face." Clyde rose and went inside the dining salon.

Drake followed slowly, still rattled enough to jump in the food line when a familiar voice said with a sneer, "I am surprised our humble entertainments appeal to you." Quartermain, with Henry at his side, glanced at Drake's plate full of Scottish salmon, Yorkshire pudding, peas, and apple tarts. He could not hide his satisfied smirk at the sight of Clyde's battered face.

Drake took a deliberate bite, chewed, and swallowed at his leisure before answering, "Tolerable, Quartermain. But your chef put a wee bit too much salt in the pudding. Would you care for me to send mine to give

The Gentle Beast

him better instruction?" Drake didn't have a chef. He and Clyde subsisted on much simpler fare than this, but his enemies didn't need to know that.

Quartermain stiffened. Henry only looked even more weary. Drake's gaze sharpened on that haggard face. Henry looked as if a strong wind would prostrate him. Drake told himself he was glad, but he could only remember the love in Callista's eyes when she looked at her stepfather.

The man in line behind Drake backed up, making room for Quartermain and Henry. Drake finished loading his plate, then looked about for a table. He spied Johnson in animated conversation with Wilkes. Wilkes beckoned to him.

Drake hesitated. The less concourse he had with Wilkes, especially in the current company, the better. On the other hand, Drake couldn't afford to be rude. Aware that Quartermain watched, Drake mentally cursed the fellow and sat down next to Johnson, across from Wilkes.

Clyde had to find another table and was soon drawn into conversation with an old man holding a speaking horn.

Johnson glanced at Drake and continued his conversation with Wilkes. "Indeed, I argue with my friend Boswell often about the Scots. I shall take him to a provincial town and show him genuine civilized life; for you know, he lives among savages in Scotland, and among rakes in London."

Wilkes smiled and responded, "Except when he is with grave, sober, decent people like you and me." Wilkes shoved the butter dish to Johnson before the good doctor had time to reach for it.

Johnson responded with a straight face. "And we ashamed of him, libertine that he is."

Drake and Wilkes laughed at his sly wink. A more moral, upstanding citizen than Doctor Johnson would be difficult to find, but he enjoyed a good time as much as the next man and numbered several rakes among his friends. Boswell, one of his closest companions, was known for keeping low company.

Drake was intrigued to note that Johnson's behavior had definitely mellowed toward Wilkes. Of course, the wine and good food had aided that endeavor. Drake doubted that either had changed his political persuasion, or ever would.

Complacently, Johnson slathered butter on his bread.

"More of that delicious salmon, Doctor?" Wilkes asked. "I shall be happy to fetch you some."

"Not at the moment, thank you, sir."

Quartermain sat down at the table. Drake didn't glance at him, even when the ill-mannered fellow's elbow butted into his. Henry set down his full plate, looked at it, held a hand to his mouth, and hurried off.

Drake stared after him, but Quartermain didn't even watch his partner leave. Drake nibbled on a bite of salmon. Henry was obviously ill. Drake was torn between delight and concern that God would finish him before the Dragon could. From somewhere came the rogue thought that Callista would be devastated if Henry died. Drake shoved it away, along with his plate.

Now Wilkes and Johnson discussed Shakespeare. Quartermain interjected, "Yes, yes, he's a ruddy giant and all that, but let us discuss something of import— such as these *Letters of Junius*. What think you of those, Mr. Wilkes?"

Johnson's mouth tightened at the rude interruption, but he only waited politely for Wilkes's response.

Wilkes shrugged. "I cannot say that I am not in sym-

The Gentle Beast

pathy with the cause espoused by the *Letters*, given that a Commons seat was thrice denied me by the high-handedness of one man. The means, however, may be questionable."

Drake hid a smile in his napkin. Indeed, the Commons lost a powerful legislator when Wilkes was denied his seat. He was a master at the subtlety of politicking.

Quartermain glanced in triumph at Johnson, expecting him to object. That gentleman, however, merely commented obliquely, "One's position on equality and democracy can really be answered by a simple test. I posed the following question to Mrs. Macaulay: If she is really so zealously fair, will she allow her footman to sit down with us? I know her answer, but as to yours . . . Tell me, Mr. Wilkes, Mr. Quartermain, do either of you dine with your servants?"

Both men shook their heads.

Johnson looked at Drake.

Drake smiled. "I dine with my servant all the time." Drake glanced at Clyde, who was shouting into the old man's ear trumpet. The old man cackled. Indeed, without Clyde's calm good sense, Drake would have been dead many times past. It was Drake who should be honored to dine with Clyde.

Quartermain followed Drake's gaze, then shifted in his seat. Drake turned on Quartermain, holding that blue gaze for a long time. He knew Quartermain took the warning: Threaten Clyde again at your peril.

Johnson looked curious at the byplay, but he only nodded at Drake. "Then you, sir, are a true proponent of democracy. As for these arguments, they are sophistry if they are not backed up by deeds." Johnson rose. "Now excuse me, gentlemen, but my bed calls."

Wilkes rose. "May I walk you out, sir?"

"Not a'tall. I am not in my dotage yet. Go ply your talents at the tables." Johnson nodded shortly at Quartermain. "Good evening. Please give your hostess my best." Under cover of folding his napkin, Johnson subtly crooked a finger at Drake.

Drake rose and followed him. On his way out, Johnson saw Simon ogling him in fascination. An indulgent smile flickered about Johnson's full lips. He stopped. "Do I know you, lad?"

Simon blushed. "No sir. But I am a great admirer of yours."

"Well, let's remedy the situation. I am—"

"Doctor Samuel Johnson, lexicographer, writer beyond compare." Simon snapped his mouth closed and went even redder, obviously embarrassed by his own effusive praise.

"You flatter me, lad. But I shall visit from time to time. You shall have ample opportunity to revise your opinion."

"It can only grow, sir." Simon scampered off, obviously tickled to have met the great man himself.

On the stoop, Johnson sighed with mixed envy and weariness. "Ah, the enthusiasm of youth." He arrowed a glance at Drake. "Not to mention the passion. 'Tis none of my concern, but that never stops me . . . that fellow Quartermain wishes you ill. But I suspect you know that. And he is ruthless, as only an ill-bred fellow can be. There is the whiff of the stables about him, despite the airs he puts on."

"I shall be careful. But I appreciate your concern."

While Johnson waited for his carriage, he appraised Drake's tall figure. "Damn, you are a strapping lad. No wonder the Lady Callista finds you irresistible. But when will you have done with these foolish masks?"

"When the time is right."

The Gentle Beast

Johnson pulled his collar up against the night air. "I only hope I am present to see it."

Drake bowed. "I am flattered at your interest."

"Do not roast me, lad. Now get yourself back in there and press your suit with the lady. Doubtless half the men present will take your place if given the chance."

Drake grinned and helped Johnson up into his carriage. "That is a very big *if*, sir, as I know from personal experience. But I shall persevere."

Johnson banged his door shut. "I never doubted it, lad. Good evening." The carriage drove off, a pudgy white hand waving out the window.

Drake searched the busy card rooms for Callista, but she was not to be found. However, he found Henry sitting, white faced, in a shadowy corner. Drake hesitated, but no one else seemed to be paying Henry any mind.

Drake paused before his old enemy. "Shall I fetch the doctor for you, Stanton?"

Henry sat straighter, then struggled to his feet. "Dash it, do you think me a fool, to put myself under the tender mercies of any sawbones you might select? Go on about your nefarious vengeance. I wish you joy of it." Henry shuffled off, but his peruked head was high.

Drake sighed. For an instant he just wished to have done with this—but only for an instant. Determined, Drake strode back into the supper room, filled a plate with the best delicacies, and broached the stairs.

The bare patches on the walls where priceless paintings had once hung tormented him, but he knew his wastrel cousin had long since sold the best art. Callista and Henry had done a good job of concealing the house's disrepair, but the new paint and wallpaper could not disguise the sagging walls and loose floorboards. Thousands of pounds needed to be spent before this

mansion could recapture its faded glory.

Soon, Drake promised himself.

Unerringly, as if some peculiar magnetism drew him, he turned down the upstairs corridor to the master bedroom. A red mist swam before his eyes as he reached the solid oak door. He tried to find the knob, but then he had to lean against the door and let the memories take him.

It had been more than twenty years since he'd stood here. The last time had been the morning before he left with his father for India. Durwood Alistair Kimball, nicknamed Drake by his father in homage to the great English explorer Francis Drake, had burst into the room without knocking. As he always did, he leaped upon the bed with his father, who lay there reading the paper.

"Be still, lad. You'll tip over my tea." Bryant Kimball calmly drained his cup and set it aside. "Are you eager to see the ocean?"

"Can I help in the rigging, Father?"

"Nay, a Kimball commands a ship. He does not sail it." Bryant stiffened as he saw a small announcement. "The blackguard! They do not suit. Just let me return from this deuced voyage, and I shall win her despite herself. Her parents will never choose Stanton, a younger son, over me."

Drake had frowned and read the small print. It announced the details of a ball, where a couple, Henry Stanton and Mary Raleigh, had scandalized the ton by dancing more than the customary two dances.

Drake had met Mary twice, on visits to her country estate with his father. She was a lovely woman, and she had the most adorable daughter, a toddler with shining red hair who reminded Drake of a little doll, she was so perfect. Drake had looked forward to the

time when she was his sister, as his father had promised.

The black scowl on his father's strong face scared Drake. Whenever Bryant Kimball wore that look, servants scrambled and aristocrats cowered. Bryant had never laid a hand on Drake; the power of that look was enough punishment. To see it now was proof of his father's feelings for Mary Raleigh. The ten-year-old boy he had been then was dismayed that his strong, aloof father could be at such sixes and sevens over a mere woman, no matter how pretty.

However, the thirty-year-old man understood exactly how strong was the allure of a beautiful woman. In a problematic present, Drake stood there, one hand on the knob, one hand balancing the plate, caught in a morass of his own making. He did not know if he could ever forgive Henry Stanton, or put a period to the man's existence as he deserved. Either course would have consequences.

One thing he did know: as usual, Clyde was right.

Blood did tell. It was the lot of the Kimball men to be fascinated by the Raleigh women. He only hoped his own romance would know a happier ending.

Or, better yet, a new beginning.

Drake shoved open the door. "Callista, I . . ." He trailed off with a gasp when he saw her. He forgot the door was open, he forgot his rage at Henry, he forgot the house full of people. The plate teetered. Only when pea juice ran down his hand did he remember it. He caught the plate just in time. Then, holding his breath, wondering if she would disappear like a dream denied, he inched toward the bed and set the plate down on the night table.

She lay on her side. Her intricate hairstyle had come loose in her sleep, and waves of living flame lapped at

the bedcovers, singeing a path almost to the floor. The dress was twisted about her hips, baring both long legs to the knee. The excuse for a bodice was strained to the limit by the bounteous flesh begging for release. He'd reached out to comply when the sight of his own shaky hand disgusted him. It dropped to his side.

The vision of this one woman in his ancestral bed inspired feelings he could scarce understand, much less master. She belonged here. She was meant to be his, to conceive and to bear his children in this bed.

Before or after he killed her stepfather?

Drake clenched his hands in denial, but no matter the path or byway, every road led to this juncture. His steps had been so sure and easy at first. Now his way was crowded by obstacles of every imaginable sort. Whichever way he turned seemed wrong. And his former eternal guide, the righteous sword of vengeance, had turned upon him.

He could hardly trust his own feelings, much less hers.

He consumed her with a last sweeping gaze. Then he forced himself to go to the door. He opened it wider. The old hinges creaked loudly. He froze, hoping she wouldn't awaken to see him slinking away like a bashful boy. He glanced at her over his shoulder.

She stirred, yawning. Her eyelashes fluttered, and then rose. She stared at him without blinking. Her welcoming smile almost blinded him with its beauty.

"I dreamed of you."

No power on earth could have kept him on his course then. He went back to her side, bending on one knee to caress her flushed, velvety cheek. "Did you, dear one? I am glad."

She kissed the back of his hand. Male laughter drifted up from downstairs. He saw the change in her

The Gentle Beast

expression as she recalled herself to where she was—and why. She tried to sit up, but he gently pushed her back. "Have you heard the old French fable about the beauty and the beast?"

She looked away. He saw that she had, but he whispered in her ear, "I have often thought how well the tale suits our relationship. Will you release the curse upon me, my beauty, and make me into a prince with the power of your love?"

She drew back. He wanted to assuage the deep sadness in her eyes, but he knew he had been the one to put it there.

She said, "It is not my love that will change you, Drake, but your own. For yourself; for the life we could have together . . ." Her voice slowly faded. ". . . for an old, sick man who regrets the misdeeds of youth."

As usual, she had a devilish knack for cutting to the heart of a matter. Since he didn't know how to respond, he offered her the plate. "I thought you might be hungry."

She nodded her thanks and balanced the plate on her lap. "Is Dr. Johnson gone?"

"Yes, he left after a most interesting dinner."

Callista wrinkled her nose. "I can imagine." She smashed a pea on the back of her knife. "Doubtless Wilkes fawned over him."

"Not to the point that he would not speak his mind."

"He is a disgusting sycophant. When it suits him." Callista nibbled a bit of ham.

"I call him practical. Johnson makes a better ally than an enemy and he quite relaxed before his plate was empty, which took some time, considering how often Wilkes helped him fill it." Drake's lips quirked in a wry smile. "Wilkes can be charming when he chooses, but nothing will ever make Johnson into a

liberal, or Wilkes into a Tory."

"And has Wilkes charmed you, too? Is that why you help him?" Callista studied her plate.

He sensed her acute attention to his answer. After a glance out at the empty hallway, he said quietly, "If you ask if I still aid him in the other way, the answer is no. Not since the other night, when he retrieved his possessions. He says I am no longer useful, since my lair has been discovered. And frankly I was weary of his constant demands. I have aided his cause because I believed in his goals, not the man himself. I knew from the beginning that his first priority was his own political ambition."

She went limp with obvious relief. "Thank God."

He took the plate away and set it on the floor. "Were you worried about me?"

She opened her mouth to lie, then snapped it shut. "Someone has to be. Forge ahead, devil take the hindmost, should be your motto instead of 'What I have, I hold.'" She bit her lip as he suited his actions to her words, pulling her firmly into his arms.

"Actually, at the moment I much prefer the latter motto. You are most pleasing to hold." He lowered his head, but she turned her face away so that his lips only grazed her cheek.

"Release me. I must go back below before I am missed." But her protest was weak, and he knew she enjoyed being in his arms as much as he enjoyed holding her.

He tried a bantering air. "But I only wanted you to thank me properly for rejecting Wilkes."

"Thank you. I much prefer your neck the length it is."

He brought his mouth a hairbreadth away from hers. "Give me a proper thank-you and I will let you go

back to those cursed ogling bucks."

She stiffened slightly, but he was encouraged when she allowed him to pull her arms about his neck. Her eyes met his steadily. Those eyes would haunt him to his death and beyond. Green they were, like new hope, like the ivy that twined around this house, rooting him to the soil of home.

This home he carried with him.

For where she went, he followed.

The simple truths shook him to his marrow. Murmuring endearments, he kissed her eyelids to break the power of that gaze. He only exchanged the sensory power of sight for the stronger force of touch. Every inch of her pleased him and teased him. She was silk and satin and living velvet, from the arms that twined about his neck, to the hair that fell over his hands. He grasped it, pulling her head back.

She sighed, whether in surrender or denial he did not know. When their lips met, the unceasing questions were swamped in a deluge of physical pleasure. His heart accelerated, his skin tingled, and blood engorged his privates. He pulled her closer, keeping his hands still on the silk of her back lest he lose control. Now was not the time, or the place. . . .

But when her shy tongue flitted into his mouth, he groaned. If not now, when? demanded his loins. He slanted his mouth firmly over hers to thrust his tongue deep, teaching her the prelude to the dance of passion. He was lowering her to the bed when an angry voice penetrated the fog of passion.

"You blackguard! Get away from her!" Henry Stanton lifted his cane to whack it over Drake's shoulders.

Drake winced and used his arm to block the second blow. He surged to his feet, but Callista beat him to Henry's side. She jerked the cane away.

"Stop it! He did nothing I did not allow." When Drake waited expectantly, she blushed but admitted, "Indeed, I encouraged him."

"Must I tell you again who he is, what he has done to us?" Henry cried.

Drake gasped. He'd assumed Callista had made the familial connection on her own. Instead, Henry had confessed it. Drake had never dreamed Henry would admit his villainy to anyone, least of all to his cherished daughter. Drake looked at Henry with new eyes. Perhaps I do not understand Henry Stanton, Earl of Swanlea, as thoroughly as I thought, he reflected. He had to force his attention back to the argument between father and daughter.

"How can I forget? Neither of you will let me." Callista clasped her stepfather's stiff shoulder. "Please, have done with this. Enough anger and hatred."

She turned to Drake. "And you. I . . . I . . ." She took a deep breath. "I admit I love you dearly." When he took a triumphant, joyous step toward her, she held up her hand. Henry closed his eyes in denial, but for the moment Drake held her attention.

"The two of you are tearing me apart. I cannot love one without loving the other. Without Henry, Drake, I would not be the woman I am."

She kissed Henry's cheek. "And without Drake, dearest Henry, I will never be the woman I could be." She caught Henry's hand; then she caught Drake's and brought the two together.

Drake hesitated. Those eyes a man had died for pinned him where he stood, leaving this final choice up to him. Callista stepped back.

Henry's hand rested limply on top of Drake's. Drake could not clasp it, but he didn't move away either. Revenge, the lodestone of his adult life, pulled at him, but

The Gentle Beast

Callista's pull was sun to earth and moon. Slowly Drake's hand began to tighten in the truce.

Henry pulled away. "No! Never will there be peace 'tween us as long as he persecutes me and mine." Henry looked away from Callista's disappointment and implacably faced his enemy. "You are a base coward, too afraid even to show your face. How can I trust you?"

Drake went to the bedroom door, closed it, and leaned against it. "You know who I am, Henry Stanton, Earl of Swanlea, murderer, but if you want proof . . ." Drake reached behind his head for the mask strings.

Callista covered her gasp with her hands, her eyes huge as he slowly lowered the mask.

Stanton paled to an ashen hue. "Dear God, you're the image of Bryant."

"Why do you think I have gone to such elaborate precautions?" Drake smiled into Callista's wondering eyes. "See, dear one, I am neither deformed nor horrible, as I know you feared."

Mesmerized, Callista stepped forward. She cupped his cheek and ran her fingers over his face as she had once before. Save this time, it was not dark. This time, her eyes tracked where her hands led her, over the high cheekbones, broken nose, and arched brows. "Like your father, you are not handsome. But dear God, you're strong. And your eyes. I have never seen eyes of such a blue."

They were so intent on one another that Henry's distress was slow to impinge upon them. But when he began to wheeze, Callista whirled. She caught him as he fell. Drake helped her get Henry to the bed.

Henry's staring eyes remained fixed on Drake's face. "Always . . . knew . . . the dashed tyrant would come back to . . . haunt . . ." His breath hissed. His body

went slack as his eyes closed.

Callista cried out and patted Henry's cheeks in a panic, but Drake took his enemy's pulse. He frowned. "Too fast. I shall fetch my doctor."

"Henry would want his own."

"It is your decision, but Hassan is the best doctor in England, I assure you."

Callista's eyes filled with tears. She looked at the still figure on the bed, then back at Drake. She stared in fascination at the compelling features, the cobalt blue eyes that a woman could gladly drown in.

He smiled. "I promise not to torment him further until he's on his feet again."

Callista nodded. "Go. Please hurry."

Drake tied his mask back on and hurried out.

Callista caught Henry's hands. "Please, Henry, hold on. I will always love you, no matter what."

Even if he came between her and Drake. She could not quite state the words, but she knew them to be true. As to the opposite, whether Henry would still love her even if she chose his enemy, Callista could not say.

"Dear Lord, do not let it come to that," she prayed. Bowing her head, Callista fell to her knees and clasped Henry's hands tighter, trying to pull him back to the light of consciousness.

In the wee hours of the morning, after the hell had closed, Henry was resting comfortably. The strange doctor, who had an odd singsong way of talking, had mixed some foul-smelling potion and forced it down Henry's throat; then he spread a salve on Henry's chest. The tortured breathing and rapid heartbeat finally eased.

Callista changed into the comfortable muslin Marian sent her and settled down for a long night. Henry's

color was better. Callista brought her feet up in the chair and clasped her arms about them, contemplating life's ironies.

Drake had devoted his adult life to ruining this man, yet in Henry's hour of need, Drake had done all he could to save him. Were the Dragon's purposes so vile that he wanted to make Henry suffer more? Or, as her eager heart bade her to hope, was Drake at last seeing the folly of vengeance? After all, he could come forward anytime now and make his claim on this house and all in it, yet he had not.

Callista closed her eyes, trying to sleep, but the image of that blessed face could not be blocked. The fading scar from Drake's brow to his high cheekbone only emphasized the indomitable will of a man who asked and gave no quarter. Yet she had often felt the gentleness in him. Whatever his feelings for the daughter of Henry Stanton, he had not used her when he had had the chance, as most men of his class and reputation would have.

Indubitably, his actions toward her were not those of a man who hated. Perhaps, in some small measure, he returned her regard? A soft smile upon her lips, she drifted off to a land where a fierce dragon guarded an earl's fiefdom. Here the lion lay down with the lamb, and the princess turned the dragon into a prince with her love. . . .

A less pleasant reality jolted her awake. Arguing male voices floated up from the entry.

She recognized Quartermain's voice first. "Get the hell off my property! You and your manservant are not welcome here—"

"I shall let Callista be the judge of that." Drake's voice was quiet, but anger bubbled under the surface.

"M'sister ain't in no condition to judge anything.

You've bewitched her," Simon said.

Clyde's voice came next. "Only one being can judge us. And surely you credit us for bringing Hassan here? He is far better than these English butchers you call physicians—"

"A blasted savage, that's all he is," Quartermain said. "Now get out before we throw you out."

"Can't stand to look at your handiwork, is that it? You barely glanced at him last night. Take a good look, and we shall see if even you do not have a conscience." Drake said quietly, "Come into the light, Clyde. Mayhap it's time to wake Callista, too."

"Come one step nearer, you bastard, and you shall regret it," Quartermain blustered.

On her way to the door, Callista paused. Creeping dread overtook her. Something was not right here.

"What does he mean, Alex?" Simon asked.

"I haven't the faintest notion."

But Callista recognized the smooth lie. She hurried to the door, frantic to see what Quartermain had done now.

Quartermain stood, his back to her, on the bottom step of the stairway, blocking it with both hands on the balustrades. Simon faced Drake and Clyde, who had both obviously just come in.

Her slippers quiet, Callista inched down the stairs, trying to get a better understanding of what had transpired. She was only three steps away when Clyde looked up, his face in the brutal glow of the lanterns by the door.

Callista gasped, catching the attention of all.

She ran the last few steps, pushing Quartermain's shielding arm away, to get a closer look at Clyde. The dear man's face looked like a tenderized side of beef. Scrapes and cuts were layered over puffy bruises that

The Gentle Beast

ranged in hue from black to sickly yellow. And his hands were bandaged.

"What happened to you, Clyde?" She had a feeling she would not like the answer.

Clyde hesitated. He glanced at Drake.

"Tell her, if you wish," Drake said quietly.

"I was kidnapped and taken to Whitefriars, where I was beaten."

"By whom?"

Clyde shrugged, but his blue eyes were not kind, for once, as he looked at Quartermain. Callista closed her eyes in disgust.

Quartermain blustered, "You surely do not connect me with this foul deed. Why, I was with Simon this time three nights ago. . . ." He trailed off sharply as all peered at him.

"We did not tell you when it happened," Drake said gently. "Not that I would credit you with enough courage to do the deed yourself."

Quartermain stiffened.

Simon shifted his feet, bursting out, "But why were you taken?"

Clyde hesitated. "For information."

"Let me guess," Callista said. "About the Dragon and his politics."

"Among other things." Clyde watched Callista's brows lower over her darkening eyes, and added hastily, "But I am much better. Thanks to Drake and Hassan."

"He got you out," Callista stated. "That's why he was mussed and dirty the other night."

"At considerable risk to himself. But it would not be the first time." Clyde glanced with affection at his employer.

Colleen Shannon

Simon looked confused. "But what has this to do with us?"

"You idiot," Callista inserted, "do you not realize yet that your dearest friend is a ruthless man who will stop at nothing, even torture and blackmail, to reach his goals?" Callista curled her lip at Quartermain's full-bore glare.

"Have a care, my dear, lest you realize just how ruthless I can be."

It was Drake's turn to stiffen. "Keep this between the two of us, Quartermain, where it belongs. If you stoop too low, you will find that I have crawled on my belly in the muck more times than you can count."

Callista waved her hand in the air. "Enough! Kindly allow me to fight my own battles."

Quartermain grabbed her hand and held it despite her attempt to pull away. "Fight? What nonsense is this? We are allies, are we not? You are only a bit ragged because of Henry's spell, right, dear Callista?"

Callista opened her mouth to retort, but Simon flung open the door. "Get out, Herrick! You expect me to believe the Dragon over one of England's greatest merchants? Your ready is not welcome here ever again."

Callista wrenched her hand away and slammed the door closed despite Simon's glare. "I have a say here, too. And I say they are welcome. We owe them courtesy, at the least, for seeing to Henry's well-being." She stalked to the parlor and pushed open the door. "It is almost breakfast time. Would you care for some tea?"

Quartermain looked as if he might explode. Instead he turned away and slammed out of the house.

Simon watched him go. Then he shook his head at his sister. "Kiss this bastard's boots if you will, but not I. Alex is worth ten of him." Simon followed Quartermain.

The Gentle Beast

Weak from the ugly scene and lack of rest, Callista caught herself against the door. Drake hurried forward to help her to a seat inside the parlor.

"I am sorry. I should have stayed away until Henry was better. But Clyde asked to see you, to help explain. . . ." Drake bit his lip and averted his head.

This uncertainty was so unlike him that Callista looked at Clyde for an explanation.

"Now that you know who he is, you deserve to know why," Clyde said simply. "Every act of the Dragon was set into motion twenty years ago by your stepfather."

Callista surged to her feet, her face white. "No! I cannot listen to this. Not now. Perhaps not ever." To hear the details would tear her apart. Not because of Henry's evil deed; because she could not face the brutality Drake had suffered.

Drake, too, rose. He slammed the parlor door closed with his boot and ripped off his mask. "Do you think this is any easier for me? But we cannot go forward until we go back, so you can understand."

Callista turned away. For weeks she'd wished to see the man behind the mask, but she had not bargained for the power of eyes that were bluer than sapphires, deeper than oceans. "I understand all too well. You repay a wrong with a wrong."

Drake growled and stepped toward her, but Clyde was there first. "My child, you must listen."

Callista whirled on him. "Why? Do you not think I am tormented by what happened to him? I have seen his scars. I have . . . felt them." Callista's anguished tone faded. "Not a day passes that my fears don't follow me into my nightmares."

"And so it is for me. But my fear is of losing you." Drake stood tall as he made the damning admission,

as if he realized he made himself vulnerable and accepted it.

Joy fluttered its hopeful wings in Callista's heart. "Then go with me. Now, to tell Henry you forgive him."

Drake closed his eyes in pain. She saw the battle in his strong face, and it was not a pretty one. His hand reached out to her, then dropped to his side. His eyes opened. The man who looked at her now was not the gentle man of her dreams.

The Dragon stood there, his face Bryant Kimball's face, his resolve Kimball's legacy. "I cannot."

Callista ran for the door. So far away, it seemed, in the blurry wash of her tears. Too far, for his tall figure blocked it.

"Sit down."

When she stood there biting her lip, her face averted, he escorted her to the nearest chair and pushed her down. "Let me have my say. When I am done, if you wish me to leave and never see you again"—he took a deep breath and finished in a rush—"I will do as you ask." He bent one arm upon the mantel and picked up the dragon-headed andiron. He stared at it for so long that Callista looked up.

From his expression, she knew he was remembering his father in this same position. Like a hunted animal, she glanced at the door. The mysteries she'd pondered for so long were about to be revealed.

She would give five years of her life if she did not have to hear them. Once she knew the facts, hope would perish. No power on earth could overcome the sick hatred Drake still held toward Henry.

But Drake's movements were so unwontedly agitated that she steeled herself to listen. This, she owed him. Let him have his say, and they could be done with each other and return to the gray reality each had

known before the rainbow of possibilities led them on this fool's quest.

She folded her hands in her lap and forced herself to listen.

Chapter Eleven

Drake stirred the embers and added more wood. He warmed his hands at the blaze as if he, too, were chilled. Then, the fire highlighting the strong planes of his countenance, he turned sideways to stare at a spot over her head.

"I will not trouble you with the details of my childhood, but it was, for the most part, a happy one. I remember little of my mother, save that my father grew more stern with every year after her passing. Until he met Mary Raleigh."

Callista stiffened. With a will of its own, her gaze fixed on his face. He was not looking at her, as if this baring of his soul were as painful for him to say as for her to listen to.

His blue eyes were focused on distant horizons as he said softly, "I remember her well. She looked much like you, but she was softer, rounder, and always laughing. She made my father laugh as no one else could. He

The Gentle Beast

had received her father's permission to wed her when she met Henry Stanton—my father's junior partner in an East India venture. Supposedly his best friend." He was suddenly eager. "Do you remember me at all, from those years?"

She could only shake her head.

His shrug could not mask his disappointment. "When I told you that first night we met at Summerlea that you looked like your mother, I still carried in my head the picture of you as a baby. You were all sass and joy, with a flaming head of hair and eyes as green as the best the earth could offer. I used to bounce you on my knee and look forward to the day I could claim you as my sister."

"But Henry never said anything—"

A harsh laugh cut her off. "Doubtless he feared to utter the name Kimball, lest questions be asked. He wanted all memory of me and my father to be buried at sea with our ship. But I digress. I did not know it then, but Henry Stanton's first venture into my life would follow an ugly pattern: what we had, he wanted. First your mother and you. Then the Yellow Rose. And finally our lives."

The ugly facts were too bare for Callista. She covered her ears, for she could not reconcile her kind stepfather with the venal weakling who had done this. She loved both of these men. How could he . . .

Drake stepped up to her and gently but inexorably pulled her hands away. "Listen, for I say this only once. My father did not know it on the morning we left for the Indies, but Henry had already coaxed your mother into running off to Gretna Green with him. As a wedding present, Henry gave her the Yellow Rose, which he had stolen from my father. They had argued over the distribution of funds from several voyages. Doubt-

less Henry, as a second son with few funds, was jealous of my father's wealth and greater portion of the profits. So when the jewel my father had purchased from an Indian potentate arrived, Henry pocketed it and claimed it did not come in with the cargo."

"But how do you know all this? If this is just hearsay—"

Those bitter eyes cut her off. "Henry's best agent in India led the supposed pirate attack against our ship. He taunted my father with all these facts before he killed him. My father died shielding me. He blocked the cabin door with his body as they broke it open." For the first time Drake faltered. He rubbed his index finger and thumb over his eyelids as if they burned. "My father saw what was happening and blockaded us in our cabin. He hugged me, told me to remember always that I was a Kimball. To take back and hold for future generations what was stolen from us. As the cabin door began to buckle, he asked me to vow that I would make Henry Stanton pay for this betrayal. And he told me what I had to do to survive."

Despite herself, Callista was on the edge of her seat. When he paused, she said, "What was that?" How could a little boy survive such a superior force?

"I jumped into the sea as they broke in. They sent a few shots after me, but I had practiced holding my breath for many years. I swam underwater to their ship, which was anchored close by. When they sent small boats after me and could find no sign, they assumed I had drowned. They stole everything of value off our ship and then burned it." His expression was proof of how vivid the memory still was to him.

Her heart raced so she could barely speak. "But how . . ."

"I climbed up their anchor chain and spent the re-

The Gentle Beast

mainder of those two days in the bilge, knee deep in nasty, salty water, rats running above my head. Luckily we docked at a small town in Arabia before I died of thirst."

The matter-of-fact way he made the comment chilled Callista to the bone. Unable to sit still, she rose to warm her hands at the fire.

"Not so luckily, two of the hired pirates caught me as I tried to slip away. They didn't know who I was, or how imperative it was that I be killed. They decided I would fetch a high price at the slave market. I was sold to a wealthy Turkish merchant. I was ten years old."

Callista grasped the mantle with both hands, bile boiling to her throat. She was not so innocent that she had not heard what strange perversions older men sometimes practiced on young boys.

"I did not make a good plaything as the man had hoped. When I always struggled against his . . . wishes, he sold me to the sultan. I was being trained as a eunuch and was about to be castrated when one of the sultan's sons took a liking to me and asked that I be his personal slave."

She was trembling now, but the dry recitation made the images in her brain that much more horrific. She sat back down weakly, her knees giving out. Dear God, she knew he'd endured something horrible, but this . . .

He fluttered his three-fingered hand. "They cut off two of my fingers when I tried to steal enough money to buy myself passage to a shipping lane where I could stow away on a ship bound for England. By the time I was fifteen, I'd tried thrice more to escape, despite the severe beatings they gave me each time. The sultan finally lost patience with me and threw me in his prison."

Drake's remote features lightened as he looked at

Clyde's puffy face. "I did not know it then, but that black day, when I was lowered into that fetid hole, would be one of the luckiest of my life. For I met Clyde there, you see. I had become almost as savage as my captors in those five years. The sultan's son taught me how to wield a knife and blade, how to kill and skin my food, how to find water in the desert, and any other number of useful things. Of Latin and science and the arts I knew little, only what I had learned back home so many years before—and struggled to forget. Memories only made my survival more difficult." Drake stirred the embers again, then nodded at Clyde.

Clyde took up the tale. "I was imprisoned for life for the crime of seeing the sultan's daughter without her veil. Quite beyond my control, it was, because I wandered into the seraglio grounds only to sketch them. I had traveled the East alone for two years, at the end of which time I intended to become a monk. I was in the prison for over a year before they threw Drake in with me."

Clyde's smile was both yearning and sad. "He was like a wildcat, hissing fury and vowing vengeance. I was a bit afraid of him at first, especially when he stole my food. But when he saw me reading my books, which were the only comforts my gaolers allowed me, he started asking questions. In the beginning I refused to answer, whetting his curiosity. A year after that, he had memorized every book I had and bartered with the other prisoners for more. We were allowed a walk a day in the grounds with the others, and by the time we escaped two years after that, Drake spoke fluent Arabic, Latin, Italian, Portugese, French, and Spanish, with a smattering of German."

"More languages than I would have learned at Eton,

The Gentle Beast

no doubt, with a far more interesting teacher," Drake inserted.

Clyde bowed his head in acknowledgment. "We spent hours discussing the classics and mathematics and science. When I grew ill and did not get better, he knew he had to get me out. My own burning desire to escape had faded over the years, but Drake . . . well, Drake will never give up."

As if she needed to be reminded of that. When Drake stirred the fire moodily, letting the silence stretch, she croaked, "How did you escape?"

"Our turnkey was replaced by an old, drunken man who was more careless than our former gaoler. I stole his keys as we were escorted back one day."

"He did not miss them?"

"We had the end cell, and I took them as he dropped them into his pocket. I waited until it was dark and quiet, and then I unlocked every cell. I knew it would be harder for them to find us among so many."

Clyde sent him a chiding look. "And he was still boy enough to set the caged birds free, even the ones he did not like."

Drake shrugged. "We hid under a pile of rugs in a wagon leaving the gates. I stole the wagon and the driver's clothes and drove Clyde, who was by now very ill, to a town in Arabia on the Red Sea. That was where we met Hassan."

Clyde grumbled. "And letting him save my life may have been the worst mistake I ever made. Now he thinks he owns it."

Drake's grin was short-lived as melancholy overtook him again. "When Clyde was better, I signed on with a pirate crew. I was eighteen, but looked older, and the past eight years had toughened me. I won the captaincy in less than three years. When the time was

right, I took my share, made my way to Bombay, and began a less hazardous, more profitable career as a merchant. 'Tis amazing the things people will say in front of people they do not believe speak their language. The majority of my wealth was made honestly, Callista, trade by trade. I swear it."

Callista took a deep breath, but she had to ask. "And . . . women? Why have you never wed?"

Drake's eyes darkened to indigo. He hesitated, then said simply, "I wanted no entanglements that would make me weak. Those years taught me a lesson my father had tried—and failed—to instill in a sheltered young aristocrat."

Callista winced and said softly, "The strong thrive. The weak perish."

He nodded. "A credo you have flourished under, I might add."

She had to look away from that piercing gaze. "Why did you wait so long to return to England?"

"Actually, my agents have been buying up Henry's debts for years. And I knew the day I set foot on these shores that my life would never be free again."

Callista held her breath. Was he understanding, at last, that a life devoted to vengeance was a life enchained?

At her wondering look he added, "Once I reclaimed my name and lands, I would have to leave the old wanderlust behind. I owe it to my father."

When Callista's face fell, he squatted before her to take her clammy hands and rub them. "So you see, I have good reason for actions that may, to you, seem heartless. My father died that I might live and see justice done. It was the last thing he asked of me. Would you have done any less?"

Callista closed her eyes so she wouldn't have to see

that earnest, increasingly dear face, but he would not allow her to shut him out. "Please, Callista, try to understand."

Feeling torn in twain, she shoved him away and surged to her feet. Warily he rose to face her. "I understand perfectly! You want my approval for your persecution of the man who did this. Perhaps he deserves all you've done, and more. You've all but ruined us, and that is still not enough for the twenty years of your life he stole from you." She leaned close to finish. "But know this: I can never love a man whose guiding principle is hatred, no matter how valid the cause. It taints everything you touch, and everything we could be together. I can never build happiness upon the foundation of Henry's ruin."

His expressionless features flickered at that, and she knew she'd hurt him. Good, she told herself as she fled to the door, unable to hold back the sobs any longer.

But her tears were not for herself.

That poor little boy no longer remained for her to comfort. As for the man, well, he did not need her. He was tensile steel, as Henry had tried to warn her. Every time she tried to get near him, he sliced her to ribbons.

No more, she told herself. But every step seemed a mile, and deep inside, she knew she distanced herself from her only hope of happiness.

Drake watched her go, stifling panic. How foolish he'd been to expect his sordid little tale to make a difference. Of course her loyalty was to Henry, and that was as it should be. Yet if she had come to him, perhaps he could have let things end as they were, half finished. He smashed one fist into the other. "She will never choose me over Henry."

"The Lady Callista is loyal to the bone. You would not love her otherwise."

Drake glared at Clyde and opened his mouth to deny it, but Clyde raised an eyebrow at him, daring him to lie. Drake whirled to the fire. He stirred the embers again, absently toying with the dragon-headed poker. "Then we are at an impasse. I can only finish this and be done with it."

"If that is your choice." Clyde collected their hats. "But it is a cold spring to put them out in the rain."

"They have Summerlea."

"For how long, with no money to run it?"

When they reached the warehouse thirty minutes later, Drake was still arguing, but his diatribe stopped midsentence when he opened the door. The main shop was in shambles. The jewelry case was smashed, all the stones taken. The silver and jade and valuable statuettes were all gone. They'd even tried to take the bed, but they hadn't been able to fit it through the door. Long gashes marred the expensive wood.

"Damn his black soul to hell! Quartermain is behind this." Drake ran upstairs, fearing the worst. Knife slashes marred the secret panel, but thank God they hadn't figured out how to open it.

Clyde had followed more slowly. He sighed with relief at the closed panel. "I shall hire guards immediately."

"That will not be necessary. I will deal with this myself." Drake smiled, his white teeth all the more sinister as they flashed under the mask he'd put back on when they drove home. "The next time they come, I shall be ready."

Callista made him weak and bumbling.

This, he knew how to deal with.

* * *

The Gentle Beast

In the late afternoon Callista awoke dreary eyed. She turned on her side in Marian's comfortable bed to stare out at the gray day. She had much to do to prepare for this evening, but she could not face the world and its wickedness yet. The tears came again, but she forced them back.

Her foundation was built on shifting sand. If Henry were capable of such greed, then nothing was as it seemed. She'd looked in on him after they had moved him to Marian's town home. He slept soundly, his color normal again.

But for how long? For all she knew, Drake's doctor was poisoning him slowly. His thirst for vengeance would probably never be filled. How could she love a man like that?

But behind her closed eyes an image grew. An image of a little boy dressed in rags, his back bloody from the whip, trying to hold back his tears and fears. Her eyes watered. She wondered yet again how Henry could have been so ruthless. She wanted to cradle that desolate boy to her bosom and keep him safe, but a powerful man had taken his place.

A man who held their fate in his wounded hands.

And a wounded beast was a very uncertain mate. As long as he hated Henry, she would always feel afraid that one day he would turn on her, too.

Callista cradled her aching head, for a moment considering going back to Summerlea. Let them savage one another; she could bear it no longer.

She tossed the covers back, intending to pack her meager belongings. When she reached for her case, the emerald on her hand winked like a warning light. She stared at Sir Walter Raleigh's legacy. He had gone cheerfully to his death, remaining true to his ideals until the end.

Colleen Shannon

She could do no less. She would never forgive herself if she deserted Henry. And Drake . . . well, Drake had made his choice, but here, at least, she could see him occasionally.

"Idiot!" The sound of her own disgusted voice gave her strength. Her step was firm as she went down the hall to the room where they had moved Henry.

He was awake, staring out at the gray day as she had done. When he heard her light steps he turned eagerly to face her. He patted the bed, inviting her to sit, then frowned at her expression as she did so. "What's amiss, my dear?"

Callista searched his lined face, looking for some hint of the monster who had ruined Drake and killed Bryant Kimball. She saw only the kindly father who had been the world to her since her real father died. "Oh, Henry," she whispered. "How could you have done it?"

He apparently caught her meaning immediately. His age-spotted hands trembled as he drew the covers to his neck. "I have asked myself that many times over the years. When Mary died so soon after we wed, I told myself God had punished me for my sins. I had stolen my happiness, so I would not be allowed to enjoy it. On that dark night at her bedside, I swore that I would spend the rest of my life doing right, and being an example to you and Simon, but God did not spare her. Now the angels get to hear her laugh."

Callista saw the moisture in his eyes. For the first time, as a woman grown tormented by choices of her own, she understood the depth of his passion for Mary Raleigh. He had not wed Mary to spite Kimball, as Drake seemed to think. Since her death eighteen years ago, he had never looked at another woman. His foul

deed had been incited as much by love for her as by envy for his partner.

He swallowed back the tears. "It is the greatest regret of my life that you have had to pay for my sins. That bastard! Nothing I did justifies this."

"Have you never wondered how a ten year-old boy survived to become the Dragon?"

Henry swallowed back more heated words. "He told you, then?"

"Yes. And you should know as well."

Henry turned his face away. "I do not wish to hear it."

"That's a pity, for you shall." Grimly Callista recounted the tale, watching Henry's head turn slowly, the growing horror in his expression, and finally the guilt that overtook him.

"I did not know he was alive," he whispered when she was done. "I swear it. If I had known, I would have searched for him." And finally, so softly Callista had to strain to hear, he said, "No wonder he hates me so."

No wonder, indeed. Callista decided it was time to let Henry stew in his own juice. She rose and went to the door, where she paused to bend a last stern look upon the bed. "Henry, have you realized yet that when Drake claims his heritage, the Kimball house will be taken from us?"

The bit of color in his face faded, leaving him almost as white as the sheets.

Callista closed the door softly, feeling a grim satisfaction that the author of this Shakespearean tragedy would pay in emotional, if not physical, coin for his deed.

As to why the punishment of her father felt so right, well, she could not dwell upon that. Not when so many obstacles stood between her and Drake.

Seeking diversion, Calista went downstairs in search of Marian. She found her friend in the salon, frowning over an assortment of fans.

Marian smiled a welcome. "Good afternoon, sluga-bed. You are just in time." Marian held up an exquisite blue lace bauble that was sewn with pearls. "This one goes well with that sapphire dress we ordered for you."

"Marian, would you quit showering me with gifts? You have done quite enough."

Marian patted the sofa beside her. "I will not desist until I have the old Callista back. This woman who runs a gaming hell has too much grim dignity about her."

Callista sat, but her laugh was hollow. " 'Tis dignity or screaming."

Marian put the fan down, her plump, pretty face troubled. "Callista, I went to Herrick's warehouse this morning to look at furniture."

"For what, pray tell?" If Marian bought them furniture for the hell, it would promptly be returned.

"Do not sit upon your high horse with me, my girl. I only wish to refurbish one of my guest rooms. Now, before I was so rudely interrupted, I was about to say that his warehouse was in shambles. Herrick was not there, but that nice man, his manager, tried to put off my inquiries." Marian shrugged, the little movement eloquent of how futile was that endeavor. "But when I persisted, he admitted that they believed Quartermain had hired the men who robbed them. And his face . . . why, he looked as if Paris had trampled him. Do you know what happened?"

Wearily Callista leaned her head against the sofa back. "Quartermain happened. He had Clyde kid-napped to force him to talk about Drake, admit who he is, and so on. I do not doubt he is also behind the

theft at the store. Quartermain will stop at nothing to embarrass Drake."

"And win you."

"If he does not have more sinister motivations."

That quieted Marian, if only for a moment. "Are you saying Quartermain will try to kill him?"

"No, he's too much of a coward for that. But he may try to have him killed." Callista stood. She paced a narrow path from hearth to chair and back. "I must warn Drake."

"Oh, I doubt the Dragon would be surprised to hear this bit of news. Doubtless he is already prepared. You should not worry about him. Now . . . which of these fans do you want?"

They were arguing over who should pay for the two Callista selected when a stir sounded at the front door. A loud banging was preceded by the excited voice of a stableboy talking to Colter.

"But sir! Primest bit o' blood I ever seen. Ye must fetch the laidy."

"Lady Callista is still abed, you oaf," Colter said loftily. "Take that beast around to the stable."

Callista ran into the foyer. "I am awake, Colter. What is it?" Her heart slammed into her rib cage as she rounded the door, hoping, praying. . . . She froze where she stood. "Paris," she whispered. Then, "Paris!"

She leaped down the steps to the two lads who were trying to hold the restive stallion. His ears pricked forward as he heard her voice. He whickered softly, going still as she caught his halter and ran her hands over him lovingly.

"We was told to give ye this note," said one of the boys, pulling his forelock bashfully. He handed over a wrinkled, smudged envelope.

Callista took it as if it were pure gold. Her hands shook as she opened it to read:

"Pax. Of all my regrets, seeing your disappointment in me is the worst. He is a fine animal, and almost worthy of you. Think of me when you train him for his first race. I shall bet heavily upon him. Yours, Drake."

Callista stuffed the note in her pocket and threw her arms about the stallion's sleek neck. Just when she had given Drake up for a lost soul, he did something like this. Would she ever understand him?

Would he ever understand her? Drake wondered as he entered the hell that night to the sound of her laughter. When he'd left her, she was in the dismals, yet now she veritably sparkled as she shook hands with Dr. Johnson, who stood in front of him in the receiving line.

Her gown of blue silk had the traditional panniers, with the skirt drawn up to reveal a white lace petticoat. White lace peeped at the low bodice and puffed sleeves. Seed pearls were sewn in a rose pattern over the silk. Her coiffure, again unpowdered in defiance of fashion, was a simple affair of loose curls falling over her bare shoulders, with braids strung with seed pearls holding up the sides. The fan she held in one hand matched the blue silk perfectly.

She was such a picture of happy grace that he almost sneaked back out. He'd been eager to see his plan to fruition, just to end his own internal conflict. She would not make him weak, blast it! And yet, seeing her thus, he hovered there, Clyde's words ringing in his ears.

"Drake, I love you like my own son, you know that,

but for once, you are wrong." That evening, as Drake had dressed, exchanging his dusty, ripped clothes for a stunning black satin jacket, white laces fuller than he usually wore, and white satin knee breeches, Clyde had said, "You have survived, and thrived, by planning a strategy and following it. Indeed, Henry Stanton deserves this last royal punishment, the fruition of the foul seeds he himself planted."

Clyde brushed off the shoulders of Drake's jacket. "But Callista Raleigh does not. Hurt her, and you hurt yourself. You will never win her by harming those she loves."

"Full stop. I shall never win her. She will not wed me because she does not love me, despite her claims."

Drake caught Clyde's secret smile in the mirror and whirled on him. Clyde's mouth went straight as Drake roared, "Leave off your nattering, blast it! I shall do what I promised, come hell or high water." Drake ran down the stairs, flinging over his shoulder, "And remember. Do not go in the basement unless you enter through the alley."

Clyde followed him down the stairs like a conscientious shadow. As Drake flung open the door, Clyde had made a last comment.

That comment rang now in Drake's ears as he stared at the woman he loved. Clyde had said, " 'Abash'd the Devil stood, and felt how awful goodness is, and saw virtue in her shape how lovely. . . . ' "

"Milton, *Paradise Lost*," said he automatically to himself. The man behind shoved him forward. Drake watched as Callista greeted Dr. Johnson.

"I hope this fine spring evening finds you well, dear sir," Callista said, with a small curtsy to her favorite author.

"As well as can be expected at my age. The promise

of your enchanting company would bring me out of my deathbed, I vow." The good doctor kissed her hand.

Callista laughed.

A muscle in Drake's jaw twitched at the happy sound.

"La, sir, if you speak thus to all the ladies, 'tis a wonder parson's mousetrap has not caught you again."

Johnson leaned forward to whisper loudly, "The joy of life is variety, dear child." He glanced over his shoulder, then looked back at Callista. "Save in those instances where true love finds two lucky people."

Callista blushed as she met Drake's eyes. She lifted the fan near her face and plied it vigorously. Smiling, Johnson went on, straight to the dining salon. Callista offered her hand to Drake.

"Welcome, Mr. Herrick. We are glad to have your company."

"We?" Drake queried. He glanced at Quartermain's cold expression. The cit stared through him, then went back to greeting the man in front of him. Drake wondered where Henry was.

Callista scandalized Quartermain by pulling Drake out of the line to a vacant card room. They stared at one another for a long moment; then Callista admitted, "I am glad you came. And as for your surprise, it was most generous, but I will send Paris back after a few days. You bought him fairly, and I no longer have the funds to train him. We spent them on the opening." Her head cocked to the side, she watched him closely as she made her last comment.

Did she know what he intended to do? The horse could be her sole source of income ere long. . . .

" 'Twould do me no good to keep him. He will not perform for my trainers. In fact he is off his feed. Misses a certain female, I suspect." He looked her up and

down, then added, "This is the first time in my life I have been jealous of a horse. Did you shower him with hugs?"

Callista smiled. "Indeed I did."

"I am glad to see the color back in your cheeks. But if you bring him in to sleep with you, you shall have to get a bigger bed." He sent her a needling look.

She did not laugh, as he intended. In fact, her eyes darkened in that expression that never failed to arouse him. "You have one large enough, as I recall."

He swallowed. " 'Tis not big enough for me and him."

Those luscious lips stretched in a winsome smile. "Who said aught about Paris?"

Drake blinked. He was reaching for her when a nasty voice said from the doorway, "I did not think you so beyond the pale as to desert your respectable guests for this . . . wastrel, Callista."

Quartermain came into the room, resplendent in gold silk and lace.

Callista gritted her teeth, but turned to face him calmly. "I can surely be spared for a moment to speak with a friend."

Quartermain snorted. "Friend? He wants but one thing of you."

Callista glided toward Quartermain. She paused at his side to tap his cheek with her fan. "The same thing you want, as you have made clear on more than one occasion." She looked between the two men, as if trying to make up her mind; then she opened the fan and shielded her face. "Since I have attained my majority, I can make my own choices, thank God. I choose . . ." She trailed off, her eyes dancing above the blue silk.

Drake knew she was teasing, but Quartermain's eyes widened eagerly. He took a step toward her.

She lowered the fan. "I choose the whist tables tonight. Variety is the joy of life, as the good doctor says." With a swish of skirts and a tinkling laugh, she was gone.

Quartermain stared after her grimly, frustration plain in his expression.

Drake barked a rude laugh. "Led you a merry dance, has she?"

Those glacial blue eyes dripped icy scorn upon him. "I have not seen your ring upon her hand either."

Drake crossed his ankles and leaned against the wall. "Yet."

"Never. She shall never be yours, you bloody bastard."

Drake studied the tip of his shoe. "Ah yes. I have noted that of you."

Quartermain tried to pretend indifference; then, goaded, he said, "What?"

"That you covet things that do not belong to you. Must be why you and Stanton get on so well."

When Quartermain merely stared at him haughtily, Drake added softly, "Or perhaps we should call a spade a spade, especially given our current location, and say that you are a master thief, hiring others but taking more than your share of the spoils."

Drake was glad when Quartermain's hands clenched into fists. He braced his feet. The cit took a step forward, looked at Drake's waiting posture, and then he pivoted and stalked out.

Drake flexed his fingers. "Pity. A good boxing of the ears would be the making of the fellow." Then he went back outside. He had only to follow the crowd to find Callista's table. The gamers were seated so close that he had no hope of drawing up another chair.

He did notice, however, that a space was vacant at

The Gentle Beast

Quartermain's table. Drake sat down in the chair, a plan forming in his mind.

Quartermain glared at him. "I have already begun to deal."

"Then begin again. Does anyone object if I raise the stakes?"

The other gamesters peered at the man in the black velvet mask, obviously wishing they could see his eyes. Drake's smile was apparent enough, however. In the leaping candle glow, his white teeth looked predatory.

"To what?" asked a bold young man. He reminded Drake of a rooster learning to crow, come good dawn or bad.

"How about a thousand pounds a point?"

Gasps rounded the table. Even the bold young lord blinked in shock. "Surely you jest."

In reply, Drake pulled a bank draft from his pocket and filled it out with bold strokes, turning it so all could read the amount: fifty thousand pounds. The sum was thrice the annual income of most of those present. "That should more than cover my losses. If I have any."

"Madness!" cried one older gentleman. "Will the house accept such high stakes?"

All turned to Quartermain. His handsome face was frozen in shock that slowly melted to outrage. "Gladly."

A general exodus followed.

"Too rich for me," said one.

"Lunatics, one and all," added another in disbelief.

Even the rooster shoved back his chair. "M'father would have my head."

Soon only Drake and Quartermain were left, staring at one another across the green baize battlefield. As Quartermain began to deal, Drake added, "And by the by, I want your personal guarantee. This house cannot cover the debt, as we both know."

Quartermain appeared to choke on rage, but with so many onlookers, he could only nod shortly. He scribbled out an IOU.

Drake relaxed and picked up his cards. Undoubtedly the poorest hand he'd ever received. Quartermain won the hand easily.

And so it went, for the first set. Drake was down forty points at the end. Quartermain was an excellent card player, and luck was definitely with him. Drake paused to sip his wine, grimly aware of his opponent's ill-concealed glee.

With every turn of the cards, the crowd around the table grew. But it was when Drake scented a familiar perfume, felt the parting of the crowd, that his luck began to change. Knowing Callista stood there before he saw her, Drake looked up at her and winked.

Her lips trembled into a smile, but she gripped the back of a chair with white-knuckled fingers. Concern for him, or the house? he wondered.

"Another ten points and I shall have to have more collateral," Quartermain needled.

Drake covered a yawn. "As you wish. But I have a request to make in return."

"Yes?"

"I should like Miss Raleigh to deal."

Quartermain stiffened. "No."

Callista sat down between the two men. "Yes." Calmly she shuffled the cards, but a close observer would have noted that her hands trembled slightly.

Quartermain puffed up like a pouter pigeon, then expelled his breath in a deep sigh. Grimly he collected his cards.

Drake concealed his delight at his hand. He had all four aces and two kings. His bid was daring, but within the bounds. Quartermain nodded woodenly and was

forced to bid low. He still lost his bid.

From that moment on, Quartermain's lead began to shrink. Five points, ten, thirty, and then, by the last hand of the last set, Drake was in the lead by ten. Quartermain took a big swig of the wine at his elbow, wiped his sweaty brows and picked up his cards.

The room was so quiet that the scrape of the cards being sorted sounded like fingernails on a blackboard. The onlookers watched, their gazes darting from each player, to Callista's tense face, and back.

Arranging his cards in his wounded hand without visible effort, Drake bit his lip. Not so good. Still, if he played the hand dealt him in the proper sequence, he could take the lead and make his run of diamonds good. Drake misled Quartermain by leading his diamonds low, making his opponent think he was not strong in the suit. The strategy worked. By game's end, Drake was up by twenty points.

Callista neatly tallied the scores, shoving the results before Quartermain. "You owe Mr. Herrick twenty thousand pounds."

Quartermain's jaw worked; then he shoved back his chair. "My secretary shall call on yours."

Drake nodded. "Thank you."

Quartermain stalked off.

Callista heard him bellow, "Simon! Come along."

She recognized her brother's light, fast footsteps.

The exterior door opened and closed. Callista's green eyes were troubled as she looked at Drake. When the other gamesters wandered off, gossiping about the strange match, she shoved back her chair. "You thrive on danger, don't you?"

Drake shrugged. "Fifty thousand is a pittance to me. It was worth the risk to put the arrogant bastard in his place."

"Pride will be your downfall one day." Her lips white, she hurried off.

No one was there to hear Drake's grim, "But not today."

He stalked off to the dining salon, hoping to calm his churning stomach with some food. Dr. Johnson was just shoving back his plate. Drake hesitated slightly on seeing him, but the old fellow waved at him merrily. Drake sighed and joined him, grimly aware that after tonight the doctor would not be so glad to see him.

Indeed, the entire ton would probably ostracize him after this night's work. Was Callista right? Was pride driving him instead of justice? Drake squashed the errant doubt and sat down beside the doctor. "Do you not play, sir?"

"Cards are not a talent of mine, young man."

Drake teased, "I am surprised there is anything you are not an expert at."

"A desire for knowledge is the natural feeling of mankind. What, think you because I am old, that reason is any less important to me? I am not in my dotage yet. If I wished to become a gambler, I could yet. I do not wish to."

Drake hastened to soothe the doctor's ruffled feathers. "No, sir, I did not mean that at all. I . . ." Drake trailed off, embarrassed. Tension was making him clumsy.

He should have allowed Clyde to come. Clyde always knew the right words to put him at ease, and to make him see the proper course of action. Then again, of late he had rejected all of Clyde's counsel. Besides, he needed someone to watch the warehouse. Quartermain was not through yet.

Johnson's stiff posture relaxed. "Never mind, young

The Gentle Beast

man. I opine that you have other things on your mind than empty platitudes."

Drake heaved a sigh of relief. "Thank you, sir." He noted that more and more people were drifting into the dining salon, staring at him with mingled dislike and interest. Under such looks, the smallest morsel would choke him. Best to get on with it. "Ah, sir, do you plan to stay awhile?"

Johnson stretched out an obviously aching leg. "Not much longer."

"May I ask that you delay long enough to partake of port with the other gentlemen?"

Johnson's plump white hand adjusted his wig. "Hmmm, and might I ask why you wish me to stay?"

"I have . . . something to say. I wish you to hear it from me rather than the gossips."

Johnson's blue eyes kindled. "As you wish."

Drake leaped up. "Good. I shall return shortly."

Johnson stared after him curiously.

Callista bathed her flushed face in the ewer, dreading her return downstairs. With Henry ill, and Quartermain and Simon gone, she had no choice but to play hostess. Where the devil had Quartermain taken Simon? His abrupt disappearance did not bode well for Drake's safety, for when he left the card room he wore an expression Callista recognized.

Sheer, flaming hatred.

Drake had bested him, at business, at cards—at love. Quartermain was not one to gracefully accept defeat. If he had to cheat to win he would do so, as he had proved when he forced them to take on ruinous debt in this place or lose their share.

Callista sipped some brandy, coughed, drank some more. She started at shadows only because she was

tired, she told herself. In this sad crush, they would be right as rain within a fortnight. But the lump of dread in her stomach was only partly relieved by the potent fire of the brandy. She snapped the glass down, straightened her shoulders, and went to the door. She was opening it when she heard an odd, dragging sound. She stepped outside in time to see Drake half carrying, half dragging a picture down the stairs.

Every muscle in her body tensed. Her little homily blew away in the whirlwind of an abrupt certainty: he was revealing himself to all. Like her, he could no longer bear this purgatory, and he would see an end to it.

With his identity went their livelihood. She had refused him too many times, and now he would have the triumph of his vengeance. Callista leaped out the door, banging it behind her, pleading words on her lips, but she bit them back, going stock-still.

Truth hit her like a body blow. They had turned his family home into a gaming hell; they were the intruders; he was right to evict them and reclaim his birthright.

The fact that their last farthing was tied up in this place was sheer bad luck, she tried to tell herself.

Or a calculated misfortune?

Already feeling the cold winds howling through Summerlea's rotting walls, Callista slowly went down the stairs, holding on to the banister for support. Her heart pounded in her ears with every step. The dining salon was empty, as she had expected. The servants had broken out the port and carried glasses and bottles on trays into the grand salon.

Callista peeked inside. The scene that met her eyes might have come from a Hogarth engraving. Bewigged and befrocked dandies, some with beauty patches and

clocks on their stockings, lounged before a great, roaring fire, sipping fine wine and trading empty sallies.

Outside, the London rabble shivered in the cold spring winds, scrounging for food. Callista shivered, well aware that she could be among their number ere long, yet her fears were not solely for herself. Drake toyed with fire by unveiling himself to this crowd who already mostly resented him. These luminaries of the upper ten thousand would not appreciate being made the fool, or welcome a man of Drake's background, no matter how blue his blood. Drake stood, one elbow braced on the mantel, directly beneath the portrait he'd apparently had a servant put over the mantel.

If Callista had doubted his purpose, she could no longer. She felt it in the resolve emanating from him, saw it in the aggressive manner in which he stood on his family hearth. Callista went inside, her head high despite the scandalized looks she received from several of the older gentlemen. It was just not done for a female to intrude on this male ritual.

Some of her panic eased as she noted Dr. Johnson seated in the place of honor—the large wing chair next to the fire. Surely with his calming influence things could not get too nasty. He looked up and saw her pulling her fan between her hands so hard that she ripped the delicate silk. He glanced up at Drake's towering figure, then back at Callista. He gave her a sympathetic smile.

There were no vacant seats, so Callista went across the huge expanse of the room and sat down on the floor before Johnson. He touched her shoulder, and the sympathy was a brace to her sagging fortitude.

After this, she told herself, she could get on with her life. She would never have to see Drake Kimball again. She could not look at him as he began, but she did

Colleen Shannon

notice Quartermain and Simon come inside, stare at the portrait, then hover beside the door.

"Many of you have wondered why a grown man would parade around London as if he were at a masquerade ball." Drake snorted a laugh. " 'Twas not by choice, I assure you."

Callista noted that Simon looked confused, but Quartermain kept glancing between Drake's tall figure and the portrait, dread growing in his expression.

"Quite simply, I could not reveal myself because I was dedicated to a cause that has guided me since I was a boy. A cause you have all, at one time or another, pursued." Drake paused, letting suspense build, then added softly, "Justice. My father was foully murdered by a member of your class."

Murmurs rippled across the room. Johnson gripped Callista's shoulder as she started.

One of the older gentlemen snorted his disbelief. "If this all happened when you were a lad, how could you possibly know who killed your father? Did the murderer shake your hand before he did the deed?"

Drake was unmoved by the skepticism and the scorn. "No, but he stole two things of great value from my father, then sent his trusted adviser to do his dirty work. This man taunted my father with the truth, in my hearing, before he stabbed him through the heart."

"Nonsense," crowed the rooster. "But most entertaining. Do go . . ." He trailed off with a squawk under Drake's raking stare.

"I barely survived, and spent seven years as a slave of the sultan of Turkey before I escaped to make my fortune in the Indies." Drake paused, watching his audience. Callista had turned sideways so she could face him, but not once did he glance at her.

Even the most cynical of them were on the edge of

their seats now. Some of the older ones began to whisper the names Callista dreaded.

"Stanton." Subtle looks were sent between her and Simon.

Others said, "Kimball. Must be Kimball's son. Thought he was dead."

Callista gripped the fan so tightly that the fragile ribs broke. Any moment now Drake would verify their suspicions, ruining what little reputation her family had left. His next words made her eyes go wide.

"I shall not name names," Drake said wearily. "But of this charade, I have had enough. It is time I take my place among you and reclaim my father's name."

Like a magnet, the portrait of the strong man and handsome little boy drew the eyes of everyone in the room.

It was left to Dr. Johnson to ask in his inimitable, rational way, "And you have proof of this, I presume?"

Drake paused in the act of reaching for his mask strings. He nodded his head in respect at the doctor and pulled a sheaf of papers from his pocket, tossing it in Johnson's lap.

The rustle of papers was the only sound as Johnson leafed through them. He set them aside. "A copy of the birth certificate of Durwood Alistair Kimball, née 1742, London, England. And the will leaving all to him, plus a copy of the letters patent decreeing the Kimball title."

Ripples of shock went through the younger crowd as they, too, made the connection. All eyes zeroed in on Callista's pale face, then looked about the room, appraising the value of the repairs Stanton had unknowingly performed on the home his greatest enemy would now reclaim. What a delicious scandal.

Drake's refusal to name the perpetrator had fooled no one.

Johnson let the suspense build before he said simply, "Interesting, no doubt, but these documents could be forged, or stolen. How do we know that you are really Durwood Kimball?"

Drake smiled and removed his mask.

A buzz swept the room. Johnson, too, seemed shocked, staring from the portrait to Drake's face, highlighted by the roaring fire.

Even Callista was stunned at his resemblance, standing as he did before the great portrait. A younger, harder Bryant Kimball stared back at them. The scar added to, rather than detracted from, the character in Drake's face.

When the universal shock wore off, the crowd's reactions began to vary.

"Deuced havey-cavey behavior, if you ask me," whispered an old gentleman loudly. "Should have come forward the instant he set foot here rather than lead Stanton down this thorny path."

Henry Stanton was liked among the gathering; Kimball had not been.

From a younger man: "Greedy of him, to take their only possession when he has so many. But from what I hear of Kimball the elder, blood will tell."

And the rooster said, his feathers obviously ruffled, "Well, I shan't waste another farthing of my blunt here. Place is bound to close, deuce take the fellow." And he rose. Without so much as a wave, he turned his back on Drake and strutted out.

Quartermain gave a last furious look at Drake's revealed face; then he strode out. Looking stunned and ashamed, Simon followed.

Many other gentlemen shoved toward the door, but a stern voice froze them in their tracks. "Who is the wronged one here, might I ask? This young man, or

The Gentle Beast

the man of your number who sent him to a life of slavery?" Johnson rose, leaning heavily on his cane, his blue eyes glowing with the strength of his convictions.

Drake had turned to stare at the fire, gripping the mantel, but Callista saw the tension in his back.

The dandy closest to the door shrugged. "Don't really matter now, does it? He's repaid Stanton in kind—stole from him, threatened his life. Even . . ." The dandy looked at Callista's white face and trailed off.

She knew what the rumors said. Her weeklong absence was still a subject of glee among the ton, and Drake's possessiveness toward her here had not quieted the gossip.

"So, repay evil with evil, then? Wickedness is always easier than virtue, for it takes the shortcut to everything." Johnson sighed wearily. "Do as you will. As for me"—he turned to put a hand on Drake's shoulder—"I say vengeance is a bitter brew that poisons the cook as much as the broth. Do as your conscience bids you, young man."

Drake still did not look up as Johnson offered his arm to Callista. She rose and put her trembling hand upon his sleeve. Only his support gave her the strength to walk down that corridor of curiosity. The gentlemen parted for them.

Drake stared over the crowd at her retreating back. An astute observer might have noticed the despair in his astonishingly blue eyes, but he stayed put under the needling curiosity of his peers. Men crowded out ahead of him. Only when they were all gone did Callista and Johnson exit from the side room. Outwardly calm again, she escorted him to the door.

Safely outside on the stoop, Callista said, "You have been my savior again, kind sir. How can I thank you?"

"By answering my curiosity. Is the fantastic tale told by that young man true?"

Callista hesitated and then nodded. "But my stepfather is truly repentent, and he had reasons for acting as he did."

Johnson looked sad, but he offered no rebuke. He kissed her hand. "Whatever the end of this, I hope I am graced by your company again."

Callista gave him a curtsy as his carriage drew up. "I shall see to it." She waved at him cheerily as the coachman drove away.

I may come begging at your door, she said inwardly, but her warm smile was genuine. The smile froze as, last but certainly not least, Drake exited.

It seemed strange to see him unmasked. And yet Callista knew that she had glimpsed the real man most often during that heady week with him, when he kept his mask firmly attached. This barefaced, ruthless lord was a stranger to her. She offered her hand out of politeness. "I . . . shall begin packing our things tomorrow."

He ignored her hand. "When I am ready to evict you, I shall so inform you."

Callista lifted her chin under the icy blast of his blue eyes. So warm they had been, once upon a time. "As you wish. Good evening." She turned to go back in before she lost control.

"Callista, I . . ."

She touched the door with desperate fingers, unable to bear the regret in his voice. Three things happened at once.

He turned to reach for her shoulder to stop her; a pistol shot resounded, so close that she smelled the burning powder; Drake fell heavily against her.

The Gentle Beast

Callista turned, horrified, to catch him in her arms. She fell backward into the house, their mutual weight shoving the door wide, the blood on his face gushing down on her hands and face like tears. . . .

Chapter Twelve

Slamming the door with her foot, Drake a deadweight on top of her, Callista screamed for the servants. Two of the burly footmen carried Drake into the grand salon and laid him on a long settee. Callista ran upstairs for her medical kit, biting out of the side of her mouth as she went, "Send for that Arab physician—Hassan, I believe his name is."

The waiter scurried away to do her bidding.

Callista ran back down and bathed the side of Drake's face. She could barely see his aquiline features through the blur of her tears, but her panicked wheezing slowed as she realized the bullet had only grazed his temple. She dropped the bloody rag back in the bowl and buried her face against him. The reassuring beat of that indomitable heart gave a curious comfort.

If he were less strong, she would not be facing poverty.

The Gentle Beast

If he were less strong, she would not love him with all her soul.

When he stirred, she wiped her eyes on her sleeve and sat up with a bright smile.

He blinked, then cradled his aching head with a loud, "Ouch! Did you hit me?"

Callista's mouth went straight at his outrage, but her eyes danced merrily. "Now why did I not think of that?"

Drake peered at her, then sat up with a surge. "Someone shot at me." He winced and hunched his head on his shoulders, as if his neck could not bear such a heavy weight. "Your illustrious partner has given up trying to best me fairly, it seems."

"This surprises you? I would suspect he will invade your home next." Callista wondered why this brought a smile from him, but Hassan and Clyde bustled into the room before she could ask.

Clyde was white with concern as he looked at the bloody rag and the red streaks on Drake's shirt.

Hassan calmly took Drake's pulse. He peered into Drake's eyes, then appraised the deep temple gouge. Then he snapped his bag closed. "That thick English skull is yet again the saving of you." He cocked his head to the side. "You shall have matching scars on both sides. Most interesting."

Drake glared at him, but Hassan merely crossed his arms placidly over his chest.

Clyde sagged into a chair, his blue eyes acerbic with the *I told you so* he might as well have voiced.

Callista rose with decision. "This cannot be tolerated. I am sending for the magistrates."

Drake's hoot of derision was spoiled when he winced and held a hand to his head. "My assailant is long gone, and we will have no way of tying him to Quartermain,

323

even if we find him. No. I shall handle this in my own time, in my own way."

Callista said quietly, "If you please. You seem to act best when you act alone." She turned on her heel, pausing when he called after her.

"Callista! Please wait." He struggled to his feet. "I . . . thank you for your concern. Under the circumstances I can hardly ask for more." He took a deep breath. "And please do not close the gaming hell on my account. I have not asked for it, nor shall I."

She whirled back around. "But . . . I do not understand. Is this not the last of your grand plan? To throw us in the street? Especially since I will not, ah . . ." She trailed away as she glanced at the two older men.

Hassan watched with interest, Clyde with foreboding, as Drake gritted his teeth under the force of his own inner battle. "This will be the last time I speak of it. I cannot bear to think of you without means of support." He gave her a short bow, his face going red under the embarrassing admission. "I bid you good evening. I regret any gossip I may have caused this night. If you post an ad, I am certain your card rooms will be filled to the brim. I shall trouble you no longer." He turned and stalked out.

Smiling, Hassan put his fingers together and bowed in Callista's direction; then he picked up his bag and followed Drake out, glancing over his shoulder at Clyde.

Clyde shook his head, waving Hassan on. Hassan left, the front door opening and closing behind him.

All the while, Callista stared into space, her ears ringing with one sentence: *I shall trouble you no longer. . . . I shall trouble you no longer.* He had washed his hands of her, then. Yet why did he spare them, when his vic-

The Gentle Beast

tory would be complete if he retook the home his father had built?

Callista started when Clyde took her clammy hand. She had not even noticed he was there.

He murmured, "I am gratified age has not addled my wits completely."

Callista blinked at him in confusion.

"I knew you would be the making of him," Clyde said simply. "If I am not too bold, will you answer me one question?"

Callista closed her eyes and turned away from his earnestness. She knew what he wanted to know before he said it.

"Do you love him?"

The words came from a wellspring she could neither tap nor cap. "With all my heart."

Clyde sighed deeply. "Praise the dear Lord. Then you must go to him. No doubt he shall have the banns posted immediately. . . ." He trailed off when she stood there, shoulders bowed, still turned away.

"'Tis not that simple. Can you imagine the scandal if I should wed him?" *But you can bed him and no one will know,* said an insinuating little voice Callista longed to listen to. She turned back around so Clyde could see her own torment. "As for myself, I care little, but Simon and Henry care deeply—"

"Yes, once. No more," said a beloved voice from the doorway. Henry came into the room, moving slowly, but dressed and vigorous. "The servants came to fetch me when Drake was attacked. Is he well?"

Clyde's features went blank with hostility. "Yes, no thanks to you."

"This was not of my doing, I assure you."

"No, but you set the whole sorry spectacle in motion with your greed and jealousy."

Henry's only defense was a weary, "A sin I have paid for grievously over the years. First I lost my Mary; then I lost my home, my lands, and my fortune, the latter with the aid of your master. When does the hatred stop?"

The words broke a dam in Callista. Suddenly she stepped between the two men, the anguish and despair gone from her expression. Instead her face was luminous with an inward epiphany. She raised her hand imperatively. "Now! It stops now."

Both men looked at her.

"Drake revealed himself to the ton this night," Callista told Henry. "He did not name you as his tormentor, though everyone assumed it was you. He told me tonight, even after Quartermain sent men to kill him—" her voice choked off with emotion before she went on—"that he would not repossess this house. That we could keep the hell open."

Henry's eyes grew wider with every revelation. "But why?"

Both of them looked to Clyde for some understanding of how their enemy had become their benefactor.

He smiled, his own anger gone under the warmth of Callista's glow. "Only one power in the universe can overcome hatred." He nodded at Callista. "And this beautiful young woman is a living example of it in all she does."

As he appraised his daughter, a welter of emotions crossed Henry's face: pride, confusion, comprehension, disapproval, and finally acceptance. He held his hands out to Callista. "Do you love him, daughter?"

She took them. "Yes, Henry, I do. As much as you loved my mother."

"Then go to him. Despite his own actions, from this day forward I can never again wish him harm. I give

you my blessing. I shall give you away at the wedding."

Callista threw her arms about his neck, sealing their reunion with a sweet kiss. "Thank you, Henry. I feel as if I have my father safe again."

Henry hugged her back fiercely, as if finally aware that his own actions had jeopardized the twenty years of good with which he'd tried to atone for the ugliest act of his life.

Clyde offered his arm to her with a flourish. "I shall gladly be your escort, my lady." Callista took his arm and walked out beside him without a backward glance.

The future beckoned.

Alex Quartermain watched from the shadows of the lawn as Clyde helped Callista into the carriage. Simon swayed beside Quartermain, the worse for drink.

Quartermain's lids shielded the nasty look in his eyes as he said offhandedly, "Damn, your sister's off to He—, uh, Kimball again."

Simon squinted after the carriage. "Sh . . . silly chit."

"Hmmm. Might even bring more scandal down upon us, hurt our business."

Simon frowned, took a step after the carriage, stumbled, and would have fallen if Quartermain had not caught him. "Must do shomething." Simon grinned weakly. "Later." Then he threw up.

Drake's hand shook as he poured himself a third glass of brandy. The ache in his head was slowly fading, but it only made his heartache worse. "You weak fool," he sneered to himself. He sat here alone, his life's work half done, with only regret to look forward to.

At least if he had carried through with his plans, he would have the satisfaction of seeing Henry Stanton

ostracized, shivering in the cold as Drake had done, hungry as Drake had been.

A face too willful to be angelic appeared in his mind's eye. Yet a sweetness of heart and mind glowed in those green eyes, bathing something cold and hard deep within him in a luminous warmth. The rock-hard lump of hatred had shifted in his breast with every smile they shared. Now it had melted, running through his veins in a soothing flow.

This peace gave him only torment.

A familiar scraping sound came. Clyde returning through the rear warehouse door, he realized vaguely, but he only leaned deeper into the cushions. He did not want even Clyde to see him in this state.

At least in the past he had purpose to guide him; now he sat here alone, aye, knowing he'd done the right thing, but no happier for it.

She would never come to him.

Grateful she might be, but how could she ever love the man who had wounded her family so? Mayhap someday she would give him the scraps of her regard, when they had remade their fortune in the gaming hell.

Scraps were not enough. He squeezed the Venetian glass so hard that it cracked in his hand. He set it down with a snap to bury his head in his hands. "Callista," he groaned, the name half prayer, half curse.

Magically she was there, her hand cool upon his brow. Thinking he'd dreamed her up, he nestled against her with a sigh. But when her voice came, soft and resonant in the darkness, blood surged through his veins in a rush that made him weak.

"I am here. I will never leave you again." The hand tenderly stroked back his tousled hair.

Tentatively he reached out, afraid to believe. Soft, living flesh met his touch. Drake groaned and hauled

her onto his lap. "Dear God, if you knew how much I have longed for you."

"I do know." She caught his cheeks in her hands and softly kissed the marks on each of his temples. "There has been enough of pain and sadness. Today we begin anew."

Drake turned up the lamp beside him, needing to see her eyes.

She stared back with a serenity that calmed the last of his doubt. Those eyes had haunted him since he first looked into the innocent, trusting gaze of a baby, to this moment when a grown woman stared at him with—He held his breath. He was afraid to believe the desire there, but when she caught his chin and slanted her mouth over his, truth became poetic justice. At another time, he would consider the irony; vengeance was a cheap price to pay for this happiness.

For now, more primitive truths clamored for acceptance.

This was meant to be.

This was right.

Nothing would ever again come between them.

Drake lay there under her eagerness, so ravenous that he was afraid to kiss her back lest he frighten her. She felt his hesitance and redoubled her efforts, slanting her mouth over his to tease the corners of his lips with the tip of her tongue. A strangled groan escaped him, but he kept his lips firmly closed. He held her waist, tense with the warring needs to crush her close or put her aside.

They were not married yet. And he honored her too much to dishonor her, especially after all she had suffered at his hands. Or so he lectured himself. But his male flesh ignored sane counsel, fairly leaping out of his breeches with eagerness. It had been so long since

he'd been with a woman, and to have this one woman his for the taking . . .

Sweat beaded his brow, but he managed to rise and plop her on the settee, taking two steps back from temptation. He shook his head when she would have risen. She sank back. "No, Callista. For once in my life I will do the right thing. We will wed with all the pomp and circumstance I can contrive, and you will become mine in the master bedroom of our town house, not here in the Dragon's lair. The Dragon and his clandestine ways died tonight with the rebirth of Drake Kimball, and I want no memory of that time to sully our new beginning."

She merely looked up at him with those Eden eyes. If she had held an apple out to him, he could not have been more tempted. He swayed toward her, then stumbled away, ramming his knee into a chair leg. Soft laughter taunted him, but when he turned back to glare at her, she was gone.

He heard the rustle of silk, and looked up in time to see her bounding up the catwalk stairs. Never had he seen her move so fast. What was she going to do?

He took deep, gulping breaths, trying to calm himself. Where the devil was Clyde? They needed chaperoning. But call as he might, Clyde was nowhere to be found. *Damn the man, what happened to his sanctimony when I need it most?*

Drake went to a mirror, tied back his hair, and put on his coat, determined to take her back to the town house as soon as she came down. He was straightening his lapels when a noise caught his attention.

Reflected in the mirror he saw the fulfillment of every male fantasy. He whirled.

Callista stood stirring the fire back to life. She'd already spread the fur rug before the blaze.

The Gentle Beast

He did not need warming, however. She was dressed—or almost dressed—in the excuse for a night rail he'd purchased to torment her. The white lace was low cut, almost falling off her shoulders, and lush white skin peeped every inch or so from the weave of the fabric. The fire lovingly glazed the little left to his imagination in a crimson glow. The effect as she glided toward him, her red hair sweeping her hips, the white lace a floating veil, was to make her a dream come true.

Was he bold enough to reach for it?

On silent feet she stepped up to him, so close he could feel the heat of her body. But for a moment she did not touch him. She merely looked at him with those long-lashed eyes that always made him think of new life aborning. His loins surged a reply to nature's call. She smiled slowly as she saw his reaction.

One by one she refuted his earlier points by taking an item of his clothing. Shocked, he stood there, their roles reversed. Now she manipulated him. And with every garment went reason, right and wrong, and lastly, male pride.

She shoved his jacket off his shoulders, dropping it at their feet. "If I have taught you the meaning of love, you have taught me the meaning of desire. It would be very wrong of you to send me away now."

She unbuttoned his shirt next, shoving it wide to bury her nose in the hair on his chest. "I care not for pomp and circumstance. I prefer we wed by special license as soon as possible. As for the death of the Dragon . . ."

This time she unbuttoned his breeches, caressing his lower stomach, but not quite touching him where he most wanted to be touched. The last few muscles in his body not already rock hard went rigid.

Her smile was sultry as she said softly, her breath

sweet upon his face, "'Tis fitting that we put a period to him here, where it all began. I, for one, shall mourn him, and hope that the so proper Drake Kimball allows me glimpses of my beast from time to time." Callista put her arms about his neck and gently but inexorably pulled his mouth down to hers, shoving his shirt off. She licked and nibbled and teased until the hands that tried to hold her away quivered upon her shoulders, then dropped behind her back to clutch her close.

The last of his wavering resolve fled when her tongue slipped into his open mouth, kissing as he had taught her. With a primitive growl, he crushed her against him, answering her teasing tongue with a passion that changed the tenor of their embrace.

Until that moment she had been in control. Now the full force of the hunger he'd denied too long broke the dam of his restraint. A tidal wave of passion swept from him to her, knocking her loose from her moorings.

Murmuring her name, he bent her back over his arm, his mouth leading her in the little sexual prelude of advance and retreat. Tongue, lips, hands begged her, worshiped her, and demanded more even as she responded. Then he was pulling the cradle of her hips over him, rubbing his loins against her as he sampled the sweet nectar of her mouth.

Callista's knees gave out. With a savage growl that might have frightened her had she loved him less, he swept her off her feet and strode up the catwalk in five great strides.

He sat her on the bed and reached to tear off the rest of his clothes. She averted her face.

He froze. From somewhere deep within, he foraged for the gentle strength that only she incited in him. "Do you want me to stop?"

The Gentle Beast

Those huge eyes went from his tense expression, to his broad, bare chest, and centered on the bulge that the sagging breeches barely covered. A shuddering sigh raised her shoulders. In reply she lay back and held up her arms in welcome.

His held breath slowly eased. He started to shimmy out of his breeches, but her gaze widened. He caught the knee breeches just in time. Damn, he didn't know how to initiate a virgin, especially a woman who only needed to look at him sideways to make him hard. He hovered there, feeling like an idiot, frantically grasping for control.

A giggle came from the bed. "This is the first time I have ever seen you hesitate. Am I so displeasing, then?"

He swooped down on her, pressing her into the bed with his body. Gently he bumped his hips against hers. "You know enough of men to realize I would not be in this state if I found you, ah, displeasing."

"Then why do you wait?"

Drake framed her lovely face in his hands. "My darling, it is always painful for a virgin, and when you kissed me downstairs, I almost lost control. I must go slow and easy."

"Why not let me lead, then?"

He stared at her. A spark glowed deep behind the forest green depths. A conflagration could flare out of hand any moment. He understood that, even if she did not. How could he bear to have those innocent hands wandering over him and not respond? Yet how could he deny her anything?

He swallowed harshly. "As you wish."

She shoved him aside and spread him out on the bed. His breeches slipped a bit more. He knew the hair at his loins was exposed, but this was her game.

It didn't seem to bother her to make up the rules as

she went. She pulled him flat, propped a knee on each side of his hips, and began light strokes on his strong neck. The tentative touch ran down his muscular arms, back up to his collarbones, over the whorls of hair covering his chest. Every muscle in his body bade him take her, now, end this torment, but part of him was equally fascinated by her expression. So he lay still, letting her toy with him.

For the moment.

She looked like a woman on a mission. The quiescent power under her hands obviously fascinated her. With every pleasing angle and hard plane, she made a little murmur of discovery.

"If you pull out a knife and dissect a piece here and there, who knows what you might discover." Drake groaned. "I swear 'twould hurt less than this agony."

Her hands stopped on his nipples, the palms flat. "I cannot help it. You are fascinating." And she went back to her exploration, rotating her fingertips on his small nipples. Drake's strong neck tensed as he had to stop himself from arching in pleasure-pain. His nipples were already pebble hard, and the light stroke was almost more than he could bear.

She scooted down to kiss his flat stomach. The muscles contracted, but somehow he stayed still, even when he felt her soft heat slide over him. The woman he'd desired from time immemorial, it seemed, was here in his bed.

And he could not do a damn thing about it.

He owed her this little revenge, but oh, he'd had whippings that hurt less. His loins were screaming now. He was so caught up in his battle with himself that he automatically lifted his hips when she pulled at his pants. They slipped down and off. She sat astride his calves now, the essence of woman so close to all

that made him man. He had only to pull her up a little. . . .

Drake swallowed a curse and tried counting backward in every language he knew. Then she touched him. His back bowed against the bed as his hungry flesh leaped into the soft warmth of her hands.

She gave a startled gasp and pulled back. He forced himself to go limp, though no power on earth could have relaxed him where he needed it most. This time he had to look at her. When he stayed still, the fear in her face receded. She tentatively cupped him in her hand, looking at him shyly. He bit his tongue, but somehow his restraint held.

When he did not move, she grew more aggressive, stroking him with sheer tactile delight. "How can you be so soft here? As soft as I am here." And she brought his limp hand inside the gaping night rail to her breast.

"Oh God," he said in a strangled voice, "kiss me or kill me." Compulsively, he cupped the round flesh, kneading her gently.

She gasped at the sensation, her gaze fixing on his face for the first time. She started to move off him. "I am hurting you."

He caught her shoulders. The loose night rail slipped to her waist, baring her bosom in all its glory. A low rumble emanated from his chest as he caught each breast in his hands. She froze, watching him as if she realized he was a force of nature about to be unleashed. But then he raised his head, and his tongue began to sample the velvety tips of her breasts.

It was her turn to squirm. Her already quickened breathing came in soft pants now. He suckled one peak, coaxing it to hardness, before lavishing like treatment on the other. "Do you feel my pain yet?" he asked against her skin.

Comprehension dawned on her face. She arched into his touch, answering in a throaty voice, "Yes. And I know what to do to end it."

"You do?" He lay back, her toy again, dark azure eyes daring her.

Callista literally rose to the challenge. Still astride him, she eased up on her knees. With a toss of her head, she flung off the night rail, baring that glorious form. He absorbed her, his heart thudding so loudly that he could barely hear her.

She stretched out a long, shapely leg next to his powerful, hairy one, comparing them. "Equals at last." That caught his attention. She slanted a taunting look at him. "At least, we're both naked. Of course, if you wish to prove your male superiority, we can switch places."

He caught a fistful of red hair and used it to pull her face down to his, tensing again as he felt her moist heat slip over him. He had to steady his breath before he could reply, "I am clay in your dainty little hands, vixen, and you know it. You win." Holding her gaze, he pulled her closer, closer. He lightly brushed at the juncture of her hips, pleased to feel the slickness there.

She was almost as eager as he was. Sheer delight coursed through him, heady because it was not merely a delight of the body. This night began something that would never end as long as they both lived.

Time to seal the bond. Just as his lips met hers, he heard her say, "No, darling, we both win."

And she proceeded to prove it by kissing him deeply, simultaneously pulling his hands to her hips so he could help her find the proper angle. He adjusted her slightly, felt her raise her hips and lower them. At the first touch, a moan escaped his clenched jaw. Callista hesitated, then wriggled her hips. Her eyes went wide

as she felt that imperative maleness seek the haven nature had formed for it. He entered, that first little bit enough to hurt.

She stopped, wincing, but then she saw the look on his face. His head was thrown back, his eyes closed, every strong angle tensed in sensual need. Callista bit her lip, raised slightly, then pressed downward with all her weight.

A scream built inside her, but he raised himself on his elbows and caught it with his mouth, staying still to give her time to adjust to his fullness. Never had his mouth been so tender upon hers. The tension went out of him as he luxuriated in the most intimate clasp he had ever known. For with Callista, it was his heart, as much as his body, that savored this melding.

He said between kisses, "Ah, my darling Athena, wise, warlike one, I am yours. Here I belong." He nibbled at her ear and added with a throaty laugh, "And here I just may stay."

The last of the pain eased with his teasing, allowing Callista to understand the true meaning of intimacy. She flexed her muscles upon him, unable to believe she could hold so much in the secret center of her body.

He choked on an endearment, sagging back against the bed.

Callista smiled. "You like that, do you not?" And she did it again. "So do I." Callista felt an odd tension building in her womanhood. She tried to pull him deeper, for it still wasn't enough. What magical things his male wand did to everything it touched. If she had known what she was missing, she would have attacked him earlier. . . .

Drake held her hips firmly, denying his own need to buck into the sheath rippling upon him with sleek female power. But when she began to raise and lower

her hips simultaneously with pulling on him with her muscles, his closed eyes popped open. "Stop!"

She rested all her weight on him, panting breaths escaping her passion-flushed lips. "Why?"

Drake brushed her hair back from her sweaty temple. "Because you please me more than I can bear."

That secret little smile that drove him wild stretched her lips. "Good." And she began anew, moving faster on the downstroke. Her hair flew wildly about her head, her breasts bobbing.

Drake's heels pressed into the bed. The ache was growing, growing beyond his control, but he could feel that the angle was wrong. He caught her hips and pushed her off.

Callista scarcely had time to gasp "What is—" before he rearranged her. The throbbing down there had grown more insistent, and she was squirming with the need to ease it when he flipped her on her back, held her legs wide, and pressed the hard head of his desire against her. But he did not enter, merely teased her with the pressure, brushing up and down upon her.

She quivered as he brought her knees up, pressing her heels flat upon the bed. This way she made a cradle for his hips that made him rub against the most sensitive part of her body. Callista tried to pull him into her, but his soft laugh swirled above them. Still rubbing, up and down, he lowered his head to her breasts, kissing and nipping gently until she was wild.

She writhed under him, little gasping pleas spilling from her lips. He drank the soft sighs and made them his own even as he took her. Gently, slowly, he merged with her, letting her feel the unbearable intimacy only lovers know.

Callista held her breath as he filled her. Inch by inch, until she was sure she could hold no more. Somehow

The Gentle Beast

he pressed deeper still, that hard heat probing for all that made her woman, and making her exult in all that made him man.

What had she been afraid of? She could not remember somehow. And then all thought ceased as sheer pleasure grew. Her eyes fluttered shut as that strange throbbing built again. This time it would not be denied.

Nor would he.

Just as gently he withdrew, poised and aching at her opening, only to delve to the end of her passage again. But he watched her face with eyes so dark a blue they were almost black. He seemed to read some hidden language she could not voice, for he moved higher when she wanted, lower when she shifted in that direction.

He still held her hips raised in his hands, leaving her vulnerable to his will, but she understood on some primitive level that he was as enslaved as she. He would no more harm her than he would hurt himself.

The cadence of their breathing grew with every thrust. They lost all sense of self, their hips joining them into one wild creature striving for a mutual end. Callista felt him harden within her.

Her eyes, full of green, glorious life, caught his as she instinctively clenched upon him a final time. She gave a little scream as the tension snapped, eruptions blowing her apart where she cradled him. Drake groaned his triumph as he thrust deep, feeling for the tip of her womb to give her back the life she'd birthed in him.

When her eyes fluttered shut at the feel of those powerful spurts, Drake said hoarsely, "No! Look at me, Callista."

Her eyes opened obediently. In the most intimate po-

sition a man can have with a woman, Drake blessed her in the fluid of their mutual fulfillment, holding her gaze all the while. If he had shouted from the rooftops of Westminster that she was his, he could not have made the joy of his possession more plain.

And the independent Callista, who had vowed never to put her fate in the hands of any man, reveled in the taking. For she finally understood life's most basic lesson: true lovers receive only in the giving.

When Drake collapsed upon her, she cradled him in her arms, tears of joy in her eyes. He felt the wetness upon his cheek and drew back in alarm, pulling away. "Have I hurt you?"

"Nay. I just never understood . . . I did not know it could be so . . ."

Unashamedly he let her see the moisture build in his own eyes before he pulled her cheek against his chest. He stroked her hair, letting their heightened senses slowly return them to terra firma. When they were calm again, he said, "I have bedded many women in my life, Callista, but I have never made love. I know that now. Aye, you are beautiful, but it is your indomitable spirit that makes me whole. I gravely regret the pain I caused you."

Callista kissed his mouth; then she jumped to her feet and propped her hands on her hips. "Well? Do you plan to feed me? I can only live on love for so long."

That cobalt gaze kindled as it raked over her. "Wench, unless you cover that delectable body, we shall sup at love's table first."

Laughing, Callista stole his dressing gown, turning back the sleeves and cinching it firmly.

He mock-scowled at her. "What am I to wear?"

It was her turn to rake him with an appreciative gaze as a fathom plus of virile male rose to face her. "Don't

get dressed on my account. . . ." Her teasing trailed away as she saw the blood on his member. She touched herself in wonder.

His face grew more gentle than she had ever seen it. "The best gift you will ever give me. I shall cherish it the rest of my life. I have only one poor substitute to offer in return." Drake went to the secret bedpost, unscrewed it, and flipped something in his hand.

It flashed golden fire as he brought it to her. The Yellow Rose dangled from his fingers, winking its promise of golden days. "I ask you formally to be my wife, and wish to give you this to pledge my troth."

She stared at him, brief flashes of the stone's stormy history in her eyes. But at his pleading look, she closed her eyelids in assent. The heavy stone dropped between her breasts, under the robe. She loosened the sash to see the necklace against her skin. The robe gaped open.

Drake stared at her in the long mirror, his breathing quickening again. How many times had he dreamed of her thus? The words came of their own accord, words he'd never intended to admit, even to her. "It is fitting that you wear this stone that was purchased, then stolen, for love of your mother. It has taken me a long time, but I finally understand what drove Henry to act as he did."

She held her breath as he touched the stone, making it dance and sparkle in the light.

"He loved your mother beyond reason, as I love you. He would do anything to win her." His voice went so soft she had to strain to hear. "Exactly as I will do all in my power to make you happy and keep you safe. Vengeance almost destroyed me, but you have truly turned a wounded beast into a happy man. You are mine, Callista Raleigh. Nothing will ever come be-

tween us again. From this day forward I devote myself to peace."

Callista looked back at the stone. It no longer felt lifeless or cold. It had taken on the heat of her body, sparkling with all the joy of her future. Callista's stomach growled, but amazingly she had a deeper hunger. Leisurely, she shrugged out of the robe, lifting her chin to meet his avid stare. "I accept. Henry has given his blessing to our union, so nothing stands in our way now. I care not what society thinks."

Drake blinked in surprise, but then his hands wandered to her breasts, testing their texture and weight. He said softly, "I almost find it in myself to pity Henry Stanton, for I know firsthand the power the Raleigh women wield over us poor helpless males."

Callista pressed her hips back against the growing hardness of his loins. "Helpless?"

"Helpless to resist you, or even to want to." Drake twirled her around, rubbing his torso against her. Her pleasurable sigh made his nostrils flare. He lifted her breasts to his insatiable mouth, saying into her skin, "Callista, are you sore?"

"Yes, a little."

He drew back in disappointment, but she only took his hand and led him to the bed. "But 'tis much like riding, is it not? The more one rides, the better one gets, and the stronger one's thighs."

And she shoved him prone, climbing in the saddle to offer her breasts.

They did indeed sup again.

But it was a long time before they ate.

They had just finished a late supper of cheese, bread, fruit, and wine when a scraping noise sounded from upstairs, at the top of the secret passage. Immediately

The Gentle Beast

Drake stiffened. "They're here. Get dressed." He pushed her ahead of him up the catwalk, but anticipation, not fear, ruled his expression.

"Who's here?" Callista tugged her clothes on quickly.

"Quartermain's emissaries." Drake shrugged into his shirt, slipped his feet into shoes, and ran downstairs, still tucking his shirt into his breeches.

Callista followed more slowly. She reached the last rung of the stairs in time to see him sticking a pistol in his trousers and calmly checking the charge of a huge blunderbuss. Callista paled. "Shouldn't we just leave?"

"I learned years ago that when you run from jackals, they devour you. We should be safe enough. They have a surprise in store." Drake dragged a heavy desk to squarely face the door to the hidden passageway just as heavy footsteps pounded down the tunnel steps. "Callista, get behind me. Do you know how to load shot in a musket?"

"No."

"Do you know how to shoot?"

"Yes, that I do."

Drake handed her the blunderbuss and pulled another across his lap to begin loading it. "It's filled with buckshot. Just aim it at the opening, but do not fire until several men have come out." As Drake loaded another weapon, he tilted his head, listening.

The distinct sound of the door being closed on the other end came. His odd smile was explained by a muffled explosion as the outside door clicked shut. Men screamed, then scrabbled at the door. A man dressed in dark clothes, his panicked face pockmarked, spilled into the room, debris on his head and clothes.

"Get ready," Drake said calmly.

Callista took a deep breath to still her shaky hands,

343

braced the musket on the desk, and sighted along it. When three more men pushed against the first in their eagerness to escape the smoke and dust filling the secret passage, Callista pressed the trigger. The weapon's kick knocked her on her backside, but she scrambled up in time to take a second musket.

The shot had peppered the men, but their loud screams were as much from outrage as pain, for it was obvious their wounds were superficial. A motley assortment of weapons flew out at Drake's command.

Drake calmly rose, leveling two pistols on the men. "Get back inside." He peered sharply at the fourth man in line, then smiled. "Why, I am honored, Mr. Norther. I never dreamed you would deign to dirty your hands yourself. I never believed you would leave your little fiefdom. Why, half the magistrates in London are on the lookout for you."

Felix Norther shoved his man aside and strode arrogantly down the last step to come into the light. He stared at Drake's revealed face, blinking. He stopped when Drake waved a pistol at him. Norther snarled, "You have the luck of a cat. But you have just used up your ninth life."

"Oh, yes?" Drake checked his pocket watch. " 'Tis your own feet you must be landing on, my larcenous friend." Drake waved him back with the pistol. "Now retreat back inside like a good little boy. You can come out and play when I am ready."

Norther's face reddened at the taunt. He reached for his boot but straightened, screaming, when Drake shot his hand.

Smoke wreathed about Drake's saturnine expression as he said softly, "Please, try it again." The second pistol was steady in its aim at Norther's heart.

Paling, Norther moved into the passage, shoving his

The Gentle Beast

men back. Warily Drake stepped forward, closing the door with his shoe. He turned a curlicue on the outside. A latch clicked home. Then he shoved the heavy desk before the door, putting several plaster busts on top of that. Finally he nodded, dusting his hands on his pants. "That should hold them until Clyde gets here. The other end of the passageway is blocked with debris."

Callista propped the musket against the wall, wiping her sweaty brow. "Who is that? And how did you know he was coming?"

"Felix Norther. The man who kidnapped and tortured Clyde, otherwise known as Alex Quartermain's partner in crime."

Callista glanced darkly at the door as everything clicked home. "He's the one who shot at you."

"He or one of his men. But they shall all be in Newgate ere long." Drake wet a rag in a ewer and used it to wipe dust from her face. "Clyde will arrive at seven this morning with the magistrates."

"But how did you know they would come now? And what did you do to trap them in the passage?"

"When their assassination attempt failed, they had to come here next. Norther hates me almost as much as Quartermain does, but I never realized how much. The magistrates will be delighted to see him. And the trap was merely an old pirate trick. A small charge set to go off when the exterior passage door closed to trap them inside." Drake set the rag aside and kissed her cheek. "I never believed you were in danger or I should have sent you away."

Callista waved an airy hand at that. "Bring them on. If I had known they were behind the attack on you and Clyde, I would have aimed below their belts."

Drake shouted a laugh, then pulled her into his arms.

"Ah, my beauty, what fine sons we shall have."

Callista cupped her stomach, blushing, as if she had not realized the night just past could bear fruit.

Drake covered her hands with his wounded one, his eyes darkening to navy. "I cannot wait to see you big with my child." He kissed her, then set her firmly aside, patting her rear. "But you shall not seduce me again, my lusty wench, until you make a proper man out of me."

Callista stuck her nose in the air, but her sideways glance danced with mirth. "We may be wed fifty years, but you shall never be proper."

Drake opened his mouth to retort, then shut it when a clock bonged six in the morning. "Come along, we must get you safely home. I do not want you here when the magistrates come." Drake wrapped her in her cape, kissed her nape, and drew her to the outside warehouse door.

Walking her one street over, he hailed a sedan chairman and paid the man generously. "Take good care of her," he bade the burly fellow. He kissed Callista's cheek as he handed her inside.

In that secret hour before dawn, when neither day nor night ruled supreme, they stared at each other in the pearly grayness. A street lantern lent a golden glow to the scene that merely accented its dreamlike quality.

Callista could not shake the feeling that she would awaken, alone again. She clutched his hand. "I do not want to leave you. I feel a chill, of a sudden."

He brought her hand to his lips. "I shall post the banns immediately. We shall wed within the w—"

"Herrick!" came the voice out of the darkness like a pistol shot. "Get your filthy hands off my sister." Simon strode up, Quartermain at his side like an evil shadow.

The Gentle Beast

Drake bit off to the chairman, "Well, go on, my good fellow."

Callista leaped out of the chair before the man could start off. "Not likely." She caught Drake's arm and stood tall, her chin raised under the condemning stares of her brother and former suitor. She knew she had the look of a woman well loved, but she owed them no explanations. "What if his hands are on me by my choice, brother?"

Simon fell back a step. "'Lista, you cannot mean that. Why, everything we own, he's coveted."

"He had a good teacher," Callista retorted, "as Henry himself admitted. Simon, 'tis time to let bygones be bygones. Drake and Henry are willing. Why not you?"

"Because I can never hold my head up in this town again if this . . . blackguard finishes his defilement of you with a travesty of a marriage. Why, you would shame the Stantons and the Raleighs both, to wed this outcast. Half the men at the hell last night will refuse to admit him to their drawing rooms. Tell me you have refused him, 'Lista."

In answer, Callista flipped the Yellow Rose out of her dress. Even twenty meters away, the lantern struck sparks off the clarity of the stone.

Simon curled his lip in disgust. "You were right, Alex. She's barmy in her noodle. He's bewitched her."

Callista stared at Quartermain's self-satisfied air. How she hated this man. If things were different, she would call him out herself. She contented herself with a verbal insult. "The words have a familiar ring to them. How many times did you make him repeat them, oh great Machiavelli?"

He shrugged. "Simon can be quite acute when he troubles to use that good brain of his."

Drake's cold stare had never left Quartermain's face.

For the first time, he spoke. "Pity he did not use it sooner. Then, perhaps, he would see you for what you are."

Simon fumbled off his glove. "I have had enough of your foul insults. She's still m'sister, and I have a care for our reputation even if she does not. You have obviously sullied her, and you shall pay the price."

When Simon clenched his glove and raised it, Callista gasped and tried to step between him and Drake. Quartermain caught her cape and pulled her back. She struggled to get free, but by the time she snatched her cape loose, it was too late.

Simon struck the side of Drake's face with such force that the sound of the slap rang in the empty street. "You shall name your seconds, if you can find anyone to stand up with you. This time tomorrow morning, the Hempstead priory graveyard. Weapon of your choice."

Drake rubbed his cheek. His face was in shadow, but those blue eyes glowed with holy fire. For the first time since Callista had found him last night, he lived up to his namesake again.

Callista jerked the glove away from Simon. "Are you mad? I forbid it, I tell you."

Gently Drake pulled her away and escorted her back to the onlooking chairman. "'Tis a point of honor, my dear. With all the gossip rampant about my background and how I earned my fortune, do you think I can afford to cry off and be branded a coward? I want a better life for you and our children than that."

Callista clutched at him, her heart pounding in dread.

Bitter experience had taught her that happiness just grasped was always most fleeting. "But Simon is an excellent shot. And so are you. You cannot kill him,

The Gentle Beast

Drake. Nor can I bear for him to kill you. I love you both." The memory of Heath, his laughing vitality cold and ashen after his duel to defend her, haunted her. She had to stop this!

He pressed a finger against her mouth. "Fear not. I shall contrive. Trust me this last time and all will be well." He stepped back and nodded at the chairman. The man took off like a scalded rabbit, obviously scared of the odd doings of the gentry.

Drake's reassuring smile turned to stone. The inimical will of the boy who'd survived torture stared out of the transformed man. "My second shall call on you." Drake gathered his black cloak around him and strode back into the darkness. His voice carried back, "And, Quartermain . . . do not smile too gleefully yet. Felix Norther is in custody. I suspect he shall gladly name the man who's hired him over the years. . . ." Drake's voice trailed off with a sibilant hiss.

And he was gone.

In the lightening street, Simon peered at Alex's sickly expression.

Chapter Thirteen

That day, dawning with such bright courage, was the bleakest of Callista's life. The sun smiled a winsome greeting on the spring wildflowers bowing their homage in Marian's garden. For the first time in months, the wind had a warm tinge to it. Everything smelled new, alive with the hope that Callista should have nurtured in her breast.

A lump of foreboding weighed her down instead. She sat in Marian's luxurious bedroom staring out the window. A cheeky robin landed on the sill, throwing back its head to chortle the arrival of spring. Callista barely saw it.

She was too tired to sleep, too anguished to rise and face the day. She had thought she was done with this purgatory, where she felt half alive, her future as bleak as her past. She buried her face in her hands, praying, as she had never prayed before, that God would not

350

The Gentle Beast

torment her with this brief taste of happiness, only to snatch it away.

Somehow she knew Drake would not kill Simon. Simon, however, had no such compunction. Callista wrapped her arms about herself, shivering despite the warming day. She had to do something. But what?

Outside, the sound of raised voices floated up from Marian's massive foyer. Callista forced her leaden limbs to move. She started down the stairs, holding on to the railing. She reached the bottom in time to see Henry slap Quartermain.

"Get out! I shall mortgage everything I have to buy your interest. You foul all you touch."

Marian waved a goggling servant out of the hall, her back against the door as she watched with concern. She looked relieved to see Callista.

His cheeks scarlet with rage, Quartermain raised his fist, but Simon rushed into the fray between the two men.

"Father, don't. Alex is the only friend who stood by us when we needed it most."

"For his own ends. Simon, can you not see that Alex has encouraged you to drink, and gamble, and now to duel? This is not the life your mother would have wanted for you."

"Why? She married you, did she not?"

Henry swayed on his feet at the low blow, standing firm again when Callista put her hand on his arm. She shook her head at her brother. "Simon, do as you must. But I tell you this: if you kill Drake Kimball, I will mourn him the rest of my life. I will never again look upon your face in the same way."

Simon reared back as if struck. Then his hurt expression hardened. "You are right. I will do as I must.

Come along, Alex. I need to practice my target shooting."

Henry roused himself enough to warn, "My secretary shall call upon you, Quartermain. We will come up with a plan for me to buy you out."

Quartermain shrugged. "If you come up with the ready, I may consider it. If it pleases me." And he tramped out on Simon's heels.

Callista's stiff spine wilted with the slamming door. Marian caught her two friends' elbows and led them each into the salon, where she seated them before the fire and stirred it to roaring life. She poured a brandy for each.

Callista cocked a wry eyebrow at the clock, which read eleven in the morning. Marian put her fists on her hips. "'Tis a bit late for you to go prim and proper."

Sighing, Callista sipped. She coughed as the spirit burned her empty stomach, but her head was clearer when the glass was empty.

Henry did not touch his. He held it up to the light, appraising the golden color, his cheeks flushed high on his cheekbones. "Odd, is it not, how one act can change the whole course of a family's existence. I shall still be paying penance for it upon my deathbed, and no doubt St. Peter shall turn me away from the pearly gates when I show up with my life book in my hands."

Henry's mesmerized expression concerned Callista. She caught his wrist, stopping the rotation of the glass. "It is never too late to atone, Henry. You have already made a good start. I know you did your best to dissuade Simon from this madness. I do not believe Drake will kill him. We can only hope for the best."

Henry jerked away, set his glass down so hard that brandy sloshed onto the fine rosewood end table, and surged to his feet. "Hope? Balderdash! There is some-

thing I can do, and I shall do it." Henry hurried to the door, appearing ten years younger, but he paused to look over his shoulder at Marian. "See she does not come to the dueling field, Marian. This is men's work." And he slammed the salon door behind him.

Only the servant in the hallway saw the secret smile on his face as he went out the front door.

Inside the salon, Callista's white-faced despair was flooded with a rush of color. She gripped the arms of her chair so hard that one of her nails broke. "Ohhh! I hate it when he says that." She looked more herself as she leaped to her feet. "Men's work, is it? Well, let us see what a woman's touch can do."

Marian watched her with foreboding. "Callista, what can you do?"

"Well, I certainly cannot sit idly by when the man I have promised to wed and the brother I love are bound by their cursed male honor to kill one another."

Marian appraised her friend; then a comprehending smile stretched her face. "Ah, I see. How was it, Callista? Is the Dragon as masterful as he seems?"

"Why have you never told me over the years how pleasurable the sex act is?" Callista turned to peer at her friend. "You gave me the bare details only, if you will forgive the pun."

"Because it is different with everyone. A woman does not find much pleasure in it unless her heart is as engaged as much as her body. So much depended upon whom you wed."

A sad, reflective look descended on Marian's pretty face. Callista knew she was remembering her own dear late marquess.

Callista whirled for the door. "And I will not lose him as I lost Heath. Marian, may I borrow your coach? I have a call to make."

*   *   *

In his office, Clyde's hands shook slightly as he helped clean Drake's favorite brace of pistols. The pearl handles and silver-and-gold inlay could not disguise their deadly precision. "Why did you let the boy taunt you into this?"

Drake sighted along one barrel. "Quartermain would have me laughed out of the ton if I had refused him. With time, Callista and I will be accepted, but not if I am branded a coward, in addition to my other sins."

"But how can you kill the Lady Callista's brother? And I hear he is a crack shot."

Drake set the first pistol back in the velvet-lined case and took the second one from Clyde's limp hands. "I will not lose my life now that I finally have a reason to live."

Clyde closed his eyes in obvious, silent prayer. Drake watched him, a smile playing about his lips. "Enough, old friend. Tell me about Norther and his friends, once the magistrates took them into custody."

Clyde's teeth were bared in a very un-Christian smile. "He made the mistake of trying to bribe them—in my presence. Their howls of outrage could be heard across the Thames, I make no doubt."

"And where is Norther being held?"

"Under dragoon guard at the local constable's, along with his men. After their trial they will be moved to Newgate. If Quartermain is to act, he must act now."

"And you are certain that Quartermain went to the constable's, inquiring, as a so-called concerned citizen, about their crimes, and trying to get his goods back?"

"Such was his excuse, according to the plump magistrate. He's quite a good chap, really. He's been much friendlier since you delivered London's most wanted

The Gentle Beast

criminal to him. He's most eager to answer any of my questions."

"And he let you in to see Norther?"

Clyde nodded. "Norther's like a cock eager to crow. Seems to think Quartermain set a trap for him, coaxing him out of hiding to get him out of the way. He wants revenge."

"Excellent. Go back to the magistrate now and suggest, vaguely enough to make him think it is his own idea, that he have men watch Norther's jail. If I survive, Quartermain's next move will be to kill the man who can prove Alex Quartermain is not the model citizen he claims to be." Drake sighted one deadly eye along the second pistol. "He shall be hoist with his own petard. A more fitting end I could not have devised for the man who's lived a life manipulating others. He will not be happy in Newgate." A loud knock sounded on the shop door.

Clyde rose with alacrity. "Do you not practice today? Will you wait for me? I will help you set up targets."

Drake put the second pistol in the case and locked them both away. "I do not need to practice for what I intend to do."

Clyde frowned, but when the knock came again, more imperatively this time, he went down the stairs. He ripped open the shop door, growling, "Can you not read? We are cl—" He broke off with a gasp, staring at the man on the stoop.

Drake arrived to peer over his shoulder in equal surprise.

Henry Stanton, Earl of Swanlea, murderer of Drake's father, bowed slightly, his expression wooden. "Good day, Kimball. May I trouble you for a short audience?"

Drake swung the door wide. "I shall say this for you,

Henry Stanton. You can still surprise me, which is a rarity for most men."

Clyde glanced between the two men, but they were civil, if not warm. Shrugging, he went on his errand, leaving the two alone.

Henry came in, shoving the door closed with his foot. "I shall take that as a compliment. From what I understand, you have seen many things in your life that most men can only dream of."

"Or dread," Drake said dryly, a hint of the old dislike in his chilly tone. But he stood back, sweeping a cordial arm before him. "What can I do for you?"

"I do not deserve it, but you can help me make my son into a man."

Drake sat down on a chair, waving Henry opposite. "How do you know I do not intend to make him into a corpse?"

Henry did not react to the goad. He merely cocked his head to the side, staring at that strong face. "Zounds, but you remind me so much of your father. Ah, the times we had together in the East Indies. Before . . ." He changed tactics as Drake stiffened. "Callista does not believe you plan to kill my boy, and nor do I. I ask you—no, I beg you—to let me serve as your second."

Drake's mouth dropped open. "Against your own son?"

"I can think of no better way to be a living example of the rejection of futile vengeance. Hatred and jealousy almost destroyed me once. I cannot bear for it to do the same to Simon. If he sees me there at your side, perhaps the shock will awaken him to how much he has been swayed by Quartermain's pernicious influence."

"Or, feeling betrayed, he will hate you for the rest of

his life." A month ago, even two weeks ago, Drake would have pounced on the offer, gleeful at this opportunity to drive a wedge between father and son. Now he did not even need to close his eyes to call up the memory of Callista's face. He would devote his life to seeing that happy smile—and often—in recompense for the misery he'd caused her.

Besides, this man had molded Callista into the woman he loved. Because of that, Drake could almost forgive him. "No, Henry. I am honored at your offer, but it would break Callista's heart if the two of you were at odds."

Henry smiled slowly. "I knew you did not intend to kill him."

"Leave me and my reasons out of this. You may have your problem solved for you, Stanton. I may never live to torment you as your son-in-law. I understand your son is a crack shot."

Henry rose and walked up to Drake. Slowly Drake stood to face this archenemy who had, disconcertingly, changed into an ally. When Henry offered his hand, Drake took it without hesitation.

"Forgive me," Henry said simply. "If I could call back my misdeeds, I would give my own life to do so. To this day I still miss your father. I swear it."

Somehow Drake believed him. The last of the shadows lifted from his heart. Drake shook Henry's hand firmly, then released it. "Good. Then you should know that I have his head for business. Wait here." Drake covered the stairs in six double strides, then came back down as quickly. He offered a legal-looking document to Henry. "I purchased the Walcome hell today for a princely sum. You can see that the deed is in your name and Simon's. The only condition is that I have a quarter irrevocable interest in it, to be paid to me an-

nually, even after the purchase price is paid off." Drake forced the deed into Henry's limp hand, unable to resist a gibe. "Since I have given up asking for your pound of flesh, good English pounds will do instead."

Henry merely stared down at the deed as if he could not believe it.

Drake cleared his throat. "And the second provision is that you sell my town house back to me for what you paid for it."

When Henry looked up, his eyes were moist. "But it is yours, to take back legally without paying a cent."

Drake shrugged. "'Tis a pittance to me. Little enough for peace in my household. As for Callista, well, I suppose I should formally ask for her hand."

A faint smile stretched Henry's face at the less than gracious offer. "Do not strain yourself. She is of age, and a more willful girl has never lived. But if it counts for aught, you have my blessing. She needs a strong man."

Blessing, not mere acceptance. Drake hid his satisfaction with a brisk nod. "Good. Now that's settled, would you care to join me for luncheon at the King's Head? A little public conviviality will surely quiet the gossips."

Henry stuck the deed in his pocket. "I should be delighted, as long as you let me pay the shot."

"Nonsense." Drake held the door for Henry. "It is my duty to seal our bargain."

They were still arguing amiably when they sauntered into the King's Head, one of London's most popular taverns, the favorite haunt of Dr. Samuel Johnson. Conversation died away as the two men entered. Those who had not seen him unmasked stared at Drake, even as he asked for a table under his real name. Whispers broke out, only to hush after the relationship between

The Gentle Beast

the two men was explained to those who did not know it.

Thus the guests at the King's Head were treated to the latest shocking development in the newest scandal. Why, it was positively decadent, the way the two confirmed enemies sat down together, all agreed. Could it be true that Stanton's daughter would marry the son of the man he had wronged? Why, a lion would as soon lie down with a lamb.

All stared, peering around corners and over tables, as Drake crooked a finger for a comely barmaid and ordered the best port, pouring it himself. The deep red color caught the brilliant sunshine; their male laughter turned the wine into rubies rather than blood.

And outside, in that unseen realm that awaits all souls, the angel of death fluttered his wings in disappointment. He flew off in search of weaker prey.

Standing at the pearly gates, St. Peter smiled and made a new mark in his book.

Callista paused outside St. Paul's, where Dr. Johnson's servant had sent her after she called. Johnson had apparently come here to attend a friend's funeral. Callista hated to bother him, but time pressed too hard for her to be deterred by the niceties. She stood outside the huge structure, the dome soaring with a majesty only the great architect Christopher Wren could have devised.

She wished seeing the lofty magnificence of man's best imaginings could reassure her; instead, she contemplated the irony of meeting Dr. Johnson at one funeral in hopes of stopping another.

Finally, men and women in sober dress began filing out the huge doors. Mournful organ music trailed after

them, but Callista tried to ignore its depressing effect as she searched the crowd.

Finally she spied him, hobbling down the steps carefully on his cane. She ran up to him. "Good afternoon, sir. May I have a word with you?"

Johnson reared back, startled. He glanced around at the curious onlookers; then he took Callista's arm and escorted her down the steps, back to Marian's waiting coachman.

"You sometimes carry your independence too far, child. A pretty young maid should never approach a man alone, even an old one, in front of so many social climbers. But I can see from your face that I do not need to tell you that."

Callista said urgently, "My last intent was to embarrass you, sir. But I must speak with you. I am somewhat ashamed to ask your help yet again, but this is a life-and-death matter."

Understanding dawned on Johnson's puzzled face. "Ah, you speak of your brother's duel with young Kimball."

It was Callista's turn to blink with surprise. "Is it the talk of the town already?"

"That fellow Quartermain has been making the rounds of the coffeehouses all day, I am told." Johnson made no effort to hide his disapproval. "The man has no grace, but if the tale is true, I cannot approve of either young hothead."

Callista looked about at the people walking slowly by, obviously straining to hear. "May we have a private audience somewhere?"

Johnson checked his watch. When Callista's stomach growled loudly at that strategic moment, Johnson smiled. "I rent a private dining salon at the King's Head. Would you care to join me for luncheon?" He

The Gentle Beast

nodded at the coachman. "Your man can serve as chaperon."

Callista tried to remember when she last had eaten. Her face flushed as she vividly recalled eating orange sections from Drake's fingers. "I shall meet you there forthwith."

And so it was that Callista Raleigh, soon to be Kimball, dined a wall away from her husband-to-be and her father, unaware of their presence. Callista controlled her impatience and let Johnson enjoy his side of beef and bread washed down with ale.

After he wiped his mouth, he folded his napkin neatly by his plate and bent that arrow-straight gaze upon her. "Now, what would you have me do?"

"Simon respects you greatly. If you were to go to the dueling site with me, perhaps . . ."

"Do I apprehend that you wish me to talk your brother out of fighting?" Johnson frowned.

"I only know that I have spoken to both Simon and Drake, and neither will listen to me."

"What you ask is impossible, child. This is a point of honor. May I ask who issued the challenge?"

"Simon."

Johnson relaxed slightly. "I am glad to see my judgment is not faulty, after all. I cannot imagine provocation great enough to make Kimball call your brother out. Drake Kimball obviously loves you dearly, as you love him."

Callista twisted her hands together in her lap, nodding. "And 'tis exceedingly frustrating, since my father and Drake have set aside their differences. It is only at Quartermain's urging that this duel is being fought, which is why I believe, with a little argument, Simon may be persuaded away from such a lawless way to settle a petty argument."

Colleen Shannon

Johnson shook his head before she finished. "Duels fought on a point of honor are less lawless than many of the wars so many strangers die fighting. No, my child. If your brother called Drake out, young Kimball has no choice but to fight. He will fight not from aggression, but from self-defense; to avert the stigma of the world, and to prevent himself from being driven out of society. Such goals, if not the means, are surely admirable. I cannot interfere."

Callista sagged back in her chair. "Then Drake may die tomorrow at dawn."

"How do you know it will not be your brother who is wounded?"

"Drake will not shoot him." Callista pushed herself to her feet. "Thank you for the lunch, sir. I shall trouble you no longer."

Johnson rose with unusual speed as she trudged toward the door. "When is this duel set? And where?"

Callista told him, not daring to hope he would change his mind. He nodded, saying nothing further. Callista went into the narrow hall, but she had to back around the corner to avoid two servants bearing laden trays. She could see into the main taproom now.

She glanced indifferently over the crowd. She froze, staring at a central table.

Drake. And Henry. Sharing a hearty lunch and a bottle of port. Callista took a step toward them, remembered this was a male domain, and shrank back. Johnson, curious at her odd behavior, came out and peered over her shoulder. They both watched the two men argue amiably, gesturing their points, but obviously agreeing to disagree.

"So you were right. They truly have made amends."

Tears blurred Callista's vision. She managed a nod as she pivoted and hurried out the back door, Marian's

The Gentle Beast

coachman at her heels. She was too upset to notice Johnson's thoughtful expression as he watched the two old enemies.

On the short ride to Marian's, Callista stared unseeingly out the window, haunted ever more frequently by the peaceful look on Heath's face as he lay in his coffin.

She had thought then that she would never feel again, much less love again. But she had been young and resilient. Now, as a mature woman, she knew beyond doubt that if Drake died, her wish for living perished with him. And to lose him in such a way, over such a foolish point of honor, well, she could not bear it.

But what else could she do? Short of taking a pistol herself, there was . . . Callista caught her breath. Her sluggish heart began a rat-a-tat against her ribs.

It just might work. If the ton caught wind of it, she would be ostracized, but she had to chance it.

The Hempstead priory graveyard boasted a high hill overlooking the Thames, with a flat plateau on top. For centuries it had been a favorite dueling site of the gentlemen of the ton. Where better to kill than a graveyard? So much aristocratic blood had been spilled here that it was a wonder the grass was not blue.

Like a painted harlot, dawn still labored under night's embrace. At five-thirty, a few streaks of color foretold her liberation, but darkness held sway for the moment.

Carriage wheels rattled on the road up the hill. A lone figure jumped out of the coach, hurried to the shadow of a huge oak, and waved the coachman on. The heavy cloak concealed much, but a white hand caught the last of the moon's glow as it pulled a pistol out of a belt to check it.

Colleen Shannon

A mere twenty minutes passed before three more coaches rumbled up. Drake, Hassan, and Clyde got out of one carriage, Henry Stanton out of another, and finally, Simon, Quartermain, and . . . Dr. Samuel Johnson clambered out of the last.

Drake tossed off his cloak, firmly affixing a black mask to his face. He was garbed head to toe in black, but his tall figure was still outlined against the grayish sky.

Simon also wore black. His face made a pale oval above the black shirt. The two opponents appraised each other without speaking. Simon could be seen swaying slightly. Quartermain said something savage to him in an undertone and Simon snapped to attention.

Then, scowling, Quartermain met Clyde in the middle of the clearing.

"Your weapons?"

Clyde handed over the case of pistols. "We choose pistols at thirty paces."

"Thirty? Twenty is more usual."

Clyde did not bother with a retort. As the challenged party, they were allowed to choose the terms. Quartermain took the case to Simon and spoke briefly. Simon nodded, wiping his brow with his sleeve.

Quartermain offered Drake his choice of pistol, then gave the last gun to Simon. Henry and Johnson stood to the side, watching grimly, not far from the huge oak. Hassan, as the attendant surgeon, looked confused at this European ritual, standing off to himself.

Henry glanced at the tree when a slight rustling sounded, but it subsided and he lost interest.

When both men had loaded and approved their weapons, Clyde pulled a white kerchief from his pocket. "First blood shall give satisfaction."

The Gentle Beast

"To the death," Simon slurred.

Clyde ignored him. "First blood." Clyde raised the kerchief.

"Wait!" Henry strode forward. He pulled something from his pocket. "I will not ask you again to withdraw the challenge, Simon, but you should know that Drake Kimball has gone into partnership with us in a new hell, at a quarter interest. He asks only that we let him buy his ancestral town house back at the price we paid for it."

Simon wiggled a finger in his ear as if he could not believe his hearing. "I cannot believe it."

"And I also want you to know that I disapprove so much of this duel that I offered Drake my services as his second. He refused, not out of hatred toward me, but out of concern for your reaction." Henry stood back. "Now, continue if you must, but the only blood that will tell will be our own: retribution, death, and dishonor handed down from one generation to the next. If Drake can forgive my sin, surely you can forgive him." Calmly Henry walked back to Johnson's side, but his shaking hands were stuck in his greatcoat.

Simon looked at Henry, at Drake's still figure, at Johnson's disapproving expression, and finally at Quartermain. "Alex?"

"Henry will do anything to get out of our agreement, Simon. Including forgiving the man who has so richly wronged you, stolen everything you have, even your sister. Still, it is your choice." Quartermain crossed his arms over his chest, but his seething fury at Drake's new partnership emanated from him like a stench.

Simon teetered in the breeze, his glazed eyes pleading for a reassurance none gave him. He pulled a flask from his pocket and took a hefty swig. He capped the

flask and put it back, standing firm. "Let's get on with it."

Henry's shoulders sagged. Johnson clicked his tongue. Quartermain smiled.

And Drake? Drake took his position, back to back with Simon, his hand at his side holding the pistol rock steady.

Under the oak tree, however, a stifled sob could be heard. As the white handkerchief fell and the two men began counting in unison, that white, slender hand poked the pistol through the leaves. Drake took large steps away, Simon small ones, as the count lengthened.

"Fifteen . . . sixteen . . ."

Johnson's lips moved as he counted silently along with the duelists. At twenty, a rustling in the trees made him turn. The sky was growing lighter by the moment, and Johnson saw the pale glint of steel. At twenty-five, he lunged for that hand as it drew a pistol bead on Simon's legs.

Johnson pulled hard on the fragile wrist. Callista, dressed in black, stumbled from beneath the tree, wild eyed with fear. "No! I only mean to wound him, to give Drake a chance."

"Twenty-nine . . ."

"Shhh. Do not distract him, child." Johnson put an arm around her and gently drew the pistol away as the count reached thirty.

In a dead quiet not broken by so much as a cricket, Callista's worst nightmare played out. She buried her face in Johnson's shoulder, unable to watch. A pile of dead leaves whirled between the two men, obscuring their visions as they turned. Simon squinted, raised his pistol, took a deep breath, and aimed, but it was clear his heart was not in it.

The Gentle Beast

Meanwhile, Drake turned sideways, raised a steady hand, and waited to see what Simon would do. When Simon tightened his grip on the pistol to fire, Drake turned even more sharply sideways, began to pull his own trigger—and swung his arm wide to shoot harmlessly.

The two pistol shots rang out, reverberating off the headstones. Drake stumbled back, letting the gun drop.

Callista screamed. Hassan glanced between the two men, picked up his bag, and hurried toward Drake, who was clutching his arm.

Simon rubbed his eyes free of grit and stared at his adversary. He ran a hand over himself, as if he could not believe he stood whole, then turned to look at Drake's mark, a crumbling gravestone. He looked back at Drake.

Finally his dumbfounded expression changed as he stared at his best friend.

Quartermain's lip curled in disappointment as Hassan ripped Drake's shirt and swabbed the graze. "Nothing to be concerned about, but it is bleeding," Hassan said in his singsong way.

Callista ran to Drake. Henry collapsed against a tree trunk, weak with relief. And Johnson, that arbiter of taste, stared at Quartermain's disgust with ill-concealed distaste.

Quartermain turned on his heel and stalked to his carriage. Without even asking Simon how he would get home, he ordered his coachman to make haste. No one bade him farewell.

Taking the mask off for the last time, Drake patted Callista's cheek, but his eyes met Clyde's over her head. He nodded slightly. Clyde took Drake's coach to follow Quartermain.

Drake sighed and rubbed his chin in Callista's hair. "Vixen. I told you to stay away."

Callista continued running her hands over Drake. When she was satisfied he was indeed safe, she stepped away in time to see Johnson surreptitiously stick her gun in his jacket. Callista smiled her thanks at him for keeping his counsel. Yet again, he had saved her from a foolish, desperate act. She went over to him, unaware that Drake had seen Johnson's action. Drake frowned.

Callista did not notice. "I thank you for coming, sir. If not for you . . ."

"Yes, well, this has made my blood run, I vow. I have not seen the dawn since I can remember." Johnson appreciatively watched the sun wink over the horizon. He yawned. "And I shall not miss making the rounds of the alehouses."

Callista's eyes widened. "Did you spend part of the night with Simon?"

"Yes. I called on him. We discussed everything but the duel, but managed to put away quite a bit of ale in the process." Johnson blandly met her smiling eyes.

No wonder Simon had been half bosky. Callista curtsied. "For once I am glad of Simon's propensity for drink."

Johnson cradled his head. "Not I."

Callista laughed. She glanced over at her brother. He was standing, talking seriously to Henry. Henry gave him a little push.

Looking like the boy he still was, Simon sheepishly came over to his sister. "Sorry, 'Lista. Lost my head, I guess. But Alex made it sound like such a point of honor. Where did he go?"

"To perdition, shortly," Drake answered, joining them. He turned so Simon could see the blood on the bandage. "Satisfied?"

The Gentle Beast

Simon reddened. "Embarrassed. I thank you for not firing at me after I gave you every provocation. I must have been wrong about you."

"You have been a nodcock, as you very well know," his sister said tartly. "I do not doubt that, between the two of you, I earned my first gray hairs this morn." She took Drake's good arm. "Can we go home now?"

Drake kissed her cheek. "We tied my horse up at the bottom of the hill, just in case we needed another mode of transport. I shall join you for luncheon, during which you can tell me how you came to be here, and what you intended to do. But I have an errand to run first."

"But Drake—"

Drake firmly led her to Henry's coach. "Wear your finest dress, and watch the announcement section in the morning paper. You will probably be getting callers today."

Distracted, Callista touched a hand to her mussed hair.

Over her head, Henry nodded approvingly as Drake's eyes met his. Drake winked, as if he could read Henry's thoughts.

It did indeed take a strong man to handle a strong woman. . . .

Henry helped Callista into the carriage, his expression serene at the match he could not even have contemplated a bare week ago. The others crowded in on the plush squabs.

A merry discussion took place on Wilkes's chances to win the mayoral election. Callista was too drained to participate. A bounce brought the Yellow Rose out of Callista's dress. It winked in the brightening day.

Henry leaned forward to catch the stone and turn it this way and that. Emotion flitted across his face. Cal-

lista reached to unclasp it, but Henry shook his head.

"No, Mary would want you to have it. I can think of no more fitting place for it to rest. It symbolizes the bond between our two families, worn by the woman who forged it." Henry let the stone go and relaxed against the cushions.

Callista clasped his hand and leaned back to let the sun caress her face. And at her breast, the Yellow Rose caught every ray, brilliant with promise.

Drake winced as he dismounted and tied his stallion outside the constabulary. Sure enough, his carriage was parked on a side street, Quartermain's carriage opposite. The cit knew that Drake would make it his life's work to see that Norther talked loud and long to the authorities. Quartermain had no choice but to act rashly.

Drake sneaked in the back door of the squat, ugly building. A soldier stood on guard in the storeroom piled with crates and ammunition. He moved to block Drake's path. "Now see here, this ain't no bleedin' street, fer ye to—"

"Never mind. Let the gentleman in," said a familiar voice. The plump magistrate came into the room, Clyde on his heels.

"There, I told you he would arrive," Clyde said.

The soldier stood back, but he eyed Drake suspiciously.

The magistrate caught Drake's arm and led him down a hall to a locked row of cells. "It seems you were right yet again, sir. Mr. Quartermain just came, asking for a word with the prisoner."

Drake started to reply, but the magistrate put a finger to his lips and tiptoed into the guardroom next door to one of the cells. Quietly, carefully, the magistrate

The Gentle Beast

flipped a peephole up and peered into the next cell.

An old-fashioned listening horn sat on a rickety table. Drake picked it up and stuck the large end against the wooden wall. If he strained, he could make out bits of conversation.

From Quartermain, ". . . no proof . . . help you in Newgate if you . . . quiet."

Norther's voice was louder. "They have already agreed to ask the court for leniency if I tell them everything. You bastard, it was your fault I left Whitefriars. It was safe, you assured me. And Herrick was too slippery a character for my men, you said. I must lead them. . . . I led them, indeed. Straight to jail. Now get the hell out of here before I add to my sentence with another murder."

Quartermain was silent for so long that Drake grew uneasy. He was wondering how Quartermain would do the deed. Nothing so messy as knives or guns, not when Quartermain would be the last visitor to see Norther alive. No, he would do it in some sneaky way that could not be traced.

"I see," Quartermain finally said quietly. "I had to try to dissuade you, you understand. I must make haste and pack for a long journey to the continent. But I truly regret your capture, and would ask you to share a drink with me for old times' sake." Drake heard something metal touch glass.

Flinging the listening horn aside, Drake gestured wildly at the magistrate, who could see, but not hear, what was going on. "Poison," Drake hissed.

The one word made the little man explode into movement amazingly fast for one so plump. Beckoning to the soldiers on guard down the hall, he had the key out of his pocket and into the cell lock in a trice. They burst into the cell just as Quartermain handed a shot

371

glass of scotch whiskey to Norther, raising another himself.

Drake knocked the glass out of Quartermain's hand and grabbed Norther's.

"What the devil?" Norther bellowed. "I . . ." But his outrage sputtered away as Drake took Norther's untouched, full glass and handed it to Quartermain.

"To your health," Drake said softly.

Quartermain snapped, "How dare you? Now you've taken Felix's away, it would be rude of me to imbibe without him."

The truth had obviously dawned on Norther. He shoved Quartermain against the wall and forced the glass to the cit's lips. "Drink, you poisonous bastard. 'Tis a fitting end for you."

Quartermain desperately turned his face away even as Norther tried to hold his head still. When Quartermain was ashen with fear, the magistrate nodded at the soldiers. They pulled the two men apart.

Drake dipped his fingers in Quartermain's pocket and pulled out a flask. He shook it, and a small amount of liquid sloshed around. He poured the remaining liquid on the floor, then carefully poured the whiskey still left in Norther's glass back into the flask and handed the lethal brew over to the magistrate. "If you have any pets who need to be put out of their misery, I suggest you use this."

Now that the soldiers had forced Norther into a chair and held him there, Quartermain had recovered his composure. "I shall say one of Norther's friends gave me the flask."

Drake lifted an eyebrow. "Doubtless you frequently hobnob with thieves and killers. Doing it a bit too brown, old chap. I doubt the court will believe you either."

The Gentle Beast

Drake's sanguine air was too much for Quartermain. With a sound of guttural rage, Quartermain grabbed a pistol from the belt of a surprised soldier and leveled it at Drake. He held his hand out for the keys. "Slowly now. If I have to flee England, I am perfectly happy to do so as a murderer rather than as a thief."

The magistrate hesitated, but when Quartermain cocked the pistol, he tossed the keys over. The soldiers reluctantly threw their weapons into the hall.

Quartermain waved them all further into the cell. Drake read intent in the cit's eyes. The instant Quartermain had them all locked in, he would stick the pistol through the grille in the door and fire.

Drake's eyes met Clyde's. Clyde nodded imperceptibly, clutched his chest with both hands, and groaned, falling to the floor.

It was distraction enough. When Quartermain's feral eyes flickered to Clyde, Drake lunged for the gun. Quartermain tried to turn it against him, but Drake slammed the cit's elbow against the wall. Quartermain grunted in pain. The barrel shifted as Quartermain tried to ease Drake's iron hold. The pistol pointed wildly about the cell.

Since the struggling men blocked the door, the soldiers could not reach their weapons. They looked at the magistrate for guidance, but the soldiers appeared none too keen to get closer to that wildly gyrating pistol.

The magistrate was intent on the battle.

No one noticed Felix Norther lift his leg and pull a tiny pistol from the sole of his boot.

Drake was winning the wrestling match—until Quartermain rammed the pistol butt into Drake's wounded arm. Drake winced. His grip slackened, giv-

ing Quartermain time enough to squirm free and level the gun.

A pistol shot retorted from the wrong quarter. The magistrate and soldiers instinctively ducked, and then all three of them jumped on Norther and pulled the smoking pistol away.

Drake caught Quartermain's gun as it slipped from his hand. Quartermain swayed on his feet, clutching the small hole in his chest. His back skidded down the door as he sank to the floor, looking like a man who needed to rest.

He laughed, an ugly, bitter sound, blood dotting his lips. "Always thought . . . I would die . . . peacefully . . . in my own bed." He squinted up at Drake, and it was obvious his eyes were growing dim.

"You reap what you sow," Drake said grimly.

Clyde nodded piously at his pupil. Lesson taught, lesson learned.

Quartermain's mouth went slack. He slumped to the floor.

The magistrate stepped back from Norther, straightening his wig and looking harrassed. "Now what do we do with you? I shall testify that you not only killed him in self-defense, but you chose a damned convenient moment to do it. But that was a damned sneaky place to hide a weapon. What say you, sir?"

Drake shrugged at the question, wincing as his arm protested. "I leave that in your capable hands. Thank you, Mr. Norther. I shall follow your trial with interest."

Norther returned a surly, "If you expect my thanks, you shall grow old waiting. I knew he would try to poison me."

Drake smiled at the obvious untruth, but he merely turned on his heel and went out into the sunshine.

The Gentle Beast

They tied Drake's horse to the back of the carriage. For once Drake obeyed Clyde's insistence and lay down against the squabs.

He cupped his aching arm, contemplating the frailties of life. One minute Quartermain was triumphant, about to kill his greatest enemy. The next he was dead.

Still, somehow Drake was glad that he had not had to kill the cit. Drake had killed enough, always in self-defense, but because of Callista things had changed. For the first time in his life, he valued it. He and Quartermain had not been so different, once upon a time.

Hatred was a canker, eating away at all it touched, good and bad impartially. A life built on vengeance was essentially a selfish life, devoted to crushing opposition for the cheap thrill of victory. And what would he have done after he tormented Stanton into death or decline or starvation? The rest of his life would have stretched before him, empty and lonely.

Nothing he did could ever bring his father back.

Producing strong heirs with the daughter of Mary Raleigh would surely be a close second.

Drake sighed and tipped his mask over his face, falling asleep on a last happy thought. He, too, hoped to die peacefully in his bed, at Callista's side.

Better yet, on top of her.

Drake's lips stretched in a smile. For the first time in a long time, his dreams were joyful.

The marriage of Drake Kimball and Callista Raleigh was to be remembered as one of the most attended events of the off season. The bride, dressed in exquisite lace trimmed with topazes to match the blaze at her throat, was surely as lovely as any princess who had walked down Westminster's long aisle.

And the groom, who should have looked severe in

his black silk jacket, white cravat, and white breeches, had such a glow in his amazing blue eyes that the women of the ton who had never seen him were agog at Callista's good fortune. Why, he was as rich as Croesus and handsome to boot. That Raleigh girl, despite the whiff of scandal that had always followed her, was a lucky chit.

Prominent among the guests at the huge reception was a certain lexicographer. He stayed long past when most of the other guests had gone. When no one but Simon, Henry, and Marian remained in the grand salon of the Kimball town house, Dr. Johnson approached the happy couple, who were lost in their own world.

Drake sipped from a champagne glass, his eyes a physical promise upon Callista's. She blushed and spilled a dab on her shoulder. Drake bent his head to kiss the moisture from her skin, his breath hot upon her.

At his insistence, he had not touched her since that night a long month ago when she had bearded the Dragon in his lair. Their heir, he informed her, would be conceived in his ancestral home, in the same bed in which he'd been conceived.

Callista had turned away to smile, for the bulge in his breeches showed just how hard it would be to live up to his lofty proclamation. She was glad that her arrogant Dragon was not completely dead. He had not pressed her about Johnson's odd behavior, but she knew he waited for her to tell him what had happened at the cemetery. If she waited, perhaps he would forget, she hoped. She was greatly upset by her foolish behavior, and wanted only to forget it.

But the Dragon had an excellent memory, as he proved when his mouth wandered in reverent remem-

brance on her skin. "Is it too early to plead tiredness? I have waited long enough."

Callista felt a shadow over them and pushed Drake away, blushing deeper. She looked up at Dr. Johnson. "May I get you more refreshment, sir?"

"No, child, it is nourishment enough watching the two of you."

Callista averted her eyes in embarrassment, but Drake only grinned under the doctor's teasing blue stare.

Johnson set a package in Callista's lap. "I thought it best that you open this privately."

Callista fumbled with the lovely paper, aware of Drake's curiosity. If this was what she feared, she had some explaining to do. She opened the box. Sure enough, inside lay her pistol, but under that was a signed copy of *The Rambler* and a book of psalms.

Drake stared at the odd assortment. "What in heaven's name?"

"An excellent choice of words, Kimball," Johnson said blandly. "For heaven has granted you the choice between violence or reverence. I just wanted you to know that I approve your choice."

Drake stared after them as Johnson asked Callista to see him out.

As Callista walked him to the door, Johnson bent to kiss her cheek. "I am extremely fond of you, child. I leave it up to you whether you tell him how I came by the pistol, but I would encourage you in that. It cannot harm your relationship for him to know how much you love him." And the doctor went on his way, whistling, as if their happiness truly pleased him.

The words were still ringing in Callista's ears an hour later when everyone had finally left them alone. Callista retired to change into her night rail and full robe,

nibbling at her lip in indecision.

When she went into the great bedroom, Drake was propped on an elbow on his huge bed, wearing naught but an open shirt and a seductive smile. Beside him was a package.

Callista's heart picked up a primitive rhythm just from the look of him, knowing that at last he was hers. When he patted the bed beside him, she sat down. He started to pull her into his arms, but she held him off.

"Drake, I . . . Well, that is, you should know. . . ." She took a deep breath and finished in a rush, "Dr. Johnson returned the weapon to me because he caught me trying to use it during the duel to shoot Simon in the leg and throw his aim off so he would not kill you."

Drake went still. Callista studied her lap, ashamed, as he seemed to be struggling for words.

When he spoke, his voice was husky with emotion. "You love me that much?"

Callista flung her arms about his neck. "You are life to me, and sustenance. I love you more than water, or air, or sunshine—"

He stopped her words with his lips. Callista was reaching to slip the shirt off his shoulders when he wrenched himself away. He was already hard with eagerness, but he merely shifted uncomfortably and handed her the package.

"Open this first." His gaze raked her breasts in the low-cut night rail. "Quickly."

Callista ripped through the expensive paper, her hands shaking. She pulled out an exquisite book. She gasped. The leather was the softest she had ever felt, and front, back and spine, it was gilded and embossed in a rose pattern. On the front was a tiny portrait of herself, facing Drake. His dragon mask dangled from her fingers as he reached to set the Yellow Rose about

her neck. Each corner of the book was set with rubies, diamonds and pearls. She opened to the heavy vellum paper and saw that the inside told the story of Beauty and the Beast. Further back was a family tree, in which she could write the names of their descendants, and behind that were blank pages for their children to add their own love stories.

Callista's eyes misted. He could not have given her anything she would treasure more. It was as if she held their love in her hands, a treasure all the greater because it had been so hard won.

Drake drew her to his breast and pressed her cheek against his strong heart.

"I love you, my beauty. Never again will I hate, or kill. I will devote myself to giving you a measure of the happiness you have given me. We have closed one chapter on our beginning, but the true depth of what we offer each other is still to come." And he kissed her, softly, sweetly, pledging his troth in the age-old way.

And there, on the bed where a little boy had last seen his father in their ancestral home, they banished their ghosts forever. A soft sound of masculine satisfaction might have sounded in that unseen realm. Perhaps somewhere Bryant Kimball was glad that his son and Mary Raleigh's daughter had found the love denied him.

But Drake and Callista Kimball were too busy building a future to dwell on the past. . . .

Prince of Kisses

Curious, Devlin Rhodes crept over the carpet toward the bed. The air left his lungs in a whoosh.

Long hair fell over the side of the bed in shimmering waves that reached the floor. The red tresses caught every stealthy ray of moonlight and cast it back; he could only wonder what her hair looked like at noon. Her eyes were closed, but her lashes were sable fans against her flawless ivory skin. Her dark brows arched wickedly above, flying away to her temples with a reckless disregard for fashion that he found enchanting.

She slept on her back, a leg half out of the covers, bare to the knee. Her ankle was slim but sturdy, a pleasing segue to the shapely calf and hidden thigh that must complete the stunning limb like the crescendo to an aria. He couldn't see her breasts, but the covers mounded in a way that proved she was very much a woman, in spite of her attempts to live—and act—like a man.

Devlin swallowed, mastering the stirring at his groin, and tore his gaze away. Despite the fact that they both owned jewelry stores, they were as far apart socially as the moon and the stars. He'd learned at an early age that wanting what he couldn't have only made his poverty hurt more.

Quietly he searched the bookcase, nudging at corners, carvings, and books. Finally, when he pressed on a medallion, part of the case slid open on well-oiled springs. A safe gleamed behind it. Devlin pulled a stethoscope out of his pack. In ten minutes, he had the safe open.

Quickly, for he heard the covers stirring, he pulled out the contents. The familiar solid feel of stones and gold comforted him. Then his fingers felt something unexpected. He pulled out a rectangular wrapped object. Deftly, he opened the oilskin rag. A book? What book could be so valuable that it had to be stowed with a king's ransom of jewels?

Devlin barely had time to glimpse an exquisite binding inset with jewels before a hiccup came from the bed. Dropping everything willy-nilly into his pack, he buttoned the bag closed and shouldered it. He pulled his glove back on and latched the safe. The bookcase slid home.

He'd almost made it back to the window when a cold feminine voice said, "Stop right there or I'll shoot you where you stand." Lady Charlaine Callista Kimball came forward into the moonlight, her thin gown revealing a voluptuous form.

However, Devlin's appreciation was somewhat spoiled by the incongruous accessory she sported. The tiny pearl-handled pistol glittered with a gimlet eye in the moonlight.

He let his gaze linger insolently on all the shadowy

383

curves and valleys his hands itched to discover. What he wouldn't give for a blazing noon sun. Still, she was intimidated enough to hunch her shoulders.

Grinning, Devlin leaned against the wall and crossed his feet at the ankles. "No need to threaten me, you know. I'll gladly stay in your bedchamber as long as you like, *chérie.*"

"Do not call me that," she said through her teeth. "Doubtless you will not find me dear when I throw you to my dogs."

A lesser man might have backed away at the threat; Devlin Rhodes merely raised a well-defined black eyebrow. "Please do. I have not found the time to play with them today."

He had to admire her aplomb when she said coolly, "Indeed? This I must see." She started to wave him downstairs, and then noticed her bare feet poking beneath her gown. Even in the moonlight, he saw her blush. Savagely she jerked up a dressing gown from the foot of her bed.

She looked at it, then at him, and finally down at the gun in her hand.

He had to smile at her dilemma. Indeed, it would be difficult to put on such a heavy garment while trying to hold a pistol on him all the while. He bowed gallantly. "I shall be delighted to hold the pistol for you."

She glared at him. She nibbled that full, sensuous lip.

"That, too, I shall be even happier to do," he said softly, his gaze caressing her mouth. "I have a feeling you do not utilize the gifts God blessed you with so richly."

"Oh!" She held the dressing gown over her form and backed to the door, her pistol still leveled at his chest. Awkwardly holding the gown over herself with an arm

384

as she fumbled for the knob, she opened the door, backed outside and locked it. He heard her light steps hurry down the hall; then she called, "Henrietta! Fetch my watchman!"

How fortunate that she thought he'd entered through the door. To his dismay, by the time he secured his pack soundly on his shoulders and straddled the windowsill, several moving torches were bobbing around in the gardens far below. Devlin heard heavy footsteps tromping upstairs.

Trapped. He gave a last desperate look at the room, but all the obvious hiding places were too small. Unless. . . . He eyed the bed. It was doubtful even her own men would search the Ice Princess's virgin bed. Quickly, he picked up the heavy glass bowl filled with flowers and water, carried it to the window, and threw it outside with all his might.

A satisfying thud sounded. One of the bouncing torches stopped. "There he be! This way!" a man called. The torch leaped toward the sound.

Devlin tossed one of his gloves at the foot of the tower. Then, pushing the pack beneath the bed, he dove under the down covers. The feather bed was so soft that his form was barely noticeable. He settled back, alert for the tiniest sound.

He was not scared; he was not tense. In fact, a rakish grin stretched his mobile face. The emotion tapping against his ribs was far more heady than fear.

And far more dangerous . . .

Some time later, Charlaine stomped back into her chamber, disgusted. In all the years the Kimballs had owned this estate, no one had ever dared to break in. Who was this fellow of the dancing eyes and the nimble fingers who could sprout wings and fly? For surely that

was the only way he could have escaped.

She slammed her bedchamber door to appraise her haven with jaundiced eyes. No man had ever set foot in here, including her own father.

Until tonight.

Again, the image of those flashing white teeth and laughing blue eyes haunted her. The man's thick black hair tumbled with abandon across his broad, intelligent forehead. His brows were untidy accents to the rest of a perfectly symmetrical countenance. Handsome nose, not too big, not too small; wide, perfectly shaped lips. And his physique! His form-fitting clothes gave her active imagination plenty to work with. Odd, that she could picture the scoundrel so vividly.

She scowled at her own weakness. Girlhood longings were for the poor and the weak. She was neither. Indeed, she was the great-grandaughter of a pirate.

What would her legacy to history be? Doubtless, no heirs would give her immortality in their own family tall tales. She would have no grand romance to add to the family—

She drew in a sharp breath and rushed to the hidden safe. The jewels were insured, but the precious illuminated book passed down from Great-Grandfather Drake Kimball was irreplaceable. Her fingers trembled as she spun the dial and swung open the safe. Her vision swam before her. She reached inside, as if her eyes deceived her. But no. The safe was empty.

"Blast and damn his black, thieving heart! You shall pay for this, and richly, I vow on the blood of my ancestors!" She slammed the safe shut and kicked the bookcase panel closed so hard that half the books fell out.

Frustrated, she flopped on the bed and tried to pull the covers over her legs. Odd. The heavy down seemed

caught on something. Come to think of it, the bed did not feel quite right. She got up on her knees and leaned toward the end of the bed to check the tucked-in covers.

She felt the opposite side of the bed move and turned, but she was too late. The covers seemed to come to life. She found herself sprawled, flat on her back in her own bed, the intruder she'd thought long since fled now master, where only she had been mistress a few scant seconds before.

No man had ever been so close. She felt every inch of his tall, muscular frame weighing her down into the soft bed. Oddly, the pressure was not unpleasant. Something about his planes and angles seemed to fit her curves just right, but the primitive feeling horrified her conscious mind, as did the strange stiffness pressing into her lower abdomen.

Innocent she might be, but she knew what *that* meant. He must have watched her standing before the fire in the thin gown. The fact that he found her as physically pleasing as she secretly found him only added to her frustrated rage. She was so stunned and still, staring up at those bold blue eyes, that his big hand eased its pressure over her mouth.

"Promise not to scream, and I will let you up."

She nodded slightly. He eased his palm away and started to move aside. She took a deep breath, but the scream had barely started before that tough, capable hand swallowed it. His grin made her quiver deep inside. He settled on her comfortably.

"Your choice, *chérie.* I much prefer this position over a chilly spring night." He squirmed atop her, grinning wider when her eyes fluttered closed. He cocked his head to one side and raised his torso so he could contemplate her pleasing shape. With his free hand, he

flicked at the high neckline of her sweeping nightgown. "Even your choice of bed attire is cold and proper." He leaned to whisper in her ear, "Save when you stand in front of the fire. There, I suspect, is the real Charlaine Kimball. Your hair tumbles down your back like liquid flame, but it is still cold compared to the passion you suppress within."

The things he was saying to her were horrible, unthinkable. Why could this scoundrel, on their first meeting, see so easily beneath the mask others took for reality? She began to buck beneath him, frantic to get away, to be safe again.

His response was unexpected. Holding her chin in one strong hand, he drew his muffling palm away. She had no time to scream, for another substance, softer, warmer, immediately covered her mouth.

She'd been kissed before, but those were furtive affairs ended promptly by her. This time, when she tried to draw back, she had nowhere to run. She could only lie there, captive to him and the feelings he aroused. His lips were so warm, so sweetly gentle. She would have expected a rough-and-tumble man like him to be brutal, to demand her surrender.

Not he. He assayed, testing her like a prospector seeking something far more valuable than gold. And he seemed to find it, for he slanted his head for a deeper angle and rubbed his lips against hers, growling his own pleasure. She felt his heart rate accelerate, and her own heart followed, as if he led her in some pagan dance.

She gasped into his mouth, but that only urged him to greater trespass. The tip of his tongue dipped into her open mouth like a hummingbird seeking life's nectar. As if only she could supply it, only he could take it. *Share with me*, he seemed to say. *We will each be the*

richer for it. Her defenses were slowly crumbling under the persuasive assault. His skillful mouth aroused in her such feelings as she had never known, nor even dreamt of. No one would know if just this once, she were weak, if she explored the great unknown of being a woman with a man.

When the teasing tip of his tongue retreated, she struggled her hands free and cupped the back of his head to slant her mouth under his. Boldly, she followed his example, dipping her tongue into his own warm mouth scented of brandy and peppermint. He showed her the dance and retreat for a full minute. When she was limp beneath him, her head swirling with his scent, his taste, his touch, he drew away slightly.

Murmuring French endearments, he lowered his mouth to her throbbing neck and stabbed his tongue into the scented hollow of her throat. And then his hands, his big, capable hands, skillfully worked at the buttons of her bodice.

A niggling doubt penetrated the pleasant fog of arousal. Something was wrong. If only she could think.

"Mon coeur," he whispered into the V of skin he was slowly exposing.

The realizations hit her like winter air: He spoke French so well because he *was* a damned frog; she was not the first, nor would she be the last, to wilt under this expert seduction.

She was a Kimball, not some harlot to play a light-skirt beneath a frog libertine!

He'd reached the fifth tiny button. He was taking his time, as if he were not a hunted thief, but a welcome guest. As if she were not the favorite of royalty, but a common chit he could have his way with and discard. Gall at his arrogance revived her formidable will-

power. She caught his big hands as they moved to pull her bodice aside.

He paused and looked down at her. "*Mon cher*, what is amiss?"

So tender his tone, as if she really were his dear. She flung his hands aside and caught his wide shoulders to push him away. He balked, catching her wrists in his hands and holding them above her head. He was gentle, but inexorable.

Like the tide. Like the sunrise. Like the seasons. She squelched the thoughts. A force of nature he might be, but she was a creature who liked her comforts civilized.

Her tone was cool, as if her voice alone could master her own fevered flesh. "An experiment, mainly. Quite pleasant, but I am finished now. You will let me up, if you please."

He froze, obviously surprised by her calm. Then he smiled. A crooked, knowing smile. "Ah, but what if I do not please?" He tilted her chin back and lowered his mouth.

"Then I shall scream loud enough to shake the rafters," she said, turning her head. Nothing stopped her from screaming. Nothing, save those sultry blue eyes.

"One day, *mon cher*, you will scream beneath me with a different emotion." The soft words had the nature of a vow, all the more troubling since she didn't understand his meaning. He glanced around, tugged the velvet cords off her bed curtains and proceeded to tie her to the bedpost. He used a strange knot that held her but gave slightly when she pulled at it.

Still, to be tied up in her own bedchamber. . . . Outrage gave her strength.

He stifled her scream with a large hand. "Promise me you will not call them for five minutes, and I will

not gag you." He eased his hand away.

"Blasted frog, y—"

Back came the hand. That long length of sheer masculinity settled back atop her. "As you wish. I will stay." His eyes filled half her world, then three quarters, and finally she saw nothing but him, felt nothing but him.

When he pulled his hand away to kiss her, she said breathlessly, "Very well. I promise not to scream for five minutes."

The kiss landed on her neck, blending with a heavy male sigh that sounded like regret. "Pity. Never have I enjoyed a battle of wills more."

Finally, his weight lifted. She heard him rummaging about. She had to wound him somehow. "How do you know I will keep my word?"

He came into her field of sight again. That maddening smile stretched those expressive, sensual lips. "The Ice Princess will never admit to the world that she was bested in her own chamber by a mere, ah, what is the term? Ah yes, a frog." He cocked his head and appraised her. "'Tis you who looks a bit green about the gills, my sweet. But fear not. We shall meet again."

At the window, he turned. With only the moon to bless his parting, he threw her an airy kiss that landed like a brand. Even as she glared at him with fury, part of her knew she would never forget the sight of him at this moment. His black hair blew in the breeze from the open casement. His brilliant blue eyes sparkled in the moonlight.

He stepped over the sill and paused astride it. "You are wasted alone up here, my Ice Princess. But not for long. Two things I promise you: When the time is right, I shall return your treasure to you. And one day, you will melt beneath my kiss, and beg me for what we almost shared this night. Until then, I will not kiss you

again, no matter how much you beg."

"You arrogant frog, never, ever will I beg you for anything! Not in your dreams—"

"But in yours, yes?" He had the temerity to wink. And then, with a lithe twist of his fit body, he dropped out of sight.

But not out of mind. Even as she stewed, pulling at her silken bonds, part of her knew she would never be the same again. An even more primitive instinct warned she *would* see him again.

She touched lips still sensitive from his touch. What would she do then? Kiss him, or call the guards on him as he deserved?